They were so screwed—a feeling Tommy was getting used to...

Sitting in the front seats, Tommy and Jack looked at each other, and for a second time, shrugged their shoulders in unison.

"Please tell me there will be no more to this hard-drive mystery," Jack said.

Tommy laughed. "Jack, you're screwed. You've gotten yourself involved in something really fucked up. You should have just ignored the letter from this Jarvis guy, and if a compliant was filed, told the bar you never received the request."

"It came via registered mail." Jack sighed.

"You are so screwed," Tommy said again, without the follow-on laughter this time, as he contemplated the implications of his friend's situation.

"Well, let us hope I did not mistakenly involve you, as well."

Ignoring Jack's comment, Tommy said, "Let's drive back around the block. I want to check out the black van again."

"Our primary goal should be to remove ourselves from this neighborhood," Jack replied, shaking his head.

"Just humor me."

Jack sighed and turned left as he departed the driveway. At the end of the block, he made another left and the black van came into view, parked alongside the curb. A soft cloud chugged from its exhaust, and Tommy leaned forward in his seat, examining the van. As they drove past, the driver, with a small head, bushy dark hair, and beady eyes, glared back at them through the open driver's window.

"That man could not have been five foot tall," Jack commented.

"Five foot two," Tommy responded.

"Do you know him?"

Silent for a moment, Tommy muttered, "What did Jarvis's note say you were to do with the hard-drive?"

"Turn it over to the FBI."

After another short moment of silence, Tommy said, "Don't."

"Don't what?"

"Don't turn it over till we figure out what's going on." Tommy sighed. "This hard-drive may be our only ticket to getting out of this mess."

"Are we in a mess?"

"The answer to your question as to whether I knew the short guy is yes. Last time I we met, he was working for an organization called the Society. If he still works for the Society, then the FBI is the last place we should take the hard-drive. The Society has members in each and every law enforcement organization you can think of, not to mention each and every criminal organization."

"What you're saying is that we are indeed in a mess."

"The term 'we are in a mess' might be a bit of an understatement."

Formerly a sought-after structural engineer and manager of complex construction sites across the country, Tommy Luck is now nothing more than an unemployed drunk. His lifestyle is simple: drink himself into a stupor each night and run each morning to minimize the effects of his nightly binges.

Assisting a friend in retrieving a hard-drive from an upscale residence in Northwest Washington DC, Tommy once again finds himself swept up in a complex web of murder and deceit. This particular hard-drive happens to belong to a powerful organization. It contains sensitive information, and they would do just about anything to get it back. The problem is the organization's standard operating procedure is to eliminate any outsider who comes into contact with the hard-drive.

Fleeing the country to escape the organization and their pursuing assassins, Tommy finds himself matching wits with his long-time rival, John Smith. As Tommy works to uncover the truth he discovers there is more to this mystery than meets the eye, and no one seems to be who they claim. Every step of headway into exposing what's really going on creates more uncertainty. The only thing Tommy Luck seems to be able to control, as he peels back the layers of deceit surrounding his situation, is his relentless schedule of drinking and running.

In *Tommy's Rival* by Patrick Ashtre, Tommy Luck is in trouble once again, but this time it's by accident. He gets a call from an attorney friend whose criminal client asks him to retrieve a hard-drive from under a floorboard in the client's house if the client doesn't contact him by a certain time. The stolen hard-drive belongs to a powerful secret society and contains sensitive information. When the two men go to retrieve the hard-drive, they run into the society's thugs, and the game is on. John Smith, Tommy's long-time rival and an employee of the society, tries, once again, to kill Tommy and his friends, but, once again, Tommy proves very hard to kill. Some people just never learn. Like the other two books in the series, this one is intense, fast paced, and chilling. You can't help but root for Tommy and his friends and cheer at their unorthodox methods. A really great read. ~ *Taylor Jones, The Review Team of Taylor Jones & Regan Murphy*

Tommy's Rival by Patrick Ashtre is the third in his Tommy Luck series. In this story, Tommy accompanies an attorney friend to retrieve a hard-drive from the home of a client after the client failed to call at the time he said he would. When Tommy and his friend Jack arrive at the house and retrieve the hard-drive, they are accosted by thugs, one of whom Tommy recognizes as working with Tommy's nemesis, John Smith. It is later discovered that the hard-drive contains sensitive information on the powerful "Society" and had been stolen from the Society by Jack's client. Since Tommy realizes that anyone who knows about the hard-drive is probably on a hit list, he and his friend flee to an island in the Gulf of Thailand, where hopefully, the Society will not be able to reach them. But the Society's reach is very long...*Tommy's Luck*, like the first two books, is compelling, intense, and intriguing. I love trying to figure out how Tommy will get out of each new mess. If you liked the

other two books, you really don't want to miss this one. ~
*Regan Murphy, The Review Team of Taylor Jones & Regan
Murphy*

OTHER BOOK
BY
PATRICK ASHTRE
AND
BLACK OPAL BOOKS

Non-Fiction

A Distant Island

Chaloklum ~ The Island of No Last Names

Fiction

Tommy's Luck

Tommy's Troubles

Author's Note

This book is the third in the Tommy Luck trilogy. While *Tommy's Rival* is a standalone story, it is my recommendation that you read *Tommy's Luck* and *Tommy's Troubles* in order, before reading this book. The linkages between the stories are numerous and many of the first and second books' mysteries are revealed in the third.

TOMMY'S RIVAL

PATRICK ASHTRE

A Black Opal Books Publication

GENRE: THRILLER/SUSPENSE

This is a work of fiction. Names, places, characters and incidents are either the product of the author's imagination or are used fictitiously, and any resemblance to any actual persons, living or dead, businesses, organizations, events or locales is entirely coincidental. All trademarks, service marks, registered trademarks, and registered service marks are the property of their respective owners and are used herein for identification purposes only. The publisher does not have any control over or assume any responsibility for author or third-party websites or their contents.

DEDICATION

To Benjamin, Alison, and Amelia

CHAPTER 1

Georgetown, Washington DC, USA, 5 December 2016:

Kelly wasn't sure what had awakened her from a deep sleep. Rubbing her eyes, she looked around the bedroom. Its daisy yellow walls draped in darkness, and took in the shadowy details. An outside street lamp cast a muted light across the room creating a medley of shadows on the ceiling and walls. A long oak dresser stood against one wall with a large oval mirror inside a gold frame hanging above. On another wall stood the doors to the en-suite bathroom and walk-in closet. A door leading to the hallway was situated on a third. The bedroom door was open, and she watched as a series of shadows danced across the hallway walls as a car drove past her house. She took a deep lung full of air and smelled the familiar scent of her slumbering husband, before glancing at a clock on a small round table next to the bed. Its red illuminated face read 0223.

Feeling warm air descending onto the queen-sized bed from an overhead vent, Kelly wondered if it hadn't been groaning contraction of the house that had awakened her, which happened when the home's furnace failed to fight off the night chill. She sat up and placed her back against the headboard, smoothing back her straight brunette hair. A thick green quilt fell to her waist, revealing a pearl white silk nightgown that highlighted her soft brown skin. Pulling the quilt back up to her shoulders, she glanced down at Stan, her husband, sleeping soundly next to her and then once again to the open door leading to the hallway and living room. Craning her head to one side, she listened to the house sounds, but heard nothing. Yawning she slipped back down onto the bed. Just as she began nuzzling her head into the pillow she heard the noise again, a shuffling sound coming through the open door from the living room. Sitting back up and craning her head again, her heart jumped when she heard a faint cough come from down the hall.

"Stan," she quietly whispered, lightly shaking her husband's shoulder.

Moaning at her touch, Stan rolled away from her onto his side, pulling the quilt from Kelly's legs.

Feeling panic building in her chest, she whispered, "Stan," slightly louder and shook him again.

"What?" He hoarsely responded, rolling onto his back and opening his left eye. "What time is it?"

"Someone's in the living room." Kelly felt her eyes beginning to fill with tears, as a smoldering terror began to consume her.

Stan slowly pulled himself up, slipping back so he too was resting on the bed's headboard next to Kelly. He looked over at his panicked wife and asked, "Okay, what is it that you heard that makes you believe someone is in our living room?"

She reached out and placed her hand on his bare chest. "I heard something. Something woke me up. Then I heard someone cough. It came from down the hallway."

"I don't hear anything," Stan replied, the hoarseness giving way to his normal rhythmic tone.

Moving her hand from his chest and clutching Stan's left forearm, Kelly looked at her husband with frightened and pleading eyes and repeated her earlier claim, "I heard someone cough. There's someone in the living room."

"All right, all right, relax, I'll check it out." Stan reached out, gently caressing Kelly's cheek with the back of his hand.

Kelly watched as he slipped his legs out from under the

heavy green quilt and placed his bare feet on the floor, rubbing his eyes in an attempt to banish the last of his sleepiness. As he stood up, the quilt fell from his red pajama bottoms, and he walked to the door, briefly stopping to see if he could hear the noise that had scared Kelly.

Looking back at Kelly, Stan whispered, "Are you sure you heard something?"

"Someone is out there." Her voice cracked. "I heard a cough. I'm sure."

Watching him disappear down the hallway, Kelly pulled the quilt tightly across her shoulders as she stared at the darkness beyond the hallway door.

Another shuffling noise then a sharp thump, followed by a second loud thud and a grunt echoed across the hallway walls. She pulled the quilt up to her neck, a tear broke from her right eye and worked its way down her cheek. A faint moan was followed by an even fainter gurgling sound, and Kelly felt a shiver snake down her spine.

"Stan." Her voice cracked. "Stan?"

Hard-soled footsteps could be heard on the hallway's wooden floor, moving in the direction of the bedroom.

"Stan? Stan?" Kelly called out again in a quivering voice.

A shadow formed in the bedroom's doorway. Kelly's mind raced and through a haze of terror a man wearing a black turtleneck sweater, heavy dark jacket, and black pants slowly took shape. The man stood silently inspecting Kelly as she held the green quilt up to her neck.

"Where is it?" The man's gruff voice echoed off the room's walls.

"What?" Kelly answered, glancing at her cell phone lying on the top of the small round bed stand, next to the clock, its face now reading a red 0227. "Who are you?"

"Where's the database?"

Reaching for her cell, she asked, "Who told you about the database?"

"Don't," the man hoarsely demanded, taking a step into the room.

Pulling her hand back from the cell and wrapping her arms around her chest, Kelly took several deep breaths, trying to quiet herself. She examined the man, his features now illuminated in the dim light coming from the lamp post outside the room's window. He was tall with wide shoulders, page boy cut blonde hair, and large dark eyes.

"Who are you?" she asked again, attempting to rein in her panic.

"Where's the database?"

"What did you do with Stan?" She attempted to summon some resoluteness, but tears now freely streamed down her cheeks. She repeated her question, "Where's Stan?"

The man took another step toward the bed and pulled an eight-inch knife from his jacket's pocket, before pointing its shadowy edge at Kelly, slowly and coarsely said, "Tell me where the database is."

"There. It's there." Her voice cracked again, all firmness gone, as she pointed to a framed picture of Stan on a sailboat someplace on the Chesapeake Bay hanging between the walk-in closet and bathroom doors. "Where's Stan?"

The man walked to the wall and pulled the picture from its mount, revealing a small greenish colored safe with a black dial, a digital screen with key pad, and silver handle. He tossed the picture to the floor. The picture's glass shattered as it hit the edge of the rug. It clattered to a stop on the wooden floor.

"What's the digital code?" The man looked over his shoulder at Kelly while placing the knife back into his pocket.

Frozen in fear, Kelly rattled off six numbers before mumbling again, "What have you done with Stan?"

The man typed in the numbers before looking over his shoulder again and saying, "If an alarm goes off, you're dead."

"The alarm was deactivated when you entered the numbers onto the keypad."

"What's the combination?"

"Seventeen, forty-two, thirteen."

Twisting the combination into the dial, the man pulled the silver handle down and opened the small heavy door. Reaching inside, he grabbed a rectangular shaped black box. From the box, he pulled a small cobalt blue and silver rectangular device with a USB port on one side, and placed it in the pocket of his jacket, dropping the box to the floor. Turning, the man walked over to Kelly and stood, towering over her, as she shivered under the quilt. Kelly could smell the man's body odor, harsh and pungent.

Roughly pushing her back on to the bed, the man grabbed the quilt and threw it aside. He then groped at her nightgown, pushing it up and revealing white panties. Terrified, Kelly pulled her gown back down, shimmying backward on the mattress. Grabbing her left ankle, the big-shouldered man pulled her back to the edge of the bed before silently taking the knife from his pocket and pointing its edge at her throat. Reaching out, he roughly grabbed the top of her nightgown and ripped it from her, showing her bared breasts and white panties.

"Take them off," he grunted, pointing the knife at her panties.

"Please don't."

"Take them off," the man growled, placing the tip of the knife against her throat.

"Please," she cried as she slipped her panties off.

CHAPTER 2

Chevy Chase, Maryland, USA, 5 December 2016:

The three older men sat in the spacious bookcase-lined study. Heavy snow could be seen falling through windows edged with frost. Beyond the falling snow, traffic moved slowly along Connecticut Avenue, providing a slow-motion light show of white headlights and red taillights flickering off of the descending flurry. Leaping flames burnt large logs in a massive stone fireplace, not ten feet away from where the men sat, and reflected off a polished wood ceiling and floor. A blue and red Persian rug lay across the center of the floor and a wide silver chandelier hung overhead. The room smelt a mixture of burnt wood, fine liquors, and old men.

Oliver Mason, a narrow-shouldered and wide-hipped man with straight white hair that resembled that of an aging monk, sat in a red velvet chair to the left of the fire. Dressed in hunter green pants with a sharp crease and a light blue shirt, Oliver turned his attention to a single piece of white paper in his hand, silently reading the typed black print for the second time.

A large plump man, Andres Tressel, with unruly curly white hair and a matching white beard, dressed in rumpled khaki pants, sat across from him on the right side of the fire in a high backed and overstuffed chair covered in a floral fabric. Wearing a paisley vest over and white shirt and wide red suspenders, Andres sat scratching his ruddy white haired cheek with his right hand while holding a glass filled with ice and brown bourbon in his left. Turning his attention from the fire and looking at Oliver, he grunted.

Sitting on a couch directly in front of the fire and between his two companions, James Tillage, a lean man with bald top and short white stubble on the sides of his head, dressed in dark tailored trousers and a white shirt, yawned. A recovering alcoholic, James picked up a crystal glass filled with ice and sparkling water that had been sitting on a small round table next to the couch, and began raising it to his lips. Midway through the process, he reversed the motion and placed glass back down on the round table, as if changing his mind.

"Last night?" Oliver asked with a distinct English accent, breaking their momentary silence. Looking over to the other two men, he reached out to a small square table beside the red velvet chair and picked up a snifter filled with brandy. "What time?"

"Early this morning. Just before two-thirty a.m.," Anders relied in a heavy Scandinavian accent.

"And Kelly?" Oliver inquired, before raising the glass to his mouth and taking a sip of its brownish contents.

"The swine cut her husband's throat when he went into the living room in an attempt to discover the source of a noise that had awakened Kelly. He then had his way with the poor girl after acquiring the database from her wall safe." Andres continued, "She's traumatized to say the least."

Oliver asked, "Where is she now?"

"With our private physician at the Hartford residence," Andres answered in his baritone like voice. "I have several men taking care of the security, as well."

"How did the thief know about the hard-drive and database?" Oliver arched his white eyebrows. "There are only a handful of people that knew it existed—even fewer knew its location—and all members of the Society."

"No idea," James said in a North American accent. "Kelly's house is one of the many safe places we store the database in a rotation process. A computer randomly selects the storage facility and the time it is to be stored, we are informed of the next storage location one day before a scheduled move, and, finally, the database is discreetly moved by one or two trusted employees. All in all, six individuals, at most, know where the database is at any given moment. But you're correct. It has to be someone within the Society. It has to be one of the six."

"I believe we can discount Kelly as responsible for communicating its location." Andres remarked. "I doubt she would have planned her husband's death and her subsequent rape in order to obtain the database."

"She, or one of the two employees charged with moving the database, might have let it slip out," James noted, picking up his sparkling water from the small round table, again.

"This move was conducted by only one individual. Only five people knew the database's location," Andres explained then added, "Or someone may have identified the employee tasked with moving the device and simply followed him. Do we use the same individuals each time it's moved?"

"Yes and no, the individuals assigned to transport the database come from a short list of vetted employees," James clarified, placing the crystal glass filled with sparkling water back on the small table, once again untouched. "Another selection randomly made by the computer."

"The contents would be devastating to the Society if it were to find its way into the wrong hands. Do we have any clue to who might be responsible?" Oliver asked.

"I called our man John Smith," James explained, brushing invisible lint from his white shirt. "He's working on the problem as we speak. He's also at the Hartford residence."

"I don't trust that man," Oliver commented up before he picked up the crystal snifter of brandy again, taking another sip.

"Whatever happen to the gentleman we wished to hire as our executive assistant?" Andres chirped in.

"Thomas Luck," James answered without hesitation.

"Mr. Luck chose to turn down the position due to our selection of John Smith to participate in the operation designed to measure his capacity to handle the unknown stress," Oliver explained, shaking his head while looking whimsically into the fire. "It was an enormous mistake. Even Caroline, our long time executive secretary, quit over our subsequent employment of John Smith."

"We chose John Smith to be a part of Mr. Luck's qualification test because they were enemies," James interjected, "They participated in the same NSA operation the year before—"

"And we still have Mr. Smith on the payroll," Andres interrupted.

"John Smith is simply a stand in until we can find an adequate replacement," James said.

"I don't trust the man," Andres said, repeating Oliver's earlier proclamation.

"We should have offered Mr. Luck more compensation," Oliver muttered.

"We did," James replied. "We offered him three times the previous executive assistant's salary and he turned it down."

"We should have offered more," Oliver repeated.

"He would have turned it down. We attempted to hire a principled drunk. Who would have known they existed," James answered, looking at his two companions and shaking his head. "The minute we involved John Smith, Mr. Luck was lost to us."

"He is indeed a drunk," Andres agreed with a slight chuckle, before pouring the remaining contents of his glass into his mouth and taking massive swallow of bourbon. "However, he is a very effective drunk."

CHAPTER 3

Hartford County, Maryland, USA, 5 December 2016:

The Mercedes's headlights cut through the night as it coiled its way through the Maryland countryside along an icy black-topped road. Thick snow fell and a thin shroud of ice clung to the branches of leafless oak and slender pine trees that crowded the sides of the narrow lane.

The chauffeur, dressed in a black suit, looked in the rearview mirror. "Won't be long now, sir."

A tall man with wide shoulders, pageboy cut blond hair, and large dark eyes looked at the reflection of the chauffeur's face in the review mirror, shifting nervously in the back seat. A short man with beady eyes and a pale complexion, there was something about the chauffeur that unnerved the tall man. It certainly wasn't the size of man in the front seat that intimidated him, but there was something unsettling about the chauffer. Pulling his dark green jacket close around his body, he replied, "Can you turn the heat up? It's freezing back here."

The driver reached up to the dashboard with an absurdly small hand and twisted a wide black knob, while saying "Yes, sir, sorry about that."

The Mercedes crested a small rise and slowed, before turning into a driveway and stopping in front of wide black iron gates covered in an icy sheen supported by tall brick columns. From the rear seat, the tall man looked up, squinting at a bright round spotlight mounted on the top left column illuminating the car. Turning, the man saw a remote camera fixed to the top of the right column, it lens slowly spinning, focusing on the car. The man wondered if the camera lens was attempting to capture the license plate or the faces within. After a few moments, the gates began opening inward, allowing the Mercedes to continue up a tight brick driveway bordered by thick leafless and snow covered shrubs. The sedan shuddered and trembled as it drove over the uneven brick road, twisting up a low hill. Rounding the hilltop an enormous three story white mansion came into view. With long paned windows lining the front of the mansion at every level, six brick chimneys gave evidence to the building's age. A large covered entry containing two wide wooden doors stood at its center, in front of an oval shaped conclusion to the driveway. The Mercedes slowly made it way around, stopping in front of the entrance. The chauffeur opened his door, flushing the car of its internal warm with a blast of cold air. Stepping from the Mercedes, the short man jogged around the front of the car, his hard soles crunching across the icy ground, and opened the tall man's door.

"Just like I said," the chauffeur said, tucking his small hands into his armpits in an effort to stay warm, "It wouldn't be long."

"Will you wait?" the tall man asked, as he stepped from the Mercedes. Standing a full foot and a half above the driver, the tall man again wondered why this little man made him so nervous.

"Yes, sir. Those are my instructions."

Making his way up the ice covered steps, the leftmost front door opened before he had a chance to knock. An equally tall, but stooped, man with short dark wavy hair, holding himself up with two silver aluminum canes, stood in the entrance as a discharge of warm air from the house swept over the tall man.

"John Smith," the tall man said, greeting the stooped man with the silver canes in the entrance. The tall man had met John Smith several days before during a working lunch, of sorts. It was the lunch where John Smith had given him an address and the description of a hard-drive containing a database that he desired.

"Mr. Jarvis," John Smith returned his greeting. "Please come in. It's quite chilly out here."

Walking through the wooden door, Jarvis stepped onto a polished wood floor topped with a long and narrow green rug with a red and gold mosaic design, presumably a Persian, as he entered the house. Oil paintings portraying former owners lined the walls of the long and wide foyer. Midway down the hall Jarvis saw an open door to the left with the glow of a fire reflecting off the opposite wall. A wide curved staircase stood on the right side of the foyer.

"The door to your left," John Smith said, directing him to the open door, pointing with one of his silver canes.

Jarvis strutted down the hall and through the open door, followed by a hobbling John Smith and the short chauffeur. Two matching curved green couches with blue piping bracketed a large stone fireplace on the far wall with flames leaping from its edges and warming the room. There was a large granite counter topped with crystal decanters and glasses to the right and three long windows with views of the oval drive to the left.

The distinct smell of stale cigar smoke seemed to seep from the walls.

"Please take a seat, Mr. Jarvis," John Smith politely told his guest as he slowly trailed him into the room.

Jarvis pulled off his jacket before sitting on the couch to the right of the glowing fireplace. He laid his jacket across the couch's backrest behind him. John Smith shuffled over to the couch to the left and, with a clear expression of pain, slowly sat down directly across from him, leaning his two canes up against his left knee.

The chauffeur walked over to the counter and poured a brownish liquid from one of the decanters into two crystal snifters, before placing them on a silver platter.

"I understand you were successful in acquiring the hard-drive," John Smith said.

Studying John Smith for a moment before replying, Jarvis observed his host's olive skin, dark eyes, and thick bushy eye brows. Jarvis assumed that he was of Arabic or Persian linage, but, based on his accent, had obviously grown up in the United States. Midwest by the sound of his drawl.

"Yes, earlier this morning."

"I understand you eliminated one of the residents," John Smith said flatly.

"You said not to leave any witnesses," Jarvis replied.

John Smith responded, "But you did not terminate all the witnesses,"

Hesitatingly, Jarvis answered, "Killing a woman goes against my principles."

"But I did tell you that it would be a woman who knew the location and combination to the safe," John Smith retorted. "And you did not indicate that eliminating her would be a problem then."

"I decided against it while I was there," Jarvis answered. "She won't be a problem."

"So let me get this straight," John Smith evenly said, peering Jarvis, "Violently raping a woman is within your principles but killing one is not?" When Jarvis did not respond to his question, John Smith changed the subject, calmly inquiring, "And?"

"We need to renegotiate the price," Jarvis coolly replied, glancing over at the chauffeur who was standing next to the granite countertop watching to two men converse.

Leaning forward on the couch, John Smith's face contorted into another painful expression. "Do you know who you're dealing with?"

"Yes," Jarvis answered, leaning back into the couch to get away from John Smith's twisted face. "But I took the liberty of checking the hard-drive's contents on a computer at the residence. It contained some very interesting and potentially damaging information. I was somewhat surprised there were no security precautions on the device."

"And what is your new price?" John Smith asked calmly, leaning back onto the couch, his agonizing expression immediately disappearing.

"Two million."

"That is quite an increase in price for a simple burglary."

"Don't forget the wet work," Jarvis snapped in response.

John Smith let out a short cluck that Jarvis assumed was his version of a chuckle. Turning his head and looking at the chauffeur, John Smith gestured for the drinks.

"Are you sure," the chauffeur asked with a puzzled expression.

"It is time," John Smith told his employee.

The chauffeur picked up the silver platter with the two crystal snifters and walked over to the two men. Stepping up between the couches and holding out the platter between Jarvis and John Smith, he waited while each took a crystal snifter. The short beady-eyed chauffeur moved back to the side of the room, next to the granite counter, noisily setting the silver platter on the countertop.

"Does this mean you accept my new terms?" Jarvis asked John Smith, raising the glass to his mouth, the ice cubes faintly rattling against the crystal.

"And if I did not?" John Smith replied. "And if I were to threaten violence?"

Taking a sip from his crystal glass, Jarvis said, "Ah, brandy. Nice on such a cold night"

"Vintage Cognac," John Smith corrected Jarvis. "It's a sixty-year-old Montifaud."

Laughing, Jarvis replied, "I thought Cognac was Brandy. It all tastes the same to me," before taking another long sip. "It warms me. That's what's important."

"Cognac is made in a region of France by the same name," John Smith calmly explained. "It is a finely distilled version of Brandy."

"If you had threatened me, I would have told you that if I

didn't show up for a scheduled meeting tomorrow afternoon that the hard-drive would find its way into the right hands and the information will become public knowledge," Jarvis said, turning the conversation back to the issue at hand.

"I suspected as much," John Smith replied with a cool look.

Taking another long sip of the Cognac, Jarvis gazed at John Smith just as coolly. Suddenly, he felt nauseous and then violently choked, leaving his mouth filled with the bitter taste of stomach acid.

He dropped his crystal snifter. It bounced off the edge of the couch and tumbled to the floor, spilling it contents onto the polished wooden floor. Lurching forward, Jarvis vomited at John Smith's feet.

Sitting on the green couch with blue piping, John Smith shook his head. "I am not one to threaten, Mr. Jarvis. The hard-drive will not be that difficult to locate and retrieve. Based on your resume, I doubt you have the imagination to keep the drive from me and my employer."

"Maybe we should have waited until we had a bit more information on the hard-drive's location?" the chauffer chimed in with a concerned tone, as he stepped toward the couches.

Terror seized Jarvis when he realized that he had been poisoned. With wide eyes, he attempted to lunge at John Smith. The chauffer appeared behind him, grabbing his shoulders and pulling him back into the green couch. Jarvis vomited again, down the front of his shirt.

"It will take close to ten minutes for you take your last breath, and it will not be a pleasant ten minutes," John Smith flatly informed Jarvis, as he laboriously began to stand with the aid of his two canes, the look of pain erupting on his face, once again. "I can make it a far quicker death if you tell me where the drive is located."

Jarvis gagged again, bile spilling from the sides of his mouth, and he began slipping sideways on the couch.

"I think he's too far gone," the chauffer commented, releasing Jarvis's shoulders. "I put a double dose in his drink because he's so big."

"Obviously," John Smith replied, looking down and examining the semi-conscious man. "Just in case you're wondering, Mr. Jarvis, I would have killed you tonight even if you had handed over the hard-drive and eliminated the woman."

Jarvis choked again and then watched in horror as John Smith limped from the couch, holding his crystal snifter of cognac between his right thumb and index finger, to the counter. Pouring out the cognac into a sink mounted on the granite countertop, John Smith turned and commented, "Such a terrible waste of good cognac."

Over his shoulder Jarvis saw the short chauffeur looking down at him with a grin on his face. As Jarvis back at John Smith, a painful spasm lashed at his stomach, and he choked again, a foamy saliva drool hanging from the corner of his mouth. He then hoarsely choked out, "Why?"

John Smith causally answered, "Simple. You were a loose end that needed to disappear. Anyone having possession of the hard-drive will meet a similar fate. The information is too damning."

"Why?" Jarvis choked again.

Ignoring Jarvis's question this time, John Smith told the chauffeur, "Steve, the doctor left for the evening. Check to make sure Kelly is still asleep upstairs and then once this thug quits breathing, place him in the trunk of the Mercedes. We'll dispose of him later tonight."

"Shouldn't we eliminate the woman as well?" Steve responded. "Jarvis was supposed to get rid of her last night anyway."

"She has security outside her room because there are members within the Society that want to protect her. The Patriarchs know she survived and is being cared for at this residence. If we eliminate Kelly now, it will draw questions and suspicion. With Jarvis gone, she's no threat. He can't possibly be identified if he disappears."

"But she had the hard-drive," Steve scratched his pale face with a small hand. "We're supposed to eliminate anyone coming in contact with the hard-drive for fear they have looked at the data."

"Please think about what you just said," John Smith replied with a faint hint of frustration. "She's an employee of the Society and the Society placed it with her for safe keeping. Imagine if the Society eliminated all of its employees that kept the hard-drive safe. There would be no employees left."

Steve scratched the side of his head as he thought about what John Smith had said. Then nodding in approval, he walked from the room.

In Jarvis's last few minutes of his life, he wondered if someone would tell his ex-wife and two children that he was dead or whether he his body would just disappear. He hoped it would be the former. He did not want his children to think he had abandoned them.

CHAPTER 4

Falls Church, Virginia, USA, 6 December 2016:

It was a two-story rectangular white wooden clabber home, with two enormous leafless trees growing in the front yard. With short eaves and the rain gutters and vinyl sheathing missing from the house on the back side, aged wooden joists were revealed. A small wooden deck, covered in Astroturf with a sliding glass door, welcomed guests at the rear of the house and provided a view of a newer outbuilding at the back corner of the lot.

Inside, holding a white envelope postmarked the day before, Jack sat at his large wooden desk in a small alcove off the living room, looking out onto the snow-laden Westmoreland street in East Falls Church In his other hand, Jack held two sheets of paper: one formal looking that allowed him access to a private residence, the other a handwritten note. The smell of simmering stew wafted around Jack and his desk.

A big burly man in his mid-fifties, Jack resembled a large bear readying for hibernation. Wide shoulders and thick legs and arms, he was either English or Canadian by birth, none of his friends could remember because the only time he would talk of his youth was when everyone was intoxicated. The one thing they could remember was that he had a green card and practiced law in the Washington DC area. With unruly wavy silver and brown hair mounted on an enormous head, he did not walk but, rather, lumbered— just as a bear wandering through the forest moved his whole body. Onlookers expected the ground to shake. His eyes, blue, appeared kind and soft, sparkling with intelligence and honesty to the novice, but those who knew him also saw the threat of long calculating sharp claws.

A large yellow county dump truck with a plow mounted to its front bumper drove down the road, chucking a plume of snow aside and dropping white salt from its slightly tilted bed. Watching the plow maneuver down Westmoreland, nervously rocking back and forth in his matching wooden office chair, its joints whispering a compliant at each sway, Jack pondered the contents of the handwritten letter and its scriber.

Sandy, his wife, sensing aggravation from the alcove, called out from the kitchen, "What is it, Jack?"

"Darling, remember that man named Jarvis that I represented last year in the blackmail case? The gentleman who attempted to blackmail the senator from Wisconsin about his relationship with a local stripper?" John answered with a pronounced English accent.

Sandy, a tall slender strawberry-blonde woman with light blue eyes, peeked around the corner into Jack's office. "The stripper's name was Lolly-Pop and you hated that guy."

"The man fooled me into taking the case," Jack replied, running a massive paw through his unruly hair. "He claimed innocence, but after he hoodwinked me into accepting the case, and all the facts were presented, he was clearly guilty."

"But you got him off."

"On a technicality," Jack replied, still gazing out the window.

"What's it all about?" she asked, stepping into the alcove. Wearing white cotton pajama bottoms covered with round pink Santa Claus faces and a green North Face fleece jacket, she canted one hip outward and placed her hand on her waist.

"He has requested that if I do not hear from him by the time I receive this letter, I am to enter his house and retrieve a hard-drive from under a floorboard."

"From under a floorboard?"

"Yes, from under a floorboard," Jack said, twisting in his office chair around to face his wife. His blue eyes locked onto her light blue eyes. "Not someplace you typically hide items the local constabularies consider legal."

"We might hide something under a floorboard if there wasn't the threat of this whole crumbling house coming down on us." Sandy mischievously chuckled with a straight face. "The floorboards are probably the only thing holding this place up."

Jack crumpled and tossed the envelope into a nearby trashcan. "Get serious, Sandy. This man is clearly a criminal."

"Then don't do it," she said, tilting her head in the same direction as the canted hip. "Ignore the letter."

"I'm still technically his lawyer."

"So?"

"Darling, listen to me, I am still his lawyer," Jack repeated, his English accent becoming more pronounced with his building frustration. "This request could involve me with something unlawful, but I won't know for certain until I retrieve the hard-drive and see its contents. Who knows who or what this man is mixed up with?"

"What does he want you to do with the hard-drive," she asked, reaching up and pushing a strand of hair from her face.

"Take it to the FBI," Jack answered.

"Then it's absolutely something illegal."

"That seems obvious. But I really have no desire to be mixed up in his affairs. And I don't feel comfortable going into that house if he is hiding this hard-drive. Hiding something under a floor board infers that there is someone else looking for the item."

After a brief hesitation, Sandy said, "Then call someone to go along with you. Don't go alone."

Sitting at his desk, Jack swiveled his chair back around and looked back out the window. "Yes, I shouldn't go alone."

After a moment of silence, Sandy offered, "I know who you should call."

Jack nodded his enormous head. "So do I."

CHAPTER 5

Arlington, Virginia, USA, 6 December 2016:

It was a bone-chilling day in Northern Virginia, and black-and-blue bruise-colored clouds could be seen rolling in from the west. Unemployed, Tommy Luck was three hours into his daily jog along one of the many trails that crisscrossed Arlington, Falls Church, and Fairfax. Dressed in an orange stocking cap, a thick dark blue sweat shirt, and baggy gray cotton sweatpants, his exposed hands and face burned from the intense cold while he sweated out all the alcohol he had consumed the evening prior. Trotting alongside of him was a blue and gray eyed dog. The dog, a mute with a black, brown, and white hair, seemed to be his bodyguard, scanning their surroundings for possible trouble. There was a wiry patch of fur between its shoulder blades. Although he wasn't sure, Tommy presumed the animal was a mixture of Australian cattle dog and some other unknown beast. Maybe terrier.

Tommy was not a big man. At the age of forty-five and standing just under six feet tall, he was tan and slender from his incessant running. His father had bestowed on him deep blue eyes, high cheek bones, and a boyish smile through genetics, but he had also bequeathed him a love for beautiful women. Having always been capable of attracting a woman with a wink and a smile, Tommy had used his looks and charm on many women. Sadly, this habit was partially responsible for his current financial woes. Having never been able to control his wandering eye, which understandably neither of his former wives had tolerated, Tommy was twice divorced with three children. Alimony and child support had long since used up all his savings from a short but lucrative career in managing complex construction projects.

This financial fact required him to creatively augment his coffers by occasionally doing odd jobs. A year and a half ago, he had taken on a short-term employment that required him to deliver a flash-drive to Bangkok, Thailand. He had been told the delivery was strictly legal but had quickly discovered otherwise. And even more surprising to everyone involved was that the flash-drive had not contained what had been advertised to the clientele bidding on the device.

While he eventually passed on the merchandize and had been well paid, it had been a difficult delivery that had nearly ended his life on more than one occasion, as several despicable people vied for the flash-drive. The job also left him with a thin scar that ran from the corner of his mouth to the edge of his jaw.

Last year, that same merchandize had reappeared in Arlington, and he had been wrongfully implicated for attempting to sell the flash-drive. He had also been linked to the death of a CIA agent. It had taken him a week to solve the mystery and extract himself from the violent mayhem. While he had indirectly worked for the CIA during the mystery surrounding the reemergence of the flash-drive and the death of the CIA agent, he had not been paid. Without funds, he had settled on mowing neighbor's lawns, raking leaves, and cleaning gutters for a living. It had been a tough financial year.

He listened to music by means of earphones plugged into his cell, his thick brown wavy hair bouncing around the edges of his orange cap in cadence with each step as he jogged down a narrow paved path packed with snow and ice. The dog ran on his left side with its tongue lolling from the side of its mouth and its small paws making a clipping sound across the ice. The trail alternated between sunlight and shade, which was produced the large leafless overhead oak tree limbs.

Tommy's eyes—surrounded by a spider web of fine wrinkles, the product of a lifetime of working outdoors—examined the trail ahead as the icy path passed beneath him. The dog faithfully looked up at his master and seemed to smile. Tommy jogged up to four hours each day, the persistent running keeping him slim and fat free. He also realized that it was a healthy counterbalance to his nightly excessive consumption of alcohol. Both the jogging and drinking had been daily rituals for a number of years. When those two aspects of his life were in balance, he was happy. He was in equilibrium. So each night he drank himself into a stupor and each day he made up for his unhealthy consumption with a long run. Today was no different.

The music in his ears faded as his cell began ringing and the dog looked up at his master, again. Slowing his pace, Tommy removed the ear buds and answered the phone with his standard greeting, "Tommy here."

"Tommy, its Jack."

"Hey Jack, what's up?" Tommy panted, slowing his pace even more. Having known each other for several years, the big man and his beautiful wife had befriended Tommy at a local community pool and taken him in while he was searching for a place to live. Their similar age, honest conversations, and mutual enjoyment for drinking had sealed the friendship.

"Do you have plans this afternoon?" Jack asked.

"You opening the backyard bar a little early today?"

"No, I have an assignment in Washington DC and was wondering if you might come along."

"You need company for an assignment?"

"I have a client that has tasked me to pick up an article from his house in Northwest," Jack answered slow and methodically. "My client is not necessarily a law-abiding individual and the item I am to pick up is located under a floorboard."

"Under a floorboard?"

"Yes, under a floorboard."

Tommy asked, "Do you know what the item is?"

"A hard-drive."

"Are you expecting trouble?"

"I'm not sure what to expect. I'm retrieving something for a criminal client from under a floorboard," Jack replied with a hint of sarcasm.

"What time?"

"What time, what?"

Tommy asked, "What time are you picking me up?"

"Let's make it three this afternoon," Jack answered, clearly relieved that Tommy had signed on to the task.

"It's a date. I'll be out in front of my house at three."

"Will you be sober?"

"Jack, please." Tommy sighed. "I never drink before five at night." Shaking his head, he disconnected the call and glanced down at the dog. "Looks like we have an afternoon job."

The blue-and-gray-eyed dog gazed up and gave off a low whine.

Looking into the dog's eyes, Tommy cocked his head to one side. "Please don't give me one of your canine intuitional communiqués that something is not right."

The dog whimpered again.

CHAPTER 6

Washington DC, Northwest, USA, 6 December 2016:

Sitting in the idling green Toyota minivan on the snow-packed street, Tommy and Jack examined the white stucco house. The dog sat on the backseat, softly panting, and watching the two men in the front seat. Located in an affluent area of North West Washington DC, the modest-size house, with a large covered porch and an ornate carved wooden door, had obviously been built during an age when craftsmanship was at its apex. Surrounded by leafless trees, stone and craftsman style houses flanked the old white house on a sea of snow and ice, in what appeared to be an abandoned neighborhood. There was not a soul to be seen on the sidewalks.

"So this guy is a criminal?" Tommy asked while examining the house.

"Crime pays at times," Jack mumbled, obviously concerned about his next thirty minutes of activity.

"I met a criminal last year who lived in an upscale Georgetown home."

"Did he have a brother named Jarvis?"

"Not likely. His name was Jacob Livingston and he was not a good guy. He probably murdered any family members he might have had if there had been personal gain to be achieved." Then looking up and down the snowy block, Tommy asked "Where is everyone?"

"Probably having high tea and crumpets at the local country club—or maybe out shopping for a new Lamborghini or Rolls Royce," Jack offered with a straight face, still gazing at the house.

"Maybe we should have rented a Mercedes or Lotus." Tommy chuckled. "We'd fit into the neighborhood a bit better."

"Maybe they'll just think we're the maids or here for snow removal purposes." Jack joined Tommy's chuckle.

"Except we forgot the 'Merry Maids' magnetic sign for the side of the car," Tommy commented. "There might be a driveway out back the house. Let's take a drive around the block. At least we won't have to park on the street."

"You're right," Jack replied, glancing over at Tommy. "Parking on a Washington DC street after a snow storm is the equivalent to writing oneself a parking ticket."

"Snow storm or not, there's a ninety percent chance of walking away with a parking ticket in this city." Tommy chuckled again. "How else do you think they pay those swollen employee ranks?"

Driving through the intersection, they began passing elaborate homes situated on snow packed lots that populated the neighborhood. At the end of the block, the minivan passed a lone black Chevy van with tinted windows, before turning the corner.

Examining the van as they drove past, Tommy commented, "Probably IRS agents. This neighborhood has got to be pretty lucrative in terms of tax dodgers."

"These people have teams of accountants and lawyers protecting their wealth. There's more money in hounding people like you and me."

"A case of quantity verse quality?"

"We're McDonalds when it comes to the IRS," Jack replied.

Nodding his head, Tommy replied, "A quick and economical meal."

Turning the corner and driving back toward the stucco house, they saw a small driveway and Jack pulled in, coming to a halt on a short icy patch abeam the home's back-door. Silently, they opened their doors and stepped out onto the driveway, the snow crunching under their weight. Misty columns immediately began curling from their mouths as they breathed out into the frigid air. The dog bounded onto the front seat then out the door and stood next to Tommy. Once again looking up, the two men scrutinized the white stucco house. Two stories high with black wood trim around each window, and a black metal roof, the house was impressive. Wearing a dark green jacket and faded blue jeans, Tommy shook his head. Jack, dressed in a dark blue jacket and khaki slacks, whistled. The dog panted.

Jack said, "And I thought this guy was an inept imbecile. He's obviously done well with his criminal aspirations."

"Makes me wonder why I wasted all those years in construction, sweating it out twenty or thirty floors up on thin metal beams. Did he pay you?"

"Who?"

"This Jarvis guy," Tommy clarified, still examining the house. "You obviously worked with him before. Did he pay for your services?"

"In cash."

Glancing at one another, and shrugging their shoulders in unison, Jack and Tommy walked up a set of wooden stairs leading to the back door. The dog followed. They found the back door slightly ajar, and Tommy pushed it open several feet.

Peering into the house, they saw the kitchen strewn with draws, and cooking utensils. Various spilled ingredients were scattered across the floor. Beyond the kitchen, they could see the living room was equally messy, with cushions thrown about and their fluffy core ripped from inside, chairs overturned, and books littering the floor.

"He never struck me as untidy," Jack said. "Always clean and properly dressed."

"I've seen this kind of work before. I had a similar rearrangement of my house a couple of months ago. Looks to me like someone else is interested in retrieving something from this house—and it looks as if they didn't find it."

"What do you mean?"

"Someone has searched this place," Tommy announced, peering into the house.

Stepping inside, the two men and the dog maneuvered past granite countertops, through the strewn pots and pans, around an overturned and broken pot of flour, and across a milk carton lying on its side, slowly leaking its contents on the floor.

Coming to a stop at the entrance to the living room, Tommy commented, "It's still warm."

"What's still warm?" Jack looked at Tommy quizzically.

"The house is still warm. The back door is open and the house is still warm."

"Why does it matter?"

"This search didn't happen too long ago," Tommy answered. "They are either still here or have only recently left."

The two men listened for noises for a moment. The only sound they heard was the house's old wooden structure contracting in the cold air. Tommy looked at the dog to see if the animal sensed anyone else in the house. The dog looked up at Tommy with an unconcerned expression, its tongue lapping at the side of its mouth.

"I think we're alone," Tommy announced.

"Then let's get this over with," Jack replied, cautiously stepping into the living room.

With the dog following, they circumnavigated the mess in the living room, making their way up polished wooden staircase. Stopping midway to the top, the two men looked up at a wooden banister with black newel posts and spindles, and a white handrail mounted along the edge of a second floor walkway. A matching balustrade stood behind them, along the edge of the stairs.

"He wrote in a note that one of the floorboards on the second level, adjacent to stairs, would slide out. It's not glued or nailed," Jack explained to Tommy.

Standing on the stairs below the second floor, Tommy and Jack began trying to move the individual floorboards, under the black and white banister. Tommy started on the right and Jack on the left, working their way outward from the center.

When Jack found one that moved next to one of the newel posts, he whispered, "Got it."

"Why you whispering?"

"It seemed the appropriate way to communicate while discovering a secret compartment."

He slipped a short section of the floorboard from out from the floor, and a cobalt blue and silver device with a USB port on one side appeared in the small confine.

"Bingo," Tommy whispered.

"Why are you whispering?" Jack looked at Tommy with a thin smile.

"It seemed like the appropriate thing to do, when discovering a secret compartment holding an alleged valuable and likely illegal hard-drive."

Suddenly, they heard a faint murmur from the living room, and the dog growled. Quickly slipping the hard-drive into the pocket of his dark blue jacket, Jack glanced down into the living room. With his hands splayed across the floor boards under the banister on the second level, Tommy looked up as a man appeared overhead, standing on the walkway above them. Bringing the sole of his shoe down on top of the fingers of Tommy's right hand, the man, dressed in a black suit, tan overcoat, and red tie, smiled. Two more men, in khaki pants and matching blue shirts, advertising a local plumbing company, appeared below them.

The man in the overcoat standing above them, six foot four with short brown hair and dazzling green eyes, looked down and began twisting the shoe that was holding Tommy's fingers in place. Silently Tommy tried and failed to remove his fingers. The dog barked and growled as the man rotated his sole across Tommy's fingers.

Looking up at the green-eyed man above them, the muscles in Jack's jaw tensed. Without a word, his blue eyes flickered and his enormous shoulders rippled, just before he threw his weight against the wooden banister, snapping it from the newel posts holding in place. Jack placed all his weight behind the unencumbered and accelerating banister as it glided downward. The rail struck the green eyed man on the right shin. A muffled splinter could be heard and green eyed man in the overcoat gave off a high-pitched shriek before crumpling forward, and falling over the top of Tommy, Jack, and the dog. His tan overcoat fluttered behind him as he arched overhead. The man then bounced off the stairway banister, the wooden railing shuddering from the impact, before he fell onto the living room floor with a loud slap. John and Tommy, having ducked when the man plummeted over them, remained standing midway up the stairs. Tommy rubbed the fingers on his right hand with his left.

The room remained silent. No one had yet to utter a word. The blue shirted plumbers glared up at Tommy and Jack. Tommy and John peered down at the blue shirted plumbers. The green eyed man lay motionless on the living room floor, his tan overcoat twisted around his body. Silently the plumbers, keeping an eye on Tommy, Jack, and the dog, gathered up the green-eyed man. Hoisting him by his shoulders, the two men dragged him into the kitchen and out the back door.

"What was that all about?" Tommy broke the silence, first looking at the dog, then at Jack.

"I have absolutely no idea," Jack replied, looking back at Tommy.

"You broke his leg," Tommy replied, with a short laugh.

"Technically, the banister broke his leg. And I believe that was the least of his worries. I heard another bone fracture as he bounced off this," Jack said, gesturing to the stairway banister with his chin. "How did your fingers fare?"

"Thank you for getting his foot off of my fingers. They're sore but fine."

"It seemed obvious that the finger routine would have a follow-on performance. I was simply trying to avoid any more unpleasantness."

"Well, thank you anyway."

The two men and the dog calmly walked down the stairs and into kitchen. After briefly examining the snow covered backyard, to ensure there would be no surprise ambush by the mysterious plumbers, they walked down the backstairs, across the yard, and stepped into the green minivan, the dog once again taking up position on the backseat.

Sitting in the front seats, Tommy and Jack looked at each other, and for a second time shrugged their shoulders in unison.

"Please tell me there will be no more to this hard-drive mystery," Jack said.

Tommy laughed. "Jack, you're screwed. You've gotten yourself involved in something really fucked up. You should have just ignored the letter from this Jarvis guy. If a compliant were filed, told the bar you never received the request."

"It came via registered mail." Jack sighed.

"You are so screwed," Tommy said again, without the follow-on laughter this time, as he contemplated the implications of his friend's situation.

"Well, let us hope I did not mistakenly involve you, as well."

Ignoring Jack's comment, Tommy said, "Let's drive back around the block. I want to check out the black van again."

"Our primary goal should be to remove ourselves from this neighborhood," Jack replied, shaking his head.

"Just humor me."

Jack sighed and turned left as he departed the driveway. At the end of the block, he made another left and the black van came into view, parked alongside the curb. A soft cloud chugged from its exhaust, and Tommy leaned forward in his seat, examining the van. As they drove past, the driver, with a small head, bushy dark hair, and beady eyes, glared back at them through the open driver's window.

"That man could not have been five foot tall," Jack commented.

"Five foot two," Tommy responded.

"Do you know him?"

Silent for a moment, Tommy muttered, "What did Jarvis's note say you were to do with the hard-drive?"

"Turn it over to the FBI."

After another short moment of silence, Tommy said, "Don't."

"Don't what?"

"Don't turn it over till we figure out what's going on." Tommy sighed. "This hard-drive may be our only ticket to getting out of this mess."

"Are we in a mess?"

"The answer to your question as to whether I knew the short guy is yes. Last time I we met, he was working for an organization called the Society. If he still works for the Society, then the FBI is the last place we should take the hard-drive. The Society has members in each and every law enforcement organization you can think of, not to mention each and every criminal organization."

"What you're saying is that we are indeed in a mess."

"The term 'we are in a mess' might be a bit of an understatement."

CHAPTER 7

Sitting on cold gray vinyl tiles in the grocery store aisle, Omid Sassani absently twisted at his shoe laces. Next to him was a box of canned tomatoes, needing his attention in stacking them on the shelves above. Tired of reaching up and placing the cans on the correct ledge, he had taken a few minutes to sit and rest.

Several customers maneuvered around him, some smiling at his boyish behavior and others shaking their heads in disgust at his apparent laziness. He didn't care. While other kids his age were out playing baseball or football during their summer break, he worked in his father's grocery store for up to ten hours a day. Omid knew that he wasn't lazy, and it didn't really matter whether he was working or not, he had no friends. In the middleclass neighborhood in which his family resided, his coffee-colored skin was surrounded by a sea of white. To make matters worse, he was a Muslim living in a predominately Christian area. Religion and the color of his skin made him an outsider, and no one knew better the cruelty that children could inflict on one another. Teased relentlessly at school, Omid was a loner. Not by his choice, but by his father's choice in where they settled.

When not working, Omid enjoyed reading. While his father would push a *Koran* into his hands each night, Omid would sneak away to his bedroom and replace the book with one of his own. Having just finished Jules Verne's,

Twenty Thousand Leagues Under the Sea, he was now read-ing Enid Blyton's, *The Secret Seven*.

Standing up, Omid picked up another can from the box, ensured that it was dust free, stood on his toes, and placed it on the shelf above. He made sure to twist the can so the cus-tomers could easily read the label. His arms and hands burned. His mind roiled in boredom. Reaching down, he picked up another can and brushed the dust from its round silver top. As he began standing on his toes to place the can on the shelf above, he was grabbed by the collar and tossed down the aisle, rolling and twisting across the floor. The can that had been in his hand broke loose and tumbled along besides him, clattering to a stop next to his head.

Looking back down the aisle, Omid saw his father angri-ly glaring at him. Omid whimpered and a tear began form-ing at the corner of his right eye. Without a word, his father turned and briskly walked away. Omid cautiously resumed stacking the cans.

That evening they drove home in silence. His head bowed in obedience, Omid allowed his father to exit the car and walk into the home before he followed. He was terrified and wondered what would happen when he entered the house after his father. Hesitatingly, he opened the car door and slowly walked up the sidewalk to the front door. He gingerly opened the door and, expecting the worst, stepped inside. He could hear his father quietly discussing some-thing with his mother in the kitchen. He assumed that the issue concerned him and whatever rule he had broken at the store earlier. He didn't know which, but the rough treatment at the store, followed by the silent car ride, told him that he had done something wrong. His infraction had likely been trivial but his father demanded perfection. Omid knew his father and that he would physically pay for whatever he had done.

As he quietly stepped toward the hallway on which his room was located, Omid heard a horrific slap followed by a quiet whimper. More hushed discussion came from the kitchen, and Omid could hear building rage in his father's hissing whispers. Another slap could be heard as Omid opened his bedroom door. Another moan from his mother drifted down the hallway. As Omid closed the door, he knew that the discussion in the kitchen was now a one-way conversation. His mother, having been punished for disagreeing, had become silent.

At seven years old, Omid began mentally and physically preparing himself for the inevitable. He removed his trousers and sat on the bed, trying to calm himself. He stripped off his underwear and rolled over on his stomach. As his father demanded, his bare bottom should be prepared for the whipping. He took deep breaths in anticipation of what was coming—and he waited. Omid Sassani did not have long to wait.

CHAPTER 8

Hartford County, Maryland, USA, 6 December 2016:

The room was heavily draped and the walls were lined with bookcases filled with classic works. The faint smell of aged wood and stale cigar smoke wafted the air around a large mahogany desk with a laptop to one side and a crystal ashtray to the other. Sitting at the desk, with drape-blocked views of the winter wonderland just outside, John Smith aimlessly rocked back and forth on a matching mahogany chair cushioned in leather. His mind swirled around the memory of the beating he took after returning from the grocery store with his father at the age of seven. The infraction turned out to have been a customer complaining about his playing in the aisles. His name back then had been Omid Sassani and he had not been playing. He had simply been a seven-year-old boy tired of reaching up and placing cans of tomatoes on the shelf above his head. The words his father had raged over him that night, before taking the leather belt from his pants and whipping Omid's bare bottom, stuck in his mind like concrete pillars. His father had screamed, "Omid Sassani, you are as worthless as woman. Your only future will be to mix with the infidels and provide a place for them to put their white shriveled manhood."

After the beating, his father removed all of Omid's books, less the Koran that he earlier used to slap the terrified boy on the head with several times, and threw them in the backyard. Dousing the books with gasoline from a small can they used to refuel the lawnmower, his father had lit them by casually tossing a cigarette on the fuel laden pile. Omid, with tears streaming down his cheeks, had been forced to watch as his prized book collection burned.

"Omid Sassani, you are as worthless as a woman," John Smith whispered while sitting the mahogany desk in the heavily draped room. John Smith had learned to hate the name his father had bestowed on his only son, and he eventually changed and attempted to forget the name Omid Sassani. With the exception of a few, there were only foul memories associated with that name.

His thoughts were interrupted by a cell phone, sitting to one side of the desk, as it began vibrating and ringing. Picking it up, John Smith looked at the caller ID before answering. "Steve, did they find the hard-drive?"

"No, and you would not believe what happened," Steve replied, sounding out of breath with excitement.

"Where are you now?" John Smith asked, his heart sinking.

"We're in the van around the corner from the house," Steve replied. "One of the guys got pretty messed up."

"Now tell me what happened." John Smith requested, envisioning Steve's tiny pale hands gripping the cell and his beady eyes darting about as they talked. "Were you with them?"

"No they told me to wait in the van," Steve answered. "They said they could finish quicker if I wasn't in the way."

"It was to be a simple search," John Smith said. "The three men we hired are supposed to be professionals at finding items that are not meant to be found."

"They were interrupted. They were in the midst of the search when two guys entered the house. These guys knew exactly where to find the hard-drive. They hurt one of our guys bad."

"We hired three men. What did the other two do?"

"It was the head guy that got clobbered. The other two gathered him up and got out. They weren't sure what to do," Steve replied, his voice still filled with excitement. "And you won't believe—"

"Did you get the license number of the car the other two men used?" John Smith, tired of Steve's excitement, interrupted.

"Yeah, yeah," Steve replied, before rattling off a Virginia plate number. "It was a green Toyota minivan."

"Did they take the hard-drive?"

"It was under a floorboard. The other two guys knew where to find it. One of our guys saw one them slip it into his jacket pocket."

"All right, then they have the hard-drive." John Smith hesitated for a moment. "I'll find out who the license belongs to. You need to put a team together to eliminate the minivan owner and find the hard-drive."

"That will take some time," Steve mumbled, his excitement ebbing. "Wet work combined with a search. It'll take a special team."

"Tomorrow night, at the latest. I don't want these people to have time to pass on the hard-drive."

"But you're not listening to me," Steve pleaded. "We know one of the men who interrupted the search, and you'll never believe who it was."

"If I won't believe, then I can't possibly guess." Then, with a sigh, John Smith asked, "Who interrupted them?"

"Mr. Luck." Steve's voice hit an apex of excitement. "It was Tommy Luck—and his dog."

"Tommy Luck?" John Smith leapt up from the desk. His back screamed in pain, and he nearly fell back into the chair, before grabbing the edge of the desk with his free hand to stabilize himself.

"Yes, Mr. Luck," Steve replied.

Slamming the cell shut, John Smith threw the small device across the room. The cell bounced off the edge of a bookcase, before exploding into pieces on the hardwood floor. Hovering over the desk, he quickly grabbed his silver canes to steady himself, before hobbling over to a side table and filling a crystal glass with whiskey from a nearby bottle with shaking hands.

"What was Tommy Luck doing at that house?" John Smith yelled at the empty room, his back screaming in agony from a spasm brought about by his stress. Picking up the crystal glass, he took a large mouth full of whiskey and swallowed. The bourbon burned as it ran down his throat, and warmed his stomach, draining the tension from his body.

Footsteps could be heard running down the staircase in the foyer, before a faint knock at the door and a muffled, "Sir, is everything all right?" It was the security guard who was stationed outside Kelly's room upstairs.

Taking several deep breaths of air to compose himself and let his back pain subside, John Smith calmly replied, "Yes, everything is fine. Could you please bring me a new cell phone?"

A few moments later, the employee returned and knocked on the study door again. John Smith hobbled over to the door and opened it the security guard. Quietly taking a cell from the obedient security guard, John Smith closed the door in the man's face without a word and shuffled back to the desk before dialing Steve's number.

"Did Tommy see you?" John Smith asked, when Steve answered the phone.

"Yes, when they left the house they drove past the van and he saw me."

After a few moments of silence, John Smith instructed Steve, "I will find out who the mini-van belongs to. I'll have an address for you within the hour. Tomorrow night, I want two teams. One will enter the home of the minivan driver and the other Tommy Luck's house. We know Tommy doesn't drive a van. He's got that old white Chevy truck."

"Yeah, I got it. Two teams to hit two houses," Steve said, acknowledging the instructions.

"I want no survivors," John Smith continued. "I don't

care who is in the houses, with the exception of children, I want everyone dead. And above all, find the hard-drive. Do you understand?"

After Steve acknowledged the instructions for the second time, he then asked, "Should I assign someone to watch their houses before we hit them?"

"Absolutely not," John Smith quickly replied. "Tommy would spot the surveillance and run. We want him to think he has time to plan. He knows who he's up against and that will give him a little confidence. I don't want to tip him off to what we are planning. Do you understand?"

After Steve acknowledged his instructions, John Smith calmly closed the new cell and painfully sat back down at the desk. After a few moments of contemplating the hard-drive situation, he looked at his watch, reached across the desk, and pulled the laptop computer from the corner, so it was sitting directly in front of him. He then reached into his pocket and pulled out a cellophane packet that contained a USB flash drive.

As he opened the packet, a barely perceptible smell of petroleum rose up and swirled around his nose. John Smith turned the flash-drive over in his hands. It was made of hard cardboard with the small USB connector protruding from the end. John Smith knew that the flash-drive, when inserted into the computer, would take over the operating system and from that moment on any activity would not be recorded on the computer, only the flash-drive.

Inserting the flash-drive, the screen momentarily blinked, and a new screen appeared, allowing for texting to other computers similarly fashioned. He typed in, *TT3*, the address of the other flash-drive he wanted to communicate with. With the cursor flashing behind his initials, JS, he typed: *We have a problem*, and waited for a response.

After a few moments, *TT3: Go ahead*, flashed across the screen, and John Smith realized the man had been waiting for his message as to whether they had recovered the hard-drive.

Behind a flashing *JS:* John Smith then typed *The hard-drive has been taken from Jarvis's house by two men. We know one of the individuals responsible for taking it and will find out who the other is shortly.*

The flashing cursor quickly spelled out, *TT3: Go ahead*, again.

Hesitating a moment, John Smith then typed, *Thomas Luck was one of the men, the same man that the Society looked at hiring last year for the executive assistant position. Luck saw Steve and must know that I am involved. I am not sure he is aware this has anything to do with the Society.*

TT3: Is that a problem?

John Smith typed, *He was the preferred man for my position earlier this year. You tell me. Is that a problem?*

After a brief delay, the flashing cursor printed out *TT3: I see your point. Will you be able to retrieve the hard-drive?*

Hesitating a moment, John Smith typed, *I know the man and I know what he will do. Because of my involvement, he will likely hang onto the hard-drive. If he's aware of the Society connection, he will also want to hang onto the hard-drive. He will know that turning the device over or leaking its contents will not be in his best interest.*

TT3: What will you do? flashed across the screen.

I am sending crews to eliminate Thomas Luck and the other individual present when the hard-drive was taken. Once they are eliminated the crews will search the houses and retrieve the hard-drive.

TT3: When? quickly flashed across the screen.

Tomorrow evening.

TT3: Too late. I want it done tonight.

John Smith typed, *Not enough time. Tomorrow is the earliest it can be arranged.*

TT3: Make time. Do it tonight or early tomorrow morning. The mission remains the same. Do not tell the other members of Luck's involvement. They must continue to believe that we are unaware who has the database. Once we obtain the hard-drive, we will proceed with our original plan.

John Smith typed, *Understood—tonight*, just before the flashing TT3 disappeared from the screen.

Sitting at the large mahogany desk, John Smith contemplated the implications of Tommy Luck's involvement with the hard-drive. John Smith had worked with and against the unemployed drunk over the last year and one half, and the man had proven to be both a worthy ally and adversary. Each encounter with Tommy Luck had been marked by proactive cleverness. Each encounter had proven Tommy Luck's unusual knack for survival. Each encounter had seen the unemployed drunk the victor. In John Smith's opinion, Tommy Luck was responsible for the two canes at his side. In John Smith's opinion, Tommy Luck had undermined his money-making ventures both in Thailand a year and a half ago, and in Washington DC earlier this year. Hatred was an understatement. John Smith despised Tommy Luck and wanted to see him dead.

Painfully reaching across the desk, John Smith dragged the crystal ashtray closer. He then pulled the cardboard sheathed flash-drive from the computer and a lighter from the top drawer. Holding the flash-drive over the ashtray, he lit the corner. The cardboard quickly ignited and John Smith dropped it, and all evidence of his communication with TT3, into the ashtray. Black smoke rose and the flash-drive crackled, spiting sparks. The smell of burning petroleum filled the room.

Picking the cell back up, John Smith called Steve for a third time that day.

"Tonight. We need to send a team to their houses tonight," John Smith calmly told Steve when he answered the phone.

"I won't be able to get two teams together that quickly," Steve complained.

"Then send one. Have them do one house and then the other."

"Which house should I do first?" Steve asked.

"Do Tommy's second," John Smith directed. "Between his uncanny knack for survival and that dog, his will be the toughest. The first house will give the team time to warm up. Make sure they know that Tommy is unpredictable. Make sure they're ready for him and that dog."

Closing the cell, John Smith began anticipating the raid into Tommy Luck's house, and he knew it would require an especially talented team. Steve would make sure the odds against the unemployed drunk were insurmountable. He considered calling Steve back to ensure he knew that, but then dismissed the idea. Steve was not an intelligent man, but he wasn't that stupid. He would know that Tommy Luck was a tough nut to crack. Steve would figure it out. Rocking back in the chair, John Smith realized that Tommy Luck would die tonight and forever be out of his life. John Smith smiled at the thought.

CHAPTER 9

Arlington, Virginia, USA, 6 December 2016:

The television flickered next to a white brick fireplace with smoke stains at its edges and the central heat quarreled with the outside night chill, the house groaning as it expanded and contracted in tempo with the sparring elements. The living room was small with an old wooden parquet floor that could have used a good sanding and refinishing. The walls were otherwise empty except for several professional awards. On his fifth Jameson on the rocks, with the blue-and-gray eyed dog at his feet, Tommy sat on a sagging brown couch in the living room, watching the evening news. A comfortable numbness had begun to develop on his brow, and he had almost forgotten the events that had occurred at the white stucco house in Northwest Washington DC earlier that day. The wind had picked up outside, rattling windows and breaking brittle branches from swaying trees, some clattering on the house's roof.

Suddenly, the dog perked up and barked once.

Looking down at the dog, Tommy asked, "What?"

The dog cocked his head to one side and then there was a knock at the front door. Looking up at Tommy, the dog gave off a low guttural whine. In his semi-drunken state, Tommy initially thought it was just broken branch, maybe dangling from its previous perch on strands of tree fiber. A second knock announced that someone was actually at his door and the dog growled. Standing from the couch, Tommy made his way to the foyer and reached for the door handle. The dog followed at his heels while watching the door with a curious expression. Hesitating a moment, Tommy looked down at the dog. The dog looked up with an unconcerned expression.

"A lot of good you are," Tommy said to his canine pal. "You couldn't even tell that those men were still in the house today." Shaking his head, Tommy vanquished any thought of the visitor being involved with the hard-drive and pulled the door open.

Standing, shivering in the night, a woman dressed in a black parka and blue jeans, smiled at Tommy. Blonde hair erupted from the edges of a black wool cap and sparkling bright blue eyes studied him.

"Hello, Tommy," the woman greeted him. "Are you drunk yet?"

"Caroline." Tommy sighed. "Not quite. I had a premonition that someone from the Society might be calling."

"Your premonitions are normally correct." She giggled. "Except, I'm no longer with the Society."

Stepping aside, Tommy said, "Well, come on in. Get out of the cold. *Me casa su casa*," while gesturing her into the house.

Caroline stepped inside and immediately stripped the black parka and wool cap. A slender woman, she stood five feet four inches, and her straight blonde hair was cut just below her ears. Her bright blue eyes were quick and danced on soft porcelain skin. Dropping the parka and wool cap on a small table in the foyer, she marched straight into the kitchen with dog following her. Tommy walked over to the fireplace and began arranging several logs to start a fire. Caroline returned, carrying a matching glass of Jameson on the rocks, and sat down on the sagging brown couch.

Glancing over his shoulder while pushing crumpled newspaper under the logs, Tommy said, "Go ahead. Tell me what's going on."

"You, my friend, are in big trouble," she commented before sipping at the glass of whiskey.

"I seem to have a talent for finding trouble where none is to be found. Who does Steve work for these days?"

"He and John Smith work for the Society."

"And you do not?" Tommy dragged a match across one of the bricks on the hearth.

"I quit after the flash-drive fiasco earlier this year," Caroline casually announced.

"But you know what happened today?"

"I have maintained several contacts in the Society, yes."

"And I'm screwed?" he asked, while placing the flaming match under the crumpled newspaper.

"Yes, you and whoever your friend happens to be. You are both in big trouble."

"Why?"

"The hard-drive you took from the house belongs to the Society. It contains the history of the Society, with documented proof of its actions," Caroline explained. "And many of the actions it has taken over the years have been questionable in terms of legality. A few people disappearing. Others meeting untimely deaths. Like instructing John Smith to kill a CIA agent in order to frame you for a job interview to test your ability to handle the unknown and pressure."

"John Smith claimed it was his idea to murder the CIA agent." Tommy stood from the fire and picked up his drink from the mantel, before moving to the couch and sitting down next to Caroline.

"That might be so," Caroline replied. "Nevertheless, there are many other instances where the Society was involved in illegal activity, and it's all documented on the hard-drive. It also contains all the Society agents, both official and criminal."

"So how about we just give the hard-drive back?"

"Too late because of its contents, anyone who has had possession of the hard-drive and is not a member of the Society must be eliminated. It's SOP—standard operating procedure."

Tommy chuckled. "I'm familiar with the acronym SOP."

"The Society cannot take the chance of someone viewing or copying the information. The only way of ensuring that none of the information is leaked, is to terminate any outsider who has had access."

"Then maybe I should give it to the television station?"

"If you recall our conversation earlier this year, while the Society was giving you the job interview and subsequently trying to hire you, they have agents in each and every major media outlet."

Tommy added, "And law enforcement organization across the globe, not mention each and every criminal organization. Yeah, I remember."

"The Society is led by two hierarchically levels of command made up of eight individuals. The top level consists of three gentlemen who devise and plan the Society's actions. They are called the Patriarchs. A second echelon team consists of the five individuals, and they vote on the plans developed by the Patriarchs."

"And what do you call them?" Tommy jokingly asked, "The Matriarchs?"

"We call them the Bishops," Caroline answered flatly. "All in all, there are eight gentlemen and/or ladies, on a rotating basis, that manage the Society. Typically the entire command structure is made up of two from Asia, two from Africa, two from Europe, and two from North America."

"What about South America?"

"I said typically." Caroline sighed. "Occasionally, the command structure has members from Southeast Asia, South America, and the middle east. The Society attempts to maintain a regional balance, focusing on areas of industrial and political power."

"Got it," Tommy said, nodding his head.

"Both the Patriarchs and the Bishops base their decisions concerning the society's activities on democratic rule. Each member of the team has one vote, and the final decision on each plan, at both levels is based on the most votes."

"What if there's a tie?" Tommy watched the flames of the fire nipping at the edges of the fireplace, while sipping his whiskey.

"What do you mean?"

"You said there are eight members who vote on the courses of action. What if four say yes and four say no?"

"The three Patriarchs design and plan the possible courses of action," Caroline sighed. "The Bishops vote. There are five of them."

"Back to the question of turning over the hard-drive," Tommy prompted Caroline.

"Just one more thing about the Society leadership," she continued, "the three members of the Patriarchs are based in Washington DC."

"Back to the law enforcement agencies," Tommy said again. "Explain to me why can't we just hand the hard-drive over to the FBI or some other law enforcement agency?"

"Most of the Society law enforcement agents are senior officials," Caroline clarified. "The Society enlists the best talent when they are young agents and those same agents rise through the ranks at the bequest of the same. In other words, if you were to deliver the hard-drive to any law enforcement agency around the globe, it would likely disappear and make its way back to the Society." Caroline went on to explain the technology and information systems the Society had at its beck and call, via the different law enforcement agencies. "It's the same with media outlets."

Standing from the couch, Tommy looked down at Caroline and asked, "So what can I do, besides allowing them to eliminate—murder—me and my pal?"

Standing up in front of Tommy and cupping a hand on his neck, she said in a serious tone, "They will be coming after you and your friend tomorrow evening. You need to get out of town."

"And where do we go?"

"The one thing I know about you is that if anyone is capable of extracting themselves from this, it's you. Earlier this year and Thailand the year before is the proof. Do what you do best. Figure a way out."

"Where does John Smith fit in to this mess?"

"He's right in the center. He is the one who has been tasked with retrieving the hard-drive."

"And who is your contact within the Society?"

"The only one that still talks to me is John Smith's right hand man, Steve. Everyone else plays by the rules. No communication about Society business except with Society members."

Tommy chuckled. "He's not a smart guy."

"Which is why I cultivated my friendship with him," Caroline replied with a thin smile on her face.

"Please don't tell me you've had sex with him," Tommy groaned.

"He hangs on with just a little phone sex." Caroline giggled before continuing, "There's something else."

"What is it?"

"There's something that seems freelance about the retrieval of the hard-drive."

"What do you mean?"

"As you pointed out, Steve is not a super intelligent guy," Caroline explained. "I had the impression, the way he described what they were doing, that there's something about this operation that's either not known or unapproved—yet. I think the Patriarchs know the hard-drive is missing, and they know John Smith is attempting to retrieve it, but there is some element of this whole operation that's cloaked in secrecy."

"Why do you say that?"

"I'm not sure. Call it a hunch," Carol said, as she drew her right index finger the length of the scar that ran from the corner of his mouth to the edge of his jaw. Standing on her tiptoes, Caroline whispered in his ear, "They're not coming until tomorrow night."

Looking down into Caroline's eyes, Tommy smiled as he began unbuttoning her blouse. Caroline reached down and unbuckled his belt while kissing him on the lips. Tommy felt himself become aroused as Caroline stroked his crotch through his jeans. Tommy slipped his hand into her pants and could feel her warm wetness, as she softly moaned.

Placing her mouth next to his ear, Caroline asked, "How drunk are you?"

"Sober enough to recognize a good deal."

Giggling, Caroline asked, "A good deal?"

Slipping her shirt off her shoulders and running his hands down her bare sides, Tommy replied, "I'll save half a bottle of Jamison while getting laid by a beautiful woman. That's a pretty good deal."

Playfully punching him in the crouch, Caroline grabbed his hands and pulled him toward the bedroom. "Thomas Bacon Luck, you're such a romantic."

CHAPTER 10

Arlington, Virginia, USA, 7 December 2016:

Rolling over on his bed Tommy saw short blonde hair budding from under a white quilt and lying across the pillow next to him. The scent of love hung in the air as Tommy examined Caroline's porcelain forearm and hand with unpolished nails protruding from under the soft white quilt. Turning his head, he looked out over his sage green bedroom and saw her blue jeans lying across the long mahogany dresser standing against the wall. A pair of black lace panties lay on the floor next to the bed and a matching bra was strewn next to the door. The faded jeans and tee shirt he had been wearing were waded up in the corner of the room.

Slipping a hand under the quilt, Tommy ran his fingers across Caroline's bare back and then down to her naked bottom. She let out a soft moan. With his other hand, he ran his fingers through his wavy brown hair and began to think of all he must do in the next few hours.

"What time is it," Caroline groggily asked, her voice muffled under the quilt.

"Just after midnight."

"Are you getting up?" Another muffled question came from under the white quilt.

"I figure I should go over to my friend's house and start making a plan for getting out of town—the sooner, the better."

"Won't he be asleep?" Turning on her side, she pulled

the quilt from her face. Her bright blue eyes sparkled with intelligence.

"They'll likely be in the backyard bar," Tommy replied in the midst of a yawn. "It's pretty popular with their friends and neighbors. It normally runs till one or two in the morning."

"What's the backyard bar? Can I come?"

"To the backyard bar?"

"To wherever you're headed to get away from the Society."

Hesitatingly, Tommy said, "Caroline, I like you, and I like sleeping with you, but I'm not sure I trust you. You claim not to be working for the Society, but how do I really know?"

Laughing, Caroline replied, "Tommy, I know where you're headed."

"How do you know?" Tommy asked. "Where am I headed?"

"I'm the one who sought you out to work for the Society earlier this year. I've read your file." She giggled, "I know exactly where you're headed."

"Does the Society? Does John Smith know where I'm headed?"

"Unlike his right hand man, John Smith is not dumb," Caroline said, reaching up and running her index finger down the scar on his face. "When you and your friend disappear, it'll take him less than a day to figure out where you're headed."

Climbing from the bed, Tommy slipped on his faded jeans from the corner of the room and walked over to the dresser. Pulling a dark blue sweater from the third drawer, he slipped it over his head before looking over at Caroline, who was watching his every move, and said, "Wait here. I should be back in an hour or two. We can discuss whether you can come or not then."

Caroline smiled and nodded her head, before slipping back under the white quilt.

Walking from the bedroom into a short hall off the foyer, he pulled his dark green jacket from a hook in a hallway closet. The dog trotted up to his feet and looked up. As he opened the front door, a cold gust of air blew into the house and Tommy shivered.

"You need to stay here," Tommy said looking down at the dog. "Someone needs to keep an eye on her," he added, gesturing toward the bedroom.

Peering up with pleading eyes, the dog gave off a low whine.

Shaking his head, Tommy gazed down at the dog and said, "You are such a worrywart. What makes you think something is wrong?"

Pushing its snout against Tommy's thigh, willing him back into the bedroom, the dog whined again.

"We've got to work on our communication. I have no idea what's bothering you." Then patting the dog on the head, Tommy walked out the front door and into the chilly night.

CHAPTER 11

Falls Church, Virginia, USA, 7 December 2016:

Driving his ancient white Chevy pickup into the snow packed and crowded driveway, Tommy had to edge past a dark blue minivan and a small red Chevy Caprice. The hinges of the pickup gave off a high pitched shriek as Tommy opened the door. It let off an equaling loud squeal when he stepped from the truck and slammed the door. Examining the two extra cars in the driveway, Tommy shook his head, recognizing the vehicles and knowing their owners. They were two people he was in no mood to deal with. Gusting wind muffled the noise of cars and trucks careening along the nearby Interstate 66 and the scent of pine wafted the turbulent air as Tommy began maneuvering through the shadowy maze of cars, toward the rear of the house.

Stepping from the icy driveway onto ice crusted grass in the backyard, Tommy saw a dim red light above the door of a small outbuilding in the far corner of the lot, evidence that the backyard bar was still open. A stiff frigid breeze cut through his jacket, and he shivered while walking past a snow covered trampoline, toward the beaconing red light. Maneuvering past several snow laden bushes, along a narrow path leading to the door, Tommy stepped up the single, and slightly uneven, concrete step that led to the entrance.

Peering through the window, Tommy sighed when he saw Betty and Markey, owners of the two cars in the driveway, hovering over a dark wooden counter. Jack, with his large shoulders slumped, looked as if he were ready to fall over from sheer boredom as he stood behind the counter waiting on his two remaining visitors.

The outbuilding was what most of Jack and Sandy's friends referred to as the backyard bar. A large single room, whose unfinished walls were decorated with objects gathered over decades of living and working in the nation's capital. One side of the room had several gray filing cabinets, presumably filled with Jack's professional records, and a long bookcase loaded with mostly non-fiction works documenting wars and political intrigue. On the other side of the room stood an ancient and meticulously carved wooden buffet with a dozen bottles of various types of alcohol on top. A large etched mirror, encased an equally detailed wooden frame, hovered on the wall above the buffet. A dark brown bar with three stools was situated so that a barman, or woman, could stand behind the counter and pour drinks from bottles on the buffet. On the far wall was a well-worn dark blue futon sofa, allowing refuge for those guests that had had too much to drink. Trinkets, pictures, posters, and several weapons adorned the walls or stood on the various tables about the room.

Taking a deep breath, Tommy opened the door and was met with a soft draft of warm air that smelt of stale beer and cigarettes. The sight of Tommy stepping through the door brought a renewed enthusiasm from the bear of a man standing behind the bar and the look of relief filled his eyes.

Dressed in her usual loose fitting gray cotton sweat pants, a baggy dark maroon sweatshirt advertising a local Catholic High School, and an oversized green parka, Betty sat on a stool, babbling at Jack across the bar. With large doe brown eyes and an attractive oval face bracketed by long brown hair, from the neck down Betty's body could have passed for a man or woman. She had sagging shoulders, a massive waist that hung like an inner-tube over her belt, and spindly legs. Hearing the door open, she twisted on her stool and greeted Tommy with a, "Hey, look who's here!" Her voice, gravelly from years of smoking, sounded as if it could have come from someone twice her age.

Markey turned as well. With a cartoonish size stomach protruding from his midsection, skeletal arms and legs, gray placid skin, and small dark eyes peering out behind thick wire rim glasses, Markey looked as if he could be a fashion model for stick figure drawing. Dressed in a white tight fitting polo shirt and gray polyester pants that embellished both his obscenely large stomach and placid skin, Markey called out a greeting as well, saying a simple, "Hey," as if he had forgotten Tommy's name. A crooked smile revealed yellowish-gray teeth that oddly matched the color of his skin.

"Arlington's finest," Tommy replied with a grimace.

Jack, shaking his head with pleading eyes, muttered, "Please save me."

Quickly twisting back around on her stool, Betty's hissed, "What did you say, Jack?"

His face taking on a slightly embarrassed expression, Jack answered Betty's question with silence, presumably hoping the offensive woman would quickly forget his slip of the tongue or pass out. Markey seemed oblivious to the comment or question, his small eyes darting back and forth between Betty and Jack.

"I can take a hint," Betty rasped in proclamation, her drooping shoulders and inner-tube waist bouncing in discord under the baggy clothing as she stood from the stool.

Markey looked at Jack and then Betty with a confused look on his face, and said, "Hey." He was clearly not following the conversation.

"Jack and I need to talk in private," Tommy announced to the room.

"So your good friend Tommy arrives and your other friends fall to the wayside," Betty complained, her raspy voice sounding like a massive wad of phlegm was caught in her throat.

Looking around in confusion, Markey smiled and

slipped off his stool, stumbling several steps before regaining his balance. Betty glared at Jack and then Tommy, as if waiting for an apology. Tommy had a hard time taking his eyes off of her sagging midsection, wondering how many beers it had taken to develop such a monstrosity and about the hydraulics of her making love to her husband. Her waist looked to Tommy like it could have a life of its own, only crawling from her limp body when she passed out each night, and wrapping itself back around when she first stirred in the morning. Jack remained quiet, attempting to act as if there were no tension in the air.

"Are you departing?" Jack meekly asked Markey and Betty, as if it he had missed Betty's complaint and Tommy's announcement.

"They're leaving," Tommy firmly requested.

With Betty glaring at Tommy and Markey examining his shoes, seemingly trying to figure out why he was standing, Jack said, "It's been a wonderful night. Thank you so much for dropping by."

Betty hissed, "Fuck you guys," as she waddled from the bar, her waist resembling oversized oars moving a rowboat to some unknown destination.

"Hey," Markey replied, once again revealing his yellowish grey teeth with a crooked grin. He pulled a gray parka from the stool and struggled to put it on, requiring Tommy to step over and help him. Once the parka was secure on his shoulders, Markey staggered behind Betty and stumbled on the threshold, falling out the door. With slow motor skills due to his over consumption of alcohol, his arms hung limply at his side as he fell face down into a snow bank.

Looking at Tommy, Jack asked, "Shall we help him to his vehicle?"

"Even if he's able to find his keys, which I doubt, he will be incapable of putting them in the ignition." Tommy chuckled, watching Markey wobble to his feet just outside the open door.

Tommy stepped over to close the door in time to see Markey fall sideways into one of the snow-laden bushes along the path. Ignoring Markey's plight, Tommy turned and looked at Jack, still standing behind the bar, and asked, "Where's Sandy?"

"Inside the house. She was ready to punch Betty in the face."

"What was it this time? Was Betty giving another sermon on her family's importance in the development of Arlington?"

"I think it was an oration concerning skin cancer and how Sandy was sure to meet an untimely death due to her light skin," Jack said in a serious tone. "Betty's sister, the doctor, has told her so, so it must be true."

"Cunt."

"Which one?"

"Cunts."

"I am just glad that the entire family didn't show up," Jack continued, "Sandy would have surely had a cerebral hematoma."

"I need to talk with you and Sandy," Tommy said, ignoring John's comment. "Right now."

"The hard-drive?" Jack asked.

"Do you still have the hard-drive?"

"Of course. You declared I shouldn't turn it over to the authorities as of yet."

The two men made their way out of the bar, down the short path, past Markey passed out between two bushes, across the icy lawn, onto the Astroturf cover deck, and into the house. Sandy, sitting in the living room watching season two, episode five of the *Game of Thrones* for the tenth time, looked up. "Is the bitch gone?"

"Yes, darling, she slithered away about five minutes ago," Jack replied.

They walked into the living room, and Jack sat on his well-worn brown leather chair to one side and Tommy sat next to Sandy on the couch.

"Okay, what's wrong?" Sandy asked, clear irritated. "Am I going to need a drink?"

Tommy looked at her and flatly said, "Yes, that hard-drive has gotten us all in a little jam."

"Okay, wait a minute," Sandy interrupted, waving her hands above her head, as she stood and disappeared into the kitchen. A few moments later, she returned with a bottle of Jose Cuervo tequila and three shot glasses in one hand and four limes and a knife in her other. As she began pouring the shots, she said, "Go ahead and give us the bad news."

Methodically taking his time, it took Tommy three rounds of tequila shots among the threesome to explain about the Society, its powerful connections, Caroline, and John Smith. He also explained about the hard-drive and its contents. Finally, he told Jack and Sandy, as they sat listening intently, about the Society decree that anyone having had possession of the hard-drive was to be eliminated.

"We are definitely screwed," Jack was the first to comment after Tommy's explanation, leaning back and tossing another shot of tequila in his mouth with his bear-like paw.

Sandy glared at Jack, saying, "I told you to not go to that house," as she handed him a slice of lime.

"We need to get out of town and find a temporary safe haven," Tommy said, just before he delivered a fourth shot of tequila into his gullet.

Her voice raising several octaves, Sandy asked, "Where can we possibly be safe from this Society?"

"Where are your children?"

"With their grandparents," Sandy quickly chirped, taking her shot of tequila before biting into a thick wedge of lime.

"Tell your parents they need to stay there for a week more or so," Tommy instructed.

Sandy said, "My father will be furious—and my kids will be traumatized. If this Society knows everything, they know where our children are and will come after them."

"John Smith is a lot of things, but he keeps away from kids," Tommy answered. "The problem is that the Society is a techno superstar. They have access to everything. They can see into our bank accounts. They have our passports and every camera across the country—the world—at their disposal. If they wanted, they would know I'm at your house right now by simply having monitored my movements on traffic cameras. Which reminds me, we need to remove the batteries from our cell phones. They are nothing but tracking devices for the Society."

"Then what can we do?" Jack asked, digging in his pocket for his cell. "They've probably already locked our accounts and canceled our passports."

"Caroline believes this might be somewhat of a freelance operation, so far. In other words, John Smith does not have all the tools he would if it had been sanctioned by the Society hierarchy," Tommy continued, as he removed the battery from his cell. "That means we have a limited amount of time to make arrangements and get out of the country before he seeks approval and assistance from the Society's Patriarchs."

"Where would we go and what good will it do if we leave the United States?" Sandy asked while pouring three more shots. "It just means we would end up getting axed in some foreign country!"

"I know a place where we can go that is out of the reach of the Society," Tommy said, smiling. "It's like the old Wild West—a place the Society can't possibly have the level of information or influence they're accustomed to. I fondly refer to it as Pirate Island."

After a moment of silence, Jack asked, "So where is the Wild West? Where is Pirate Island?"

Taking one of the shot glasses glimmering with yellow tequila, Tommy said, "Thailand," and tossed it into his mouth. "More specially, an island called Koh PhaNgan."

Looking over to Tommy on the couch next to her, Sandy calmly asked, "You want a lime?"

Out of the corner of his eye, Tommy saw a shadow cross the backyard. "Someone's outside." Leaping from couch, he turned the kitchen light out before slipping into the narrow galley kitchen and peering out the window into the darkness. He could only see the tops of the trees swaying in the wind.

"It was probably just Markey," Jack commented, throwing back another shot of tequila before hoisting his bulk from the leather chair.

"Markey has either perished from hypothermia in the bushes or dragged himself to his car. Whatever was out there was moving swiftly and with an obvious goal."

"We've got raccoons and foxes around here," Sandy added as she rose from the couch, leaving her shot of tequila untouched on the coffee table. "A fox scared the hell out of the dog last week. He wouldn't go on the deck for days!"

"Too big," Tommy replied, still looking outside. "Turn all the lights in the house off—quickly please. Do you have any weapons?"

"Jack, you turn the lights off." Sandy took command, as she ran up a set of stairs at the rear of the living room, calling out, "I'll go to the gun safe."

As Jack began turning the lights off, Tommy could hear the hundred year old floor joists overhead squeaking and moaning as Sandy maneuvered around the second floor. As the final light was turned off, Tommy saw a shadowy figure moving across the back lawn, to the side of the house, followed by the faint squeal of the ancient wooden garage door in the basement being forced.

Sandy returned from the second floor and handed Tommy a 9mm Glock, and Jack a .22 rifle that he recognized belonged to their twelve-year-old son. Sandy held what looked to Tommy, from the shadows, like a Colt .45 M1911.

"Sandy, you cover the front door. Jack you watch the French doors here in the kitchen. I'm going down into the basement," Tommy instructed. "Move up against a wall and behind something near each entrance. When they come, they might use a concussion grenade followed by a lot of firepower. Keep your mouths open until the grenade goes off. I'll be right back."

The couple quickly took up position. Jack moved behind the kitchen counter and Sandy to the stairs leading to the second floor.

Moving to the far end of the kitchen, Tommy slowly pulled open the door leading to the basement and was met with a damp cold draft smelling of mildew and fabric softener. The narrow staircase moaned as he placed his foot on the top step. Halting for a moment, Tommy listened to the sounds coming from the garage. Hearing nothing, he took one huge leap down the staircase, crashing into the cinderblock wall at its base, and rolling flat onto the floor next to a tool chest. The small area lit up with suppressed gunfire, rounds ricocheting off the cinderblock walls and tearing through stored boxes. In the strobe like light of the assailant's weapon, Tommy saw the man, dressed in black with a matching balaclava, midway across the garage. When the man stopped firing, the room became pitch black again, and eerily quiet. Quietly opening the tool box, Tommy reached in and extracted a large monkey wrench. To distract his assailant, Tommy aimed and threw the monkey wrench in the direction he had last seen the man. A loud thud was followed by a groan, and then the clatter of two metal objects hitting the floor. Assuming one of the metal objects that hit the concrete floor was the man's weapon, Tommy jumped to his feet and sprinted across the darkness. He ran headlong into the man, and they became entangled before falling to the floor. As he was falling, Tommy aimed his Glock at the shadow next to him and pulled the trigger. A bright flash illuminated the man. Tommy adjusted his aim and pulled the trigger again. The loud reports of his weapon reverberated in the small garage and the smell of spent gunpowder filled the air. Tommy abated his fall with his free hand, as the man limply dropped to the concrete floor next to him. Just to be sure, he fired two more shots at the shadow on the floor, ensuring the man was dead. He lifted the black balaclava covering the man's face. Empty staring eyes looked up at him. Yes, he was most certainly dead.

Quickly turning and racing back toward the stairs, Tommy could hear silenced rounds begin ricocheting off pots and pans, penetrating walls and smashing pottery on the first floor. Reaching the top of the stairs, Tommy heard two distinct cracks of what sounded like Sandy's .45 Colt being fired. Running into the kitchen he saw the .22 rifle lying on the linoleum floor with a broken butt, and Jack struggling with another man, also dressed in black wearing a hood over his head, who was holding what looked to be an eight-inch knife. The scene seemed surreal as Jack's powerful arm easily took the wrist of the assailant he was struggling with and forced the man to plunge the knife into his own neck. Leaping over Jack and the now very dead thug, Tommy sprinted past another man dressed in black lying on the kitchen floor with a piece of the .22 rifle's butt lodged in his crushed forehead. As he rounded the corner into the living room, Tommy witnessed Sandy double tap a man in the chest with the .45 Colt at five feet. The man collapsed onto another assailant who had obviously been shot several seconds earlier. Sandy turned and, even in the shadowy living room, Tommy could see her triumphant smile.

"Close the door," Tommy said, smiling back at the tall light-blue eyed woman, as he reached down and turned on one of the living room's lights.

As he walked back toward the kitchen, the house was silent. Tommy flicked a light switch on the wall, illuminating the kitchen. The light revealed Jack standing in front of the sliding glass door breathing heavily, with a man also dressed in black, holding the muzzle of a silenced UZI SMG pressed against his thick neck. Tommy and Sandy silently raised and pointed their weapons at the man holding Jack hostage.

Shrugging his shoulders, Jack said, "I subdued two. Three was just asking too much."

"I nailed two," Sandy announced, cocking her head to the right.

"It was my fault," Tommy confessed, "I only got one."

"Shut up," the man growled, "Get me the hard-drive." His voice was muffled beneath the black balaclava covering his face.

"And then you kill us?" Sandy laughed. "No way."

"Get the hard-drive, Sandy," Tommy said, repeating the thug's request.

"We have two choices here," the man dressed in black hissed. "One, I kill this big guy and you two kill me. Two, you hand me the hard-drive, and I walk out of here. Or three, you hand me the hard-drive, and I kill the big guy and you kill me. From my perspective, there's only one way out."

"That's three," Sandy sarcastically chirped, shaking her head.

The man dressed in black looked confused. "What's three?"

"You said we had two choices and then you gave us three," Sandy spat.

From outside the French doors, there was a sudden movement. Two hands swiftly reached up and grabbed the intruder's neck and jaw, jerking his head violently to the right. A distinct crack rang out in the narrow galley kitchen and the black-clad thug dropped lifelessly to the floor.

Jack stepped aside. A tall slender man with wire-rimmed glasses and a chiseled face stepped through the door and stood over the crumpled form. Tommy, Sandy, and Jack all sighed in relief.

"Jesus!" Sandy exclaimed, running her hand through her strawberry-blonde hair.

Jack wiped his ruddy face. Tommy chuckled.

"Jim," Tommy asked, "what are you doing here?

"I came over to see if the bar was still open," Jim replied in his slightly high-pitched voice. "I was getting ready to leave when I saw and heard all hell break loose in the house."

"Where did you learn that trick?" Tommy asked, gesturing to the man at Jim's feet.

"I've told you many times," Jim said with a hint of aggravation, "I was a Navy SEAL."

After a brief hesitation, Tommy confessed, "I never believed you."

A moment later, Jack admitted, "Actually, Jim, neither did I."

Sandy quickly divulged, "I didn't either. I mean, I know you were in the Navy, but—Jeez, Jim, I guess I'll never doubt you again! You sure came in handy!"

CHAPTER 12

Arlington, Virginia, USA, 7 December 2016:

Stepping into his white Chevy pickup, Tommy began driving back to his house. Moving down the dark streets of Arlington, with the snow heaped along their edges illuminated by large overhead lampposts, he considered his actions and conversation with Jack and Sandy before leaving them, wondering if he had forgotten something—anything.

Pushing Jim out the door, after thanking him for saving Jack's life and convincing him to give up his cell phone, they had dragged Markey from the bushes into the backyard bar, where they appropriated his cell, as well. Tommy then explained to Jack and Sandy that the most critical and pressing issue would be pooling enough money together to allow them to live in Thailand for several weeks. This would give them time to devise a way to extract themselves from the problem of the hard-drive and the Society in general. Tommy knew from experience that once John Smith realized that they had eliminated his hit team, he would cancel their credit and debit cards, and likely lock their bank accounts. That would probably occur before sunrise, which meant one trip to the ATM for each card. Even if each were to take money out, the three hundred dollar ATM limit would only provide $900 in cash. That would not purchase even one ticket to Bangkok. Even if they were to purchase their plane tickets through another source, $900 would supply only enough cash for about ten days, if they watched their money and had no other requirements other than to eat and sleep. It certainly would not provide for alcohol, a requirement in Tommy's mind—undoubtedly, Jack and Sandy's too. It also didn't take into account unforeseen expenses. Surprising both Tommy and Jack, Sandy dug through her closet and pulled out a shoebox containing nearly twelve thousand dollars cash. When Jack had questioned her and expressed surprise as to why she had that much cash in a shoebox, Sandy retorted, "It's my money and I'll do what I want with it—and aren't you glad I have it?"

Jack had quickly informed her that she sounded like a J.G. Wentworth commercial.

Tommy had then instructed them to book three tickets to Bangkok, via Munich, departing from Dulles International Airport at six a.m., which was only a scant three hours away. He told them to pack only what could fit in carry-on luggage, making sure they remembered the Society's harddrive.

"Don't over pack, Sandy. You only need gear for warmer weather," Tommy had requested.

Once those simple tasks had been accomplished, he told them they needed to get out of the house and walk five or six blocks, before calling for a cab on the cell they had acquired from Jim. From there they were to make their way to the airport and wait for him.

"You think this John Smith asshole will ask if any taxis came to this address shortly after we kicked his hit team's ass," Sandy had knowingly commented. "The cab driver would tell him where he took us and our escape would be halted before we started."

Quickly confirming her suspicions, Tommy had said, "Exactly—five or six blocks minimum. The farther, the better. Our escape will be based on how far ahead of John Smith we can stay. It could come down to minutes."

Pulling up to his home, he sat in the idling Chevy pickup and examined the small white house. Lights glowed from behind the thick burgundy curtains in the living room and steam rose from the furnace vent at the rear of the house. Looking down at the truck's glowing dashboard, it donned on Tommy that with all that had happened, he hadn't considered the possibility of two hit teams. Had there been a second hit team? Had a team hit his house at the same time as Jack and Sandy's but found him absent? Looking back up at the house, he scrutinized the house again. Nothing seemed abnormal. Nothing seemed out of place. His gut instincts did not sound the alarm.

Keeping his eye on the house, Tommy slowly pulled the handle and the driver side door loudly squealed in displeasure as it opened. The frigid air swept over him as he stepped from pickup, closing the door. A matching shrill noise pierced the night. Standing next to the pickup, Tommy considered what Caroline had told him. She had said that John Smith was arranging for a team to hit his and Jack's house the next night. Was she still an employee of the Society? Had she purposefully misled him? Was there a second team? Were they lying in wait for his return?

Slowly walking up the steps to his front door, Tommy continued to study the house. Moving from the steps, he walked along the side of the house, his shoes crunching through ice-crusted snow, peeking into the dining room window. The house was orderly and quiet. No one had searched his home. He moved through a chain link fence gate. A faint squeal rang out as its hinges swung it open. Stepping into the backyard, he slowly opened the back door, stopping and listening for noise within. It was quiet. Stepping inside, Tommy calmly walked through the kitchen to the bedroom. Caroline's clothes were gone and the bed was made. The sage green room was empty.

"Dog," Tommy called out.

When dog did not come trotting up at his master's call, Tommy moved to the living room. The television was off and the last embers in the fireplace were smoldering. Tommy moved about the house looking for a note from Caroline or clue as to what had happened to her and his dog. He found none.

Giving up his hunt, Tommy packed the leather satchel John Smith had given him, during the delivery job to Thailand a year and a half earlier, with jeans, shorts, T-shirts, flip-flops, and his laptop computer. He also slipped in his running shoes. There would be no need for warm clothing where he and his friends were headed. He then pulled his passport from the top drawer of his bedroom dresser. Looking at his watch, Tommy walked into the kitchen a pulled a glass from a cabinet next to the refrigerator. He then filled the glass with whiskey from a bottle of Jamison sitting on the counter. Whiskey sloshed over the edge of the glass as he dropped two ice cubes. Quickly downing the glass's contents, Tommy repeated the procedure until he felt a comfortable numbness building on his brow.

The room spun slightly as he picked up the leather satchel and swung it over his shoulder. As he opened the front door, a cold gust of air washed over him. The whiskey worked quickly, and he could feel a smoldering drunkenness began to take hold. Departing the small white house, Tommy walked down to the Westover shopping area, six blocks away, with the leather satchel over his shoulder, and used Markey's cell to call a cab.

CHAPTER 13

Kimball, Nebraska, USA, 4 August 1992:

Walking down the side of the street, Omid random-ly kicked tuffs of grass growing through cracks in the sidewalk. It had been another tough day in the small farming town with the other kids teasing him in what seemed an endless procession of abuse about his fami-ly and his heritage. Omid Sassani came to the town once a year to visit his maternal grandparents—an old white-skinned farmer and his Persian grandmother. It was the town his mother had grown up in.

A local farmer's son, Donny, and two other boys, scared him the most. Usually leading the parade of insults, they had left him alone that day, studying him from a distance. Watching, whispering, and smiling to one and other. Omid felt an uncommon dread about the change in their tactics. He could deal with the insults. He could deal with the shoves, the pushes, and the occasional fight. But not know-ing what those three were up to terrified him.

Taking his usual shortcut, over the rail road tracks, through the thick bramble of shrubs into the back lot of the Comet Motel, and then up the hill to the small neighbor-hood of ranch style houses where his grandparents had re-tired and lived, Omid kept looking over his shoulder. Step-ping up to the brambles, he could see the Comet Motel's sign, depicting a pink comet with a yellow tail on a faded green background overhead. He was almost to safety. He was almost back to the comfort of his grandparent's house.

As he stepped through an opening in the thick scrubs behind the motel, three sets of hands grabbed him and threw him violently to a ground covered in short dry grass.

"I hear you Arabs like to get poked in the ass." The red-plaid-shirted Donny laughed, looking down at Omid. "I hear rag head men prefer boys to girls."

Scooting backward on his bottom, Omid bumped into the thick wall of scrubs. The sharp branches scratched his neck and back. One particularly sharp branch ripped a hole in his shirt. He then scampered to his left, but was met with a swift kick by one of Donny's friends, this one with blond buzz cut hair and wearing a white western style shirt. Laughing, Donny grabbed him by his shoulder, twisting him to his hands and knees. Omid quickly twisted back to his bottom, facing his attackers. Donny's two friends reached down and grabbed him, throwing him to his belly, holding him down. Donny grabbed the waist of his blue khaki trousers and pulled them down to his hips, his belt holding them from going any farther. Lying on his belly, Omid could taste dirt in his mouth. He could feel the dry abrasive grass on his cheek. Feeling a rising terror, he let out a loud, high-pitched scream.

"Shut up rag head!" Donny hoarsely whispered, pulling at Omid's pants again.

Seizing his belt with his right hand, Omid vainly tried to hold up his trousers. He tried to twist over on his back but one of the boys held him down while the other stepped on his head, holding it on the ground. Omid let out another scream.

"Shut up!" Donny yelled, kicking him in the side.

With his head held in place by a foot and his right cheek on the rough ground, he could see Donny loosening his belt. One of the other boys pulled at his pants again, dislodging them from his thighs and jerking them down to his ankles. His underwear caught up on his knees. He watched as Donny dropped his blue jeans and white jockey underwear, revealing an erect penis. He watched as Donny knelt behind him. He cried out again, no words just a high-pitched guttural cry. He could feel someone forcefully spreading his legs. Clutching the dry grass next to his head, Omid prepared himself for the inevitable. Screaming one last time, he closed his eyes. He could feel tears coursing down his cheeks, mixing with the dry dirt.

Suddenly, there was the sound of someone running across the brittle grass and then the noise of a fleshy impact followed by the clamor of brambles being crushed, punctuated by two distinct thuds. The foot that had been holding his head on the ground suddenly vanished. Omid opened his eyes.

A tan muscular arm and hand reached down and grabbed Donny from atop Omid. He felt the weight of Donny being thrown from him.

Omid twisted over and sat up, the dry grass now scratched at his bare bottom. A shoeless slender and young man in dirty blue jeans with a bare chest took a step toward the trio that had attacked him. The young man had wavy brown hair and deep blue eyes that seemed to capture everything.

The young man glared at Donny and his friends, growling, "What the fuck are you doing?"

"Mind your own business, mister," Donny screamed as he stood and pulled up his pants. His rage was directed at the young man.

"The little rag head deserved this," one of Donny's friends yelled.

"That's right, this rag head deserved this," Donny said, repeating his friend's claim as he buckled his belt.

"You fuckers are going to jail. This is a small town and you can't hide," the young man declared.

Looking up with dark innocent eyes, Omid wondered who this man was. The young man glanced down at him. Swiping his wiry dark hair from his face, for a moment Omid wondered if this man might be homeless. As quickly, he decided the young man must be a resident at the Comet

Motel. Maybe he worked on one of the local oil rigs? Maybe he was just passing through?

The wavy brown haired young man looked back to the three teenagers, roaring, "Now get the hell out of here before I kick your ass!"

Donny and his friends quickly began maneuvering through a small opening in the hedge. Just before disappearing through the gap in the hedge, Donny turned and said, "He's no good. You're on the wrong side, mister."

"No one deserves what you were trying to do, jackass. No one," the young shoeless man growled in response.

The young man turned toward Omid and reached his hand down. Staring into the young man's blue eyes, Omid took his hand. He could feel a quiet strength in the young man as he was pulled to his feet. It was more than physical strength. It was a balanced strength. It was a pure strength. It was strength that seemed to encompass every element of the young man's being.

In a calm voice, the blue eyed young man said, "Now, get your clothes on."

Clumsily, Omid first pulled up his underwear and then his blue pants before looking back up at the young man.

"What's your name?" the young man asked.

Omid mumbled his name.

With concerned blue eyes, the young man then asked, "Do you know those boys?"

With tears beginning to fall from in his dark eyes and roll down his cheeks, Omid silently nodded.

Dropping to one knee, the young man took Omid's shoulders into his hands and said, "What happened to you today was unfair, and it should never happen to anyone. But life is not fair. Life is never fair. Some people get all the breaks and others get nothing. You should never look back and worry about your past misfortune—or look forward and hope for a break. You just need to realize that life's not fair and forge ahead, recognizing it's ultimately out of your control. Happiness is based on who we associate with and how you treat the people around us. You can choose to live a life feeling sorry for yourself, wallowing in self-pity, and looking out for only yourself, or a life where you choose your friends and are loyal to those friends, supporting each other when things get tough."

Omid immediately knew what the young man meant. Growing up in Kansas City and visiting this remote farming town once a year, life had never been fair to him, a young boy of Persian linage. He had already learned the truth of the young man's words from a daily dose of abuse and insults by his fair-skinned neighbors and classmates. Not all of them tortured him. Some were nice, but not enough to make living anything but pure agony.

"Let me take you home," the young man calmly said in a low voice, still holding his shoulders.

As much as he wanted to be escorted home by this young man, Omid knew his father would be furious. His father would blame him for bringing this cruelty onto himself. His father would be enraged that Omid was beholding to a white man for saving him. He knew he could never let his father know what had happened. He abruptly twisted out of the young man's grip and ran through the opening in the bramble of scrubs that ran along the motel's back property line. He ran away from the person that had saved his honor in this godforsaken town.

CHAPTER 14

Hartford County, Maryland, USA, 7 December 2016:

Sitting at the large mahogany desk, in the bookcase-lined room, John Smith gazed out upon the snow covered lawns and ice strewn trees through long windows with thick dark green drapes pulled aside. The faint smell of aged wood and stale cigar smoke wafted the air around a large mahogany desk, as he contemplated his childhood memory of nearly being raped by the three boys in Kimball, Nebraska.

His silver canes propped up next the desk was a reminder of what the young man had told him that day, "Life is not fair. Life is never fair." The young blue-eyed man was right. "Some people get all the breaks and others get nothing." To John Smith, survival had become a matter of going through life having to fight for each and every break. They never came naturally or by chance. He had learned to fight hard for each victory, for they would never come without a struggle. He learned that the breaks were found when he only thought of himself, ignoring those around him. He often wondered what had happened to the young man. Had he chosen his friends well? Did he and his friends struggle against odds together or had the young blue-eyed man finally given in to the unfairness and wallowed in self-pity? Had he learned, like John Smith, life was a lonely struggle, not one undertaken as a team? He knew the young man with quiet and balanced strength would never approve of his life or the course he had chosen, struggling against the unfairness alone. John Smith had never found happiness or friends, but he had survived through deceit and revenge in a constant battle to defeat his peers. Sitting at the mahogany desk, looking out the long windows on to the snowy scene, he was certain that the blue-eyed young man would never approve of his life choices.

The study door suddenly burst open to reveal Steve, with his short arms and legs flailing. Resembling a child, he sprinted into the room, skidding to a halt on the polished wooden floor.

Looking at Steve, John Smith could feel his heart drop in his chest. He knew by the look in the little man's beady eyes that Tommy Luck had survived the night.

"Our hit team?" John Smith muttered, tapping his fingers in disharmony on the mahogany desk.

"Dead," Steve puffed, in excitement. "All of them are dead."

"Don't tell me," John Smith said, feeling anger building within, "they hit the first house with success and then were killed at Tommy's?"

"No!" Steve bellowed. "I found them all dead in the first house—at his friend's house."

"All right, calm down," John Smith told his assistant, attempting to control his frustration. "Tell me what happened."

"You told me to instruct the hit team to hit Mr. Luck's friend's house first. It was a team of six. These people were professionals and had all the right qualifications. They were ex-servicemen, good with firearms, and hand-to-hand combat—you name it, they had it. These guys had worked together before. They knew what they were doing," Steve explained. "They were supposed to meet me when the job—"

"Jobs," John Smith interrupted. "There were two jobs."

"Yeah right, jobs," Steve corrected. "They were supposed to meet with me when the two jobs were done. They figured it would take them an hour at each house and planned on meeting me at four in the morning to hand over the hard-drive. When they didn't show up at four, I waited a little longer, thinking there may have been a delay. At seven in the morning, I realized they weren't coming so I drove over to Tommy's friend's house, first. The doors were closed and no lights were on—everything was quiet. So I drove over to Mr. Luck's house and found the same thing. Doors were closed and no lights were on. I then drove back over to his friend's house and parked around the corner. It was nearly nine in the morning and a lot of people were about the neighborhood. So I walked up to the front door and knocked. No one answered. So I walked around the back of the house and some skinny guy with wire-rimmed glass and a big belly came stumbling out of a building in the back corner of the lot. I asked him if he had seen Mr. Luck's friend and he said yes. He had seen him last night. I asked him if he had heard any disturbances and he said no, that he had been in the building all night and didn't hear a thing."

"So how do you know that the hit team is dead?" John Smith asked, his anger being to be replaced by frustration at the length of Steve's story.

"Well, as I'm helping this guy into his car—he smelled like a distillery—I noticed that this old garage door leading into the basement had been forced and was partially open. So once this guy drives off, I walk over and peek inside," Steve said as his dark beady eyes darted around the room.

"Please tell me what you saw."

"All six hit team men stacked up like firewood on the garage floor."

"Tommy appears to have friends with the same unique talent as he," John Smith muttered, looking back out the window at the winter snow scene. "Was the green mini-van still at the house?"

"Yeah."

"Was Luck's truck at his house?"

"Yeah, boss."

"Get on the phone with the Society and have them look

into the local cab companies' databases. I want to know if any cab departed from either Tommy or his friend's house between midnight and six this morning."

"That means we're going to bring in the Society support?" Steve asked.

"Yes, but strictly Society support. I don't want to reach out to any other agencies yet," John Smith answered. "We need to try and get control of this without aid from any government agencies. We don't want things to spin out of control, but we don't want to advertise the fact that the harddrive has been stolen."

"Got it, I'll find out if any cabs were called to either residence." Steve replied, as he began turning to leave.

"Wait a second," John Smith calmly requested. "Also check their credit cards for charges since two in the morning. See if they bought tickets on planes, trains or buses—check for rental cars, as well."

"All right," Steve replied as he began to turn again, rubbing his small hands through his dark bushy hair.

"Wait a minute," John Smith requested again. "I'm not finished. If they're on the run, then we need to have the Society cancel their credit cards and freeze their bank accounts."

"Okay," Steve replied and he began to turning once again.

"Stop!" John Smith howled, raising his voice several octaves. After taking two deep breaths, he calmly said, "Finally, make an appointment for me with the Society Patriarchs, and get a cleanup team over to that house. We need to get rid of the remains of the hit team." When Steve remained standing, looking at him with his beady eyes as if he was waiting for more instructions, John Smith yelled, "Go! Get out of here," as he picked up one of his silver aluminum canes and slammed it on the desktop, the computer and ashtray jumping at the impact.

John Smith painfully leaned back in the matching mahogany chair and after a few moments of contemplating his instructions to Steve, he reached across the desk and pulled the laptop computer from the corner, so it was sitting directly in front of him. He then reached into his pocket and pulled out another cellophane packet containing a USB flash-drive.

Opening the packet, the barely perceptible smell of petroleum once again rose up and swirled around his nose. Inserting the flash drive, the screen momentarily blinked, and the alternate texting screen appeared. As the previous day, he typed in, *TT3*, the address of the other flash drive he wanted to communicate with. With the cursor flashing his initials, *JS*, he typed: *We have a problem*, and waited for a response.

John Smith waited patiently for twenty minutes, before the cursor typed *TT3: That seems to be a common phrase with you. Go ahead.*

John Smith then typed *The hit team failed. All are dead and Luck and his friends have disappeared.*

The cursor quickly spelled, *TT3: Go ahead*, again.

Hesitating a moment, John Smith then typed behind his flashing initials, *Checking all modes of transportation, now. Have canceled all credit cards and frozen bank accounts. We should know soon where they have gone.*

TT3: Full tech support?

Yes, we need full support. Tommy Luck is good at disappearing. We will need full support to find him.

After a brief delay, the cursor printed out, *TT3: I will inform the other Patriarchs that Mr. Luck is responsible for stealing the hard-drive.*

I have requested a meeting to update the Patriarchs. I should know where he is by then.

TT3: How will we now acquire the hard-drive and proceed with the plan?

Once I have the hard-drive in my possession, I will tell the Patriarchs that it was not on Tommy Luck at the time of his termination. I will tell them that he had already passed it off to another agent, John Smith typed. *I can claim that I am still searching. We will have possession of the hard-drive and the other Patriarchs will not be the wiser.*

TT3: Sounds risky, quickly flashed across the screen. Then, *TT3: but it seems our only course*, appeared a few seconds later.

JS: Risky but the only course of action available, John Smith concurred. *We can then proceed with the original plan.*

TT3: Concur, appeared on the screen just before the flashing TT3 disappeared.

As if reenacting his actions from the day before, John Smith painfully reached across the desk and pulled the crystal ashtray closer. He then pulled the cardboard sheathed flash-drive from the computer and a lighter from the top drawer. Holding the flash-drive over the ashtray, he lit the corner and it ignited. He dropped the flaming device into the ashtray. All evidence of his communication with TT3 began to go up in a black smoke as the flash-drive crackled and spat sparks.

CHAPTER 15

Suvarnabhumi International Airport, Thailand, 8 December 2016:

As economy passengers, Tommy, Jack, and Sandy were nearly the last people to disembark the aircraft at Suvarnabhumi International Airport, just outside of Bangkok. Walking along the wide crowded corridor, past restrooms, female janitors dressed in yellow smocks, and a smoking room, Tommy could feel the drastic change in humidity and began to smell the scents he associated with Thailand. He could feel his lips begin form into an instinctive smile. It was like a fragrance rolling over him. A pleasant mixed bouquet of the tropical milieu and Thailand's unique cuisine, with a dash of scented oil used in body massages wafted the air.

Just before reaching the ramp leading to the immigration counters, Tommy gestured his travel companions to the side of the passageway, dodging other new arrivals traveling for the same destination. "We need to chat before heading through immigration."

"I'm exhausted," Sandy complained as they stepped to the side of the corridor. "We've been traveling for nearly eighteen hours. And, I need a shower. I look and smell like a pig."

"You should try the cheaper route via Tokyo." Tommy chuckled. "Twenty-three hours. I've learned to hate that flight."

Jack yawned. "I am ready for a very long nap on a soft bed, preferably one with a swimming pool just outside my room."

"Then that will be my goal, Jack, a room with a swimming pool just outside its door," Tommy replied, smiling.

"Excellent." Jack yawned again.

"But first, let's make sure we get out of this airport. We all need to take different lines, and I would like you to ensure that I get to the immigration desk about five people before you," Tommy explained. "If John Smith and the Society have already figured out our destination, the Thai Royal Police could be waiting for us. They will be looking for three Americans traveling together, and they'll know our names. If you see them usher me off, you need to find another way out."

"We've never been in Thailand before," Sandy snapped. "We don't speak Thai, and you want us to try and get past immigration if you're caught? What about a stamp in our passports? What about a visa? And where do we go and what do we do?"

"Thailand is the land of financial encouragement. If I'm shepherded off by guys in brown uniforms, find an exit and bribe anyone standing in front of you and freedom." Writing down a name and number on a piece of paper, Tommy said, "When you get out of the airport, call this guy at this number, tell him you're friends of mine, and he'll get you to Koh PhaNgan."

"And then?" Sandy asked, yawning herself.

"Give him the hard-drive, and he'll help you figure out what to do," Tommy said, handing Sandy the slip of paper.

Pulling the slip from Sandy's hand and examining it, Jack asked, "Who is this gentleman?"

"He's no gentleman." Tommy laughed. "He's the mafia boss for a large portion of PhaNgan Island."

"This is a French name," Jack said, looking at Tommy.

"Alain is indeed a Frenchman—one of the few Farangs who have gathered enough respect and fear among the

Thais to hold the mafia boss title. He's also got some big brass balls to have ever tried to achieve that status in Thailand as a Farang," Tommy said. "Look, chances are that John Smith is still trying to figure out where we've gone, and I'll make it through immigration. This is simply a precaution."

"Please clarify the expression Farang?" Jack asked, rubbing his red-rimmed eyes.

"Thais primarily identify foreigners, not by their nationality, but by the color of their skin," Tommy explained. "Light-skinned folks like you and me are referred to as Farangs, Blacks are referred to as Chocolate, Japanese as Nippon, etc. etc. Farang comes from the term Franzie which refers to the first French colonists in Southeast Asia."

"This is who you plan to contact if we can escape this airport. Can we trust this Alain guy? We hate French people," Sandy retorted, taking the slip of paper back from Jack with a glare.

"Yes and no," Tommy replied.

"Yes and no?" Jack looked puzzled and concerned, all at the same time.

"Alain is a good friend, but he will place his survival as Mafioso boss above all else," Tommy explained. "On the other hand, he loves a challenge. And we are a challenge."

"What are his views in regards to violence and powerful societies that have the ability to squash any man on impulse?" Jack asked.

"He didn't achieve his current position by shying away from a fight. And like I said, he loves a challenge, especially ones that entails a little violence."

"Sounds like our man," Jack commented, nodding.

Walking up the ramp, the threesome found themselves at the end of a very long line leading up to ten separate immigration counters.

Each counter was manned with a brown-uniformed immigration officer who looked as tired and expressionless as their American counterparts. As directed by Tommy, Jack and Sandy delayed getting into separate lines until he was well ahead of them.

The lines slowed and surged as people shifted back and forth, attempting to see why it was taking so long. Tommy finally found himself in front of one of the immigration desks with a small round silver camera resembling the alien's vehicles in the movie *War of the Worlds* atop a matching silver stand, pointing at him. The immigration official took Tommy's passport, and he could hear it being swiped through a small device behind the counter. Adjusting his feet to the two yellow guides on the floor under him, Tommy smiled at the camera.

The immigration official behind the counter scowled "Please, no smile. Again please."

Looking back into the round silver camera eye, Tommy frowned this time, and the immigration official scowled again, shaking his head. As the official typed away on a keyboard hidden behind the counter, Tommy could hear the man stamping his passport. Tommy let out a sigh of relief as the immigration official placed his passport on the counter and gestured him through. Walking into the baggage claim area, Tommy glanced back at Jack and Sandy, who were still in line, and smiled. They nodded and smiled back.

Once Jack and Sandy had been processed by and moved through immigration, they all made their way down the long line of silver baggage carousels, crowded with luggage and surrounded with people, toward the customs area. The officials at the customs counter eyed the threesome but did not stop them as they walked through the *Nothing to Declare* exit from the baggage claim into the airport's busy terminal. The sights and smells of Thailand always brought Tommy's spirits up. He found it to be a fascinating country and culture that always surprised him when he least expected it. As he stepped into the crowded airport lobby, with Jack and Sandy at his side, he felt at home.

They were immediately engulfed into a sea of hawkers, calling out one deal or another: taxis, limousines, hotels, resorts, and good times. While the scene was chaotic, it was Thailand's orderly chaos that Tommy loved the most. In Tommy's mind, Thailand's uniqueness was derived from a bizarre mixture of their Buddhist roots and their intense nationalism. Thais were all very aware and proud of the fact that no western power had ever colonized their country, the only nation able to make that claim in Southeast Asia. Thais were a proud, competitive people, softened by the gentle teachings of Buddha. A perfect mixture in a crowded room, everyone knew what they wanted and aggressively strove for it with manners and a smile.

Tommy ignored the tradesmen and led Sandy and Jack outside, through large turnstile glass doors. With the hot sun hovering overhead in a bright blue sky, the morning air was heavy with humidity, and the unique smell of spicy Thai food seemed to swirl around him. Tommy knew Thailand would slow down as the sun came up and the heat began consuming the early morning's coolness. Glancing down from a walkway hovering over traffic, they could see rows of yellow and green and hot pink taxis on the street below. Lines of people waited. Attendants filled out destination forms and flagged down empty taxis. With his hand on his forehead, blocking out the bright light, Tommy began leading his two companions across the walkway to a three-lane thoroughfare, busy with limousines, vans, and buses.

A lone middle-aged woman carrying a clipboard and dressed in a black polyester suit approached them and asked, in near perfect English, where they were going. Tommy told her Bangkok and she rattled off a price which he immediately refused in the Thai language. The woman smiled and gave Tommy a new price, speaking in Thai.

"What was that all about," Sandy asked.

"There are typically two prices in this country." Tommy chuckled. "A Farang price and a Thai price, and it's all about the language you speak, not about the color of your skin."

"How do you say, I need a billet and bed? I am highly

fatigued," Jack muttered, standing behind Sandy, wiping sweat from his brow with a large pinkish forearm.

The black suited woman led them to a white van, where the driver handed her a slip of paper and then opened the doors of vehicle for his new passengers.

"You have no luggage?" the driver asked.

"Traveling light," Tommy responded.

Sandy chuckled as she climbed into the van. "Yeah, we're running from some insane organization that call themselves the Society and didn't have time to pack anything."

"They are out to kill us," Jack corroborated, looking pleadingly at the driver as he followed her into the van.

The van rocked as John placed his enormous foot on the edge and hoisted himself inside.

"Pay no attention to them," Tommy said to the confused-looking driver, as he stepped into the van. "Their very tired and need some rest."

With the air conditioning blasting away inside, the van had a white hand-painted diagram of a temple at the center of its brown dashboard, surrounded by gold leaf pressings, and white and purple lotus flowers strung up in a garnish hanging from the rearview mirror. The driver jumped behind the wheel and smiled as he looked back at his weary passengers. With three wide bench seats, Sandy took the rear seat, Jack the middle, and Tommy the one right behind the driver. As the van pulled away from the curb, Jack and Sandy stretched out on the bench seats, disappearing from view as they passed palm trees and banana groves, with a clear blue sky overhead. Cool air cascaded down on Tommy and brought with it the mixed scent of fresh flowers and mildew.

Driving out of the departure zone, the van began making its way out of the airport. Tommy said to the driver, "Actually, we'd like to go the Pattaya Beach."

"Pattaya?" the drivers asked.

"Pattaya?" Sandy's voice called out from the back seat.

"Yes, Pattaya," Tommy replied. "I know it's farther and we'll pay the difference. I would also like to avoid the toll booth south of the airport. I can pay extra for that, as well."

As the driver nodded his head, Tommy could see a smile on his face through the rearview mirror.

"I thought we were headed for Bangkok and a soft bed," Jack groggily commented from the middle bench seat.

"So does the woman who just arranged our ride," Tommy answered. "So will whoever tracks her down and asks her where the three Americans went."

"Smart move, you clever bastard," Sandy mumbled from the backseat.

Farms surrounding the highway were occasionally interrupted with small communities, wooden shanties selling trinkets and food, and ancient-looking gas stations. At one point, the driver took a side road and looped around several farm fields, before returning to the highway. Tommy figured that he was following instructions, and avoiding the toll booth that had a surveillance video. Back on the highway, they came to a complex built around the interstate, jam-packed with retailers, grocery stores, and a Seven-Eleven and KFC. Cars were parked along the shoulder of the highway, as their passengers crowded into the stores. Tommy asked the van driver to stop, and when the van pulled up to the curb, he jumped out, walking past a KFC, and disappeared into an electronics store, quickly returning with a new cell phone and several new SIM cards.

Thai cells were all prepaid and recharged with more minutes at any local convenience store—in Tommy's view, a far better and cheaper system than used in the United States, not to mention more discreet. Most cell phones in Thailand had no name associated with the device, and Tommy knew it would take an incredible long shot for the Society, or one of its agents at NSA or Thai intelligence to discover what cell phone he was using. When they did, he would already be using a different SIM card with a different number.

Climbing back into the van, Tommy gestured the driver to continue, as he was slipping a SIM card into his new phone.

"What do you have there," Jack, who was lying on the bench seat behind him, called out without raising his head.

The rhythmic cadence of breathing could be heard in the back where Sandy had lain down, telling Tommy and Jack she was sound asleep.

"I need to make a phone call," Tommy replied.

"Calling the Mafioso Frenchman?"

"No, the problem with getting to Koh PhaNgan is that there is a lot of territory in between, run by various mafias and police chiefs. I'd like to travel through the island of Samui, as it is the quickest route, but it has a very powerful mafia. If the Society's figured out where we're headed, they have undoubtedly contacted that local mafia and have already agreed to pay a high price for our capture."

"And you know someone on this Samui island who can help?"

"I have a good friend that's very connected with that mafia," Tommy explained. "He is the island boss's right hand man."

"Another Farang?"

"My friend is a Farang, yes," Tommy answered. "But the Samui Mafia boss is pure Thai and a ruthless man."

"What about the police?"

"The police are controlled by the mafia on Samui."

"So it's a matter of making a deal with the ruthless mafia boss?"

"No, the Society can buy his loyalty, but my friend has a different brand of allegiance than his boss or his fellow mafia companions. His version of loyalty is to friends, as opposed to money or his coldblooded boss and heartless fellow employees."

"Are you sure?"

"Absolutely."

"Is he friends with the Frenchman?"

"Absolutely not. They can't stand one and other." Tommy laughed. "In fact, if they were to accidently run into one and other on the street, I think one would leave the encounter in a body bag."

"And your other friend's name?"

"Chandler," Tommy replied.

"The name sounds like a fellow countryman," Jack commented.

"Yeah, he's a south Londoner. He owns villas on both Samui and PhaNgan. The PhaNgan villa falls within Alain's territory, but there is an undeclared truce to avoid each other when Chandler is on the island."

"You certainly have some interesting friends," Jack muttered, before rolling over on his side and quickly falling asleep.

The van careened along the highway, dodging the other traffic, and the tropics closed in on the interstate. As they climbed a low set of hills, Tommy could see a large Buddha carved into a jungle-lined cliff face before they descended the other side. More and more structures began crowding sides of the highway, the closer the van came to their destination. Suddenly, a large black and blue cloud appeared overhead, and punishing rainfall pelted the top of the van. As quickly as it had appeared, the storm ebbed when they approached the Gulf of Thailand and the city of Pattaya Beach.

CHAPTER 16

Chevy Chase, Maryland, USA, 8 December 2016:

Standing next to the dormant stone fireplace, John Smith leaned against his two silver canes, looking down at the three older men, none of whom had offered him a seat. It was a spacious room, and like the room at Hartford, it was a bookcase-lined study with tall narrow windows showing a wintery scene of snow and ice. Beyond the lawn and trees burdened with snow, traffic moved slowly along Connecticut Avenue. Beneath his feet, a blue and red Persian rug covered a polished wood floor, and above his head hung a silver chandelier. The room smelled like a mixture of burnt wood, fine liquors, and old men.

Oliver Mason—with his narrow shoulders and wide hips rendering an odd pear shape—sat on a red velvet chair to his right and looked up at John Smith. "Mr. Smith, we understand you have a lead on the hard-drive."

Painfully shifting his head to look at the old man on the red velvet chair, John Smith answered, "Yes, Mr. Mason, we have discovered who stole the hard-drive and raped Kelly."

Dressed in crisply creased navy-blue pants, Oliver pushed his monk-like white hair back with one hand and raised a crystal snifter of brandy with the other, saying, "Go ahead," before taking a sip.

"We discovered that the man the Society evaluated for a position last year is responsible," John Smith lied.

"Go ahead," Oliver directed, again.

"We were able to discover that Thomas Bacon Luck—Tommy Luck—entered Kelly's house, killed her husband, took the hard-drive, and raped her."

Sitting on a couch directly in front of the dormant stone fireplace, James Tillage, a lean man with bald top and short white stubble on the sides of his head, dressed in dark tailored trousers and a light green shirt shook his head. "That seems a bit odd. A man who would not accept our invitation for employment due to our choice of unsavory evaluation tactics and the seedy staff participating in that evaluation," he commented, looking directly at John Smith, "would slit a man's throat, steal a hard-drive, and then viciously rape a woman." Picking up a crystal glass filled with sparkling water, ice cubes faintly tinkling on its sides, he continued, "We all agree he chose to not accept our invitation due to his lofty principles, why would he suddenly throw those principles aside? Why would he now throw them aside in such an unpleasant and sleazy fashion? It makes no sense."

Grimacing in pain as he shifted his body again, John Smith, replied, "Perhaps he is seeking revenge?"

"Revenge for what?" James, chirped

"Revenge for our tactics in the evaluation. We did kill a CIA agent and frame him for the murder. We did make it appear as if he was attempting to sell a classified flash-drive containing a virus and drew his family into the evaluation, as well," John Smith retorted.

"That's ridiculous," James spat. "And we did not draw his family into the process. That was the buffoon of an inspector general at the NSA. As for the CIA agent, that was your misguided decision."

"I was working for you," John Smith retorted. "He's sees my actions as nothing more than a proxy to the Society as a whole."

"What proof do you have?" the large plump Andres Tressel interrupted with a thick Scandinavian accent. Sitting closest to John Smith in an overstuffed chair covered in floral fabric, Andres, with his unruly curly white hair and beard, was dressed in rumpled khaki pants and a white shirt with thick red suspenders strapped over his shoulders. He brought a crystal glass filled with ice and bourbon to his lips, taking a large swallow, waiting for John Smith's reply.

Shifting from one leg to the other in an attempt to alleviate the throbbing pain in his back, John Smith explained, "We captured his truck's image on traffic cameras headed in the direction of Kelly's house. We were also able to find a nearby Seven-Eleven surveillance camera that secured footage of him stepping from his pickup and walking in the direction of Kelly's house at the time of the incident—that same camera shows him returning to his parked truck shortly after the incident." John Smith had taken the precaution of having a technician create a video depicting Tommy arriving and departing from the scene from other footage, in the event these old men decided they wanted to personally witness the evidence. Standing next to the stone fireplace with his throbbing back, John Smith hoped they would.

"Do you know where Thomas Luck is now?" James asked.

"Thailand," John Smith answered.

"Thomas Luck is in Thailand?" Andres groaned, scratching his ruddy bearded cheek with his free hand. "How did he escape the country? Why did you not have his passport canceled?"

Dropping his head, John Smith awkwardly answered, "Initially, I was reluctant to involve our contacts in official agencies because of the contents of the hard-drive. I felt it better if we tried to handle it in-house without assistances. So we strictly used the Society IT support team. There was a slight misunderstanding between myself and my assistant. I asked him to utilize the Society IT assets to check their credit cards, and all modes of transportation. He understood that I just wanted him to check credit cards for purchases involving transportation—not checking with the actual carriers in the event they used cash. We resolved the issue but the delay allowed Tommy Luck and his companions time to make the trip and exit the airport in Bangkok. It's now clear we need to involve law enforcement and other external assets to track him down and retrieve the hard-drive."

"Sounds as if you need a new assistant," Oliver commented, taking another sip of brandy. "Companions?"

"Yes, he is traveling with another man and his wife," John Smith explained. "We discovered what flight they were on and its destination about thirty minutes after they had landed. I coordinated with our contacts in the Royal Thai Police but Tommy and his companions had already cleared immigrations and customs. The police canvassed the area with their description. A woman recognized them and claimed to have arranged for a van to Bangkok. We immediately shifted our search accordingly. We also tagged the van license number and began sifting through toll booth videos. No booths in the direction of Bangkok processed the van. Neither did the lone booth south of the airport. We were lucky when a KFC security video captured Tommy at what was described to me as a truck stop of sorts. He passed the camera twice on foot walking along the sidewalk out front. We are currently attempting to track down the van's driver. There is only one significant population center in the region South of Bangkok—Pattaya Beach. Thence, we are now working on bringing our assets to bear in Pattaya to continue our search."

"That was quick work with a private surveillance video," James commented, nodding his head in approval.

"All footage from Thailand KFC surveillance cameras are electronically recorded at a central hub," John Smith explained to the old men. "Apparently, many of the larger chains do the same: Seven-Eleven, KFC, and Family Mart, to name a few. With face recognition technology, it has become a simple process. It was actually the idea of one of our Royal Thai Police agents that we check."

Oliver commented, "KFC? I'm surprised there are Kentucky Fried Chicken stores in Thailand."

"Apparently, they are very popular in the country." John

Smith shifted again in another attempt to alleviate the building pain in his back.

Andres grumbled, "Mr. Luck seems to be staying one step ahead of the world's best law enforcement and intelligence agencies."

"It would appear so," John Smith confessed. "I've contacted the local mafia in Pattaya, Koh Samui, and Koh PhaNgan, offering a reward."

"Why Samui and PhaNgan?" Oliver queried. "Are they close to Pattaya?"

John Smith responded, "No, but I believe he will head back to an area in the country that he is familiar and most comfortable with. That would be Koh PhaNgan. Samui, with an airport, is an obvious step in that direction. Koh PhaNgan has no airport. The island is only accessible via ferry options from several different ports, one of which is Koh Samui."

Oliver, scratching his chin asked, "Are you going to cover those other ports as well?"

"Not at this stage," John Smith answered. "All the ports with ferries to Koh PhaNgan are in the southern region of the country. The easiest way for him to get to PhaNgan from Pattaya is by air to Samui, where he will have to catch a ferry."

After a moment, James asked, "What other actions have you taken?"

"I'm also sending two Society action teams directly to Pattaya and plan on shifting them to Koh PhaNgan if Tommy makes it that far. I would rather our teams intercept and dispose of the threesome to limit the exposure of the harddrive."

"And when will they arrive?" Andres asked.

"They will be flying out with me on the Society's Gulf Stream this afternoon. We will all arrive tomorrow afternoon."

"What are the issues?" James asked.

"I have worked with and against Tommy Luck on several occasions. He is clever and unpredictable. I have taken the liberty of employing a woman he was temporarily involved with to help. Between my knowledge of him and her more intimate familiarity, we will find and eliminate Tommy and his friends, and retrieve the hard-drive but it won't be easy."

"And his Achilles heel?" James asked a second question.

"Tommy Luck's weaknesses?" John Smith asked. "That's easy, he has two. He's a drunk and he's fiercely loyal to his friends. If it's a choice between his safety and the welfare of a friend, he will choose his friend. If it choice between drinking and not, he'll drink."

James, his white stubble hair now brimming with perspiration, looked at John Smith with a hint of revulsion, commenting, "Have you considered that Mr. Luck might select friends with the same traits?"

CHAPTER 17

Pattaya Beach, Thailand, 8 December 2016:

Taking an off ramp, the van joined a two lane high-way that passed a small university, seemingly out in the middle of nowhere. The farm fields fringed with jungle gave way to more and more buildings, housing factories and businesses. The highway eventually led to another junction and elevated ramp that emptied onto busy four lane road, trimmed with businesses and teaming with motorcycles, cars, and trucks.

As the van passed a hospital it came to a halt at a turn lane stoplight, allowing for motorists to cross the converging lanes, also thick with traffic. In no particular order, the traffic packed into the turn lane. Scooters shifted into any free space, cars jockeyed for better position, and trucks honked their horns. Jack and Sandy both sat up in the rears seats, looking around at the frenzied sight.

"Are we close?" Jack asked.

"Very," Tommy responded.

"Are we safe?" Sandy inquired, examining the hectic scene.

"Not necessarily," Tommy replied in a perfect serious tone. "However, if we can make it across this road without being broadsided, we should be okay."

The light changed to green and the van driver firmly stepped on the accelerator, dodging scooters and cars, alike. A taxi swerved in front, two scooters collided, and a truck jerked forward before stalling, as the mob lurched ahead.

Resembling bumper cars at a carnival, the participants all aggressively jockeyed for a position on the intersecting street. Tommy could see a trickle of sweat roll down the driver's temple as he maneuvered his van in the chaotic traffic, finally sighing when they had found a spot on the bisecting street.

Furniture outlets, plumbing suppliers, clothing boutiques, and electronics stores filled the buildings alongside the street. These began to slowly give way to restaurants and then to bars. Still early in the day, the restaurants and bars had few customers and fewer girls tending to the clientele.

As they turned onto a coast road, a thin ribbon of rough brown sand marked the edge of the Gulf, with nearly a hundred boats of various types bobbing on its brownish surface. Jet skis, with gray water plumes trailing their path, weaved in and out of the bobbing boats, and speedboats dragged high flying para-sails. Once again, the scene had a disorderly feel, and onlookers would not have been surprised to see two speeding boats or para-sails collide.

The shore was crowded with people and packed with faded striped fabric beach chairs and overhead umbrellas. Droves of hawkers maneuvered among the tourists, selling their wares: wood carvings, massages, and food, to name a few.

An elaborately designed sidewalk, with intertwining colored bricks, planters holding enormous palm trees and other tropical foliage, and brass statues, separated the busy beach road from the gravelly brown sand.

Middle-aged men with pot bellies and placid skin moved along the sidewalks, and younger men sat sunning on the beach, or negotiating with jet-ski and motorboat operators.

"The water looks gross," Sandy commented, examining the beach activity and the water beyond.

"Pattaya is really too close to Bangkok and its runoff to be a great beach getaway," Tommy answered. "The sewage systems in Thailand are several generations behind what we're used to. I wouldn't swim here, but most do and walk away healthy."

"The use of the term 'most' implies that some don't," Sandy pointed out.

Jack scratched his head. "Why has this become a popular tourist destination?"

"Pattaya's primarily trade is sex tourism," Tommy replied. "The beach is just an added incentive. Look at the tourists, most are middle-aged men. You don't see a lot of western women roaming around."

"Thanks, Tommy," Sandy chirped from the back seat, "for bringing me to a city filled with young golden- skinned hot chicks."

"You're welcome. This is a really fun town. The bars are crazy, but there's a lot more to do than just get drunk."

"Yeah," Sandy flatly retorted, "you can always get laid."

"Come on, darling," Jack interjected, sensing Sandy's building anger, "we're here because it is the last place the Society would expect us."

"You should have seen this place in the late seventies," Tommy continued. "It was a sleepy little beach town. Small resorts mixed in the some of the heavy hitters, but it wasn't cluttered at all. There was one small red light district, probably the genesis of the Vietnam War, but all in all, it was a great vacation spot."

The van moved along the beach road, passing massive resorts and shopping malls. Small sois, or streets, bisected the coast road between the resorts. Bars, businesses, and restaurants filled the space between, and lined the street. Sandy and Jack looked left and then right, taking in the gulf scene and city. When the road ahead came to a barricade with a neon banner above reading *Walking Street*, the traffic turned left, moving away from the beach. Another left turn, and the van was now traveling in the opposite direction of the coast road, and one block deeper into the interior of the busy city.

At a slight bend in the road, and abeam a small shopping

mall with an enormous advertisement for Ripley's House of Horrors hovering overhead, Tommy directed the driver to turn into the Pattaya Beach Marriott. When the van came to a stop at the imposing Marriott entrance, two bellboys dressed in tan tunics and baggy brown cotton shorts opened the van's side door. Heat poured through the open door and easily overwhelmed the vehicle's humming overhead air conditioning. One by one, Tommy, Jack, and Sandy stepped out into the stifling heat. Tommy paid the driver and the bellboys attempted to take their few belongings. Turning from the driver, Tommy thanked the two men and told them they would not be staying at the Marriott.

"Don't tell me," Sandy yawned. "You figure someone will track down the driver."

Jack's shoulders slumped and he mumbled, "I was so looking forward to Marriott quality lodgings, not to mention, a civilized man could easily get heat stroke if exposed to these elements too long."

Throwing his leather satchel over his shoulder, Tommy smiled and gestured them forward, saying, "It won't be long now."

Leaving the Marriott, the threesome walked along the sidewalk, dodging hawkers and old men holding hands with young Thai women. They passed bar after bar, and an occasional restaurant or massage parlor. Still too early, the bars were quiet, with young women still cleaning up the mess from the night before. Tropical foliage sprouted from vacant spaces, and an occasional palm tree broke up the concrete landscape. Empty beer bottles and an assortment of trash that looked as if it had spawned from the local Seven-Eleven or Family-Mart clung to the edge of the sidewalk, and a unique aroma that seemed both musty and humid at the same time, mixed with the exhaust of the passing traffic. The heat beat down on their shoulders as they trudged up the sidewalk as scooters and trucks careened past them.

After what seemed an eternity, to Jack and Sandy, in the stifling heat and humidity, especially after the frigid cold of northern Virginia in winter, Tommy turned down a narrow Soi lined with palm trees to one side and a white cinderblock wall to the other. More trash was heaped along the base of the wall, with thick bright green foliage popping up between. Near where the narrow street intersected with the coastal road, Tommy stopped in front of a long three story white stucco hotel, tucked away on the narrow street. The wide concrete steps led to an entrance highlighted in dark stained wood trimmed with short wide palm trees and more bright green tropical foliage. Ascending the stairs, they found themselves standing in a modest reception area.

A simple wooden desk acted as the reception counter, and a young Thai woman, with exotic almond shaped dark eyes and silken black hair, greeted the guests. A small alcove opposite the reception desk offered several chairs with unobstructed views of the gulf.

Booking two rooms, Tommy turned to Jack and said, "Sorry, no swimming pool, but the rooms are quite large and clean."

"You've stayed here before?" Sandy inquired.

"Do the rooms include air conditioning and televisions?" Jack asked, placing a large hand around Sandy's waist.

"Yes, yes, and yes. I need to make a couple of phone calls. Let's meet up around seven. The sun will be down, and it will have begun to cool outside."

Finding his room on the second floor, Tommy fiddled with the lock and opened the door. Heat and humidity spilled out from the open door, and he quickly found the air conditioner, turning it on and adjusting it to its maximum setting. The room was vast, with white stucco walls. A long dark wood cabinet, with a thirty-six-inch television on top and a refrigerator underneath, and a matching desk stood on one wall. A king size bed with a red and gold bedspread stood to the other side of the room. Sliding glass doors leading to a small porch, with views of the narrow street, took up the third wall.

Tommy stepped to the bathroom door, pushed it open, and examined the long room with two porcelain sinks and a bathtub hidden behind a clear shower curtain. It was the exact way he remembered the room from his last stay four years before. The only difference was that he was alone this time.

Throwing his leather satchel on the red and gold topped bed, he stripped his clothes and wandered into the bathroom. After a long cold shower, he wrapped a white towel around his waist and sat down on the bed, the box springs under a firm mattress giving off a faint squeal of complaint at the added weight. With the cool air blowing across his bare shoulders, he reached into the satchel and pulled out his new cell phone.

Dialing in a memorized number, he held the phone to his ear and waited.

"Hello," a familiar voice answered with a distinct English accent.

"Hello, Chandler," Tommy greeted his friend.

"Tommy, where the bloody hell are you?" Chandler's south London accent marked his voice, "You're in some big shit, my friend."

"I'm well aware of my predicament." Tommy chuckled. "So the Society has already contacted your boss?"

"And my boss, knowing of our relationship, contacted me. You and your friends are to be eliminated on sight and whatever belongings you have held until they can arrange for pick up."

After a brief hesitation while he contemplated the information, Tommy asked, "Can you get me to PhaNgan? As you pointed out your boss knows of our friendship, and he might have passed the information on. If they're listening, I've already told them which city I'm in. I'd rather not give them the equivalent of a grid coordinate."

"Of course, I'll fly up tomorrow and meet with you. Let's meet at the bar you've told me about a thousand times. The one with the distinctive owner you always talk about when you're drunk."

"I know which bar you're talking about. What time?"

"Let's say two-ish," Chandler answered. "I'll have arranged for your transportation by then."

"Thanks, Chandler."

"You're very welcome, my friend. I look forward to seeing your septic ass."

Tommy laughed and said goodbye to Chandler before closing the cell. He then took the SIM card from the cell and tossed it into a small trashcan next to the desk. Reaching into his satchel, he pulled out a second SIM card and placed it into the cell phone.

Dialing a second memorized number, Tommy once again held it up to his ear and waited for the owner to answer.

"Who is this," a heavy French accented voice answered the phone.

Tommy chuckled. "A wayward American in a lot of trouble."

"Tommy! I thought you might call," Alain replied. "You're in some big trouble, my friend."

"So I've been told."

"You are in Thailand, yes?"

"Yes, and I'm on my way to PhaNgan if you'll have me."

"But of course." Alain laughed. "I would consider it an honor. Anyone who can piss off the most powerful organization in the world is more than welcome. You will be safe here."

"Are you sure?"

"But of course. This organization—this Society—sent an emissary this morning. They have offered me to...how do you say elimine?...eliminate you and your friends. When I turned them down, the man actually threatened me," Alain exclaimed, laughing, "I laugh at them. Ha! I killed their emissary for threatening me. They are nothing on this island."

"What about the other Mafioso on the island?" Tommy asked, "Will they not try and collect the reward?"

"But of course," Alain replied. "They will try, and I will defeat them. Then I will take their property—their turf—it is all good for me."

"My friends and I should be there in a day or two."

"How will you arrive?"

"Don't concern yourself with that," Tommy answered, not wanting to mention Chandler's name due to their intense dislike for one and other. "I've got a plan. I just wanted to make sure you didn't mind having a fugitive hanging out in your territory."

"Fugitive, ha!" Alain laughed again. "You will be under my protection. You and your friends will be safe. Come to Koh PhaNgan. Let them come to Koh PhaNgan. They will learn that their big Society is not so big on this small island."

Closing the cell, Tommy could not help but smile. Alain was right. The Society would learn that they were not so big on the little island of Koh PhaNgan. The rules were different. Thailand was the Wild West, and Koh PhaNgan was the OK Corral. Chuckling to himself, Tommy realized that would make him Wyatt Earp, and, in-turn, make Jack Doc Holliday. Quickly grasping the implications of calling Jack Doc Holliday, Tommy decided that it might be best to keep that joke from his companions. Sandy might be offended if he were to imply she was Big Nose Kate, Doc Holliday's long-time girlfriend.

CHAPTER 18

Chevy Chase, Maryland, USA, 8 December 2016:

Happy that the meeting was coming to an end, John Smith shifted again, attempting to reduce the pain in his back. He had been standing next to the stone fireplace, leaning on his two silver canes, for nearly three hours. The sun had dropped below the horizon, and a light snow had begun to fall outside. The head and taillights of cars and trucks began slowing on Connecticut Avenue, due to both environmental factors.

"Before you leave, I would like a copy of your evidence against Mr. Luck—the Seven-Eleven surveillance video," James, sitting on the couch sipping sparkling water, demanded.

"Yes, of course," John Smith grumbled, painfully bending down and retrieving a CD from a leather satchel at his feet. Shuffling over closer to the couch, he leaned forward and handed the CD to James, his face contorting into a mask of an agonizing pain as he bent down. Straightening up, he asked, "Will there be anything else?"

The three old men looked at one and other, before Oliver, with his monk like white hair, gestured for John Smith to leave with a brush of his hand. "That will be all, Mr. Smith. Please ensure we're updated as to the progress—or not, of the search and capture of Mr. Luck and his friends."

"We might consider keeping Mr. Luck alive for questioning," Andres added, with his thick Scandinavian accent.

James looked at John Smith and then at Andres, saying, "That is a topic we need to discuss—after Mr. Smith departs."

Throwing his satchel over his left shoulder, John Smith began shuffling across the Persian rug toward a set of wide wooden doors. "If there is any change in your position concerning Tommy's fate, please let me know. As of right now, I have instructed our agents to kill him and his friends on sight."

"We will let you know," James replied over his shoulder, as John Smith stepped from the room, closing the door behind him with a push by one of his silver canes.

The bookcase-lined room was silent for a moment, as the three old men examined one and other. James reached over his head a snapped his fingers and a thin gaunt man dressed in a white jacket appeared from a door at the side of the room.

"A fire, please," James instructed the man, who silently began preparing the fireplace.

Sitting in the red velvet chair, Oliver said, "I do not trust Mr. Smith. I have not risen to the position I have by not being able to detect deceit. John Smith is not telling us something."

Andres, shifting in the overstuffed floral, said, "He is doing the best he can. He was not our first choice to fill the position he currently holds."

"Nor the second," retorted Oliver.

"I detest the man but we all agreed he was a suitable substitute until we can find a replacement for the executive assistant position," James said, watching the white jacketed man kneeling in front of the dormant fireplace.

"I would like to see his evidence," Oliver said, gesturing for the compact disc.

Ignoring Oliver's request for the CD, James replied, "I see no reason why it would benefit Mr. Smith to falsely accuse Mr. Luck."

Oliver laughed, "We hired him last year due to his hatred for Mr. Luck—Mr. Smith would do anything possible to discredit Mr. Luck."

"Yes," Andres commented. "We need to view the evidence on the compact disc."

"That will be easy enough," James hesitatingly replied. "After I seen the video, I'll pass it along to you two."

"About Mr. Luck's fate?" Andres asked, adding, "I say we put his elimination on hold until we can sort out the surveillance video."

"Guilty or not, Mr. Luck is nothing to us," Oliver disagreed. "I say let the termination order stand, for now."

"I agree," James added. "Unless we have some tangible reason to suspect that he has been falsely accused, I don't want our uncertainty to be the cause of a missed opportunity by our agents overseas."

CHAPTER 19

Pattaya Beach, Thailand, 8 December 2016:

At just past seven in the evening, Tommy wandered down to the small lobby to find Jack, clad in khaki shorts and a Hawaiian shirt, and Sandy, wearing white linen shorts and a blue blouse, sitting in the small alcove, gazing out onto the narrow street. Handing his key to the same receptionist that had checked them in, Tommy turned and walked into the alcove, saying, "Are you two ready to get something to eat?"

"Famished," Jack said, pulling his giant body from the chair.

"Where's the closest Denny's?" Sandy joked, standing up. "I could clean out their all-you-can-eat specials, and that's tantamount to poisoning oneself. Do you always dress in faded jeans?"

"I like well-worn jeans. I find them comfortable," Tommy replied with a shrug. "What kind of food do you want? This town has it all."

"No seafood," Sandy commented, gesturing out to the gulf. "I have a feeling that it would taste like that water looks."

"The seafood is brought in from elsewhere."

"It doesn't matter," Sandy said. "After looking at the water as we drove in, I've spent that last four hours of sleep having nightmares about deformed brown fish with sharp teeth and red eyes. I can eat anything but seafood."

"Sandy, listen to the man, the seafood is brought in from elsewhere," Jack piped in, running a massive hand through his unruly silver and brown hair. "Seafood sounds marvelous to me. Actually, anything sounds marvelous to me."

"How about Mexican?" Tommy offered.

"Mexican sounds good," Sandy answered, glaring at Jack. "Anything but seafood."

"Yes, Mexican," Jack muttered. "We find ourselves in Thailand for the very first time and we eat Mexican. There is likely a law against such an infraction."

"Keep it up, Jack, and you'll need to bring home one of those forty-kilo brown rice burners that Tommy is so enamored with," Sandy spat. "You won't be touching me."

"Sandy, darling—" Jack began.

"Jack, quit while you're ahead," Sandy interrupted. "Let's go eat Mexican. You'll have all night to grovel at my feet, apologizing."

The threesome stepped out of the hotel, down the concrete steps, and onto the narrow palm-tree-and-trash-lined street. The sun was nearly down, and the heat was quickly giving away to a cool evening. The musty gulf breeze blew up the Soi and ruffled their hair as they walked away from the water.

Stepping out onto the main road, Tommy flagged down a pickup truck with vinyl covered benches on each side of its aluminum roofed bed. Climbing into the bed via a heavy metal grated rung, Tommy, Sandy, and Jack took up one side of the pickup's bed. A pretty black-haired woman with wide shoulders and narrow hips, dressed a short white miniskirt, smiled from the other side. Her small but firm bosom pushed against a black blouse, threatening to pop its top three buttons.

Tommy reached up and grabbed a long round metal rail, for steadying oneself, that ran the length of the bed just under the roof. Small lights flickered above the rail, illuminating the interior, and advertisement stickers decorated all available space. Scooters and cars racing past

"Don't you have to tell the driver where we're going?" Sandy asked, as the pickup began slowly moving down the frenzied street, looking for more passengers.

"This is a baht-bus," Tommy explained. "You can hire them individually or just hop on one if you just want to take the inner city loop. We're just going a couple of blocks on the loop."

The pretty woman across from them pressed a small button on the overhead and a faint buzz could be heard coming from the cab. The baht-bus pulled over and came to a halt. Stepping from the bed, the woman walked up to the passenger window of the cab and dropped some change into the hand of the driver.

Jack, shaking his head, said, "Something was definitely peculiar about that woman."

"I can't believe it." Sandy laughed. "We haven't been out for ten minutes and Jack's already drooling over with the rice burners."

"Sweetheart," Jack began explaining. "I am just saying there something was odd about that woman. Yes, she was attractive but something was amiss that I cannot put my finger on."

"I know she was beautiful," Sandy responded, smiling, "but we haven't been out of the hotel for ten minutes and you're already salivating—"

"She had an Adam's apple," Tommy announced, interrupting their bickering.

Both Jack and Sandy looked at Tommy, as the baht-bus began rolling along the crowded street again.

"Your subconscious probably noted that she had an Adam's apple."

Sandy laughed. "No way!"

Jack chuckled. "Oh, dear."

"Oh yes." Tommy smiled. "That was what the Thais refer to as a katoy. A common fixture in any setting around the country. A man dressed like a woman. I'll explain the whole dynamics of katoys later, if you want."

"But she had boobs," Sandy exclaimed.

"They take estrogen. The estrogen grows boobs."

Reaching up, Tommy punched the button on the overhead, the faint buzz could be heard again, and the baht-bus pulled over and came to a stop. Piling out onto the sidewalk, Tommy handed the driver thirty baht and gestured his companions forward.

Turning down a narrow street, with a blue and white overhead marker identifying it as Soi Seven, the threesome walked past more hotels, bars, and restaurants. The street was busy with chubby middle-aged men hovering around the bars. Bargirls, dressed in alluring clothing, called out to Tommy and Jack, offering cold beer and more. An old stooped woman with silvering hair, dressed in a faded blue sarong, stopped in front of Sandy. Smiling, the old woman reached up and touched Sandy's strawberry blonde hair. She then reached into a basket and handed Sandy a small flower.

Tommy handed the old woman ten baht, and said to Sandy, "it's to put in your hair."

Smiling down at the stooped woman, Sandy placed the flower behind her right ear, saying, "I can't remember which side you're supposed to place a flower to show you're taken."

"Tell the old lady I want one too," Jack said smiling. "I'll place mine behind my left ear, and we can see which one of us ends up with a date for the night."

"That from a man who thought another man dressed in a skimpy white miniskirt was attractive," Sandy commented, with a wry smile.

"Sweetheart, you thought she—he—was attractive, as well," Jack replied.

Passing a cluster of open air bars on the left, with dueling music and girls waving at passing tourists, Tommy saw their destination on the right. Gesturing toward a white stucco and red brick building, they walked up several concrete steps into The Tequila Reef Cantina.

Taking a seat at a window table, they immediately ordered a round of tequila from the barmaid. The barmaid brought over three shot glasses and a plate filled with lime wedges and salt, before pulling out a bottle of clear liquid with a red sombrero on top from a leather holster wrapped around her waist.

"No way," Tommy quickly declined the tequila. "Do you have Jose?"

"What's wrong with that tequila?" Sandy asked.

"That stuff is rot gut. You know I love tequila, and I know good tequila. I have never taken a shot of Sierra Tequila without gagging."

Sandy laughed. "I want to try it."

"I believe I will trust Tommy on this particular issue," Jack commented.

"You're such a pussy." Sandy elbowed her husband. "I'm going to try the Sierra stuff."

The barmaid poured the clear liquid into her shot glass and then looked at Jack. Jack halfheartedly nodded, with a grimace on his face, and she filled his glass, as well. When the barmaid looked at Tommy, he placed both hand over his shot glass, shielding it from her, while shaking his head and saying, "Jose, please."

"You are such a wimp," Sandy poked at Tommy.

"I may be wimp, but you'll be so sorry."

Sandy and Jack took the shot glasses in hand, looked at one another, and tossed the contents in their mouths. Sandy immediately sprayed the tequila across the table, dousing Tommy, coughing and gagging. Jack swallowed his shot. His eyes seemed to lose focus, and with a single cough, he began to turn pale. The barmaid returned with a bottle of Jose Cuervo and poured the shimmering yellow liquid into Tommy's shot glass, as he wiped the residual of Sandy's discharged shot off his face.

"Tommy, I am so sorry." Sandy coughed again. "That stuff was shit!" she declared, while gesturing the barmaid to fill her shot glass with Jose Cuervo.

"That was dreadful," Jack said, wiping newly sprouted sweat from his brow with his forearm. He gestured for Jose Cuervo, as well.

After a large dinner, the threesome chatted about Pattaya and how they should entertain themselves. Tommy looked out the window and spotted two men standing near one of the open air bars, ignoring the bargirls, and watching the Tequila Reef. The men, dressed in khaki pants and neatly pressed shirts, looked out of place on the slightly raunchy street. A brown rat ran past one man's shoes, into a nearby gutter.

"Let's get going," Tommy announced. "Let's head down to Walking Street. Every newcomer to the city has to experience one night on Walking Street."

Examining Tommy for a moment, with narrow light blue eyes, Sandy asked, "Okay, what's up?"

"What is it about your sixth-sense?" Tommy laughed. "It's like you're plugged into the people around you. Jack, how can you live with this?"

"It is a living hell, and I have often contemplated suicide over this very topic many times," Jack solemnly replied. "It is like living with a mind reader. You can have no secrets, nor hidden agendas."

"What's up Tommy?" Sandy asked again.

"Don't look, but there are two men across the street, watching us."

"Do you think they could have already found us?" Sandy whispered, looking at Tommy.

"With the Society, anything is possible."

"What can we possibly do?" Jack asked, with a concerned look.

"I don't think those two guys will do anything with all these people around," Tommy responded. "I say we head down to Walking Street, and when given a chance to lose them, we lose them. There are too many hotels in this town for the Society to check them all. And the night staff has come on duty, so there's no one there to identify us. The morning staff is next, and they haven't seen us, either. The earliest they'll be able to find where we're staying is tomorrow afternoon, when the afternoon staff comes back on duty. And by then we'll hopefully be on our way to Koh PhaNgan."

After paying their bill, the three walked down the busy street to the coastal road. Flagging down another baht-bus, they climbed in the back. Before the bus got going, one of the men in khaki trousers stepped into the back and sat down directly across from Jack. The baht-bus began moving down the busy street and Jack, with a grimace, began staring at the man. The man in the khaki trousers avoided his ogle, looking out over his shoulder at the darkened Gulf of Thailand.

Reaching up, Jack grabbed a small rail above his head, and looked over at Tommy, on his left. Tommy looked back and shrugged, confused as to what Jack was attempting to communicate. Swiftly, Jack lifted himself up on the bar above and swung both meaty legs out, smashing the man in the chest with his feet. The man's head slammed into the edge of the roof before he tumbled out the side of the pickup and bounced across the pavement. A speeding sedan ran the man over. The traffic behind them swerved and screeched to a halt, as the baht-bus continued down the coastal road.

"Seemed like the ideal time to lose the gentleman following us," Jack calmly commented, as he put his large feet back on the floor and removed his hands from the rail.

Looking up to the pickup cab to ensure the driver hadn't seen what occurred in the back, Tommy laughed.

Sandy looked over at her husband, shaking her head. "I am married to a Neanderthal."

They stepped off the baht-bus and paid the driver when it arrived at the entrance to Walking Street. The driver looked confused, when he glanced back and didn't see his fourth passenger, asking Tommy in Thai what had happened to the man dressed in Khaki pants. Tommy told him that the man had jumped off the bus just after getting on. The driver shook his head and made a disparaging comment about some customers. Tommy agreed with him.

Stepping into a sea of men and a few women, of various ages and health, they began moving up the street, passing a magician with a crowd circled around watching the show. The loud music between the competing bars and the chatter between the tourists and hawkers was deafening.

As they passed by a bar called Lucifer's, Tommy yelled over the noise, "What do you want to see?"

Sandy yelled back, "Something that's a mixture of elegance and raunchiness. Licentious yet demure!"

Turning and heading back toward the entrance to the street, Tommy knew exactly where to take them. A few minutes later, he led them down a narrow alley and stopped at an entrance covered by a two heavy bolts of red fabric, that resembled drapes on a window. A neon sign overhead advertised the Beach Lounge, and two men stood outside beckoning potential customers into the bar. Tommy gestured Sandy to the entrance.

They stepped inside. The narrow room had a long elevated dance floor with five brass poles running down the center of the room. The base of the dance floor was made of Plexiglas and illuminated from underneath. Ten women, dressed in plaid schoolgirl skirts, danced on the illuminated floor. Some had white blouses. Others had nothing, revealing brown nipples and round bosoms. Barstools were situated around the edge of the stage. Up against the walls were two rows of tiered seating, covered in red vinyl with black piping.

The barstools around the stage were filled with men hoisting potbellies and double chins. Gray hair out numbered other colors, and they all stared up at the girls with longing in their eyes. More clientele with similar features filled the tiered seating. Taking a seat on the back row, they ordered beer from a waitress dressed in a black skirt and white blouse.

"Those men are just staring up the women's skirts," Sandy commented. "It's like they're in a trance, or something."

"The girls have no panties on," Tommy calmly announced.

Sandy face contorted and she cried out, "Are you *serious*? That is so disgusting!"

Jack, with a licentious smile, said, "Maybe we should reposition ourselves," gesturing toward the barstools.

"You asked for elegant yet raunchy." Tommy commented, as the waitress delivered three beers.

Sandy muttered, "I'm not sure how long I can stand this place."

"Now, let's not get in a rush, sweetheart," Jack added.

Sandy asked, "Do they sell Jose?"

"Sierra only in this joint, I'm sure."

"Order three. I'll try and keep it in my mouth this time." Changing the subject, Sandy then asked, "How do you think they found us so quickly?"

"Sierra?" Tommy asked, ignoring her question.

"Yes! Order me another shot," Sandy snapped. "If you two wimps want to drink beer, fine. I'm drinking tequila, even if my tongue rots and teeth fallout from its toxicity. Now, tell me why and how those men found us so quickly."

After ordering three shots of Sierra tequila, Tommy said, "They have obviously figured out we didn't head for Bangkok. Probably because the van wasn't seen passing through any toll booths. That leaves only one other populated area near the airport to hide in, Pattaya. Or maybe they're looking in both cities. Who knows or cares? The Society has likely contacted both the police and local mafia for help in both Bangkok and Pattaya. There are probably fifty people out combing this city for us. I think the two we saw back on Soi Seven were nothing more than a chance encounter."

The shots arrived and the threesome tossed them back. Jack replicated his earlier reaction, Sandy swallowed the repulsive liquid before coughing and choking for a solid ten minutes, and Tommy gagged, excusing himself to the bathroom, where he threw up.

After consuming six rounds of beer, Jack turned to Tommy. "I'm growing tired of the drooling men and the school girls and allegedly panty-less, entertainment. Can we move on and find something a bit bawdier?"

"Bawdier." Sandy laughed. "I'm not sure Tommy can top this place."

Laughing, Tommy said, "Bawdier, aye," as he stood up and began making his way down the tiers and toward the exit. With Jack and Sandy following, Tommy led them farther into the alley and through a narrow dark door. The bar was similarly fashioned as the last, an illuminated stage running up the center of the narrow room and black vinyl tiered seating. The sound system blasted out tinny hip-hop music and on the stage, completely naked women with numbers attached to garters on their thighs, danced for a similar crowd of fat middle-aged men. Taking seats on the first tier, the threesome ordered another round of beer.

"Do you think they have Jose?" Sandy asked.

Tommy looked over at her, saying, "You've got to be kidding me. This place is about low rent as it gets on Walking Street, the chance of them stocking good tequila is equivalent to their having a bottle of Dom Perignon Champagne tucked away in the backroom."

Waving the waitress over, Sandy asked her, "Jose? Do you have Jose Cuevo tequila?" When the waitress nodded her head and scurried off, Sandy turned to Tommy with a thin smile, saying, "Some Thailand expert you are."

Tommy silently smirked back.

Gesturing toward the stage, Jack grimaced. "These girls certainly do not meet the standards of the Beach Lounge. I think number twenty-four has recently undergone a cesarean section."

Looking at the stage, Tommy examined number twenty-four, a plump girl with a fresh scar across a protruding abdomen. The girl next to twenty-four, number fifteen, seemed as if she was at the end of her lifecycle as a nude dancer, her sagging bosoms and ass as evidence. Both had pleading eyes looking out at the crowd. Sandy frowned and pointed to another girl with enormous dark circles under her eyes, looking completely stoned.

"You asked for raunchier," Tommy replied to their gawking.

"Raunchy and gross have two different definitions," Sandy informed Tommy.

"I believe gross and raunchy are shared alternatives in any thesaurus," Tommy retorted.

"I asked for bawdy," Jack corrected them both.

"Bawdy, gross, raunchy—all shared alternatives," Tommy said, defending his bar choice.

The waitress returned smiling, holding out a bottle of the red topped Sierra tequila in one hand, and three shot glasses in the other. Sandy dropped her head in defeat, as Jack gestured for three shots.

Throwing the tequila back, Sandy turned pale as tequila dribbled from the edges of her hand covered mouth, John's brow immediately broke out in sweat and his eyes lost focus, again, and Tommy tossed the beer from his mug onto the floor and threw up in the empty glass.

After one more round of beer, they decided to move to a quieter part of the city, and left the bar. Catching another baht-bus, they got off on Soi Yamato, two blocks past the Marriott. Soi Yamato was lined with six story narrow buildings, each housing a bar or restaurant, filled with a preponderance of middle-aged and older men. It was obvious this was not a street younger men hung out on. They walked past a hawker with a portable pizza cart, busy filling the requests, and then a man pushing a cart stacked high with stuffed animals and balloons. Another pushed a cart filled with ladies fashions while the bargirls crowded the bar entrances gazing upon his wares.

Stepping into a narrow bar named The Exodus, playing soft rock and roll music, they sat down on a several chairs next to a small pool table. Three girls hovered around the bar, each with heavy makeup and dressed in tight fitting clothes. Tommy smiled at an attractive twenty-five-year-old woman dressed in a short jeans skirt and tight-fitting black top. Her long silken hair folded over her shoulders, and her large brown eyes shined with intelligence. Calling her over, Tommy ordered three beers. Silently, she went behind the bar and produced three ice cold beers.

"I prefer this to that panty-less place any day," Sandy commented. "I've always loved little dives. Especially ones with English names."

"I think Exodus is biblical as opposed to English," Tommy mumbled, hoping Sandy would not scold him.

"Speak for yourself, Sandy." Jack chuckled. "I might require a return trip to the panty-less pub before we retire to our rooms."

"You go back there before retiring to your room and you won't have a room to retire to," she said, shaking her head.

After another hour of small talk and three rounds of ice cold beer, Sandy said, "I'm hungry again."

"I second that motion," Jack added.

"Let's have one more beer and I'll take you to the Waffle House of Pattaya," Tommy answered.

Arching his eyes in misbelief, John asked, "Pattaya has a Waffle House?"

"No, of course not." Sandy laughed. "He's being factious."

Calling over to the attractive, twenty-five-year-old, Tommy whispered in her ear. She, once again, went behind the bar and produced three more ice cold beers, before disappearing into the back room.

"What was that all about?" Sandy asked, looking at Tommy quizzically.

"What?" Tommy replied, feigning ignorance.

"You have got to be kidding me." Sandy laughed. "She's half your age!"

"Hey, not only is it the oldest profession in the world, it

was a simple and acceptable business transaction in this town," Tommy retorted. "She has something I desire and I possess the cash to buy the item."

Laughing again, Sandy said, "You're hiring a prostitute!"

Jack, initially looking confused at the banter between his wife and Tommy, suddenly began laughing.

"Just drink your beer," Tommy said. "I'm just taking her out to get some food."

"Yeah, right," Sandy sarcastically muttered.

Several minutes later, the young woman now stripped of all makeup and dressed in faded jeans, a green long sleeve silk blouse, and brown flats appeared at Tommy's side. Tommy handed her three hundred baht, that she, in turn, paid to a woman behind the bar, and the foursome stepped out onto Soi Yamato.

With the young woman at his side, Tommy led them down to the main street, one block off the beach road, which they crossed when a break in traffic appeared. Walking down uneven sidewalks, past more bars, they stepped into The Kiss, a wall-less all-night eatery.

After a lively conversation, where they found that the young woman spoke reasonably good English, the food arrived. After two Thai omelets, a serving of Pad Thai and fried rice for Jack and Sandy, and green curry and som tam, or papaya salad, for Tommy and his date, they all pushed their chairs back.

Sandy looked at the woman. "Are you really going to go home with this guy," she asked, gesturing toward, Tommy.

"He has nice eyes and calmness that I like," she responded, smiling.

Sandy asked, "Why do you do this—go home with men? You're attractive and obviously smart."

"Sandy, please do not do this," Jack interrupted.

Tommy sat back in his chair and smiled at the young woman.

"It is okay. I do not mind speaking about this. Before I

came here, I worked in a factory north of Bangkok," she explained. "It was barely enough to feed myself and I also had to support my mother and two sisters in Isaan."

Raising one eyebrow and cocking her head to the side, Sandy asked, "Isaan?"

"Northeast Thailand," Tommy interjected.

"Yes, Northeast Thailand," the young woman continued. "Now I make enough money to support them and myself. I can buy nice clothes, and I meet very interesting men."

"But you go home with despicable people who here simply for sex with young women," Sandy exclaimed.

Tommy chucked at Sandy's comment before saying, "Thanks."

"I pick and choose who I go home with. I do not go home with everyone that asks me. I am very careful."

"The bar must make you go home with everyone that asks." Sandy shook her head. "It's how they make money."

"Maybe in your country, but we are Thai. We are Buddhists. It is different here."

Sandy looked quizzically at the woman. "There but for the grace of God go I, Jack."

Jack sighed in relief, and the woman took Tommy's hand and squeezed it.

After another round of beer, Sandy and the young woman went to the bathroom to freshen up.

Sitting in silence, Jack and Tommy looked around the restaurant and out onto the still busy sidewalk and street, observing the drunken middle-aged men with younger Thai woman.

His eyes narrowing, Jack began gazing at something across the room.

Seeing Jack's curious expression, Tommy asked, "What is it?"

"Possibly two more ruffians."

"It was just a matter of time. What do they look like?"

"They are Thai men, but different than the last two. They seem a bit rougher around the edges."

"Mafia."

"Are you implying that I booted a policeman out the side of the baht-bus earlier?"

"Police or mafia, our troubles with the Society trump them all," Tommy replied, still seated with his back to the thugs.

Sitting back, straightening up in his chair, Jack said, "They're heading this way."

Tommy slumped back in his chair, waiting for the inevitable confrontation.

"Mr. Luck?" a hoarse and heavily Thai accented voice called from behind.

Twisting in chair, Tommy looked up at the man before quickly turning back, and facing Jack. Dressed in pressed blue jeans, a black shirt, and red velvet jacket, the man had blood shot eyes, and half of his left ear was missing. His partner, several years younger and unscarred, had a black jacket covering a T-shirt advertising Harley-Davidson Motorcycles.

"Yes, can I help you?" Tommy kept his back to the thug.

The red velvet jacketed man queried, "Where is your friend's wife?"

"You need to ask him that question," Tommy responded, still not turning around.

The red velvet jacketed man, glared at the back of Tommy's head. Then looking to Jack, he asked, "Where is your wife?"

With a hint of a smile on his face, Jack answered, "You're about to discover the answer to that question," just before two wooden chairs crashed across the heads and shoulders of the two thugs.

The two men dropped to the floor. The other restaurant patrons began scurrying around and chattering away in excitement, as Tommy and Jack leapt from their chairs. Sandy and the young woman stood behind the crumpled men, smiling.

Sandy laughed and put an arm around the waist of the

young woman. "I'm beginning to like this chick."

Tommy quickly searched the unconscious men, pulling a .38 special from under the blood-shot-eyed man's red velvet jacket, and a .45 Colt M1911 from the other. The foursome quickly departed the restaurant, caught a baht-bus, exiting on the coastal road near the Soi where their hotel was located.

Standing in lobby, the receptionist sleeping soundly behind the desk, Tommy pulled their keys from hooks on the wall behind, before handing Sandy the .38 special.

"Just in case they discover where we're staying," Tommy explained.

Taking the weapon from Tommy, Sandy looked at the young woman and said, "There's still time to change your mind."

"Oh, Sandy, please leave it alone," Jack muttered. "It's a simple business transaction."

"Please do not worry," she replied, looking at Tommy. "I will be fine."

Jack took Sandy by the arm and gently twisted her in the direction of their room, saying, "It's time to go to bed, sweetheart."

"Goodnight," Tommy called out as his two friends began climbing the stairs to the second floor.

Sandy looked over her shoulder, and told Tommy he was a pig. Jack muttered something indiscernible. The young woman took Tommy's hand and kissed him on the cheek. Tommy smiled down at the silken haired woman holding his hand, knowing that he would forget about the Society and all the danger that lie ahead for the next hour or two.

CHAPTER 20

Pattaya Beach, Thailand, 9 December 2016:

Opening his eyes, Tommy looked around his hotel room. Bright light flooded into the room through the windows, illuminating her neatly folded clothes on the dark wood cabinet. He then looked at his clothes crumpled and tossed in the far corner of the room. He felt a hand trace down the center of his back then a soft kiss on his right shoulder. Twisting over, he found himself face to face with her large brown eyes. Her silken black hair coiled across the pillow, the sight was enough to help Tommy forget the pounding ache in his head, the dusty taste on his tongue, and the rolling nausea in his stomach. Moving one hand to his face, she ran her index finger down the thin scar that ran from the corner of his lip to the edge of his jaw. Her other slid down across this belly to his groin, where she playfully stroked him.

"I've forgotten your name," Tommy confessed, feeling himself become aroused.

"Pakpao," she answered smiling. "And yours is Tommy."

Looking into her eyes, Tommy asked, "What shall we do now, Pakpao?"

"Maybe a good morning present." She giggled.

With one great pull, Tommy tossed the red and gold bedcover from the bed, revealing their naked bodies. Pushing him over onto his back, she climbed on top and straddled him. Her long black hair fell across her bare chest and her eyes sparkled with mischievousness. He could feel her hot dampness and reached up, taking her small brown breasts into his hands. Reaching down, she placed Tommy inside of herself, emitting a soft moan, and began slowly rocking back and forth.

Twenty minutes later, Tommy climbed from the bed and left Pakpao sleeping under the covers. Placing two thousand baht on top of her folded clothes, he donned baggy blue sport shorts and an olive drab T-shirt. Stepping out the door, Tommy headed out for his traditional morning run. It was early enough that it was still somewhat cool, as the brown gulf water lapped against the gravelly beach. With the sun three fingers above the horizon, Tommy ran along the cracked and uneven sidewalk, passing tired looking bargirls with smeared makeup and disheveled clothes, obviously returning home from one hotel room or another. Two men were picking up trash along edge the coastal road, using long poles with sharp ends. A pack of four dogs chased a rat into a gutter.

Running over empty beer bottles, and other rubbish, Tommy thought about the beautiful woman currently sleeping his bed. Having been with many Thai women, Tommy had come to love their Buddhist attitude about life, happiness, and misery. The misery started the day you were born, and your level of happiness depended on how you looked at your misfortune. It meshed well with his view of life: an unfair journey at best. Some seemed to get all the breaks while other got nothing. Happiness was a matter of finding a little goodness in the world each day and focusing on that single element. Today, Pakpao was that for Tommy.

The sidewalk led him past Walking Street and then up a small hill south of the city. Passing several temples at the top, the road winded down into the small town of Jomtien Beach, where the sand seemed finer and water a bit cleaner.

As he ran, he began considering their situation, with the Society and all its assets after them. He knew that until they reached the shores of Koh PhaNgan, their chance for survival was slim. Once on the island, they would have time to contemplate their circumstances and, hopefully, find a way out of the madness. But how? What was the path out? Caroline had said that the operation had seemed freelance, somehow. Why had John Smith not immediately requested the full support of the Society? Was he playing two hands with the Society? That certainly would not surprise Tommy. John Smith was always looking for a payoff, even at the expense of others. Maybe that was where he needed to focus his attention, once on Koh PhaNgan. May be John Smith was the key to extracting themselves from this mess.

Finding himself on Sukhumvit Road, headed back to Pattaya, Tommy glanced down at this watch. He would have just enough time to return to the hotel, shower, and eat before his meeting with his friend Chandler. Hopefully Chandler would have cobbled together transportation to Koh PhaNgan for Tommy and his friends.

The door to his room was unlocked with the air conditioning still purring on the wall. With steam curling from under the edge of the bathroom door, Tommy could hear Pakpao humming an Isaan song as water struck the shower walls. Stripping his T-shirt and shorts off, Tommy stepped into the bathroom and pulled the shower curtain aside.

Pakpao turned and smiled at Tommy. Momentarily mesmerized by her golden glistening body, Tommy reached out and pulled her close to him, feeling her warmth.

"Where did you go? I've been waiting for you."

"I left money on your clothes," Tommy replied. "Was it enough?"

"It was too much." She giggled, taking his hand and pulling him into the shower. "Most men give me half that."

Taking a small bar of soap from the edge of the bathtub, Pakpao began lathering Tommy's chest and arms. Tommy playfully took the bar from her, spinning her around and scrubbing her back. After rinsing off, the two stepped from the shower, each taking one of sinks and mirrors, silently dried and combed their hair.

"Will you be in Pattaya long?"

"No, we will hopefully be leaving today."

"The men last night, I know them," she admitted. "They are not good people. They will find me and make me pay for helping you."

"I can't take you with me," Tommy said, looking over at Pakpao. Her eyes suddenly appeared frightened.

"May be I will go to Bangkok and find work," she replied. "Soi Nana and Cowboy are always looking for bargirls."

"It would be far more dangerous for you to come with me. Bangkok is probably a good decision."

After they had dressed back into faded blue jeans, Pakpao kissed Tommy and handed him a slip of paper, saying, "This is my phone number. Please call me when you return. I will come see you if you like."

"I will," Tommy replied, smiling one last time at the beautiful young woman. "Thank you for last night. It was wonderful."

"And this morning." She giggled, before stepping out the door, leaving Tommy by himself.

Tommy called Jack and Sandy's room, and they arranged to meet in the lobby at noon. Sandy asked if the young woman was still with him and he told her that Pakpao had already gone home. Once again, Sandy called him a pig before hanging up the phone.

The city was slowly coming to life as they walked down the coast road toward the Marriott. Baht-buses, scooters, and cars careened along the street, bars began opening their doors, and the jet skies, with their pluming gray water tails, and speedboats pulling the lofty para-sails, crisscrossed the edge of the gulf. Bargirls, dressed in alluring clothing, shared the sidewalk, clattering past in high heels.

Two blocks before the Marriott hotel, Tommy led them down the Soi Yamato with its high, narrow, weather-stained buildings standing side by side. Halfway down the street

Tommy stepped up three dirty concrete steps into the Legless Arms, a small pub, just down from the Exodus.

Two tall black tables stood just outside the pub, with matching tall chairs. A they took a seat, a plump woman, dressed in a silk dress, stepped up the table and asked them if they wanted something to drink.

"It's a little early for me," Tommy admitted, looking at Jack and then Sandy.

Sandy said, "It's all right for you to sleep with a woman half your age, but you can't possibly have an early drink."

"Sandy, darling, please leave it alone," Jack responded, placing his massive hand on her forearm. "I am sure Tommy paid the young woman well."

"I won't leave it alone until I'm ready," Sandy snapped. "And yes, I'd like a shot of tequila—no, I want two."

"A beer for me," Jack requested.

"Okay, a beer for me, as well," Tommy added. "And a shot of tequila. I don't want Sandy doing shooters alone."

The waitress returned quickly with the ordered drinks. Sweat broke out on Tommy's brow when he saw the clear Sierra tequila shimmering in the three shot glasses, wondering how the detestable liquor was going to taste on a hot afternoon. Sandy pushed one of her shot glasses toward Jack, who dropped his head submissively at the sight.

The threesome downed the tequila in unison, Sandy gagging, Jack letting out a tremendous belch, and Tommy excusing himself from the table to vomit in the gutter next to the sidewalk.

"Why do we continue to inflict that kind of pain on ourselves?" Jack asked, wiping his forearm across this mouth.

Sandy mumbled, between coughs, "Because we're not sissies."

"It's a waste of money for me," Tommy groaned. "I can never keep it down long enough for my body to absorb any of the alcohol."

A second round produced the same results, as they waited for Tommy's friend to show up.

At the end of the street, Sandy pointed out a man about Tommy's height walking with a slight gimp. Tommy identified the man as Chandler, explaining the gait was due to soccer-injured knees. The man had slightly freckled Gallic skin and auburn hair. With a beer belly protruding from a white polo shirt, Chandler had green eyes and thin scar on his right cheek.

"He looks like a pirate," Sandy commented, watching Chandler approach. "All he needs is an eye patch and a wooden leg."

"Don't forget the parrot," Jack added.

"He is a pirate." Tommy chuckled. "A modern-day pirate albeit, but a pirate nonetheless."

With a wide smile, Chandler mounted the dirty concrete steps, and climbed up to table.

"Hello, septic," Chandler said, greeting Tommy, shaking his hand, and pulling the chair out next to him.

"Hello, motherfucker." Tommy returned his greeting, before introducing Jack and Sandy.

"Where are you from, Jack—" Chandler asked, hearing his English accent.

Tommy quickly interrupted, saying, "Jack can't tell you where he's from unless you're drunk and won't remember the next day."

"That's true," Jack admitted, slowly nodding his head. "It's a personal rule that I vowed to adhere to as a young man. People tend to listen to what I have to say more, hoping to catch a hint to my origins."

"He's Canadian," Sandy snapped. "Everyone can hear it's a fake English accent."

Ordering a vodka and soda, Chandler sat down. "Your transportation has been arranged."

"Excellent," Jack muttered.

Tommy asked, "When do we leave? It can't be soon enough. They know we're in Pattaya. We had two run-ins with their agents last night. I'm sure they're scouring the city looking for us as we speak."

"Is two hours soon enough?" Chandler answered as the waitress delivered his drink. "Anyone hurt?"

"Last night?"

"Yes, did you injure anyone?"

"One, presumably a Royal Thai Policemen, fell out of a baht-bus and was run over by a fast moving sedan," Tommy calmly explained. "And two men, likely mafia, were beat over the head with chairs and knocked unconscious."

Chandler laughed. "That sounds entertaining. I wish I'd flown up last night."

"You didn't tell me it was policeman that Jack kicked from the bus," Sandy exclaimed.

Shaking his enormous head, Jack replied, "Sandy, dear, does it really matter?"

"Of course it does," she answered. "It's one thing to slam a mafia thug over the head with a chair—an entirely different thing to push a policeman from a moving vehicle."

Changing the subject, Tommy asked, "How are we getting to PhaNgan and where do we meet our ride?"

"A fishing vessel," Chandler explained, taking a sip of his vodka soda. "You'll be departing from the southern end of Jomtien beach in two hours. The ship is blue with orange markings and will be flying the stars and stripes just under its Thai flag. The captain has instructions to cruise directly to Chaloklum. You should be there by morning."

Their conversation was interrupted when a commotion broke out just down the street. Squinting his eyes, Tommy looked down the street for the source, before jumping to his feet and sprinting from the table. Chandler, and then Jack and Sandy followed.

Tommy arrived at the Exodus just as the man with half an ear and the red velvet jacket pulled a knife and pointed its tip at Pakpao, who was held from behind by the young thug wearing the Harley Davidson T-shirt. At a full sprint, Tommy jumped up the steps leading to the bar and tackled the knife-bearing thug from behind, knocking them both over the pool table.

Chandler was next up the steps and maneuvered around the pool table, so he standing in front of Pakpao and the young thug. The thug threw Pakpao aside and pulled a knife of his own from the small of his back. Smiling, Chandler grabbed a pool stick from the table and took a step forward. The young hooligan thrust the knife at his midsection, and Chandler expertly parried the jab, rotating and swinging the heavier end of the pool stick up, catching the young thug lightly under the jaw. Falling back two steps, the young man rubbed his jaw with his freehand.

The velvet-jacketed man rolled over the top of Tommy, brandishing the weapon above his head. Tommy punched the man in the nose, knocking him back against one of the pool table supports. Reaching into the slot holding the pool balls, Tommy pulled the eight ball out and slammed into the man's open mouth, breaking four of his front teeth.

Jack stepped into the bar and leaned against the wall. Sandy appeared by his side and wrapped her arm around her husband's waist.

Flicking the pool stick upward again, Chandler caught the young thug in the left ear, followed by a thrust into the man's belly. The young man stumbled backward, tripping on an overturned barstool, and fell on his back.

Using the pool table to stabilize himself, Tommy pulled himself to his feet and stood over the red-velvet-jacketed man. The man dropped his knife and reached up with both hands to pull the eight ball from his mouth. Tommy calmly bent down and picked up the knife, drawing up next to the man's right ear.

Chandler drew the pool stick high over his head, and viciously swung it down, putting his shoulders in to the swing to increase its momentum. The pool stick struck the center of the young man's forehead with a nasty thwack. The young hooligan's arms limply dropped to his sides.

Choking on bits of teeth lodged in his throat, the red velvet jacketed man pulled the eight ball from his mouth. Flipping the knife up, Tommy cut the red-velvet-jacketed man's right ear off, the loose piece of cartilage and skin dropping on the floor next to his thigh. Sandy put a hand over her mouth at the sight, and Jack grimaced.

"He's now got a matching pair," Tommy muttered, as Pakpao ran over and put her arms around him.

Chandler turned to Tommy. "Is there some reason other than chivalry, that we just mopped the floor with these two ruffians?"

"The girl's a friend," Sandy offered, stepping over to console Pakpao. Then looking at Tommy, Sandy said, "We should take her with us. These guys aren't going to stop till they exact some revenge for the other night."

"It's a lot more dangerous coming with us," Tommy explained. "Pakpao needs to get out of Pattaya and go to Bangkok."

"To sell herself in the big city?" Sandy protested, "You can't let her do that."

"Darling," Jack called from the side of the room. "Tommy is right. She'll be safer away from us."

"The septic is correct," Chandler said, confirming Tommy's advice. "Her chances will be better away from you three. Your problems eclipse that of a couple of thugs looking for her."

"I will be fine," Pakpao said to Sandy, while for watching Tommy's reaction. "The work there is the same here. There is no difference."

Saying farewell to Chandler and Pakpao, Tommy, Jack, and Sandy collected their luggage from the hotel, walked down the coastal road and flagged down an empty baht-bus. Stepping up the passenger window, Tommy negotiated with the driver and hired the baht-bus to take them to Jomtien Beach.

As they climbed into the back, the baht-bus jumped forward, knocking them sideways on the bench seats.

CHAPTER 21

Jomtien Beach, Thailand, 9 December 2016:

Standing on the beach, scanning the boats bobbing in the water off Jomtien, Tommy had his hand over his brow, attempting to shield his eyes from the bright sun. He saw an old wooden fishing boat painted blue and orange, anchored a hundred years off the shore. The red, white, and blue United States flag could be seen fluttering under a larger red, white, and blue Thai flag on the mast.

"There it is." Tommy pointed to the boat. "Out there."

Sandy asked, "How are we going to get out to it?"

"We can hire a long-tail."

"Please enlighten me," Jack requested, looking at Tommy.

Now pointing to a colorfully painted long wooden boat anchored just off the beach, Tommy said, "That's a long-tail," as he began walking toward several men sitting in the sand under a palm tree smoking hand-rolled cigarettes.

Speaking to the men in Thai, Tommy explained what he needed. Nodding his head, one of the men jumped to his feet and waded out into the water to the Long-Tail, a long narrow boat resembling an oversized canoe. The long-tail had a propeller mounted at the end of a very long driveshaft attached to a large engine, on the back.

"Now that's an outboard." Jack chuckled. "That engine appears to have come from a large Chevy truck."

"I'd be more surprised if it hadn't," Tommy replied.

The long-tail rocked precariously to one side its captain climbed on board. With a long handle welded to the rig, he rotated the entire engine and the long driveshaft to the stern before dropping the propeller into the water. Hitting the starter, the engine roared to life and black smoke plumed from the exhaust. After making a few adjustments, the captain turned and waved to them. Tommy, followed by Sandy and then Jack, waded out into the water, holding their belongings above their heads. The narrow boat rocked wildly as the three climbed over the edge onto boat, the captain moving his body aside to counter the additional weight each time one slipped over its wooden side.

Each of the trio taking seat on one of three tandem small wooden planks, the captain throttled the engine and the long-tail accelerated across the surface of the water with a white plume sprouting from the propeller some five feet behind the boat. The wind buffeted their hair and sea spray blew over the bow, providing a cool counterbalance to the blazing sun overhead. Smiles erupted on Sandy and Jack's faces as the long-tail raced toward the fishing boat.

Pulling up to the fishing boat, the long-tail bouncing off its wooden side, the captain raised the engine up, pulling driveshaft and propeller out of the water. Two thin men, wearing tattered shorts and T-shirts appeared on the deck above and grabbed a line from the captain, tying it to a cleat on the fishing boat.

One of the crew, a tall man with a scar across the top of his nose, reached down, offering a hand to Tommy. Tommy took Sandy's arm and helped her off the wooden plank she had been sitting on. The scar nosed man took her hand and hoisted her aboard the fishing boat. The second crew member, a small man with close-set eyes and thick lips, reached down and took Jack's hand. Unable to pull Jack's bulk from the rocking long-tail, the tall man with the scarred nose took his other hand and the two heaved him up and over the edge of the fishing boat. Tommy grabbed the side of the fishing boat and pulled himself aboard. The rope securing the long-tail was untied and the captain dropped the propeller back into the water. The narrow boat sped away, back toward the beach.

It was not a large ship. A small wheel house, with a long cantilevered roof protruding out over the fantail, sat at the stern of the boat. A single mast sprouted from the main deck just forward of a covered hold at the center of the deck, and a long pointed prow stood on the bow. Tommy knew that when fishing, the hold would be uncovered and filled with ice and the ship's catch.

The captain, a short stocky man, dressed in blue shorts and a tan short-sleeved shirt, walked up to Tommy and grunted, "You going to Chaloklum?"

"That's right," Tommy answered in Thai. "I understand we'll arrive tomorrow morning?"

Ignoring Tommy's question, he barked orders and one of the crew trotted up to the bow and pulled in the anchor line. The captain began walking back to the wheel house. Tommy followed him and gestured Jack and Sandy to do the same.

"A man of few words," Jack offered, walking behind Tommy.

"This is a pretty small boat," Sandy observed, stepping over a pile of fishing nets on the deck next to the mast, then over the covered hold.

"And a surprisingly large crew," Tommy commented, scrutinizing the three motley crew members preparing for their departure, "for such a small boat."

The captain stepped up on the narrow edge of the boat and held on to a small metal rod attached to the wall to ensure crew didn't fall overboard while transiting past the wheelhouse, as he moved to the stern of the ship. Tommy, then Sandy and Jack, followed in a single line. The captain gestured to a stool next to his, in front of the wheel, and Tommy took a seat. Sandy and Jack looked around and finally settled on two side by side hammocks, hanging from the cantilevered roof of the wheelhouse.

The engine coughed, a dark cloud of exhaust erupted from the side of the boat, and the bilge pumps began sputtering. The captain, advanced a small silver throttle, and the boat lurched forward.

CHAPTER 22

Kansas City, Missouri, USA, 12 March 1995:

It was a cold and windy day as fifteen-year-old Omid Sassani trudged down the alleyway behind his father's grocery store, carrying two heavy black plastic bags full of trash. Wearing a thick blue parka and a black New York Mets baseball cap, Omid was a large teenager for his age, nearly six foot tall with muscular arms and legs. The alley was bracketed by the back red brick wall of grocery store to one side and a tall unfinished wooden fence to the other. Scrub grass grew through cracks in the pavement. Several tall skinny trees, scuffed by passing traffic, had found footing near the fence.

Omid was tired. Not due to the undemanding physical work in the grocery store, but because of his father's relentlessly harassment. All Omid wanted at this point in his life was to get away from the Koran-brandishing man who could see no good in his only son.

But Omid had a plan, and each day at school, he worked to achieve those designs. Having decided long ago that he would not take over his father's frugal grocery store, a business that he had come to despise, Omid had worked hard to follow another path. He would use his intellect to accomplish something greater. Through his studies he would win a scholarship to a university and become exactly what his father feared the most. He would become a model American citizen, through and through. He would cleanse himself of Islam and its subjugation of woman. He would become a businessman. He would become an American, and he would disappear into the white-skinned landscape of the United States. He would convert to invisibility.

Lifting the lid to a rusted green trash dumpster with a wide yellow sticker advertising the local trash disposal company, Omid was met with the stench of decomposing vegetables and festering meat. A loud metallic bang rang out as he dropped the bags inside, and then another when he dropped metal lid back onto the dumpster. As he turned, brushing the dirt from his pant legs, Omid heard a dog barking and growling, and boys laughing at the end of the alley.

From his vantage point, Omid saw three teenagers swinging sticks, laughing, and kicking something much smaller at the far end of the building. Taking several steps in the direction of the ruckus, Omid realized that the three boys were beating an animal tied to a tree. Two more steps and he realized a dog was the focus of their malevolence.

Recalling, as he did many times, the day the blue-eyed young man had saved him from uncertain peril, Omid began steadily walking toward the commotion. As he recalled how the young man appeared out of nowhere and saved him from the teenagers, his walk turned into stride. As he recalled the young man's words, "Life is not fair. Life is never fair," Omid's pace quickened to a jog. Remembering the young man's parting words of wisdom, "Happiness is how you look at the world around you. You can choose to feel sorry for yourself and wallow in self-pity, and looking out for only yourself, or a live a life where you choose your friends and are loyal to those friends, supporting each other when things get tough," Omid began sprinting. In the alley behind his father's grocery store on that cold March day, Omid decided, right then and there, he would not spend his life just looking out for himself. He would choose a life where he would find loyal friends and support them—even if his first was to be nothing more than a dog.

"Hey!" Omid called out, sprinting toward the three stick brandishing teens.

Two of the teenagers stopped, turned, and watched as Omid raced toward them. One dropped his stick and the other tapped the third boy on his shoulder.

"Hey!" Omid called out again, getting closer.

The third boy stopped beating the dog, and turned. The three teens looked at one another and then back at Omid at a full sprint, pumping his arms to keep his speed up.

"Get away from that dog!" Omid screamed, as he ran headlong into the three boys, pushing two. The two young men silently stumbled backward several steps. Omid turned and pushed the third boy. He mimicked his friends, taking several steps back without saying a word. Not one of the boys uttered a sound, as if they were trying to read Omid's mind. It was as if they were trying to decide why this large teenager was defending the dog.

The three teens, with their arms hanging loosely at their sides, looked at Omid quizzically. They examined his irate dark eyes and bushy eyebrows. They took in the intensity of his scowling expression. They listened to his heated panting. They took in his anger.

One of the three mumbled, "Let's get out of here," breaking their silence.

The three boys silently turned and calmly walked down the alley, leaving Omid alone with the barking dog.

The dog, a bushy brown collie with matted hair, began barking and snapping at him as Omid watched the teenagers retreat. He scratched his wiry-haired head, astonished at their silence, even more so at their reaction to his aggression. Had they suddenly realized what they had been doing was wrong? Or had they seen something in his demeanor that had told them to not challenge his aggression? Looking down, he kicked one of the sticks across the alley that they had been using to beat the dog. It skidded and scrapped along the pavement. He sighed as he felt his anger wane. Looking back at the retreating boys, he wondered if the blue-eyed young man would have approved of his actions. He wondered what had become of the young man who had saved him behind the motel in that lonely town all those years ago.

He wondered what would become of himself.

CHAPTER 23

42,000 feet above the South China Sea, 9 December 2016:

Sitting in a gray leather chair next to a small oval window, John Smith contemplated his childhood memory of the three boys beating the leashed dog. The dog he had saved angrily barked and snapped at him after the teenagers had silently walked away. Only held back by the rope that tethered it to a skinny tree, Omid knew it would have attacked him if he were to let it free. It didn't matter that the dog couldn't comprehend how he had saved it from uncertain fate. He knew what he had done. He had done something good, even if there was to be no appreciation for the act. He remembered thinking that that day might define his future, that single act delineating a path of good. Looking out the window, John Smith shook his head as he considered how that thought had been so wrong. The unfairness of life had eventually turned him into something that Omid, on that cold windy day in the alley behind his father's grocery store, would have thought to be repulsive. John Smith, Omid, would end up just like the tethered dog: angry, alone, and unappreciative of the world around him.

The small jet lightly buffeted and a black laptop computer, sitting on a small table extended over his lap, rattled from the light turbulence. Reaching out, John Smith grabbed a small Styrofoam cup filled with coffee that threatened to overturn in the event of another bounce. Looking back out the window at his side, John Smith could see churning clouds hovering over the bright green Vietnamese

Coastline in the distance. Having changed planes in Manila two hours prior, John Smith sent the two Society action teams to Utapoa Airport, south of Pattaya. He and Steve hired a Cessna Citation to deliver them to Bangkok, where he would wait for word from the teams searching for Tommy and his friends.

A stewardess stood from her seat behind the cockpit and walked back to John Smith, saying, "Mr. Smith, you have an incoming call."

Stepping up to the bulkhead next to his seat, she pulled a white in-flight phone from its mount.

Taking the phone from the stewardess, John Smith answered the call, "John Smith."

A hissing and crackling voice, replied, "Mr. Smith, we believe Mr. Luck departed from Jomtien on a fishing vessel several hours ago."

"And his destination?"

"PhaNgan," the voice relied.

"Do you know that for certain?"

"A source on the island relayed information concerning his escape plans."

"Is it a reliable source?"

"I'm not sure, so we backed it up with other sources. We found the driver of a baht-bus that was hired by three people meeting their description. They instructed the bus to take them to Jomtien Beach, south of Pattaya. On Jomtien Beach we came across a long-tail captain who delivered the same three people to a fishing boat. The captain indicated that the boat departed, heading south. He did not know its destination."

"They have obviously have been given some aid in escaping," John Smith surmised. "Anything else?"

"The local mafia picked up a bargirl that had spent the evening with them last night. She was unable to tell them where they were going, or refused to do so."

"I'd like you to deliver her to Bangkok so I can talk with her myself," John Smith requested.

"That would be impossible," the hissing voice answered. "The man interrogating her went a bit too far."

"Is she dead?"

A simple "Yes" fizzled through the phone.

"Having her alive would have helpful in the capture of Tommy Luck," John Smith growled in frustration.

"The local mafia captured and questioned her," the voice explained. "We had no control over her treatment. She aided Mr. Luck and his friends in eluding several of their agents and the local boss wanted to send a message to other Thais in the city."

"Is there any way to intercept them on the high seas?" John Smith asked, changing the subject.

"We have commandeered command of several Thai Naval vessels, and they are attempting to intercept but there is heavy weather building in the center of the gulf."

After a moment of silence, John Smith then said, "Let's shift our search area to Koh PhaNgan since that's his likely destination. Notify the local mafia on the island. I'll divert the action teams to the island, as well."

Hanging up the phone, John Smith sat back in the gray leather seat and looked over at Steve, sitting across the aisle. Busy playing a computer game on a laptop on the folding table in front of him, Steve looked at John Smith with his beady eyes, asking, "What was that all about?"

"Tell the captain to divert to Samui," John Smith said. "Tommy has made it out of Pattaya. Also tell the captain to contact the Gulf Stream carrying our action teams and tell them to do the same."

Pulling the in-flight phone from the bulkhead, again, John Smith dialed a number and waited for an answer.

"Yes," John Smith was greeted on the phone by another crackling and hissing voice.

"He's on his way to Koh PhaNgan," John Smith said.

"Go ahead," the hissing voice requested.

"I'm shifting the search to the island."

"The other Patriarchs are concerned that you are not telling them everything. They don't trust you."

"Then you need to alleviate their concerns," John Smith challenged his boss. "I can find Tommy Luck and retrieve the hard-drive. You need to keep the Patriarchs off my back until I do so. Once I have the hard-drive, it really doesn't matter what they think. They will comply with all our demands."

"They are contemplating keeping Mr. Luck alive so they can talk with him," the voice cracked. "I have your video implicating Mr. Luck but they have requested it to be tested for authenticity. If they discover it's a fake, they will demand you capture him alive."

"Our plan is sound, but you must keep the video from being tested and ease their concerns about me. I will kill Tommy Luck and his friends and retrieve the hard-drive."

CHAPTER 24

Sixty-five miles north of Koh PhaNgan, Thailand, 9 December 2016:

It was a dark night. The wooden fishing boat chugged south as five-foot swells pitched the small craft to and fro. Jack and Sandy, laying in side-by-side hammocks strung from a cantilevered roof over the fantail, rocked back and forth. Deep snores from Jack rhythmically matched soft whispers of sleep coming from Sandy. Five single light bulbs twisted and swung from electric lines hung from the single mast protruding from the center of the forward deck. Sitting next to the ship's captain in the small wheelhouse, Tommy could see a line of lights on a distance coast off the starboard bow. The boat peaked over a large swell and Jack's swinging hammock brushed the back of Tommy's head.

"What's that?" Tommy asked, pointing to the lights.

"Koh Toa," the captain grunted, glancing at the lights, "but that is our problem," he said gesturing off the bow.

Looking over the bow, Tommy could see line of thunderstorms, sporadic lightening illuminating its leading edge. "I would assume by referring it to as 'being our problem' that we are going to go through it, and it is going to get rough."

The captain stuck his head out the side window of the wheelhouse and yelled, "Ohi," to his three crewmates.

The three men, who had been sleeping against the fishing nets piled on the deck, calmly stood and stretched.

Tommy suddenly felt a tension in the air that had not been there before, writing it off to the approaching storm.

"*Diaao Nee*?" the tallest of the crewmembers called out, peering at the captain in the dim light provided from the overhead bulbs.

A light rain began to fall, splattering against the wheelhouse window, as the crewmembers began working their way back to the fantail. Tommy watched one of the crew reach under his T-shirt and pull out a long-bladed knife.

Looking over to the Captain, Tommy asked, "How do you prepare for a storm?"

"We first dump our cargo," the Captain hissed, pulling a knife from his tunic and slashing out at Tommy.

Tommy pushed himself off the stool and fell back against the starboard wheelhouse wall, its small Plexiglas window shattering into five pieces before falling over the edge into the water. The knife's edge cut a shallow groove across the right side of Tommy's neck. The force of the captain's swing was too strong and the knife continued its course well after its intended target, cutting the rope holding up Jack's hammock. The hammock, with Jack still wrapped inside dropped with a resounding thud onto the wooden deck.

Tommy lunged forward and grabbed the wheel with his right hand, spinning it to the left, while simultaneously smashing his fist into the captain's nose. The boat, heaving hard to the left, surprised the crew working their way around the wheelhouse, knocking one off balance and into the churning waters. Releasing the wheel with his right hand, Tommy grabbed the captain's greasy black hair, and smashed his head against the bulkhead. The captain brought the knife about and jabbed at Tommy's midsection. Seeing the incoming blade, Tommy rotated slightly to the right, and the knife harmlessly cut through the side of his dangling T-shirt.

Stumbling to his feet, Jack quickly realized what was occurring and brandished a boat-hook that had been lying on the deck. The first crewmember to come around the edge of the wheel house, carrying a knife of his own, was met with a vicious jab to the face with the boat-hook handle, pushing him over the edge.

Tommy grabbed the captain's wrist and slammed his forearm down on the edge of the console. The captain let out a shriek and dropped the knife as his forearm broke and folded.

The second crewmember was able to dodge Jack's attempt at a second jab with the boat-hook, and leapt at the bear of a man. Jack retracted the boat-hook, flipped it around, swiftly swinging it up and hooking its end under the man's groin before raising him up and tossing the final crewmember over his head into the sea.

With the captain's greasy black hair still in his right hand, Tommy pulled the man's head down and thrust his right knee up, creating a massive collision between jaw and knee cap. The captain limply fell to the deck, under the wooden-spoke wheel.

With a thin ribbon of blood running down his neck, Tommy looked over at Jack and then at Sandy, still sleeping soundly in her hammock.

"That was an interesting way to wake up," Jack calmly commented, rubbing the back of his head. "Cut from my hammock, my head slamming into the deck, only to be accosted by several ruffians."

Wiping the blood from his neck, Tommy asked, "What do we do with him?" gesturing to the captain lying at his feet.

"Do you know how to operate this vessel?"

"I can figure it out, and I know where we are," Tommy said, gesturing to the lights of Koh Toa on the horizon. He pointed to the approaching storm. "There is the slight issue of that."

"Broken arm and jaw, I doubt he'll be much use," Jack observed. "He might shed some light on who employed him."

"Is there any doubt who hired him?"

"That's true. He's of no use whatsoever."

Tommy smiled. "Dump him?"

"Dump him," Jack responded, nodding his head in approval.

"Should we wake Sandy?"

"This ceremony should be celebrated among the participants. She might have differing opinion as to his fate. And you know me. I will capitulate, given the correct amount of marital pressure."

With Tommy holding the captain's feet and Jack his shoulders, the two men swung the captain overboard. The body disappeared into the darkness. A splash in the darkness confirmed the captain's fate. Moving to the wheelhouse, Tommy took the wheel and turned the bow south, toward the brewing storm. Lightning surged along the storms frontal boundary and the rain became more resolute, pounding the wooden deck, and the window and roof to the wheelhouse. Shaking Sandy, Jack whispered, "Darling, it time to rise and shine. We have a slight issue to deal with."

Opening her left eye, she sleepily groaned, "What is it?"

"A storm is approaching and the weather will undoubtedly become rough," Jack answered.

"God, I could sleep for a year in this hammock. All this rocking is like taking a mouth full of valium."

"I found it to be more like an aphrodisiac," Jack replied with a straight face.

"You find everything to be like an aphrodisiac," Sandy commented, rolling out of the hammock. Looking around the boat, she asked, "Where's the captain? The crew?"

"Somewhere back there," Jack said, gesturing behind the boat.

"What?" she snapped, canting her hip and head to the right, and placing a hand on her waist.

"It's a long story, darling," Jack calmly replied, placing his hand on her shoulder. "We just found it beneficial to lose the crew."

"Okay, tell me what I missed," Sandy said, sweeping his large hand off her slim shoulder, while looking at Tommy in the wheelhouse peering at the weather.

CHAPTER 25

Twenty miles west of Kansas City, Missouri, USA, 15 September 1996:

They waited at the stoplight in the small faded green Toyota sedan, Omid with his hand on Debora's knee and a smile on his face. Slightly plump with sparkling intelligent brown eyes and mousey blonde hair, Debora looked over at Omid with a smile of her own, looking at the young man she had first given herself to. The young teenage couple was inseparably in love. Each school day they would meet up between classes. Each afternoon they would walk home hand in hand and each weekend they would spend hours together.

The stoplight was in a small farming community west of Kansas City. Only two buildings marked the intersection, a Seven-Eleven to the right and an old and dingy looking gas station to the left, with a rusted Esso sign leaning against a side wall. The young couple had gone for a drive into the countryside to escape the turmoil of the big city, stopping at a small remote restaurant on a lake that they often frequented on weekends. As the sun began to find refuge behind an endless horizon of bright green corn fields, they had decided it was time to drive home.

The light turned green and Omid shifted the car into first gear, stepping on the gas pedal, and as they pulled across the intersection, it happened. A thunderous explosion of glass and metal, Omid's head slammed against the driver's side window and his left arm and shoulder smashed into the door. He could feel his ribs give way, cracking and splinting. He could see Debora out of the corner of his eyes, flailing sideways against her seatbelt. The Toyota took flight, careening over onto its roof then side. Shattered glass danced across the car's interior, all to a hideous background of twisting metal, as the small car skidded across the pavement, before roughly coming to a stop against a telephone pole.

Unable to move, Omid was pinned beneath a crumpled dashboard and steering wheel, each breath of air sending a painful spasm across his chest. Examining his left arm, limply hanging at his side, he saw boney protrusion amidst his tore shirt and skin. Turing to Debora, Omid came face to face with a bloodied warped head containing lifeless dull brown eyes.

A helicopter lifted Omid from the intersection to a Kansas City Hospital, and he was taken directly into surgery upon arrival. The next morning, after four hours of surgery the previous day to repair his left arm, a collapsed lung, and shattered ribs, Omid lay in a hospital bed, blankly staring out the window.

Omid's father quietly entered the room and took a seat next to him. Seeing his father, Omid wiped a tear from his cheek. His father glared down with disapproving eyes.

"Why?"

"Allah is a powerful force and when you displease him, he is ruthless," his father replied in a flat emotionless voice, shaking his head.

"But what happened?" Omid asked, looking pleadingly at his father. "And what does it have to do with Allah?"

"You were hit by a tractor trailer that ran the red light."

"But why?" Omid asked again.

"You are Muslim and you have displeased Allah," his father explained. "There are some things that Muslims cannot do. Socializing with infidels displeases your god."

"You say that Allah is responsible?" Omid responded as another tear broke from the corner of his right eye and worked its way down his cheek. "A tractor trailer ran a red light because Allah was displeased? Do you really believe our god is cruel? If he is displeased with Muslims and Christians sharing time, then why did he create a love between us? Why did Debora and I fall in love?"

"To teach you a lesson," his father brusquely replied. "To teach you that Muslims do not mix with infidels—a lesson you will never forget."

"But I survived," Omid chocked. "Why not take me if I am an unfit Muslim?"

"You survived because you are Muslim and your friend is dead because she is an unbeliever. It is a simple as that."

"You talk of about life as if it were designed to look favorably upon Muslims and unfavorably on all else."

"You live to serve your god. Life is lonely and religious solitude is good. You survived because of your faith. Your friend did not."

"You sound heartless," Omid hissed, turning his face from his father's. "My friend is dead, and all you can say is that my religion has saved me? What about all the Palestinians and Iraqis that perished at the hands of the infidels? Why did their faith not save them?"

"You must learn that life is a lonely journey and you exist to serve Allah. Your only warmth is your faith. Without your faith, you will shrivel and die. You are placed on this earth to serve your master," his father explained. "You can never trust an infidel. They are the unbelievers. Their self-serving and gluttonous ways will lead you astray."

"Is there no such thing as happiness? I am here simply to serve Allah?" Omid sarcastically snapped, glaring into his father's dark eyes.

"The only happiness you will find is in your Muslim faith. We have not been put on this Earth to find happiness. We are here to serve our master."

"Your faith has blinded you," Omid curtly declared. "There is more to life than serving Allah. We should seek happiness."

Looking down at Omid, his father firmly said, "You have a choice right this moment, you can quit feeling sorry for yourself and recognize that you are here to serve your god, or you can choose to live a life with the infidels. A life that is never filled with the warmth of your god. Which will it be, Omid Sassani?"

CHAPTER 26

Koh Samui, Thailand, 10 December 2016:

Sitting in the gray leather chair, as the jet banked for final approach, John Smith contemplated his childhood memory of the death of his girlfriend. His father was a devote Muslim and his religion had consumed his life. So much so that he had decided that any other form of faith, whether it was Christian or Jewish, was wrong and made their followers evil. Even in his youth, John Smith found himself disapproving of the intensity of his father's faith and he despised the hatred it had invoked. Where his father had come to hate all things non-Muslim, John Smith had come to relish a life filled with anything but Islam or its consuming religion. Shaking his head as he looked out the small oval window at the twinkling lights below, John Smith considered how completely he had dismissed the Muslim faith and swore off a life of pleasing a god that had, in his estimation, destroyed any goodness in his father.

The small Cesena Citation touched down, with a bump and screech, at Samui International Airport just after sunset, where it taxied up and parked next to the larger Society Gulf Stream jet. With a slight drizzle falling, John Smith slowly maneuvered down the narrow ladder from the jet onto the tarmac. Hobbling over to an open-sided and white canvas-topped bus, waiting to take the new arrivals to the terminal, he and Steve climbed on board. The open-sided bus resembled a hybrid between a bus and golf cart, and had a Koh Samui beach scene painted on its side. An eerily muted light, that seemed to dance in the falling drizzle, was cast down on the side-by-side jets by tall silver lamp posts situated around the concrete tarmac. Men in white overalls passed luggage from a small compartment at the rear of Citation to an awaiting tug and others dressed in grey pulled a thick black hose from a nearby fuel truck. The heavy tropical air smelt of aviation fuel mixed with that of a lush jungle. As John Smith and Steve sat down on polished wood plank bench seats, a gust of warm wind blew through the open sides of the bus, splashing them with a light mist. Suddenly, it began to rain heavily, and the downpour beat the bus's canvas top.

The Koh Samui airport was new and modern with ornate wooden pillars and beams supporting enormous white tent like roofs. Tall palm trees stood between the buildings and walkways, all illuminated by spot lights hidden in the foliage and positioned high in the palms. They climbed off the bus under a large covered entryway leading to the baggage claim area, where they retrieved their belongings from a clanking silver rotating carousel before proceeding to a small conference room near the airport terminal entrance.

Twelve stern-faced men sat in blue plastic chairs surrounding two white topped tables, all looking at John Smith and Steve as they entered the room. Five were cleaning disassembled weapons on the tables in front of them, three were inspecting maps of Koh PhaNgan, and the final four were examining folders with pictures of Tommy, Jack, and Sandy.

Several had cigarettes dangling from their lips or in small ashtrays on the table, and a smattering of soda cans littered the room. Cigarette smoke mixed with the scent of weapon lubrication oil, giving the room a customary military odor.

Hobbling across the room to one of the white tables, John Smith turned to a short stout man dressed in jeans and a crisp white short-sleeved shirt with a clip board in his hand.

Inquiring of the clip board barring man, John Smith asked, "Is there any further update?"

"Apparently," the short stout man began, "a Society agent and local mafia member arranged for the crew of the fishing to terminate Mr. Luck and his companions during their transport to PhaNgan."

Giving a short dry cluck, John Smith said, "Does this Society agent have any idea who the crew was up against?"

"Sir?" The short stout man asked, looking slightly confused.

"Does the Society agent who arranged for a Thai fishing crew to dispose of Tommy Luck and his friends have any idea of Tommy Luck's knack for survival?" John Smith asked. "Assuming you've read his record, you must see that he is more than capable of taking care of himself."

Looking directly at John Smith, the short stout man nodded his head before replying, "We won't know if the crew was successful until they pull into port this morning. They should be arriving in the small fishing village of Baan Tai on the south end of the island around eight this morning."

"And if they are successful, what of the hard-drive?"

"They are to confiscate all belongs and deliver them to us."

"Gentlemen," John Smith began to address the crowd of men as he pulled a chair out from the nearest table, "I have arranged for speed boats to deliver you to Koh PhaNgan early tomorrow morning. As you know Koh PhaNgan is or was the likely destination of Tommy Luck and his friends. As you just heard, one of our agents arranged for a fishing boat that was to pick the three up on the mainland. The crew of the boat was instructed to eliminate them en route to the island, delivering their belongings to a small port in the village of Baan Tai on the south end of the island. However, Tommy Luck has proven to be clever and unpredictable in the past and has an uncanny talent in regards to survival. Because of this, we will proceed with a plan that covers both a highly doubtful elimination at sea and his successful arrival on the island."

Handing his canes to Steve, John Smith placed both hands on the table to steady himself as he lowered onto the chair. "Four of you will proceed directly to the village of Chaloklum," John Smith continued after sitting down, "and begin surveillance on a building owned by Tommy. The remaining eight will proceed to the village of Baan Tai where they will meet with the fishing boat crew that was tasked with eliminating the three at sea. If the fishing boat crew was successful, this team will retrieve Tommy Luck and his friend's belongings before terminating the crew. My assistant and I will proceed to the resort area of Thong Nai Pan, on the east side of the island, meet with the local mafia boss, and await my orders. Any questions?"

Met with a muted mumbling and shaking of heads, John Smith turned toward Steve. "You need to contact her and tell her I want her to meet with Tommy, assuming he survived. She is to tell him that if he turns the hard-drive over, we'll leave him and his friends alone."

Looking up at John Smith with beady eyes, Steve replied, "I've already told her to do that. She said that if Mr. Luck knows that she's in cahoots with you and me, he'll kill her."

"We're paying her to do a job," John Smith retorted. "Tell her again. Tell her if she doesn't do as I say, we'll dispose of her ourselves."

"She claims that while he may have a calm demeanor on the outside," Steve continued, running one of his small pale hands through his dark bushy hair. "He's capable of anything and we'll still need to eliminate Mr. Luck and his friends after we've gotten the hard-drive."

"Obtaining the hard-drive is the priority," John Smith said, his eyes flashing at Steve. "The hard-drive is critical to the rest of the plan."

"But we'll still need to eliminate Mr. Luck—"

"Tell her," John Smith snapped. "We'll eliminate Tommy Luck, but we need the hard-drive first."

CHAPTER 27

Thirty-eight miles north of Koh PhaNgan, Thailand, 10 December 2016:

The wooden boat pitched fore and aft, and side to side, as the swells intensified. As a large wave crashed over the bow, the old ship shuddered, and its internal beams groaned. The fishing nets, piled near the mast washed to one side of the deck and lightning flashed overhead, a thunderous boom shaking the timbers under their feet.

Holding on to the wooden-spoke wheel, Tommy set a southerly course, directly into the oncoming waves. Jack and Sandy, standing next to him, held on to whatever was available, trying to maintain their footing. Rain began pelting the wheelhouse window in front of them and the cantilevered roof above. A flash and tremendous clap shook them again. Another wave struck the bow, sending gallons of saltwater across the deck and rinsing the fishing nets into the sea.

"We are so fucked!" Sandy screamed above the turmoil.

"We just need to get through the leading edge of the storm," Tommy yelled back. "It should weaken on the other side."

"You're an aviator," Jack shouted. "Not a sailor. This weather is going to strengthen. I believe I will agree with my lovely wife on this one point. We are so fucked."

A third wave came over the bow, striking the wheelhouse window, and shattering it. Shards of glass spilled across them and saltwater drenched them. A loud crack could be felt and heard under their feet. A lone bilge pump could be heard banging away over the racket of the storm, attempting to empty the ship's bowels of water. Four of the five light bulbs hanging from the mast popped and broke, throwing the forward deck into near darkness.

"Jack, we need to check the bilge," Tommy bellowed. "This boat seems to be getting sluggish, like it taking on too much water. I'm worried that one of the pumps has stopped and the ship is sinking. I had the same thing happen to me a year ago not too far from here, and the boat ended up getting swamped."

"Check the bilge?" Jack laughed, gesturing toward the waves breaking across the bow and onto the deck through the remains of the wheelhouse window. "You would like me to attempt to traverse that?"

"There should be a hatch on the fantail," Tommy shouted. "Check for a fantail for a hatch that accesses the engine."

Looking back toward the stern, Jack and Sandy inspected the deck below the hammocks. Sandy grabbed Jack's soaking shoulder and pointed to a silver colored latch at the center of the deck. The seams of a hatch could be faintly seen. Using the swinging hammocks to try and maintain his balance, Jack stumbled over to the hatch and dropped to his knees. Grabbing the latch, he pulled up with all his might, but the small hatch didn't budge. Reaching across the deck, he grabbed the boat hook he had used to toss the attacking crew members over the edge earlier. Wedging the hook into the seam of the hatch, he stood and used its handle as leverage. The wood around the hatch splintered but the hatch didn't move. Dropping the boat hook, Jack stumbled back into the wheelhouse console.

"That hatch must be locked from within," Jack yelled over the storm.

"I'm worried we're sinking," Tommy shouted, looking over to Jack. "The bilge pumps don't seem to be pumping enough water. If too much water gets into the bilge, the engine will be swamped, and we will truly be fucked."

"Tommy, he's not going out" Sandy began saying, before being interrupted by an enormous wave smashing into the wheelhouse, knocking her and Jack to the deck.

"Okay, Jack, take the wheel," Tommy screamed over the roar of another clap of lightning, as Jack pulled himself from the deck.

"Tommy, you can't possibly be thinking of going out there!" he yelled back, helping Sandy to her feet.

"Someone needs to check the bilge pumps," Tommy exclaimed. "We need to make sure they're working, and we're not filling with water!"

Laughing, Jack shouted, "Is there any doubt we're not filling with water?"

"We need to make sure the pumps are working!" Tommy exclaimed, again.

Yet another wave smashed into the boat and another loud crack could be felt and heard under the wheelhouse deck. More rain pelted the wheelhouse roof and came through the broken window, stinging their eyes and soaking them further.

A flash of lightning illuminated the seas around them, revealing violently churning waters. The boat jolted to the left when a swell hit them broadside, knocking all three to the deck, each grabbing at the wheelhouse bulkheads so not to be tossed overboard.

Scampering to his feet, Tommy grabbed the wheel and spun it to the right, bringing the bow back into the oncoming waves. Jack stood, grabbing the remains of the side window that Tommy had knocked out earlier during his fight with the ship's captain. Sandy reached up and grasped one of the wildly swinging hammocks, pulling herself to her feet.

"I'm beginning to lament our decision to dispose of the captain," Jack screamed over the storm.

"I'm beginning to regret your decision, as well," Sandy

cried out, wiping soaked hair from her eyes while still hanging onto the swinging hammocks.

"I not sure what value he'd be right now," Tommy shouted, looking over at Jack and Sandy with a crooked smile. "With broken jaw and forearm, he wouldn't be a lot of use, and let's not forget, the bastard tried to kill me."

"May be he could provide some moral support," Jack shouted back. "I'm feeling a bit apprehensive about our immediate future at the moment."

Changing the subject back to the bilge pump problem, Tommy repeated his early request, yelling, "Take the wheel! Someone needs to check the bilge pumps."

With his feet slipping sideways, Jack staggered over to the wheel and took it from Tommy, asking, "Which way do I steer this ship?"

"Head into the waves," Tommy shouted.

Releasing the hammock, Sandy attempted to move farther into the wheelhouse, but fell back to the deck. Reaching down, Tommy grabbed her by the armpits and pulled her up next to Jack.

Grabbing a heavy duty flashlight from under the console, Tommy climbed up and pushed himself through the shattered wheelhouse window, falling on the forward deck. Slipping and sliding, he reached out and grabbed a rope dangling from the base of the mast as another wave struck the boat, sending more saltwater across the deck. The last light bulb hanging from the mast popped. A mist of glass mixed with the wind and blew across the deck, plunging the forward deck into complete darkness.

Jack and Sandy watched as Tommy's shadowy figure grabbed the rope while squirming on the forward deck. The bow bucked when a large wave struck the boat, and saltwater poured across the deck and over Tommy, nearly tossing him into the sea.

Grabbing the edges of the covered hold, Tommy pulled himself forward. He could just make out the mast in the darkness. Dragging himself across the covered hold, he reached out and wrapped his arms around the base of the mast, momentarily catching his breath. Saltwater coursed down his body and burned his eyes. Pulling himself around the mast, he reached forward and grabbed the shadowy hatch leading to the ship's bilge. When the ship's bow rose up on another tremendous swell, he placed his feet on the mast. As the bow dropped down the opposite side of the swell, he pushed the hatch open and straightened his legs, falling into the bilge and bouncing down the wooden steps. The hatch slammed shut above him.

Smelling of fish, soaked timbers, and engine oil, the bilge was damp and dark. The noise of water swirling around the outside of the boat competed with that of the struggling engine, both roaring in the confined space of the bilge. Fumbling with the flashlight in shin-deep water, Tommy turned it on, revealing dark skeletal timbers. Crawling on all fours, he maneuvered around the outside edge of the hold and worked his way aft until he found two large bilge pumps. One was banging away, pumping. The other was silent. He placed his hands on the silent pump. It was cool, as if it hadn't been working for some time. He checked the wires protruding from the pump and found they were still intact. He followed the wires back to the generator mounted on the diesel engine, chugging away, just inches above the waterline, and discovered that both bilge pumps were connected to the same generator. He looked up and saw that one of the ship's timbers had broken loose and wedged itself against the hatch that Jack had attempted to open earlier from above. He crawled back to the bilge pumps, and in a moment of frustration slammed the flashlight down on the silent pump. The pump sputtered for a moment and then stopped again. Looking around the hold with the beam of the flashlight, he spotted a rusty hammer hanging on the bulkhead. He reached out and grabbed it from its mount. Raising the hammer above his head, he smashed it against the silent bilge pump. It sputtered again and then came to life, banging away next to the other operating bilge pump.

After watching to ensure the second bilge pump would keep running, Tommy crawled back around the outside of the hold to the wooden stairs leading to small hatch near the bow. Looking back, he examined the compartment with the beam from the flashlight. The water level was noticeably lower, as both pumps could be heard thumping away side-by-side.

As he climbed the stairs, another wave slammed into the side of the boat, tossing Tommy backward. He struck his head on one of the bulkhead beams at the base of the stairs.

In the wheelhouse above, Jack and Sandy, standing side-by-side fought the foul weather. The rain intensified and the swells continued to grow. The waves mercilessly beat the old wooden ship. As the boat's timbers creaked and groaned in the churning chaos, Jack held a southerly course. Both Jack and Sandy silently began wandering what had happened to Tommy. Both thought the worst. Both thought he had been washed overboard in the darkness.

CHAPTER 28

Chaloklum, Koh PhaNgan, Thailand, 10 December 2016:

It was an enormous white villa, situated on a steep slope next to beach littered with large rocks, boulders, and fine sand filling the space between. Minimalistic in design, the villa's straight lines and flat roof meshed seamlessly with the surrounding dense jungle. A large patio topped with chase lounges and bright colored umbrellas terminated with an infinity swimming pool before dropping two stories into the jungle below.

A slender and wiry man of about forty, with dark curly hair, a matching goatee and dark brown eyes, sat on a lounge under a red umbrella sipping a greenish cocktail from a tall glass, sweating condensation. He was dressed in blue and white swim trunks.

A silver platter topped with slices of pineapple and mango sat on a small end table next to his prone and tan body. His sunglasses reflected the shimmering Gulf of Thailand as he peered out onto the morning horizon. Small white clouds floated across a bright blue sky. A light breeze brought with it the scent of jungle flowers mixed with salt.

The sound of a vehicle coming to a halt on the driveway below interrupted his late morning ritual of meditation while sipping a mint filled Caiperiana.

A man of many routines and rituals, Alain would next swim fifty laps in the infinity pool, followed by a Pastis, and then an hour on the beach, reading. The noise below was replaced by several demanding voices, and the scuffle of feet climbing the concrete stairs leading up to the deck.

"Pann," Alain called over his shoulder in a thick French accent, "They are here."

A slim woman, wearing a red and blue sarong appeared next to a sliding glass door leading into the villa. With large brown eyes and long black hair, her golden skin radiated young, beauty, and a natural calmness.

"One moment, Alain," her soft soothing voice replied.

The scuffling feet became louder, and heads appeared bobbing up the steps. A short stout man in his mid-fifties, with a barrel chest, and muscular arms and legs, dressed jean shorts and a white T-shirt advertising Lotus Divers led a group of seven, as they stepped up on the patio. He had a bald top and stubble on the sides of his head, and a face that resembled that of a bulldog, with the exception of his blue eyes, which were soft and peaceful. The next four men, all of obvious western birthright, had lowered heads, wrists bound with plastic ties, and various levels of contusions on their bodies. The last in the procession, two Thai men with dark menacing eyes and shaggy black hair, held handguns loosely at their sides. The stout bulldog of a man stood aside as the two trailing Thais directed the four western men to the far side of the patio. Laying in the chase lounge drinking his mint laced Caiperiana, Alain ignored the procession and continued to examine the horizon.

Once again appearing in the sliding glass door, Pann gracefully maneuvered across the patio, delivering another silver platter to the side table next to Alain. Lying on the top of silver tray was a silenced black 9mm Berretta. The four bound men glanced at the dark menacing weapon with concern. Still looking out to the far horizon, Alain reached out and took the Berretta into his right hand.

Looking over to the bulldog of a man, Alain asked, "Calvin, que, where did you find these thugs?"

"We found two in the blue hotel," Calvin, replied with an English accent. "Another in the French bakery, watching the front, and the last in the Two Brother's restaurant, watching the back of the building."

Alain finally turned and looked up at the four bound men standing next to the edge of the deck, with fronds of the palm trees as a background. The first in line was a small man, bright blue eyes and short sandy hair. Dressed in Khaki shorts and a red T-shirt, his scowling face looked down at the concrete below his flip-flop clad feet. The next was a tall skinny man in his mid-thirties, wearing tan cotton shorts, a brown silk shirt, and deck shoes; his narrow set green eyes, glared at Alain. The third was big boned and well muscled. Dressed in swim trunks and a baggy blue shirt, with a void look on his face, he was shoeless. The final man was a mixture of the other three, short, narrow eyes, and well muscled. Dressed in a baggy white silk shirt, brown shorts, and leather loafers, he stood at the patio edge with darting eyes, as if looking for a quick escape.

Calvin tossed four passports on the patio at the feet of the bound men. "One American, two English, and one Frenchman."

"They arrived by speed boat, yes?" Alain inquired.

Nodding his head, Calvin answered, "Yes, sir, very early this morning."

"Which is the Frenchman?" Alain asked.

With a thick finger Calvin pointed to the man at the end of the line in leather loafers.

"Where did you find him?"

"At the blue hotel," Calvin replied.

Still laying on the lounge, Alain calmly brought up the Berretta and pulled the trigger. A muffled pop and the round smashed into the Frenchman's left cheek, followed by his lifeless body spinning and tumbling back over the wall into the jungle two stories below. The other three men looked at one another in disbelief before once again dropping their eyes to the concrete deck. The scent of spent gunpowder mixed with that of jungle flowers and wafted the deck around Alain and Pann.

"Frenchmen are arrogant fools," Alain explained to the remaining three. "He would be of no use except to prolong our conversation."

"But, Alain," Pann said, the soft tone of her voice kind and reassuring, "you are French."

"Yes, that is true, Pann," Alain looked up at his beautiful wife with a serious expression, "but I am different."

"Yes," she calmly replied, lightly laughing and nodding her head. "You are different."

Turning his attention back to Calvin, Alain asked, "Which one of these was in the Two Brother's?"

Again, with a short stout finger, Calvin silently pointed to the first in line, the small man with the bright blue eyes and sandy hair. The small man looked at Alain with a panicked expression as sweat beaded on his forehead.

Alain again brought the Berretta up and pulled the trigger again. Another muffled pop was followed by the big boned man with the void look on his face duplicating the Frenchman, tumbling back and lifelessly dropping over the edge of the patio into the jungle below. Once again, the aroma of spent gunpowder and jungle flowers swirled around Alain and Pann. The couple looked at each other and smiled.

"Now we have the leader and the most junior man in the team," Alain proclaimed. "Which one shall tell me the *vari*?"

Smiling, Pann translated, "Who shall tell him the truth?"

"How did you know?" Calvin asked, scratching his bald head with thick fingers. "How did you know that the leader and the lowest man in the pecking order are the two remaining?"

"They have just arrived in the village," Alain began explaining his reasoning, as a teacher would to a pupil. "The most junior will be assigned the lowest job of watching the back of the building. The second lowest would have been assigned to watch the front of the building. The leader and his lieutenant would have been relaxing at the hotel."

"How did you know the Frenchman was not the leader," Pann asked.

"There was an American in the group. No American would ever follow a Frenchman into a potentially dangerous situation, and this one—" Alain pointed to the tall skinny one with his Berretta. "—this one is the only one who has made eye contact with me. He is the leader."

Calvin and Pann both nodded their heads, in unison.

"So, which shall talk first?" Alain asked again, laying the Berretta back on the silver platter.

CHAPTER 29

Haad Thong Lang, Koh PhaNgan, Thailand, 10 December 2016:

Water was sloshing around his waist when Tommy came to and found himself in complete darkness. The smell of fish and engine oil clung to the damp air. After a few moments, allowing his head to clear, he remembered falling from the stairs after fixing the bilge pump. Feeling around himself, Tommy realized he was leaning against the bulkhead at the base of the stairs.

The boat swayed and rocked, but not nearly as viciously as it had been when he fell. Using his hands, he felt his way to the base of the stairs, and crawled up the steps on his hands and knees. Reaching up, he pushed the hatch open. A dim light illuminated off a low overcast sky that was filled with falling rain. Poking his head through the hatch, Tommy looked back and saw Sandy's shadowy figure, through the broken wheelhouse window, standing at the helm.

To the east he could see a faint red glow reflecting off the low clouds, signifying an approaching sunrise. Climbing from the hatch, he stepped over a stump where the mast had been located and walked across the covered hold. He maneuvered back toward the wheelhouse, maintaining his balance on the water-slick and rocking deck. As he stepped up to the window, Sandy had her head down, seemingly peering at something on the console.

"Sandy," Tommy said softly.

There was no reply.

"Sandy," Tommy said slightly louder.

Again, there was no reply.

Taking a deep breath, Tommy shouted, "Sandy!"

As if prodded with a power jolt of electricity, Sandy's head shot up, and she stumbled backward, releasing the wheel. Tommy reached through the shattered wheelhouse window and grabbed her wrist to keep her from falling backwards.

She looked at Tommy with wide light blue eyes and screamed, "What are you, a fucking ghost?"

Tommy laughed. "You were asleep."

"No shit, you try driving an ancient wooden fishing boat through a vicious storm for six straight hours. One wave was so big it broke the mast off and hurled it into the sea."

"Where's Jack?"

"Where have you been?" Sandy answered his question with one of her own. "We thought you'd washed overboard. We did silly turns out in that shit looking for you. We nearly killed ourselves trying to find you!"

"I fell off the stairs and knocked myself unconscious in the bilge. I just came to. Where's Jack?"

Gesturing back to one of the hammocks filled with his massive body swinging under the cantilevered roof, Sandy said, "Don't tell him I told you so, but he was magnificent last night. Calm, cool, and level headed. At one point, I told him I thought we were going to die, and he turned to me, in his fake English accent, and said, 'Don't be silly, darling, don't you recall Gilligan's Island? There's a small desolate island out there someplace waiting for us.'"

Smiling, Tommy turned and looked at dark mountainous island directly south of them, pointing and saying, "You did more than keep us a live last night. That's our destination. Flawless navigation."

"It's beautiful," Sandy commented while examining the shadowy island.

A low groan came from the hammocks, and Jack stretched his arms. Rolling out of the hammock, he sauntered up to the console and looked at Tommy. "It's about time you showed up. You missed one incredible evening of superb sailorship."

"Sailorship? I'm not sure there is such a word," Tommy replied with a chuckle.

"Only due to George and Charles Merriam, and Noah Webster never witnessing the feat that Sandy and I pulled off last night."

"Seamanship," Tommy mumbled under his breath.

After Jack and Sandy described their hellish night of battling the storm, Tommy said, "We don't want to take the boat into a harbor. We need to swim ashore in a fairly remote area."

Shaking his massive head with its unruly silver and brown hair, Jack asked, "And what odd necessity does not allow us to find a safe harbor and step ashore like a civilized people?"

"Because it will be proof to those people looking for us that we've made it to the island," Sandy answered. "It would be better if we were not seen arriving and the boat were to disappear. Whoever arranged for our disappearance on the high seas will think that the boat, crew, and passengers perished in the storm."

"That's right," Tommy agreed. "We'll bring the boat abeam a small cove called Haad Thong Lang, turn it toward open water, jump off, and swim ashore."

"How far?" Jack asked.

"How far what?" Tommy rubbed the back of his head where it had struck the bulkhead the night before.

"How far ashore? Just how far will we need to swim?" Sandy clarified.

Thinking about the question for a moment, Tommy finally answered, "One hundred yards should be enough. I'll turn the boat to the northeast to avoid any land and throttle it up. There are no fishing boats out due to the weather, so it should cruise over the horizon undetected."

Twenty minutes later, as the sun was just beginning to

peek over the horizon, Tommy turned the boat to the northeast as Jack and Sandy jumped overboard with their carryon luggage over their heads. Tying the wheel in place with a piece of rope, Tommy then pushed the throttle forward and leapt over the side with his leather satchel looped over his shoulders.

It took them nearly an hour to swim the one hundred yards. The sun had risen and was heating the island up, but the waters kept the trio cool. As they approached the shore, they had to pass over a shallow reef before crawling up a small gravelly beach ringed with tall palm trees with long trunks bending over and displaying their green floppy tops above the sand. Silently, Tommy led them through a small palm-tree-laden valley and then up to a steep hillside covered in dense tropical foliage. With Tommy in the lead, the threesome began pushing tall grass and wide flat leafed bushes aside as they struggled up the hillside.

"Do snakes inhabit the island," Jack asked innocently, trailing the group through the dense vegetation.

"Please don't tell me you have the Indiana Jones affliction to snakes." Tommy chuckled, hanging onto a thin rubber tree while pushing aside a large bush.

"Let's say I am snake challenged," Jack replied.

"Oh, please Jack," Sandy muttered. "Please don't, all of a sudden, become a sissy after what you did last night."

"Sandy," Jack retorted. "You know I dislike snakes and have always disliked snakes."

Stopping and turning, Tommy said, "There are two types of snakes on this island." "Green is good. Black is bad."

Sandy and Jack came to a halt behind him.

Wiping his vast forearm across his brow, Jack requested, "Could you elaborate as to why black is bad."

"Pythons. The black are pythons. Every time you trek in the jungle, you run a risk of running across a python. It's sort of like rolling the dice."

With wide eyes, Jack looked at Tommy then Sandy, before saying, "Enlighten me, if there were to be a line of three people trekking across the dense jungle of this island, which of the three do you think would be most likely find a snakes fangs penetrating the skin on their ankle—by the roll of the dice?"

"The first to pass alerts the snake, unless he or she is unlucky enough to step directly on the reptile," Tommy playfully explained. "Then it depends on the time of the day and health of the snake as to whether I would like to be number two or three."

Sandy asked, "Time of day?"

"The heat," Tommy replied as he turned and once again began pushing up the hill through the dense foliage.

"Given a healthy snake and this temperature," Jack called out from behind, "Where would you like to be?"

"It's pretty hot out so the snakes are going to be slow right now," Tommy called over his shoulder. "Let's just say I'm not swapping positions with you."

Finally stepping out on to a dirt road grooved with deep ruts, Jack sighed in relief. Following the rutted road, which continued up the hill, they walked deeper into the jungle. Dogs barked, monkeys shrieked, and birds screamed as they struggled up the hot dusty road.

At the top of the hill, Tommy led them to the left, down a narrow path of fine sand into a small assembly area of tall palm trees and four concrete bungalows atop stilts. With red tile roofs and covered porches, the bungalows had a nice view of a large bay with colorful fishing boats bobbing on its crystal clear waters.

"Hey, mate," a tall wide shouldered man in a baggy white T-shirt, who resembled an oversized Cary Grant, called out from the nearest bungalow. With bushy prematurely white hair, the big man looked upon the threesome from the bungalow's porch with a wide grin, and said, "Tommy! Where the bloody hell are you coming from?"

"Just a little swim down at Haad Thong Lang," Tommy called back. "When did you get back on the island, Gary?"

"Just last week, with F-One winding down, I needed a

bit of a breather," the Cary Grant lookalike answered. "I haven't seen you around. When did you get back?"

"Just now," Tommy replied, before introducing Jack and Sandy.

"You're Australian?" Sandy asked.

"Aw, no way." Gary frowned. "I'm Kiwi. You want to come up for a beer?"

"That sounds like a marvelous idea," Jack called out with sweating coursing down his cheeks. "Let's call it a victory drink for successfully traversing a jungle full of snakes."

"Not for surviving a torrential storm at sea on an ancient wooden boat?" Tommy asked.

"Give me foul weather and a canoe before a snake-saturated terrain any day," Jack confessed. "I absolute detest snakes, particularly ones that have a venomous bite."

"Do you have tequila?" Sandy asked, ignoring the repartee.

From the next bungalow down, a wide-shouldered man in his mid-sixties stepped out onto his bungalow porch and called out in a New York accent, "Hey what's going on over there?" With neatly combed silver hair, light blue eyes, and a deep tan, the man stood on his balcony dressed only in plaid boxer shorts. Placing his right hand above his brow, the New Yorker asked, "Tommy, is that you?"

Looking at Tommy, Sandy asked, "What? Does everyone on this island know you?"

"On the north side of the island, most do," Tommy admitted. "I used to own the local pub. I know all the drunks, and everyone on this side of the island is a drunk."

The New Yorker stepped back into his house, reappearing moments later in tan shorts carrying a platter of salami, cheese, and crackers. With a glass of vodka and orange juice in one hand, the New Yorker carried the platter over to Gary's deck, and Tommy introduced Don to Sandy and Jack. Gary delivered three ice cold cans of Singha beer and the five sat on his porch drinking, eating, and talking about the recent island news.

With the soft jungle sounds around them and the occasional faint noise of a motor scooter racing by on an unseen road some fifty yards farther down the hill, Don asked, "So what brings you guys to the island?"

Sandy eyed Tommy, before saying, "An insane organization calling themselves the Society is out to kill us."

"Yeah, no shit?" Don leaned back in his chair, resting his glass of vodka and orange juice on his tan bare chest. "I might have heard about this Society while I was tending bar in the village—Greenwich Village—the New York village, that is. Well, anyway, Bob Dylan and some congressman came into the Corner Bistro, where I was working. The Bistro is allegedly the oldest pub in the village. It used to be a speakeasy back during prohibition. Well anyway, Bob and this congressman were smashed and talking all sorts of shit. This congressman began telling me about how some society organization was trying to force him to vote on some issue…I can't remember what it was all about. He explained how this society was made up of business and political leaders from around the world and how they had their hands into everything. It had some strange structure, three men at the top making plans and a couple of more at the next level to vote on whether to execute those plans. "

Laughing, Tommy muttered, "It's amazing what you can learn while tending bar in New York."

Don continued, "This congressman said that he wasn't going to do it. He was going to tell this society that they could kiss his ass. He died in a car accident a week later."

"How many years ago was that?" Sandy asked, before taking a sip from her can of beer.

"Oh, geeze, that had to be thirty years ago or more," Don admitted, looking up at the ceiling, as if contemplating the memory.

"And you remembered all that after thirty years?" Gary asked.

"What I remember is that when it came time for Bob and this congressman to pay, they realized they had no money. They had credit cards but no cash. This was at the beginning of the credit card craze and the Bistro owner was too cheap to buy all the gear needed to process a card. I think the Bistro is still a cash-only joint," Don replied. "Well anyway, I loaned them five bucks and they never paid me back. That's why I remember."

"Sounds as if the congressman's death was well warranted," Jack chimed in. "Five dollars was a lot of money in those days."

Sandy, looking over at Jack with narrowed eyes, sarcastically asked, "And what of Bob Dylan? Did he get what he deserved? All those horrible disadvantages as consequence of his fame and fortune?"

Taking a large swallow of beer, with a straight face, Jack replied, "Isn't that about the time he became a born again Christian? Maybe there was a higher power involved."

"Gary," Tommy asked, interrupting the building banter. "You think you could call Alain? We need to arrange a ride to Chaloklum."

"Certainly," Gary responded, before stepping into his bungalow. The faint noise of a conversation came from the doorway, before he stepped back out and sat down. "He's sending a couple of his ruffians over to pick you up. Apparently, there was a ruckus in the village a little earlier. Alain said something about having picked up four men keeping watch on your building."

"God help those four," Tommy commented with a chuckle. "Alain isn't known for his hospitality to strangers. What else did he say?"

"That was it." Gary shrugged his shoulders. "His ruffians picked up four gentlemen keeping an eye on your place in the village."

Several beers later, a white four-door Nissan pickup pulled up to the bungalows with Calvin sitting next to a scowling Thai driver in the cab.

"Hello, Tommy," Calvin called, his thick elbow hanging out the open window and bald head glistening with sweat in the sunlight.

"Nice to see you, Calvin," Tommy called out, standing and picking up his satchel. "How's the boss?"

"He's doing all right. You ready for a lift to the building?"

"Absolutely," Tommy answered, walking down the steps from the porch with Sandy and Jack following. "Is he expecting a visit from me today or will tomorrow do?"

"He didn't say," Calvin replied. "But knowing the boss, it might be a good idea for you to see him today. You don't want to give him the impression that you're unappreciative."

The threesome, with their luggage in tow, climbed into the bed of the pickup, and Tommy slapped the top of the cab to indicate they were ready. Without saying a word, the driver put the truck in gear and the pickup began bouncing along the path, snaking its way through the tall palm trees, out onto the dirt road.

The pickup drove deeper into the island along the rutted road and then turned left onto a paved road. Three scooters with brightly clad tourists whisked past the slow-moving pickup. The hard-topped roadway dipped down into a small ravine with another complex of white bungalows, looking more like a Swedish village than a tropical getaway, built to one side. Climbing out of the ravine on the far side, the pickup crested a hill and the occupants were provided a spectacular view of a northern bay, the blueness of the water radiating against the bright green of the surrounding jungle. Several red and blue roofs could be seen in the distance at the center of the bay over thickets of palm trees. A soft hot sea breeze blew across the truck's open bed, and Tommy smiled.

CHAPTER 30

Chaloklum, Koh PhaNgan, Thailand, 10 December 2016:

This is Chaloklum?" Sandy asked, not seeing Tommy's smile. "You've talked about Chaloklum."

"Yeah," Tommy replied, as he looked out across the bay's sparkling waters while his wavy brown hair tousled against the warm wind.

Descending the hillside, the road wound its way past resort entrances and open tropical fields with grazing black water buffalo and scrawny brown cattle. Small wooden buildings dotted the roadside. They passed a wooden gasoline booth, resembling a child's lemonade stand, with an old fashion glass tank filled with golden fluid, and then a decrepit building with a hand scrawled sign tacked to the side advertising *Bank* in red paint.

"That looks secure," Sandy sarcastically muttered, observing the sign while holding her hair back from her face.

Jack chuckled. "I'm sure they have some form of depositor insurance."

"Yeah, like every jilted client gets two chickens and a pineapple," Sandy said, laughing.

The closer to the village they drove, the more and more small buildings and businesses appeared on the side of the road. Occasionally to the left, they could catch a glimpse of the bay between the buildings or through palm trees laden meadows. To the right they passed a building with a wide porch advertising Wake Up Wake Boarding, then a little bit farther down the road, a complex with a large sign announcing the Lotus Dive Center. The truck finally took a hard left, under a faded banner declaring Fisherman's Village.

Bright sarongs and dresses fluttered in the breeze at a clothing retailer on the left situated in old wooden building, and bungalows on short stilts lined the other side, tucked between thickets of lush tropical foliage. The truck followed the street as it made a hard right, and began paralleling the shoreline. The air had a heavy smell of garlic and roasted chili peppers, creating a sinus burning aroma, and then the scent of fresh bread swirled around them.

They drove slowly down a road lined with bookstores, bakeries, shops, and restaurants, dodging bathing-suit-clad tourists. A minimalist Chinese flair to the architecture attested to the village's heritage. Jack and Sandy, balancing the carryon on their laps, careened their necks left and right, trying to take in the sights. The bay was obscured except for the narrow spaces between buildings as they drove down the street. At one empty lot on the beach, they passed by racks of drying squid lying in the hot sun, its odorous presence unmistakable. Beyond the squid racks and shoreline, the bay was filled fishing boats moored on its clear waters.

Passing more Chinese minimalist buildings, concealing the bay once again, the truck stopped at a faded yellow building with tall royal blue accordion doors. Stepping from the pickup, Tommy thanked Calvin and examined the street's occupants. Several tourists, walking past speaking in French, scrutinized the threesome. Another group standing across the street purchasing cigarettes from a vendor talked in Russian. Yet another couple spoke in Italian as they walked past.

Tommy directed Jack and Sandy down the narrow space between the yellow building and a white one next door. Sandy slipped into the space and easily walked between the buildings. Jack moved sideways order to fit his massive shoulders. Tommy, with his leather satchel over his left shoulder, followed the two down the passageway.

At the end of the passage, they stepped out on a terrace next to the crystal clear waters of Chaloklum Bay. Water lapped against a wide ribbon of fine white sand that sat below a four-foot-high concrete seawall protecting the buildings along the beach from the seasonally turbulent bay. Tommy gestured to a set of steep wooden steps leading to a deck attached to the second floor of the building, overlooking the beach and waters beyond. At the top, he dug into his satchel and pulled out a set of keys, unlocking two large glass doors that led into an upstairs apartment.

Tommy smiled again as they entered a gray tiled living area. With a slight musty smell, the room had white walls with long teak-colored water stains pointing to the floor. A polished wood planked ceiling with two dusty white ceiling fans stood overhead. A small arched space containing two wooden doors leading into the bedrooms stood at the rear of the room next to a wide set of steps with a thick concrete banister and blue porcelain newel posts, leading to the building's first floor. To one side of the living area sat a long wicker couch with soft green cushions and to the other was another wooden door leading to one of the apartment's two bathrooms. Next to the bathroom door stood a small refrigerator and washing machine.

"I need to meet with Alain," Tommy said as he turned the overhead fans on, sending a fine veil of dust from the fins as they began to whirl. "And you need some sleep. You had a rough night keeping us afloat."

Jack chuckled, saying, "Yes, and all the while, you were lounging in the bilge."

"I can't believe he's not complaining about being exhausted due to stress of negotiating the snake-infested jungle," Sandy mockingly commented, looking sideways at her husband. "I can see it now. He'll sue the Society, claiming Post Traumatic Stress Disorder brought on by the trek through the jungle."

"As a matter of fact, the trek through snake-infested jungles was draining, and the idea of arguing a PTSD case against the Society in civil court is very appealing at this point," Jack replied. "However, a simple lack of sleep over the last twelve hours is the primary source of my exhaustion."

Looking at Tommy, Sandy said, "Do you have to see this Alain character right now? You must ready for some sleep, as well."

"It's best if I see Alain now. I need to find out who the four men were they found casing this place earlier. We're safe in this village, but it's time to go on the offensive. We've been letting John Smith call all the shots so far. I need to make a plan for us to call a few."

"And we'll be safe?"

"I'm sure Alain has arranged for our protection," Tommy consoled her. "I imagine he has four or five of his employees stationed around this building, keeping an eye on things. You can wander around the village, but don't stray too far. Stay within the village proper."

After directing them to the guestroom and adjusting the room's air conditioner, Tommy stepped into the master bedroom, stripped off his cloths, and took a cold shower in the en-suite bath. After drying himself off, he opened a closet sheathed in spider webs and pulled from it a pair of tan cargo shorts and an olive drab T-shirt. After dressing, he then dumped all his clothes from his satchel, and those he had been wearing the previous night, into the washing machine in the living room. He could hear Jack snoring from the guestroom as he began working his way down the concrete steps to the first floor.

CHAPTER 31

The concrete steps led to a small downstairs kitchen, which was attached to the building's business area—a bar, with terracotta tiled flooring and a high ceiling. The room's white walls were water stained, and spider webs clung to the corners of the walls. In the bar, a long wooden counter stood to one side with two large refrigerators on the far side, and a blue topped pool table sat in the center. An enormous round colorful mural of a dog in a Hawaiian shirt was painted on the wall behind the bar. Around the edges of the room stood sofas and heavily cushioned chairs. An indoor balcony hung above the long wooden counter, only accessible from the second floor guestroom. An old red Honda scooter leaned against its kickstand next to the pool table. Walking past the counter, furniture, pool table, and scooter, Tommy stepped up to the tall royal blue accordion doors and removed a long wooden rail holding them in place and pushing two of the tall shutters open.

Pushing the scooter through the open shutters, he set the kickstand down again and closed the doors behind him, locking it with a small silver lock. With the tropical sun beating down, he climbed onto the scooter's worn black seat, turned the ignition on, and pressed the start button. The scooter sputtered, spit, and then started, releasing a dark oily cloud from its exhaust.

Driving away from the building, Tommy maneuvered through the midday tourists dressed in various swim attire sharing the same street, looking through small shops, and eating in the local restaurants. A warm gust sea air tousled his hair when he drove past a large white hotel on the left. The pungent smell of dry squid wafted the air as he drove past a long concrete pier, jutting out into the clear bay. Colorful fishing boats were jockeying for position alongside the wharf to drop off their catch. He passed a wide open area that resembled an unkempt park, filled with tall palm trees and grass. Rounding a corner at the end of the street, he could see a Seven-Eleven at an intersection ahead, swarming with more colorfully clad tourists.

As he turned left at the Seven-Eleven on a side road, the tourists gave way to Thais, diligently performing various tasks under the hot midday sun. Over a bridge the road turned to dirt and a plume of dust rose from the rear wheel of the scooter. A short time later, the road once again returned to concrete and turned steeply upward. The scooter struggled against the pitch of the road as it climbed the hillside, finally topping at a small resort with more views of the bay.

The road descended and then coiled along a steep mountainside with astounding views of the Gulf of Thailand on the left. Screeching monkeys and birds announced his passing. A large monitor lizard waddled across the road ahead, its snake like tongue darting in and out. Slowing, Tommy turned the old red scooter down a driveway that led to a large white minimalistic flat roofed villa. Surrounded by bright green foliage, the villa's calming straight lines nicely mixed with chaotic lushness of the jungle. Beyond the villa, Tommy could see the brilliant blue Gulf of Thailand, shimmering on the horizon.

Driving past the villa, Tommy parked the scooter under an overhead patio, some two stories above. Climbing up a long staircase, Tommy stepped out onto an enormous concrete deck that terminated with an infinity pool, with a stunning view of the beach and water, below, wiping his brow at the top of the stairs. A breeze blew across his face, bringing with it the scent of jungle flowers and sea breeze.

A porcelain-skinned woman dressed in a black one piece swim suit with large sunglasses and a wide brimmed white hat laying on one of the chase lounges sitting under a bright red umbrella, raised her head, and said, "It's about time. What took you so long?" Short straight blonde hair, cut just below her ears, jutted from below the rim of the wide hat.

"Caroline?" Tommy asked as he walked toward the woman. The blue-and-gray-eyed dog suddenly appeared from a set of sliding glass doors and ran up to Tommy. Tommy knelt down and scratched behind the dog's ears, asking, "How in the world did you get here?"

Caroline softly replied, "Who else would fly halfway around the world to a man with a limited life expectancy."

"Not to mention, bring his dog."

Caroline giggled. "Not to mention, bring his mini-me."

"I've got to listen to this dog more often. He knew things were fucked up from the start."

"Like I said," Caroline yawningly replied. "He's your mini-me."

Standing, Tommy walked over and sat down on the lounge next to Caroline, its wooden legs faintly moaning at the added weight. The dog followed and sat down next to him on the concrete deck. Caroline placed her hand on Tommy's forearm, her warm skin sending a tingling sensation up his back. He reached down and stroked her soft cheek with the back of his hand.

"When, why, and how did you find Alain?"

"Yesterday, and I figured you could use the help." Caroline yawned. "And, as I've said many times before, I've read your file. This was your destination." Reaching to a side table, she picked up a bright blue cocktail and sipped its contents through a straw.

"Blue Hawaii?" Tommy asked, gesturing to the drink in hand.

"Is there such thing as a Blue Thai?" She giggled again.

"I doubt it. Does the Society know you're here?"

"As long as I wear this ridiculously large hat," Caroline

replied, "and never look up, they'll never know I'm here."

"What?" Tommy looked at Caroline with a confused expression.

"Satellites. They will have targeted this villa to see who might be here, by now. Some technician in Florida is probably on the phone notifying some technician at the Society that you have just arrived. It'll take another five minutes for that technician to notify John Smith that you're talking to some woman with a wide-brim hat."

Tommy scratched his head. "What about the dog?"

"As far as I know, the NSA facial features identification technology has not gone so far as to include canines."

"Good point." Tommy laughed and shrugged his shoulders. After a moment, he announced, "The hit team you warned me about in Arlington showed up a night early."

"I heard."

"When?"

"I got a call from Steve at three in the morning," she explained. "I tried to call and warn you but your cell was off. I was relieved to find out that you managed to escape."

"I took the battery out," Tommy replied, before asking, "Steve called you at three in the morning?"

"The man has no sense of time. He was bored waiting for the hit team to return and called."

"Out of the blue?"

"That's what Steve does." Caroline yawned again. "When he's bored, he likes to call."

"Looking for a little phone sex?"

Shrugging her shoulders, Caroline said, "Probably."

"He's trying to get into your pants."

"More like trying to get into my chastity belt when it comes to him. He'll have better luck playing the lottery. I would have to be simultaneously drunk and drugged, and they'd have to put me on suicide watch directly after the act."

"And my dog? How did you get yourself and my dog here undetected by the Society?"

"Cash, well-connected friends, and this big hat." Caroline laughed. "I had a friend drive me to a small airport on the Maryland eastern shore and took a private jet to Chicago. Your dog and I transferred to another private jet which delivered us, after several stops, to an old Vietnam era airstrip in Thailand. From there a boat picked us up in Satahip, and we cruised to this lovely island. Even Thailand doesn't know I am here."

"I imagine it wasn't a wooden fishing boat that brought you here."

"Of course not, it was Alain's private sailing yacht. Three staterooms with all the trimmings and a great staff of professional sailors."

"I wish I had been so lucky." Tommy shook his head. "Just the idea of a professional staff of sailors not attempting to take my life would have been nice." He then asked, "What of the four men Alain scooped up from Chaloklum this morning? Who are they?"

"Who were they," she corrected.

"Okay, who were they?"

"Society agents arranged to watch your building by a man with two silver canes," Caroline answered, slipping the sunglasses down on her nose, revealing bright blue eyes. "According to those agents, there was a little adventure planned for you on the high seas. They were the back up in the event you survived."

"I survived," Tommy said flatly.

"This morning's interrogation of the Society agents happened right here on this deck and was another event likely watched and passed on by a Florida satellite technician."

"And the fate of the four men?"

"This Alain friend of yours is fairly ruthless. I was out walking the dog when the Society men were unceremoniously rounded up and brought here. I missed the festivities. Apparently, Alain extracted the information he wanted and then killed them, tossing them over the balcony," Caroline said, pointing to the edge of the deck. "He then had his men cut off their left feet and sent them to one of his competitors in a place called Thong Nai—"

"Thong Nai Pan," Tommy interrupted. "Who told you what happened?"

"Pann, his wife," Caroline answered in a serious tone. "She seems to enjoy his ruthlessness, as well. They seem the perfect couple. One enjoys dolling it out, the other watching. Apparently, the Thong Nai Pan competitor is aiding the Society in retrieving the hard-drive."

"Alain is ruthless, but a good friend," Tommy replied, looking over his shoulder at the glistening gulf. A large tanker was on the horizon, and the loud sputtering sound of a passing long tail could be heard above the soft jungle sounds.

"Tommy!" Alain called, stepping through the sliding glass door with a tall glass filled with yellowish milky pastis in one hand and a can of Singha beer in the other. "You have finally made it."

"And glad to be here," Tommy replied, standing and walking over to greet Alain. "I hope you're doing well."

"*Merci, et vous?*"

"I'm very good, and as I said, I'm glad to finally be here. Where's your right hand man, Calvin?"

"He's checking on the village. I am glad to see you survived the fishing boat."

"Barely. Not only did we have to contend with the crew, but Mother Nature had a little surprise in store for us, as well. Who told you about the fishing boat?"

Handing Tommy the can of beer, Alain gestured to two rattan chairs under a bright yellow umbrella. "A man with the group of Society people we picked up in Chaloklum this morning. It took some minor convincing. The leader, how you say '*sans mot dire*' would not say a word. Once I got rid of the leader, the lowest ranking man told me everything. And who arranged this fishing boat ride?"

"A friend," Tommy replied, not wanting to mention Chandler's name.

"Who?" Alain asked again, in a stern demanding tone, as he followed Tommy to the rattan chairs. "You must tell me who."

"Chandler," Tommy admitted, sitting down, resting the beer bottle on its wide rattan armrest.

"You can be such a fool at times," Alain said, shaking his head, sitting in the chair opposite of Tommy. "You are too trusting."

"Like you, he's a good friend. I do trust him."

"He is English," Alain spat, before sipping the pastis in his hand. "Only the French are worse."

"You're French," Caroline commented from her lounge, before taking another sip of her cocktail.

"Yes, but I am different," Alain quickly replied.

"He is different," Tommy just as quickly agreed before taking a long swallow of beer.

"But your lieutenant, Calvin, is English," Caroline interjected again.

"Yes, and I do not trust him," Alain responded with a perfectly straight face. "I keep my eye on him at all times."

"That makes no sense," Caroline muttered, just loud enough for Tommy and Alain to hear.

"This Chandler, he is the Society agent for the island of Samui," Alain changed the subject back to Tommy's friend and his choice of transportation. "He is the liaison for this organization that is out to kill you. You are fool at times. Why did you not ask me for transport?"

"I thought my friends and I could possibly fly to Samui and catch a ferry to PhaNgan with his help. He explained that was impossible, given the circumstances, and offered to arrange for our transportation."

"And where are your friends?" Alain asked.

"At the building in town. Are they safe there?"

"*Absolument*, I have my men stationed around the village and your building." Alain then repeated his earlier claim, "Chandler is one of them, and you are a fool."

"And I think you're letting your dislike for the man cloud you judgment," Tommy responded, shaking his head. "Chandler and I have been friends for a long time."

"What will you do next?" Alain asked. "What is your plan?"

"Meet with Chandler," Tommy offered. "Find out what he knows and who he's working for."

"But your plan." Alain looked quizzically at Tommy. "What is your plan to rid yourself of the Society?"

"It's a work in progress," Tommy muttered.

"Oh, dear," Caroline commented, from her lounge chair, pulling the hat down over her eyes.

"*Quoi*?" Alain responded, with a surprised expression.

Looking at Alain, Tommy admitted, "I have no plan."

Taking a large mouthful of pastis and swallowing in one tremendous gulp, Alain then mumbled, "*Incroyable*," in disbelief.

CHAPTER 32

With the dog sitting on the platform between the handlebars and seat and Caroline sitting behind him, Tommy retraced his earlier route along the coiling mountainside road, maneuvering the scooter through the jungle with the monkeys and birds announcing his passing. Caroline shifted from side to side, taking in the sights. The dog seemed mesmerized by the sounds echoing from the surrounding jungle. At the top of the steep hill, Tommy stopped at the resort with views of Chaloklum bay.

Caroline, looking quizzically at Tommy, asked, "Where are we going?"

"I need to make a phone call."

"Why here?"

"Why not?"

Raising her eyebrows, Caroline shrugged her shoulders and said, "Okay."

Stepping into a large open-sided restaurant, Tommy and Caroline took a seat at a table near the edge looking down onto the bay. The dog followed them into the restaurant, sat under the table, and began licking its crotch.

Looking down at the dog, Tommy asked, "No doggily intuition?"

The blue-and-gray-eyed dog gazed up and barked twice before returning to the task of cleaning between his legs.

"You talk to that dog like understands you," Caroline teased.

"He's a smart dog."

Shaking her head, Caroline said, "He's a dog."

Tommy shrugged his shoulders.

After ordering beers from a slender Burmese waitress in an oversized floral dress, Tommy pulled his cell from the pocket of his cargo shorts and punched in a number.

"Hello," Chandler's voice chirped from the cell.

"Hello, Chandler," Tommy greeted his friend. "Which island are you on?"

"Hello, septic, I am on pirate's island at the moment—at the villas. Why do you ask?"

"Can we meet?"

"Of course we can," Chandler replied. "By the way, how was your trip to this lovely paradise? I trust everything was up to snuff."

"Big storm, but otherwise uneventful."

"I'm glad to hear that. As far as our meeting, I'd rather like to stay away from Chaloklum—avoiding the chance of running into your good friend Alain. How about the villas, or I can meet you in Thongsala?"

"How about the villas in ten minutes, or so?" Tommy asked, as the Burmese waitress delivered the beers.

"Where are you?"

"Belvedere resort."

"Can you give me thirty minutes?" Chandler inquired. "I just need to tidy up a bit."

"Sure, thirty minutes. I'll be there."

"Sounds grand. I look forward to your arrival."

"See you then," Tommy confirmed before closing his cell.

"You didn't tell him about the crew trying to kill you," Caroline casually remarked.

"I thought that might best be kept secret until I can see his reaction."

Nodding her head, Caroline asked, "Do I get to go with you? Do I get to see his reaction?"

"Might be best if I go this one alone. We've been friends a long time. He's more likely to open up and tell me the truth if we're alone."

Sitting at his table with magnificent views of the bay, Caroline and Tommy sat drinking their beers, listening to tourists chattering around them, watching scooters struggle up the hill, and observing Chaloklum bay. The bay was busy with activity. Long tails crisscrossed its blue waters, five fishing boats huddled around the pier, and ten more moored to the west end. On distant beaches, they could make out tourists lying on white sands. A line of dark clouds could be seen building on the western horizon. Draining the last of his beer, Tommy stood up and walked over to the cashier in time to see the white Nissan pickup pass by with Calvin looking over the steering wheel with his short powerful arm hanging out the open window. Tommy imagined that he must be returning from a security check of the village, realizing that his passing signified his friends were safe. Caroline drained the last of her beer and joined Tommy at the counter, as did the dog.

Climbing back on the ancient red Honda scooter, the threesome drove down the steep hill, firmly holding both the front and back brakes to ensure the bike stayed in control. Then onto the dirty road, dust pluming behind, and over the bridge. Tommy drove through the Seven-Eleven intersection, with its busy tourist traffic, and down the village main street, pulling up to the faded yellow building.

As Caroline was climbing off the back of the scooter, Tommy pointed to the dog and said, "Dog, you stay here."

Caroline asked, "You don't want to take the dog as backup?"

"Chandler's got dogs as well. Rather than risk the distraction of breaking up a dog fight, I want to focus on getting the truth out of my friend."

Nodding her head, Caroline slipped into the passageway and began walking toward the back of the building. The dog reluctantly followed, looking back at Tommy before slipping between the buildings.

Tommy rode the scooter past Lotus Divers complex, meandering through jungle meadows with grazing water buffalos and cattle, up the hill providing more spectacular views of the bay, and down into the ravine with the white concrete bungalows mounted on the side of a hill.

CHAPTER 33

Haad Thong Lang, Koh PhaNgan, Thailand, 10 December 2016:

Turning onto the road that led to Gary and Don's bungalows, Tommy drove past the sandy path and down the hill that he, Jack, and Sandy had walked up earlier that day, avoiding its deep ruts and rocks. He followed the road as it suddenly turned to the right, and the dirt and ruts were replaced with a hard-concrete surface. It tracked along the mountainside and up a small steep hill. At the top of the hill, Tommy could see four or five villas of various sizes and designs built overlooking the small cove of Haad Thong Lang. Directly below him, stood two side-by-side modest-sized white stucco villas. A large swimming pool with a Jacuzzi at one end separated the villas from the beach along Haad Thong Lang.

At the base of the hill, Tommy took a left into a small driveway next to a tall bamboo gate, with dogs barking on the far side. A brightly colored carved wooden sign mounted on an exposed white stucco wall advertised, Chok Dee Villas, with a green and brown palm tree centerpiece. As Tommy dropped the kickstand, Chandler's voice could be heard yelling at the unseen dogs to be quiet, before one of the tall bamboo gates began to noisily slide to one side.

"There he is," Chandler called out, his green eyes mounted on an auburn-haired head peeking through the gap in the bamboo gates. "I hope the delay wasn't inconvenient."

"I enjoyed a beer at Belvederes and took in the sights."

Stepping aside, Chandler said, "Well, come on inside, let's see how these dogs take to you."

As Tommy slipped through the bamboo gates two dogs bounded up—a yellow Labrador and a smaller black mutt. The dogs sniffed his legs and before running off, around the corner of the closest villa.

"Well, that's a relief," Chandler commented. "It's never fun when your dogs don't mix with your friends."

"Sounds like a metaphor," Tommy replied. "Maybe a metaphor concerning my two mafia pals who both happen to live in the same archipelago in the Gulf of Thailand."

"And in that metaphor, who would represent a dog and who would represent your friend?" Chandler smiled, as he turned and began walking toward the villas.

"Wrong metaphor. You're both dogs," Tommy flatly replied.

Following Chandler into the closest white stucco villa, they walked past a kitchen area separated from a spacious living room by a dark wood counter topped with grey granite. At the base of the counter, Tommy noticed a small trash bin filled with three cans of Leo beer, their rims still wet. Chandler led him into the living room, with a high ceiling and crisscrossing beams and filled with a large couch and two overstuffed chairs. The living room ended at an enormous sliding glass door trimmed in teak. Two doors stood on each side of the room, leading into large bedrooms bracketing the living area.

"Red wine okay?" Chandler asked, gesturing him toward a round table on the covered patio outside overlooking a Jacuzzi and swimming pool, and then the beach along Haad Thong Lang.

"Sure." Tommy walked out the sliding glass doors to the table. An overhead roof shielding them from the hot afternoon sun. The supporting beams were wrapped in bright green foliage and the water in the swimming pool glistened below. As he pulled a chair out from the table, Tommy no-

ticed an ashtray at its center with four self-wrapped cigarettes butts smashed in the base, one still smoldering.

Sitting down, Tommy asked over his shoulder, "You
have a cigarette I can borrow?"

"I didn't think you smoked," Chandler called back,
"With all that running you do, I would think it might be a
detriment."

Chandler walked out of the villa with a glass of red wine
in each hand. Handing one glass to Tommy, he pulled a
pack of L&M blues from his shirt pocket and dropped it on
the table. A large bladed fan slowly spun overhead, and a
soft breeze blew in from the water. Due to the remoteness
of Chandler's villas, the only sounds that could be heard
came from the jungle. The two dogs raced about, barking at
one another.

Sitting down across from one another, Chandler locked
his green eyes on Tommy and asked, "So what's this meeting about, my friend?"

Looking directly into his friend's eyes, Tommy asked,
"Are you employed by the Society?"

"Yes, I am," Chandler replied with an expressionless
face.

"And you arranged for me and my friends' demise on
the fishing boat?"

"No, absolutely not," Chandler said, rocking back in his
chair, with a shocked expression. "Someone attempted to
kill you on the trip down?"

"The crew."

"I had no idea. I really had no idea."

"Then who arranged for the extra service beyond our
transportation?"

"I don't know," Chandler answered, shifting around and
looking out across Haad Thong Lang. "I had no idea there
was any plan other than transporting you here. I had no
idea."

"Then who?"

Looking back at Tommy and placing his elbows on the table, Chandler explained, "I arranged the transportation through Alain's people. I have always trusted them to do the right thing on this island. You can't trust any of the other organizations on Pirate's Island, but you can trust Alain's. While Alain and I do not get along, I try and maintain a good working relationship with his employees. I arranged your transportation through his people."

"Who of Alain's people did you arrange the transportation with?"

"I'd rather not say. If Alain were to find out who had helped me, that person's chance of survival would be slim to none. I need to talk with the man myself and find out who else knew of our arrangement," Chandler continued. "Alain's sense of justice is how well you survive a 9mm slug to the chest."

"So you don't trust me to keep a name secret?"

"No," Chandler admitted. "Your brand of friendship is telling the truth, no matter the consequences. You think that being open about everything to your friends and letting them work out their differences is better than keeping a secret. And while I hold you as a trusted friend, your tact in dealing with dueling friends is naïve and immature. This world is ruthless and violent. In the end, money has no relatives or friends."

Sitting back, thinking about his friend's response, Tommy finally said, "So tell me about the Society. How can I extract myself from the current mess I find myself in?"

"The Society is an enormous organization. It consists of numerous departments and handlers. I have a handler who works with the organization's criminal division. Whoever is working with Alain's organization likely uses the same handler—"

"There's a Society member or agent in Alain's organization?" Tommy interrupted, somewhat astonished.

"Absolutely," Chandler answered. "Alain doesn't know it, but there is a member who provides liaison and information."

"Do you know who it is?"

"Once again, even if I knew who it was, I wouldn't tell you."

Looking out across the horizon, Tommy watched the approaching storm, black and blue clouds churning at its forefront. As he sat back, contemplating Chandler's comment, his cell began vibrating and ringing in his pocket.

Reaching into his pocket, he opened the cell and answered, "Tommy here."

"Hey, Tommy," Don called, greeting him with his thick New York accent, "I may have something more on that Society—something I remembered from tending bar in Sarasota, Florida."

"What you got?"

"Can you drop by the bungalow?"

"After the storm passes, yeah."

"Come on by and I'll tell you what I know," Don said. "It might not be much but you never know."

"See you in a bit," Tommy replied before closing the cell. Hesitating for a moment, he then said, "Tell me more," to Chandler, sitting across the table.

"The Society has existed for generations. I don't know how long," Chandler explained. "But there has always been turmoil at the upper echelon. Consider for a moment that a successful businessman as nothing more than a successful crook. So, over the years the Society evolved. It has attempted to become democratic in nature to diminish the influence of the criminal element. The organization has three planners at the top of the command structure they call the Patriarchs. Another five outside of the upper echelon, identities unbeknownst to the Patriarchs, to provide a democratic vote as to whether the Society should pursue their plans. And then add rotating seating every five years based on a wider vote to ensure that there would be no totalitarianism.

It is a brilliant structure. But through the years there have been attempts to manipulate that structure to take control of the Society."

"Is that what's happening now?"

"I have no idea," Chandler replied. "I'm nothing but a foot soldier in an enormous organization that pays well."

"What did they tell you about me and my friends?"

"I was instructed to eliminate you and your friends—Jack and Sandy—and secure whatever belongings you had."

"No mention of a hard-drive or the contents."

"I don't even want to know," Chandler admitted, pushing away from the table. "I don't want to know what it is they're looking for. That kind of knowledge is equivalent to the kiss of death in Society circles."

Taking a mouthful of red wine and swallowing, Tommy asked, "So, explain to me why should I trust you?"

Sipping his red wine, Chandler asked, "Why do you trust Alain? He's a criminal and criminals are inherently dishonest. And he likes to kill people."

"He's a loyal friend."

"My point exactly. Loyalty is the central key to friendship, but it's not defined by honesty. What if I told you that I thought most Americans are like a fat child at someone else's birthday party, crying because they received no presents? Would that endear you more to me? I think not. So I keep my opinion about Americans to myself."

"Actually, I think you have told me that." Tommy chuckled. "And you're still pissed that the Americans beat the redcoat's ass at Saratoga. So anything you say about my heritage is tainted by jealousy."

Looking quizzically at Tommy, Chandler asked, "What?"

"Saratoga, New York, was a turning point in the Revolutionary War," Tommy explained. "The ragtag American army beat the British. It was the final battle that convinced French to assist."

"Let's not forget that the tiny island nation of Great Britain was also busy at Waterloo," Chandler parried Tommy's joke with one of his own.

"Honesty is a part of loyalty," Tommy retorted, returning their discussion to friendship. "You didn't bother to tell me that you were a member of the same organization attempting to kill me and my friends. That would have been a useful bit of information, amongst friends, as I sorted out my situation."

"You're definition of friendship was born on rough construction sites across the States. Mine in the violence and poverty of South London. Is that much different?" Chandler offered. "Let's say you're balancing one a beam several hundred feet above the ground helping your mate move a large joist into place. Let's say you knew that your mate's wife was cheating on him. At that moment, would tell him that? No, of course not. You wouldn't want him to be pondering which of his mates back home were shagging his wife and not paying attention to the job at hand and his survival. At that moment, your loyalty is to your mate's survival, not his domestic difficulties back home. Truth and loyalty are not necessarily bedfellows."

A strong gust of wind blew across the deck, nearly upending the table at which they were sitting. The ashtray filled with self-rolled cigarettes fell from the table, sending its contents across the deck. The tops of the surrounding palm trees bucked. Both men looked up at the cloud formation moving in from the west, its leading edge dark with a rainy turmoil erupting from underneath. A thick bolt of lightning reached out from the storm and struck the top of Koh Mae, a small island just west of Haad Thong Lang, its thunderous clap echoing across the deck. The two dogs scampered inside with tails between their legs.

Empting his glass of red wine in one swallow, Tommy asked, "So you're telling me that I should trust you, even though you're a member of the same Society attempting to kill me and my friends?"

"Yes, you should trust our friendship," Chandler replied, then joking, "I'd quit the Society as proof, but the pay is too good."

Looking out across the horizon, with rain beginning to beating the roof overhead, Tommy asked, "How much red wine do you have?"

"Enough to weather this storm, my septic friend."

CHAPTER 37

Kansas City, Missouri, USA, 12 April 1998:

The obligatory Friday service was over and nineteen-year-old Omid Sassani stood from his prayer mat. The prayer hall with its large dome overhead was filled with shoeless men, silently picking up their mats and walking toward the exit. Several boys Omid's age began moving toward the side of the room, and through a small arched door leading to the madafa, a room for religious training.

The mosque's imam silently walked over to Omid and touched his shoulder, gesturing toward the arched door. Looking down at the small-statured imam, Omid shook his head.

"Please," whispered the imam, whose eyes filled with softness. "Please join us. It will please your father if you join us."

Dropping his head as if in defeat, Omid relented and walked with the imam through the door. The room was filled with teenage boys, ranging from twelve years up. The group silently sat on the floor, in no orderly fashion, and faced a single meticulously carved wooden chair, stained black. Omid sat cross legged among his peers and waited for the imam to sit on the black wooden chair.

A young boy brought out a silver tray filled with small porcelain cups, passing them out amongst the seated teenagers. Another brought a silver kettle, steam rising from its spout, and began to fill the cups with strong tea. The imam took a seat and silently waited for the final cup to be filled with tea.

As the imam began to talk, Omid's mind turned to his plans to leave this religion behind. He pondered what day he should inform his family. He contemplated his father's reaction. The imam's words seem to pass over his head. He was not listening.

A word caught his ear, bringing him back to the small room with the other teenagers sitting around him. He began listening to the imam and what came from his mouth was hatred and extremism. The imam spoke of the weak American spirit. He spoke of the death of fellow Muslims and how they must all fight for their brothers and sisters in harm's way. He spoke of infidels and how their blood must be spilled. He spoke of Jihad.

Omid silently stood and the imam stopped preaching. The entire room turned and stared at Omid in silence. With his head bowed and without looking at the imam, Omid walked to the door and exited the room. He walked across the prayer room, with its enormous overhead dome, to the mosque exit. He walked across the courtyard, past the ablution fountain without washing his hands. He walked out on the streets of Kansas City and dropped his prayer mat in the gutter. He walked home.

It took Omid two hours to make the walk from the mosque to his house in the predominately white neighborhood. Walking through the front door, he made his way directly to his bedroom and shut the door. Lying down on his bed, Omid stared up at the room's white ceiling and waited for his father.

The door burst open several minutes later and his father stood, silently seething, in the doorway.

"What?" Omid broke the silence, looking over at his father. "What do you want of your worthless son?"

"You dare to speak to me after embarrassing this family at the mosque?" his father spat. "You dare to say a word to me? You should be on your knees praying for forgiveness."

"He's your god, not mine."

His father strode across the room, picking up the *Koran* from a desk, and threw it at Omid, striking him in the head, before saying, "You are no son of mine. You are my daughter. A worthless daughter."

Shifting on the bed, Omid placed his feet on the floor and sat up, looking directly at his father who was shaking in anger.

Omid calmly asked, "I am your daughter?"

"You are worse than a daughter," his father hissed. "You are a dog."

Standing, Omid walked over to his father, stopping directly in front of the raging man.

"The mosque is filled with hatred—your hatred. I do not want to be filled with the same," Omid said to his father. "You claim to be righteous, but your soul is filled with blackness."

Seething with anger, his father slapped Omid in face.

"The very people you hate, I admire. The very people you chastise, I look up to. I am an American, not a Palestinian or Egyptian or Persian. I am American and proud of my country. I have no affinity to the Muslims who die by the hands of the Americans in the Middle East. They have brought this upon themselves."

With eyes brimming with hatred, his father screamed and pushed Omid to the floor, before saying, "The day you graduate from school will be the last you live in this house. You are no son of mine."

As his father strode from the bedroom Omid called out, "I do not want to be a son of yours. I have never been a son of yours."

CHAPTER 35

Bophut Fisherman's Village, Koh Samui, Thailand, 10 December 2016:

Sitting on a small patio in a heavily red cushioned rattan chair overlooking a thin ribbon of a beach and then the sound between Koh Samui and PhaNgan, John Smith recalled the day he abruptly left the meeting in the madafa at the mosque in Kansas City. A television in the room behind the patio loudly aired a CNN newscast and traffic could be faintly heard on the other side of the building. Wide leafy bushes and tall palm trees bracketed the small patio. The space between was cover in neatly manicured grass.

John Smith had heard the imam's hatred before, and it had always left him feeling empty and hollow. Having never been to the Middle East, he could not relate to the daily dangers or poverty. He watched the evening news describing the unrest and listened to the pundits spouting off about whether America was to blame or not. What he came to believe was that whether the Americans were there or not, the people of the Middle East would still be dying. The difference would be that they would be dying by their own hands. If America was to blame for anything, it was trying to teach a people filled with hatred about respect for human life. In his view, all Muslims like his father and the imam in his Kansas City mosque were filled with a loathing that had no bounds and was not anchored to anything but hatred itself. As long as the Muslims of the Middle East and Southeast

Asia turned to violence, they should expect no different from those around them. Once again, his thoughts were interrupted by a ringing cell.

Picking the cell up from a small round cast iron table next to his chair, John Smith answered.

"Mr. Smith, this is Kenneth in Maryland, the lead tech manager for your project," the unfamiliar voice announced. "Can we go covered?"

"Yes, of course," John Smith acknowledged, before pressing a small green key on his cell phone.

Two beeps signified the phone was in cover mode and John Smith said, "Go ahead, Kenneth," as he watched a huge thunderstorm begin working its way over the western edge of Koh PhaNgan.

"I've got some imagines from several of the locations you tagged as targets," Kenneth's voice answered in a much tinnier tone than before.

"Go ahead," John Smith requested again, observing distant sheets of dark rain erupt from the thunderstorm.

"It appears that four men were brought to the villa on the east side of Chaloklum and were executed."

"Have you identified them?"

"I haven't validated the identification yet, but it appears to be several members of the Society action teams."

Sighing, John Smith then asked, "Have you identified the woman who arrived yesterday?"

"No, she continues to wear a large hat and never looks up," Kenneth responded flatly, the tininess sounding as if he were in a small room. "We did run a check on arrivals in Thailand and none come up as associates with any of the three individuals we're attempting to track. But I have identified one of the new arrivals at the building in Chaloklum. One is clearly Thomas Bacon Luck."

"Then chances are the other two are his companions," John Smith acknowledged, watching a large bolt of lightning striking someplace northwest of Koh PhaNgan.

"Yes, it would seem so."

"Any other activity?"

"One hour ago Thomas Bacon Luck departed the building in the village and rode a scooter to the villa on the east side of town where he met with the unidentified woman and Alain, the owner."

"And?" John Smith asked as a soft breeze blew across the patio, as he wondered who the woman was that the satellite had seen.

"He then departed the villa and rode to another villa complex on the western side of the village, in the Haad Thong Lang area, were he met with another man."

"Have you identified that man?"

"Not yet," Kenneth admitted, "but we're working on it."

"Is that all?"

"Yes, sir," Kenneth replied. "That's all for now. We'll keep watching."

"I want you to tag the villa complex in Haad Thong Lang as a target, as well. Keep a watch on it and try to speed up your identification the man Tommy Luck met with there. That could be an important element of this operation."

"Yes, sir."

Closing his cell phone and placing it on a small round table at his side, John Smith called over his shoulder, "Steve!"

"Yeah?" Steve said, poking his dark-bushy-haired head out a set of French doors leading to the room. His beady eyes shifted around, taking in the scene.

"We need to make arrangements to move to Thong Nai Pan."

"What's going on?" Steve asked, grasping the edge of the door with one of his small pale hands.

"It would appear that Tommy and his companions—" John Smith explained, still watching the thunderstorm on the next island over, "—did indeed survive their trip to Koh PhaNgan."

"That would make sense," Steve added. "Our people did

say that the fishing boat never arrived in Baan Tai."

"And it appears that the mafia boss in control of Chaloklum has eliminated our action team members assigned to watch Tommy's building."

"Those members are overdue for checking in, and Tommy and that mafia boss are friends," Steve said, stepping out onto the patio, his short skinny arms hanging loosely at his sides. "That Alain guy and Tommy, that is."

"That is the second obvious comment you've made," John Smith replied, trying to control his anger.

"Sorry, but it all makes sense—"

"Just shut up and make arrangements for us to move," John Smith snapped at the short beady eyed man.

"When do you want to go?" Steve hesitantly asked, as if trying to remember whether John Smith had already told him the answer.

Sighing, John Smith said, "Tomorrow morning."

Steve disappeared back into the bedroom, and John Smith picked his cell back up from the table, selecting a number from its speed dial list.

"Do you have any idea what time it is?" a harsh voice answered after five rings.

"I was under the impression that you desired updates as to what is going on," John Smith replied. "If you want the update, we will need to go covered."

After a brief delay the voice said, "Going encrypted."

John Smith pressed the small green button on his phone again and waited. A few moments and two beeps later, a less caustic voice replied in the same tinny sounding tone as his previous call, "Go ahead."

Over the next five minutes, John Smith give the person on the other end a complete rundown on what had occurred.

"It seems that Mr. Luck continues to get the best of you," the voice calmly told John Smith.

"Yes, sir," John Smith replied with a sigh. "It would seem so, but we knew from the beginning that Tommy Luck is clever and unpredictable."

The tinny voice asked, ignoring John Smith's excuse, "What's your plan?"

"I'm traveling to Koh PhaNgan tomorrow morning. I will discuss my options with our mafia counterpart on the northeast side of the island. They are the ones allied in our effort to retrieve the hard-drive."

"Had you considered what you would do in this situation?"

"What do you mean?"

"Did you consider what you would do, finding yourself in a position where Tommy Luck was alive on the island and your surveillance of his building eliminated?"

"I have been working several other alternative courses of action," John Smith replied, running his hand across his short wiry hair. "I feel that I need to talk with our counterpart before I choose which course of action I should take. That island is proving to be a hard nut to crack and our mafia counterpart has better knowledge of the surrounding area. I want to use him as a sounding board."

After a momentary hesitation, the voice replied, "Next time, I hope to hear better news."

"Understood," John Smith responded. "I'm sure we'll make some headway."

"I'm not sure headway is good enough," the tinny voice responded, "Results, Mr. Smith, it is results we're looking for, not headway."

Closing his cell phone, John Smith noted that the thunderstorm over Koh PhaNgan had moved to the center of the island and the skies were beginning to clear to the west. Two tourists in skimpy swim suits walked by on the beach, past his patio, hand in hand. Soft music could be heard from a bar with a small half-moon counter off to his right where two women silently drank mugs of beer, peering at the distant Koh PhaNgan.

As he reached down to pick up his silver canes, his cell phone began ringing again, and he reversed his motion.

Opening the cell, he held it against his ear, saying "John Smith."

"It's Kenneth again."

"Yes, Kenneth, what do you have?" John Smith asked, hoping for good news.

"The man you wanted identified, I have his name."

"Yes, who was it?"

"The owner of the property on which they met," Kenneth answered. "To be accurate, this man simply opened the villa and let our target in. We didn't actually see them talking.

"Who is this man?" John Smith queried again, ignoring the extra details from Kenneth.

"Do you want to go covered?" Kenneth asked.

"No just keep it simple," John Smith answered.

"He's is one of our agents."

"Why is one of our agents meeting with our target without my knowledge?" John Smith mumbled to himself out loud.

"I couldn't answer that, sir."

"Yes, of course, I knew that," John Smith replied. "Do you have this gentleman's number?"

"Yes, sir."

"Send his name and number via encrypted texted, please," John Smith requested, before disconnecting the call.

A few moments later, John Smith's phone beeped, signifying a text had arrived. Looking down at the text, the name Chandler was followed by a local Thai phone number.

"Why is a Society agent meeting with Tommy Luck?" John Smith asked himself again, scratching the top of his head. "Why is a Society agent meeting with him without my knowledge?"

CHAPTER 36

Chevy Chase, Maryland, USA, 10 December 2016:

There's something he's not telling us," Oliver stated in his crisp English accent, looking out one of the long windows onto the grounds behind the mansion with patches of snow clinging to the garden beds and corners of the lawn. The gray-wool slacks and a white shirt he wore somehow intensified his pear-shaped profile. Running a hand through his white monk-like hair, he turned and looked at James, sitting on the red-velvet chair behind him. "There must be more than simple bad luck hindering him from retrieving the hard-drive."

Seated in the overstuffed floral chair next to James, Andres shifted his massive body and scratched his unruly white beard, before saying, "He's doing the best he can, given the circumstances." Dressed in oversized green chino pants held up by wide red suspenders, Andres pushed his rotund body from the chair and walked across the blue and red Persian carpet to a black granite topped counter between two bookcases on the far wall. Six short crystal glasses, four decanters, and an ice-filled bucket sat atop the counter. "He has been successful in locating Mr. Luck. That must count for something."

"What proof do we have that Mr. Smith is incompetent or being deceitful?" James asked, picking up a short crystal glass fill with sparkling water from a small round table next to the red velvet chair, the ice cubes inside rattling against the sides. Dressed in neatly pressed wrangler jeans and a white shirt, he added, "A gut feel is not enough to prove either."

"We were wrong to trust John Smith," Oliver insisted, turning back to the window. "I don't believe that Tommy Luck killed Kelly's husband, nor do I believe he raped the poor woman."

"What would you have us do?" James asked before taking a sip from the glass in his hand. "Do we need to hire a handy man to watch over our handy man?"

"We need to check to ensure this man is not up to foul play," Oliver replied, turning and walking over to the large gray stone fireplace, resting an elbow on its polished wood mantle while leaning against it. "My success in life can be partially attributed to gut instincts. We all know that facts and proof can be elusive at times, and deceit is a universal unpleasantness."

Pouring himself a glass of bourbon from one of the crystal decanters, Andres said, "That's fair, James. We should take precautions concerning Mr. Smith. After all, his immense hatred for Mr. Luck is a non-elusive fact." Taking a sip of the brownish bourbon in his glass, Andes turned and walked back to the floral chair, before plopping down. "The question is what precautions we shall take?"

"I see no use in this entire dribble," James commented with frustration. "We hired John Smith as a handy man to deal with issues such as this. And now we've decided that he is either incompetent or out to extract revenge on a man?"

"Let's not forget, he was hired as a temporary substitute," Oliver retorted. "We are only utilizing him until we can find a suitable replacement for the handy man position."

"That's not a bad idea," Andres said, placing his thumb under his left suspender and running it in an up and down motion.

"What's not a bad idea?" James asked, placing his glass of sparkling water back on the round table.

Looking over at James, Andres said, "As you recommended earlier, we should hire someone to check out our handy man. We should employ someone to check on Mr. Smith's activity concerning the hard-drive."

"I was being facetious," James moaned, dropping his head on the red velvet chair's backrest. "It was sarcasm."

"Nonetheless, it is a good idea and would alleviate Oliver's concerns," Andres replied, shrugging his plump shoulders.

Sighing, James slumped in the red velvet chair, muttering, "This is ridiculous."

"What about Caroline?" Andres offered.

Shaking his head, Oliver said, "I've been attempting to contact her for days. She seems to have disappeared."

Perking up, James straightened up in the chair and asked, "Disappeared? What do you mean?"

"I had planned on convincing her to return to her former position as the Patriarch executive secretary at the Society, but her phone has been temporarily disconnected and she has not replied to any of my emails."

James asked, "Temporarily suspended? For how long?"

"Yes, she is retaining the number for a future date but has had it disconnected. It's a service many people use when traveling overseas. It has been suspended for nearly a week."

After a brief hesitation, Andres arched his eyebrows and asked, "What was her relationship with Mr. Luck?"

"Only professional," Oliver answered, "as far as I know."

"Were they friends?" Andres queried Oliver again.

Shaking his head, Oliver said, "I don't believe so. Caroline was very professional in her duties. I doubt she would have crossed that line when dealing with Mr. Luck. In addition, the fact that he is heavy drinker would have been a barrier for any other type of relationship. Caroline is very careful about the men she associates with."

"That's interesting," Andres said, rubbing his white beard.

Removing his elbow from the mantle and walking across to the granite counter, Oliver said, "Back to my concerns about Mr. Smith, I would like to show a picture of Mr. Luck to Kelly. Let her identify the man that raped her. If she identifies him as the culprit, my concerns about Mr. Smith's activities will be eased, for the time being."

"What about the video of Mr. Luck's vehicle being in the vicinity of the crime?" James commented. "We ought to check it for authenticity."

"That was a swift shift in opinion," Oliver commented, looking over his shoulder at James from the counter.

"We're a team," James said, "and you're obviously dead set to check out our current handy man. If we're going to do something, then it should be done right."

"There's no reason to employ someone to perform these simple tasks," Andres said, rocking his glass back and forth and creating a miniature whirl pool of brown bourbon. "I would be happy to attend to both matters."

Using small tongs to drop ice cubes from a silver bucket into another short crystal glass, Oliver said, "That is acceptable to me."

"Not to me," James sternly stated. "The reason the Society's authority has been structured the way it has ensures that we plan and operate as a single entity. Given that the retrieval of the hard-drive is not a voting issue, we don't need to have our actions authorized with the lower voting body. But we need to maintain the integrity of Patriarch structure. Anything we do must be done together or have an outside source execute the task. We need someone outside this group to perform whatever tasks we feel obligated to accomplish in regards to John Smith."

Chuckling, Andres said, "You don't trust me?"

"It's not about trust, Andres," James replied. "It's about maintaining the structure. It's why we have a handy man in the first place."

"And look where that has led us," Oliver absently commented, pouring brandy from one of the other crystal decanters.

CHAPTER 37

Haad Thong Lang, Koh PhaNgan, Thailand, 10 December 2016:

The rain storm had passed, and Tommy said his farewell to Chandler, leaving him standing next to the bamboo gate. Tommy drove up the dirt road with water still coursing down its ruts. The air smelled of damp foliage, and water droplets broke free from their former perch on the feathery palm tree leafs, splattering the road around him.

At the top of the road, Tommy turned down the sandy path into the complex filled with the four concrete bungalows on stilts, their red roofs glistening with wetness. Parking the bike next to a tall palm tree, Tommy walked past Gary's bungalow and through a small garden to a set of concrete steps leading up to Don's wide porch. Sitting on the porch, dressed in plaid boxer shorts sipping an orange drink, Don swung back and forth on a hammock as he looked out across Chaloklum at the thunderstorm punishing the far side of the bay.

"Hey, Don," Tommy said, announcing his arrival at the bottom of the stairs.

"Hey, buddy, come on up," Don said over his shoulder, the New York roots apparent as he climbed out of the hammock. "You want something to drink?"

"Sure, what'd you got?"

"I'm working on a screwdriver."

"Sounds good."

Disappearing inside, Don called out, "How about a double?"

"Sounds doubly good."

The sun was beginning to set and red and orange tinted clouds shown across the sky. Reappearing on the deck in tan shorts, Don handed Tommy a drink and gestured to a wooden-topped table. He ran his hand through his neatly combed silver hair while taking a sip from his glass and sitting down. Taking a seat across from Don, Tommy took a long drink of the vodka and orange juice.

"It was in Sarasota, Florida, a couple of years ago," Don began, his light blue eyes flashing under silver eyebrows. "I was back in the states, taking care of my ailing mother, and had taken a part-time job at a local watering hole. Well anyway, this guy comes in and looks like hell. I mean this guy looked like he hadn't slept in days. He was unshaven and had these red-rimmed eyes that looked like makeup they were so bright. So I ask him what's up. He starts talking about this Society organization. I immediately knew what he was talking about because of my conversation all those years ago with the congressman."

"And Bob Dylan," Tommy added, before taking another drink. "So what'd this guy say to you?"

"Yeah, right, Bob Dylan. This guy told me that he works for the Society and was running for his life," Don replied, looking down and wiping a droplet of spilled screwdriver from his bare chest.

"Why?"

"He says that the Society just voted on the replacements for the top three planners. I think he called them the Patriarchs. Well, anyway, they do that every four or five years. This guy tells me how one of the new people voted in was really a bad dude. He tells me that he tried to warn the other members about this person, and that he was now being hunted down. He was running for his life."

"How did he know this person was bad?" Tommy looked over Don's shoulders at the thunderstorm pushing across the ridgeline on the east side of the bay. The jungle around them was darkening as the sun dropped farther below the horizon, and lights began twinkling from Chaloklum in the distance.

"He'd worked with him on one of the Society projects," Don explained. "This bad dude apparently went well beyond what the Society had authorized, all for personal gain. And the guy running for his life had proof of what the bad dude had done."

"Did he say what the project was?"

"It was something about a contract to build something for the Society. And this bad dude built into the contract a kick back—a significant kick back, from what I can recall. And when one of the people working for him called him on it, the bad dude had him knocked off."

"Did he mention any names?"

"This was a couple of years ago." Don chuckled, as he stood and flipped a switch near the doors leading into his bungalow, illuminating a light above them. "And my memory is not what it used to be."

"You remembered Bob Dylan and the congressman," Tommy responded, raising an eyebrow, "and that was a lot longer."

"Yeah, but money was involved with Bob and the congressman. When cash is involved, I always remember every detail, especially when I am the jilted party."

Sitting back in his chair, Tommy considered the new information Don had just given him. Caroline had commented that this operation seemed to be cloaked in secrecy and that there was a freelance element about it. Tommy wondered about the odds of a bad Patriarch and John Smith teaming up. Knowing John Smith and his lacking of a moral compass, those odds didn't seem too obscure. "How long ago was this?"

"Just a couple of years ago," Don replied, taking a sip of his drink.

"That would mean the bad guy that the employee had attempted to warn the Society about is still assigned to their leadership. That would mean that he's involved with the retrieval of the hard-drive to an unknown extent."

"That's right," Don said. "That makes your situation even more volatile and adds a new level of mystery to the whole affair. This guy could be involved and you could be the centerpiece of one of his self-serving business deals."

After a brief hesitation, Tommy commented, "Or I could have placed myself in the midst of one of his self-serving business deals. A business deal he is pursuing with John Smith."

"John Smith?" Don asked.

Tommy replied, "Another very bad and self-serving dude."

CHAPTER 38

Chaloklum, Koh PhaNgan, Thailand, 10 December 2016:

Sandy and Jack sat at a bamboo table in the restaurant on Malibu Beach, a large sandbar at the west end of Chaloklum Bay, and watched the rain pelt the small fleet of colorful fishing boats. A thatched awning kept them dry, but an occasional gust of wind carried the dampness into their protected setting.

"Have you ever seen a storm like this?" Sandy asked her hulking husband, who was sipping a bottle of Singha Beer.

As streak of lightning reached down from the churning clouds above and touched the jungle on the far side of the bay, Jack calmly replied, "Yes, darling, last night. The exception is that I now find myself sheltered on solid ground with a cold beer in my hand."

Behind them sat two slim Thai men, silently watching. Glancing over her shoulder, Sandy commented, "The difference is that we've got menacing looking foreigners following our every move. Last night we were protected by Mother Nature. A form of safety that I find far more comforting. These guys look like they could turn on us at any given moment."

"I believe that we are the foreigners in this scenario," Jack replied in a perfectly serious tone. "But you are correct, given an acceptable price, I imagine those men would hastily abandon their duties. I wonder what Tommy is up to. His presences would at least give us an advantage of numbers."

Sitting drinking their beer, Jack and Sandy watched the rain slowly move off of Malibu Beach and across the bay. The sun was setting and the sky above turned into blurred bands of red and orange, resembling a Monet watercolor painting. Bright colorful lights, resembling Christmas tree lights, came on overhead and the surrounding humidity created halos around each bulb. The gusting breeze subsided and the air wafted with the scent of the wet jungle.

As the last evidence of the sun vanished, Sandy and Jack stood and looked down the beach. They could see the lights twinkling from the upper deck of the faded yellow building some two hundred yards down the beach. Between them and the edge of the village, coconut trees hovered over the beach and the jungle appeared dark, menacing, and deserted. A monkey screeched and large shadowy bat flew out across the bay.

"It would have been prudent for us to have made the return trip before the sunset," Jack commented, setting his empty beer bottle on the bamboo table. "The return route looks slightly threatening."

"We've got Curly and Moe to protect us," Sandy replied, setting her bottle on the table next to Jack's.

"That's my concern, Larry is missing and he's the one in charge," Jack replied, running his enormous hand through his unruly brown and silver hair.

Stepping from the thatched covered awning with their shoes dangling from their fingers, the two began walking back toward the village and faded yellow building in the soft damp sand. Sandy glanced back to affirm that their two bodyguards were following. The two Thai men had stood from their table and were shifting through their pockets to pay their bill.

"This is such a lovely place," Sandy commented, looking up at a partially obscured moon peeking out from the clouds.

Jack maneuvered down to the edge of the bay, stepping in the lapping water. "The kids would love this place, assuming their parents did not require bodyguards to have a beer on the beach."

"It does take some of the fun out of this place," Sandy agreed, looking behind them for the Thai men again. "It would be nice to explore this place without the threat of the Society around every corner. Speaking of which, where are they?"

"Where is who?"

"The Thai guys looking after us."

Halting on the beach, Jack looked back at the thatched shrouded restaurant. "That is odd. They were there a moment ago."

"We need to hustle out of here," Sandy remarked, peering at the restaurant and then into the jungle. "We need to get back to the building. Something's not right."

"A perfect assessment of our current situation. Let's keep moving."

Jack and Sandy briskly walked toward the lights of the village and the faded yellow building, looking over their shoulders every few steps. Midway down the beach, four men stepped from the jungle, two carrying long machetes and two with long knives. The blades of the weapons glistened in the moonlight, as two of the men maneuvered behind Jack and Sandy.

The other two stood between them and the illuminated village, one hundred yards ahead.

"I find it somewhat amusing that our conversation concerning acceptable prices being paid to persuade our body guards to abandon their posts has seemingly come true," Jack calmly commented, dropping his shoes to the sand.

"I find it disturbing that you find it amusing," Sandy replied, mimicking Jack and dropping her sandals.

Pulling the Midnight Special Tommy had given her from a purse hanging across her shoulder, Sandy pointed the snub nose revolver at the closest man who was carrying a knife. The man smiled, revealing dark crooked teeth.

"Do you think he knows something we don't?" Jack

asked Sandy while reaching down a retrieving a wooden oar from the sand at his feet.

"Perhaps he knows we suffered through a torrential storm last night and that the revolver was soaked, and the gunpowder is likely damp," Sandy replied, shifting her aim at the machete brandishing men in front of them, extracting the same toothy reaction.

"The price on our head must be quite high for these men to disregard a revolver wielding woman with crazed eyes."

"And an oar-wielding mountain of a man," Sandy added. "These guys can't be but half your size."

"They can't be half your size," Jack commented. "Of course, I mean in height only, darling."

"Of course," Sandy grumbled.

The men cautiously stepped closer, and Jack pointed the oar at the man bearing the machete. Sandy pointed the revolver back at the crooked-toothed man with the long knife and pulled the trigger. A dry click echoed across the beach.

At the sound of hammer coming down on the firing pin, the four men rushed Jack and Sandy. Jack parried the machete brandishing man in front with the end of the oar and Sandy threw the Midnight Special at the knife-carrying crooked-toothed man, striking him in the side of the head and knocking him to the ground. Spinning, Jack brought the oar around and struck a man behind them in the neck, pushing him into the other machete armed man. Then he thrust the oar handle into the belly of the machete-brandishing man, now behind him, whom he had parried earlier. Surprised at the ferocity of Jack and Sandy's reaction, the four men took several steps back to reassess the situation. Suddenly gunfire erupted on the beach and lit up the jungle. The four men fell lifelessly to the sand.

Stepping from the dark jungle with four men at his side, a thin man with dark curly hair and a goatee asked in a thick French accent, "Where are the men watching over you? Where's Calvin?"

"Last we saw them, they were at the restaurant back

there," Sandy answered, pointing back to the thatched roof restaurant. "And we haven't seen Calvin."

"The fucking English," the man shouted down the beach at no one in particular, running his hand through his thick curly hair. "Where the fuck is Calvin?"

Suddenly three shadows could be seen jogging down the beach from the restaurant, and the curly haired man and his men raised their weapons. Calvin and the two Thai men tasked with watching Jack and Sandy emerged from the darkness.

Dropping his weapon to his side, the curly haired man screamed at Calvin, "Where the fuck have you been? Why did you leave these people to their own devises?"

Huffing, Calvin replied, "We were right behind them, sir. I was just giving these two instructions for the watch tonight."

"You were not right behind them. You were well behind them. They nearly were killed by these thugs," the curly haired man bellowed, pointing at the lifeless figures lying on the beach with his handgun. "And how did these men get into my village without you knowing?"

"I don't know, sir," Calvin replied, his voice cracking slightly, "but I'll find out."

Now waving his handgun at Calvin, the curly haired man hollered, "You fucking English. You are worthless to me."

With wide blue eyes shimmering in the moonlight, Calvin responded, "Sir, it won't happen again. You can trust me."

Glaring at the stout Englishman, the curly haired man silently walked up to him and placed the muzzle of his weapon against Calvin's forehead. Jack and Sandy looked at one another with raised eyebrows. The other men glanced at each other, as if silently betting on the outcome.

"You will escort Tommy's friends back to the building," the curly haired man growled, still holding the muzzle against Calvin's forehead. "You will make sure they are safe and guarded. If you do not, if they even stub a toe, I will put a hole in this ugly bulldog face of yours and feed you to the fish. Do you understand?"

"Yes—Yes, sir," Calvin stuttered.

Pulling the weapon from Calvin's forehead, the curly haired man shot one of the lifeless bodies lying on the beach three times, before turning and saying to Jack and Sandy in a calm voice, "I am Alain, Tommy's friend. You will be safe in my village. You need not worry about this happening again."

"Thank you saving us from certain death, Alain," Jack responded in his English accent. "And thank you for taking care of us during this debacle with the Society."

Silently looking at Jack for a moment with a frown on his face, Alain shook his head and muttered, "The fucking English," before walking away. His men briskly turned and followed.

"He's Canadian," Sandy called out to Alain's shadowy retreating figure. "And I'm an American."

Continuing his trek into the dark jungle and waving his weapon above his head, Alain called, "He sounds like a fucking Englishman to me." Then stopping and turning, Alain said, "But you'll be safe—just may be not the fucking Englishman standing next to you."

"He's my husband and Tommy's friend," Sandy yelled back.

"He's fucking English. No one can save the English," Alain called from the shadows. "They eventually kill themselves with stupidity and incompetence."

"Then why do you trust Calvin?" Sandy firmly called back. "Why do you let a stupid and incompetent Englishman work for you?"

"I do not trust him," Alain replied, pointing at Calvin with his weapon again. "I keep my eye on him. That is why I was able to save you tonight."

"Then why do you let him work for you?" Sandy asked again.

"Because no American wants to work for a Frenchman,"

Alain responded. "That leaves me with a choice between a Frenchman and Englishman."

"So why not hire a Frenchman?"

"Because the only thing a Frenchman can do is talk. The English know they are too stupid to have an intelligent conversation, so they work hard to please their employer."

With a quizzical look on her face, Sandy asked, "But aren't you French?"

"Yes, but I am different."

CHAPTER 39

Kansas City, Missouri, USA, 15 July 1999:

Stepping through the wooden double doors, Omid Sassani examined the courtroom. Long benches filled with both lawyers and their clientele stood to each side of a red carpeted isle. A waist-high matching wooden railing separated the seating area from that where the accused, their legal representatives, and judge conversed. Within that area a single podium, for the accused to present their case, stood just beyond the railing and directly in front of the judge's high bench.

A man in a cheap blue suite carrying a clipboard walked up to Omid and asked how long he would need before the judge. Omid shrugged his shoulders and said he had no idea.

The man then asked why Omid was in court, and he responded, "To change my name."

"Then it should be quick," the man responded, scribbling on the clipboard. "Name changes are normally under five minutes. Please take a seat. You're scheduled as the second to stand before the judge. Do you have a lawyer or representative?"

Responding "No" to the cheap blue suited man, Omid found a seat on the isle, near the front.

A guard, dressed in a khaki uniform and armed with a .38 Smith and Wesson hanging from a thick black leather belt, announced, "All rise."

The crowd seated in the benches noisily stood. The

judge, with short white hair and a long nose and dressed in a long black robe, followed by a woman carrying a stack of folders, entered the room from a side door and silently walked to the bench.

The woman placed the folders in front of the judge and then took a seat, behind him. The guard called out, "Please take your seats."

After a few moments, the judge nodded to the blue suited man and he called out, "Jeffery Simpson, please approach the bench."

A young blond man in blue jeans and a white shirt, accompanied by a short man in a rumpled gray suit, stood up at the rear of the courtroom and walked down the aisle, past the waist-high rail, to the podium.

After several minutes discussing the issue at hand, a drunk and disorderly violation, the judge announced his verdict and the young man and his lawyer shuffled away.

"Omid Sassini," the blue suited man called out.

Moving to the podium, Omid looked up at the judge and said, "Yes, sir."

"It says here, you've received an appointment to the Naval Academy," the judge said, looking up from the paperwork on his desk.

"Yes, sir."

"And what is it you would like to do for the navy?"

"Intelligence, sir," Omid responded, shifting his weight from one leg to the other. "I would like to become an intelligence officer."

"Why intelligence?" The judge asked.

"I think it would be fascinating work, sir," Omid confidently replied. "I enjoy puzzles and intelligence is nothing more than trying to solve puzzles—what the enemy is up to, what they plan next. That kind of work."

"Is the navy aware that you have requested a name change?" the judge asked, looking back down at the file on his desk.

"Yes, sir, the paperwork for the navy should be in the

file before you," Omid explained. "Your signature on the naval documents is all they need."

"And you have requested the name, John Smith," the judge commented, looking back to Omid. "Why this name? It seems a little mundane."

"I wanted something all American."

"Omid Sassani is all American in my books. John Smith is a name you request when you're looking to disappear into the masses." Then chuckling, the judge added, "John Doe is another."

"It seems all American to me," Omid responded.

"Very well," the judge said, shrugging his shoulders. "I hereby grant your request for a name change. From this day forward you will be known by the name, John Smith. Congratulations, Mr. Smith, and good luck at the Naval Academy."

CHAPTER 40

Thong Nai Paan, Koh PhaNgan, Thailand, 11 December 2016:

The small speed boat bounced across white caps as it turned into an enormous bay. A fine mist of salt water plumed over the bow as it plowed through the water, cooling the speedboat's occupants. Sitting on the stern, with Steve by his side, John Smith considered his memory of the day he changed his name. It was an event that would have inexplicable consequences throughout his life. That one moment set him on a course away from Islam and his family. The mundane name of John Smith would lead him down a path that would seem unavoidable at times. The long-nosed judge had been right when he asked John Smith if he wasn't attempting to disappear into the masses. And as many times as he had tried, John Smith had never been able to achieve that desire.

The speed boat raced across a bay with two massive half-moon-shaped beaches on either side. Large resorts bristled along the sand with a backdrop of emerald green ridgelines that contrasted against the deep blue bay water. The driver turned the speedboat toward the south side of the bay and slowed as it approached the wide sunbather-spotted beach.

"Where are we meeting them?" John Smith called out over the noise from the engine directly behind him.

"A bar called the Flip Flop Pharmacy," Steve yelled his reply.

"The Flip Flop Pharmacy?"

"That's what they told me," Steve said, shrugging his small narrow shoulders.

The driver turned the engine off, and the boat bobbed to a stop ten yards from the shore. Several tourists on the beach stood, examining the vessel, as the driver turned and gestured toward a small thatch-covered bar. The faint scent of sea breeze mixed with that of lush jungle swirled around the boat as it floated next to the beach. From his speed boat vantage point, John Smith could see a rounded concrete counter lined with wooden stools with a small beat up pool table standing in the back corner. Bottles of liquor adorned the walls behind the bar, and the remaining walls were covered with memorabilia, indicating that that particular establishment had been in operation for quite some time.

Taking his shoes off and rolling up his trouser legs, John Smith painfully climbed from the speedboat. Steve handed John Smith his aluminum canes before following him over the side. With Steve holding John Smith's right elbow, the two men slowly waded to shore. The engine jumped to life behind them, and looking over his shoulder, John Smith watched the speedboat turn and race from the bay, a small rooster tail of water marking its wake.

Steve helped John Smith negotiate the soft sand as they walked up to a set of concrete steps leading into the Flip Flop Pharmacy. Two men sat at the bar with their backs to the beach and eight more stood behind the building on a dirt path surrounded by bright green banana trees and other tropical foliage, leading into a parking lot. John Smith slowly climbed the steps from the beach, his aluminum canes clicking against the concrete. The two men turned at the unusual sound.

A short man with long black hair tied in a ponytail sitting at the bar, dressed in dark trousers and a light blue silk shirt, grimaced at the sight of the crippled man climbing the stairs. With a receding chin and sloped forehead, the man had small dark eyes. The second man watched John Smith negotiate the stairs, as well. Dressed in pressed blue jeans and a red and white plaid shirt, this man had short dark hair graying at the temples and a crooked nose that had obviously been broken several times. At the top of the steps, John Smith wobbled over to the men and leaned against the bar.

"Mr. Smith," the man with the sloped forehead said.

"Mr. Patchacarn?" John Smith asked, leaning his aluminum canes against the bar.

"That is correct," Patchacarn replied. "This is my Thongsala counterpart, Jimmy."

"That's a very western name," John Smith commented, wiping his brow with a white handkerchief.

Laughing, Patchacarn replied, "It is more pronounceable to westerners than his real name—his Thai name."

"May I take a seat?" John Smith asked, pulling a stool out from the bar before Patchacarn had a chance to reply.

"But of course."

A short chubby female bartender quietly approached the three men and looked at John Smith with a smile. John Smith asked the woman for a coke. When she looked at Steve with the same smile, he requested a Heineken beer. A red can of coke with a straw and a green bottle of Heineken quickly appeared on the bar.

Painfully slipping onto the stool, John Smith rested his elbow on the bar to stabilize himself before saying, "What do you have for me?"

Steve knelt and slipped shoes back onto John Smith's feet.

"We have arranged a villa for you just outside Thongsala. Your men are waiting for you at the villa. Once we finished with our meeting, a van will take you there," Patchacarn replied. "What is it that you have for us?"

Pulling a small map of the island from his jacket pocket, John Smith laid it out on the bar before saying, "From what I've been told, Alain's forces have set up two rings of security around the targets. This has been verified by our satellite assets. The first consists of checkpoints along four routes leading into the village." Using his index finger, John Smith pointed at each as he described them, "There is a checkpoint on each of the main roads, here to the west and here to the south. There is also an unlit government dirt road to the southwest that accesses the village. The checkpoint along this route is in a pass, here. The final checkpoint is along a trail coming from Bottle Beach to the east. Each checkpoint has at least one machinegun position in support."

"That looks correct," Patchacarn replied. "That is what I would do if I were Alain."

"In two night's time, I have arranged for a breach in Alain's security surrounding Chaloklum. I plan on slipping my action team through the unlit government road southwest of the village. Apparently, this checkpoint has two supporting machinegun positions."

After translating to Jimmy, Patchacarn turned to John Smith. "It is a new dirt road, as you pointed out, that circumnavigates the main roads that come from the south and west. I know where it is."

"Two nights from now, I need you to create a diversion at ten-forty-five p.m. along the main road leading into the village from the south," John Smith explained, pointing at the position where he wanted the diversion. "The diversion needs to take place here, on the pass between Madeua Wan and Chaloklum. This diversion will allow my contact within Alain's forces to shift those machinegun positions to support the perceived threat from the south, thereby allowing my men to overwhelm the checkpoint and proceed into the village unscathed."

Nodding, Patchacarn again translated to Jimmy before saying, "Yes that will work for a few minutes. But once they realize that the commotion is nothing more than a diversion, they will focus their effort directly into the village."

"That's why I need your diversion to be convincing and last at least twenty minutes," John Smith replied. "I need your men to attempt to breach the pass between Madeua Wan and Chaloklum. Make them believe that is the route we are using to enter Chaloklum. Twenty minutes should give my men time to enter the village and terminate the targets."

Shaking his head, Jimmy spoke in broken English, "Twenty minutes of a convincing diversion will cost many lives of my men. It will cost to pay the families for their deaths."

"The Society is willing to pay," John Smith responded. "This is an important termination and retrieval."

"What of the inner ring of security?" Patchacarn asked.

"Made up of five men at various places around the building they are staying in," John Smith explained. "He also has a reserve force staying east of the village made up of an additional ten men. My contact claims those forces will also be committed to the diversion and not be able to react in time once my men are in the village."

"And?" Patchacarn asked.

"And what?" John Smith responded, looking into the man's small dark eyes.

"And what is it you must retrieve?" Patchacarn clarified. "The word is that the Society is looking for something these people possess."

"That is of no concern to you," John Smith answered, waving his hand as if dismissing someone. "You will be well paid for creating the diversion."

Patchacarn and Jimmy looked at one another and then turned to John Smith nodding with unsmiling faces. Jimmy then gestured to a man standing just out back of the building. The man came into the bar and then ushered John Smith and Steve to the awaiting van.

Slipping into the van's backseat, John Smith pulled his cell phone from his hip pocket and scanned the speed dial list. The air conditioner cascaded cool air down onto John Smith and Steve as the van maneuvered from the parking lot out onto a paved road. John Smith found the number he was looking for and pressed the call button.

The van drove up a small hillside onto a wide tropical meadow as John Smith held the phone to his ear, waiting for an answer. On the fourth ring, the phone was answered and John Smith said, "We need to go covered." Pressing the green button on his phone, a few moments later John Smith heard two faint beeps, and said, "We're covered."

"Go ahead," a tinny voice said.

"I've been using our Society liaison agent embedded with Alain's mafia on the north end of the island," John Smith began. "He arranged the attempted termination on the fishing boat during their trip down to the island and a second failed attempt on Tommy's friends in Chaloklum."

"He seems as proficient as you," the tinny voice replied with thick sarcasm.

Ignoring the scornful statement, John Smith continued, "I have several irons in the fire that should work in conjunction with one another. Tomorrow a woman that Tommy was once romantically involved with will meet with him and convince him to handover the hard-drive. My contact in Alain's mafia will be arranging a failure in security the next evening, allowing me to use that breakdown to bring this fiasco to a quick end, and terminate Tommy and his friends."

"And if the woman can't convince him to turn over the hard-drive?"

"I plan on offering him immunity which he will undoubtedly reject because he won't believe me. She will meet with him and tell that my offer is truthful. His and his friend's lives for the hard-drive," John Smith explained. "He will have been mulling over the sincerity of my offer and when she comes to him he will want to believe her because he will realize he has no other choice. He will hand over the hard-drive to her. Once he has given her the hard-drive, his guard will be down. This will allow me to slip the action team into the village and terminate him and his friends the next evening."

"And if the woman can't convince him to turn over the hard-drive?" the tinny voice repeated.

"I will proceed with taking advantage of the security breach and terminate Tommy and his friends and also retrieve the hard-drive," John Smith replied. "It is a perfectly flexible plan."

"And if your people fail to terminate Tommy and his friends, or retrieve the hard-drive?"

"Then I will need to find some other way."

"You might want to check and see if Caroline has made a recent trip to Thailand."

John calmly asked, "Why do you recommend that?"

"She has disappeared and temporarily disconnected her cell number," the tinny voice answered. "It is a common procedure to hold one's number when going overseas for an extended period."

"Yes," John Smith responded.

"You don't seem surprised at the possibility."

"I'm not."

"And why is that?"

"Let's say I am aware of another western woman's presence in Chaloklum."

"Is she Mr. Luck's pervious lover? Is she the one who will be convincing Mr. Luck to handover the hard-drive?"

"Let's just say I knew there was another woman and there will be a woman contacting Tommy to convince him to hand over the hard-drive."

"And why the secrecy about who will be contacting Mr. Luck?"

"She requested that she not be identified to the Society," John Smith replied. "I plan on honoring that commitment."

"That's a surprise, coming from you." The tinny voice chuckled. "I didn't think you knew the definition of commitment."

"You might be surprised at what I know," John Smith grunted before closing his cell and disconnecting the call.

CHAPTER 41

Chevy Chase, Maryland, USA, 11 December 2016:

The two older men sat side-by-side, in front of the massive gray-stone fireplace. Oliver's thin arms rested on the red-velvet chair's wooden armrests and Andre's bulky mass slumped down in the overstuffed floral chair. Each man held a crystal glass filled with brownish liquid and ice.

Reaching up and smoothing his unruly white hair, Andres commented, "I'm not sure what to expect in regards to the initial report about the validity of John Smith's allegations concerning Mr. Luck." His Scandinavian accent clearly marked his heritage. "When do we expect hear something from the man we hired to check into the issue?"

"I imagine we should hear something by tomorrow," Oliver replied in his crisp English accent, while looking out one of the long windows providing views of the wintery grounds outside. "The investigator was given two simple tasks: show a picture of Mr. Luck to Kelly to ascertain that he was indeed her assailant and have the video footage of Mr. Luck's vehicle arriving near the scene of the crime validated."

"And?" Andres asked, looking over at Oliver and shrugging his massive shoulders.

Shifting his pear shaped body in the red velvet chair, Oliver replied, "I know precisely what to expect. John Smith is most certainly deceiving us and the entire assertion that Mr. Luck is responsible is ridiculous."

Andres asked, "Then please tell me how Mr. Luck came to have the hard-drive?"

"Does he?" Oliver quickly retorted looking over and locking eyes with Andres. "Does he really have the hard-drive?"

"Then tell me why John Smith has used all of our assets to track Mr. Luck to Thailand and gone to all the trouble of following him over there?" Andres remarked, "Please explain that little mystery."

"Simple revenge." Oliver took sip of brandy from his glass before continuing, "John Smith detests the man and blames him for several of his past failures and his current physical situation."

"Revenge?" Andres chuckled. "I doubt that revenge is the catalyst. I believe Mr. Luck does have the hard-drive, and I believe John Smith is attempting to retrieve it from the man. The question is to what end."

Suddenly, the wide oak door on the opposite end of the room burst open, and James strutted in, announcing, "It's not good news," as he walked directly over to the black-granite counter topped with crystal decanters and glasses and bracketed by floor to ceiling bookcases.

Oliver raised an eyebrow before asking, "What has our errant handy man John Smith done now?"

"It's not about John Smith," James replied, opening a small refrigerator beneath the counter with shaking hands and extracting a bottle of sparkling water. "It's about our man investigating John Smith's allegations concerning Mr. Luck."

"Stop with all the crime novel antics, James, and tell us what you know," Andres calmly demanded, while running his fingers through his white beard. Shifting his massive body in the overstuffed floral chair in order to see James better, he continued, "What in the world has made you so edgy?"

"If you recall, he was to show a picture of Mr. Luck to Kelly, allowing her to identify him as the man who raped her," James began, sweat glistening on his bald head and the short stubble on his temples. "Our investigator was also to have the video of Mr. Luck's vehicle checked for authenticity."

"Yes, we were just discussing our investigator and his tasks. Has he reported back?" Oliver asked, also shifting in his chair to see James.

Looking across the room at his two companions, James replied, "Yes, he has reported that he was unable to accomplish either task."

Running his thumbs down his wide red suspenders, Andres chuckled. "More incompetence? I thought John Smith had the corner on the market for ineptitude."

"No, he was unable to accomplish either task because Kelly has been murdered and the video has disappeared."

Oliver abruptly stood and turned, his brandy sloshing over the edge of the glass, and Andres silently took a large swallow from his short glass filled with bourbon.

"Kelly was murdered yesterday evening," James explained. "Someone drugged the security guard stationed outside her door, entered her room, and suffocated her. I entrusted the video to our files clerk. He informed the investigator that he had placed it in a locked filing cabinet. The cabinet was forced open yesterday and the only item missing was the video."

"Evidently someone doesn't want us to know the truth about the allegations," Andre's calmly replied.

Talking another sip from his glass filled with brandy, Oliver angrily asked, "But who?"

"Who knew that we were checking out John Smith's allegations?" James queried, pouring the sparkling water into a crystal glass on the granite counter.

"Only the three of us," Andres announced, arching his bushy white eyebrows.

"And the man we hired," Oliver added.

"He would have no motivation to hinder his own investigation, and he was told to keep it quiet," James replied, "not to tell anyone about it."

"Then one of us?" Andres asked.

"Then one of us," James said matter-of-factly, picking up his crystal glass filled with sparkling water, turning, and facing the two other men.

"What possible motive would one of us have to hinder an investigation into John Smith's allegations?" Oliver snapped.

Looking first and Andres and then Oliver, James said, "You suspect John Smith of not being totally honest in his dealings with us. Possibly one of us is in cahoots with John Smith. The question is, how would one of us benefit from working with him? John Smith is attempting to retrieve a hard-drive filled with Society historical data. Full of damning information, actually. The information contained on the hard-drive is enough to put the Society out of business."

"If a single individual were to have control of the hard-drive, that person could theoretically control the Society," Andres added, nodding his head, "through coercion."

"If a single individual were to acquire the hard-drive," James continued, "they not only could control the Society through intimidation, but blackmail many of the Society's powerful members. The information contained on that hard-drive could send many of our members to prison."

"That's absurd," Oliver rejoined, shaking his head. "The thought of one of us allying himself with the likes of John Smith is ridiculous."

"I've often wondered why we kept such a record of our activities," Andres asked, ignoring Oliver's comment. "Why create record that could destroy our organization?"

"I'm not sure that was the intent," James explained. "It is normal for organizations to scribe and track their history. It gives one the ability to look back and not have to reinvent the wheel. Take NAFTA for instance, the Society was the driving force behind the agreement. It took us six years to convince the three nations to sign the treaty. That same process was used in a trade agreement between the Republic of Korea and the United States. We were able to go back into our records, review how we succeeded with NAFTA, refine the process, and apply it to the KORUS FTA. That agreement took one year thanks to our recorded experience with NAFTA."

"Yes, of course, but why record names?" Andres shrugged his enormous shoulders again, "And why record the seedy aspects? We have done nothing but place our members in a threatening position."

"This discussion is absurd," Oliver said again. "To even consider that one of us is attempting to take control of the hard-drive for personal reasons is preposterous."

The three men silently looked at one another, before James walked across the room and leaned against the fireplace, resting his elbow on its polished wooden mantle. Oliver sat back down on the red-velvet chair, as Andres began once again running his thumb up and down his wide red suspenders.

Breaking the awkward silence, Andres said, "So how do we discover whether one of us is up to no good?"

"This is outlandish," Oliver exclaimed. "We are a small team. A team voted in by the greater membership, which implies trust and confidence. To even consider that one of us is out to acquire the hard-drive for personal gain is ludicrous."

Ignoring Oliver's comment, James looked over at Andres and said, "We do nothing."

"Because the thought of one of us scheming against the other two is foolish," Oliver said, shaking his head. "It is obvious that John Smith discovered we were investigating his allegations and took the necessary action to conceal the evidence."

"John Smith did not discover anything," James said. "I asked the investigator if he had told anyone about his inquiry. He said absolutely not. He had not told a soul."

Taking another drink of bourbon, Andres looked at James and asked, "And you believe we should do nothing? If we suspect that a member of our small Patriarch team is up to no good, shouldn't something be done to discover the offender?"

"I said we should do nothing," James replied. "I didn't say that nothing should be done."

Shaking his massive head, Andres said, "I'm confused, James, please explain."

"We put Mr. Luck through a very complex test of his ability to extract himself from a dangerous and difficult situation several months ago," James began explaining. "If you recall, he passed the test with flying colors."

"And subsequently turned down our offer for employment," Oliver added.

Andres chuckled. "Yes, and for reasons that are being verified today."

"Yes," James continued, "and now Mr. Luck finds himself at the center of another life-threatening mystery."

"And what does this have to do with finding out if one of us is up to no good," Andres asked, once again shifting his plump body in the floral chair.

"Everything," James said, smiling. "I would submit to you that the situation Mr. Luck currently finds himself is not as nearly complex as that of last year. I would submit to you that the man who turned down the handy man position is currently working diligently in that assignment. We do nothing because Mr. Luck will eventually extract himself from the devious intentions of John Smith. Tommy Luck will lead us to the truth, and he will discover whether one of us is cahoots with John Smith."

"Are you implying that John Smith will fail in his dealing with Mr. Luck?" Andres asked.

James chuckled. "Was there ever any doubt who would come out on top?"

CHAPTER 42

Chaloklum, Koh PhaNgan, Thailand, 11 December 2016:

The five were sitting on the upper back deck of the faded yellow building, waiting for Alain to arrive. Nervous about the impending meeting between Chandler and Alain, Tommy sipped on an ice cold bottle of Singha. It was more than just anxiety about the looming meeting, something else was bothering Tommy. Looking around the deck, Tommy first examined Jack. Dressed in khaki shorts and a faded brown and green Hawaiian shirt, the bulky man sat at a green-topped table, causally looking out across the bay. Sandy, dressed in linen shorts and a green bikini top, sat next to her husband, running her long index finger around the top of a bottle of Singha beer.

Tommy looked over at Chandler. The auburn-headed and green-eyed Englishman was swinging in a hammock, seemingly completely unconcerned about a run in with Alain at the upcoming meeting. Caroline, dressed in a black one-piece swim suit with a red and green sarong wrapped around her waist, sat in a blue cushioned rattan chair watching Tommy. With only the ends of her short straight blonde hair sticking out from under the oversized hat, she had a thin smile on her face and also seemed completely relaxed. Finally, Tommy looked at Calvin, his stout body sitting on a heavily cushioned rattan lounge, sipping a can of Leo beer. Dressed in jeans shorts and a white T-shirt advertising Chang beer, Calvin seemed as nervous as Tommy. Beneath Tommy's chair, the dog was curled up sleeping.

"How can you drink that swill," Chandler asked Calvin. "You bring those cans of slop every place you go and turn down perfectly good alternatives."

"I like Leo," Calvin retorted, defending his choice in beer. "I especially enjoy it from a can."

"It's the cheapest beer in Thailand," Chandler retorted, swinging back and forth on the hammock.

"It tastes good," Calvin countered. "A lot of people like it. Just because you don't like it doesn't make you right."

"Are you sure he's coming?" Tommy asked Calvin, trying to change the subject.

"He'll be here," Calvin answered, "and he knows the rules. No arguing with Chandler."

Chandler chuckled. "Personally, no killing Chandler might be a more comforting regulation for this meeting."

"He knows you're here," Calvin replied. "He knows you're here to help."

"He also knows you're an agent for the Society," Tommy added. "This is going to be an interesting encounter."

"First one in five years," Chandler commented.

"What happened at your last encounter?" Caroline asked, looking from Tommy to Chandler.

"He shot a friend of mine," Chandler said matter-of-factly.

"He shot a friend of yours?" Sandy asked in an astonished voice, "Did your friend survive?"

"He shot my friend when we ran into each other in Thongsala," Chandler explained. "He was shopping with his wife, Paan, and we ran into each other at the Big A grocery store. Without a word, he pulled his Berretta and shot my friend in the chest."

"He didn't say a word?" Caroline asked.

"After he shot my friend, he said that he would have rather shot me but his friendship with Tommy precluded that course of action. So he shot the closest person to me—and, no, my friend did not survive. He was dead before he hit the floor. And Alain's wife, standing next to him, smiled as if nothing unusual had happened. She acted as if shooting an unarmed man in grocery stores was a common event."

"Scary," Caroline muttered. "She does seem to enjoy his violence. I've seen it for myself."

Calvin pulled a leather pouch from his pocket and opened it up, revealing tobacco and rolling papers. As he began rolling a cigarette, a soft warm breeze blew across the deck, bringing with it the faint scent of diesel fuel and drying squid, a nauseating mixture.

The dog abruptly woke and barked once, before curling back up at Tommy's feet.

"That dog," Tommy muttered under his breath.

Caroline asked, "What?"

"He's like some creepy doorbell," Tommy replied. "It's like he's psychic."

At that moment, there were footsteps on the wooden stairs leading up to the deck, and Alain's head bobbed into view. At the top of the steps Alain glared at Chandler, swinging on the hammock, and then turned to Tommy, smiling. Carrying his black Berretta in his right hand, Alain maneuvered across the deck and over to the green-topped table.

"Tommy, let us get started," Alain commanded in his heavy French accent as he sat down. "Let us figure a way for you to get out of this mess."

Standing up, Tommy said, "If you don't mind, I'd prefer that Calvin leave."

Chandler caught Tommy's attention and silently shook his head. Slumping his shoulders, Calvin looked as if he had just been demoted. Alain looked at his American friend quizzically.

"And why do you wish to dismiss my lieutenant?" Alain asked, tapping the muzzle of his Berretta on the top of the green table.

After a brief hesitation, Tommy answered, "Because I don't trust the English and three is too many for one meeting—two is tolerable."

Chandler, still swinging in the hammock, rolled his eyes and smiled. Calvin stood up, and Jack, sitting at the green-topped table, seemed impervious to the mockery and ignored the sarcasm.

"He's Canadian," Sandy mumbled, knowing that no one would listen.

"Ah, you are not as stupid as I thought." Alain laughed. "Calvin get out. I will meet up with you at the villa later."

After Calvin had left, Tommy began, "I need to establish an advantage over the Society. I need something that will convince them to leave me and my friends alone—indefinitely."

"May be our local Society agent has an answer to your dilemma," Alain growled, glaring at Chandler.

Chandler sighed. "Alain, I am the Society liaison agent for Samui. I am also but a small cog in an enormous machine. And I know only so much about my employer."

"Yes, you are a little cog," Alain spat. "You are a little cog selling yourself and your honor."

Laughing, Chandler replied, "Are you are such a big important man? You control a small piece of territory on an unimportant and semi-lawless island."

Standing from the table and holding his Berretta at his side, Alain glared angrily at Chandler. "You best keep your mouth shut, Englishman. The only reason you are still happily swinging in that hammock is because our mutual friend requires our assistance. When this is over, and Tommy is safe, that allegiance will be gone, and I take personal pleasure in ending your pathetic, easily bought life—"

"Gentlemen," Tommy interrupted, "hold your horses. Your squabbling is doing nothing for the problem at hand. As I was saying, I need a clear advantage over the Society in order to extract me and my friends from danger."

Sitting back down, Alain began scratching the dark curly hair on his temple with the muzzle of the Berretta. "But you have the advantage. You have their hard-drive. You can *démasquer Society comme étant.* You could threaten to expose them to law enforcement."

"You're both right," Chandler offered, placing his feet on the wooden deck and sitting up in the hammock. "Tommy has a slight advantage, in that he has the hard-drive, but that in its self is not enough. The Society is an enormous organization with agents all over the globe. Simply threatening to transfer the hard-drive to a media outlet or law enforcement agency is not enough. They have the ability to intercept and defuse such transactions. There needs to be more."

"Exactly," Tommy replied, walking across the deck and leaning against a wooden pillar supporting the roof. "I need more than just the threat of exposure. I need something to convince them that it would not be in their best interest to come after me or my friends."

"You need to get them on your side." Caroline jumped into the conversation, leaning back in a blue cushioned rattan chair, running her fingers through the edges of her short blonde hair. "You need to show them you are both a worthy ally and a threatening adversary. You need to convince them to choose the worth ally."

Chandler asked, "The question is, how?"

Tommy looked around the room at each of the meeting's participants, before saying, "There is evidence that there is more going on here than just the retrieval of the hard-drive."

"What is this evidence?" Alain asked, his dark eyes locked onto Tommy.

"The theft of the hard-drive in the first place," Caroline stepped in to explain. "The hard-drive, and its contents, is very valuable to the Society and its security was well thought out. It randomly rotated between safes along the US eastern seaboard. The transfer in the rotation cycle was conducted by thoroughly vetted individuals. At any given moment, only five or six people knew its location. The three individuals deemed the Patriarchs, the one or two individuals conducting the actual transfer, and the keeper of the safe it was stored in."

"So one of those individuals had to have been involved in its theft?" Chandler asked.

"Yes," Tommy replied. "In this particular instance, the keeper of the safe was brutally raped and her husband was murdered. For the sake of expedience, let's say she is likely not involved. That leaves us with five."

"Four," Caroline clarified. "This transfer was conducted by one individual—a bit of information I wheedled out of Steve."

"The question is who had the most to gain by stealing the hard-drive?" Sandy queried, sitting at the green topped table, next to Jack and across from Alain.

"Not the individual conducting the transfer," Chandler clarified. "The Society retains control of its employees and agents through excellent pay and benefits. However, there is also an indirect method of control that is always looming overhead. Every individual working for the Society knows if they fail to remain loyal, their days are limited. This is particularly true for individuals working on high-value operations, such as the transfer of the hard-drive. The individual who conducted the transfer would know that if he were even slightly implicated in the theft, he would not see the next sunrise. Nor would he have a place to hide to avoid that threat."

"What about threatening this man's family?" Alain asked, once again frowning at Chandler.

"The individuals tasked with transferring the hard-drive have no families, no loved ones," Caroline said, enlightening the meeting participants. "They recruit them out of orphanages or find them elsewhere. But they have no father, mother, brothers, or sisters. They have no wives and no children. It's a requirement."

Looking at Caroline, Alain then asked, "Then why is the safe keeper allowed—"

"Once again for expedience," Tommy interrupted, "let's

say that the individual who conducted the transfer is not involved."

"That leaves us with one of the three Patriarchs," Sandy announced in a bewildered voice while sitting up straight in her chair. "A member of the top planning tier was involved with the theft."

"Exactly," Tommy replied. "I had a conversation with Don the other day and he told me a story about someone who attempted to warn the Society that one of the individuals voted into the Patriarchs was clearly 'a bad dude,' to use his description. Based on when Don met this guy, the bad person is still in office."

"Who is Don?" Caroline asked, cocking her head to the side.

"A bartender," Alain replied.

"A bartender knows about the Society?" Caroline blurted out, sitting up in the rattan chair.

"Bartenders know everything," Tommy replied.

"That's true," Chandler added. "Bartenders are incredible sources of information."

"So a Society employee told Don, the bartender, that one of the individuals voted in as a Patriarch was bad?" Caroline asked, as if in disbelief. "And this happened when?"

"Don met the Society employee a couple of years ago. This employee had apparently worked with the bad man on a previous operation," Tommy continued, giving the details of his meeting with Don. "When he was voted in as a Patriarch, the employee attempted to warn the Society. This employee was running for his life when Don met him. The Patriarch was out to silence him."

Shaking her head, Caroline slumped back down into the rattan chair and muttered, "A bartender."

Tommy chuckled. "So much for secrecy."

"So where does all this leave us?" Sandy asked.

Tommy looked over at Sandy and Jack sitting at the table across from Alain and said, "We suspect that there is more to our situation than simply terminating us to retrieve a hard-drive, we know John Smith, who is a bad man him-self, is in charge of the termination and retrieval, and we suspect that one of the Patriarchs is corrupt."

"You need to expose the corrupt Patriarch," Alain said, his dark eyes darting back and forth between Tommy and Caroline. "You need to expose this man and the other dom-inos with fall. Whatever plan he and this John Smith man have will be revealed."

"And how do we do that?" Tommy asked.

"Meet with John Smith," Alain explained. "Tell him that you wish to resolve the hard-drive issue. Tell him that you wish to negotiate you and your friends' lives for the hard-drive. Set the stage for a later request. A request that you will only turn the hard-drive over to a Patriarch. If there is some other tortueux underlining plan, then the corrupt Pa-triarch will be the one who arrives to retrieve the hard-drive."

Raising his eyebrows, Tommy asked, "And how does that help?"

Nodding her head in agreement, Caroline said, "You ex-pose this individual to the other Patriarchs and show that you are a worthy ally."

"If there is a nefarious underlining plan," Chandler add-ed, "the corrupt Patriarch will not tell the other Patriarchs he is retrieving the hard-drive. We ensure that the other Pa-triarchs are aware of the transfer, and he and his plan are exposed."

"He might be exposed but his plan will not be," Sandy retorted. "And he will be able to wiggle out from under sus-picion. He can just tell them he was attempting to retrieve the hard-drive."

"If he attempts to retrieve the hard-drive without the oth-er Patriarchs consent, it will raise suspicions," Caroline ex-plained. "The structure of the Patriarchs tier is designed so that no member can act alone. They all have to be in-volved."

"That is why Tommy needs to meet with John Smith and

set the stage," Alain said. "You find out as much as possible about his true motivations concerning the hard-drive. Do not yet request to hand over the hard-drive to a Patriarch, set the stage for a later request. This John Smith will suspect something if you request a meeting with a Patriarch at your first meeting. Bide your time. Let them think you are trying to find a way out of this situation. But you use the information gained from a talk with John Smith when you eventually request a meeting and talk with the corrupt Patriarch man."

"John Smith is not a dumb man," Tommy said, shaking his head, "he won't give up much information—if any."

"But his right hand man Steve might." Caroline snickered. "Get Steve by himself and he might spill the beans."

"With you?" Tommy shook his head.

"No, it needs to be someone else. Steve is dumb, but if I show up and start asking questions he is sure to figure out what's going on. The fact that I'm in Thailand with you will raise his suspicions," Caroline replied. "It needs to be someone who is good at extracting information from unsuspecting people. Someone Steve doesn't know."

A series of small rattling explosions echoed across the bay and Sandy jumped in her chair. "What the fuck was that?" she asked, looking around to see if anyone else had been surprised.

"Firecrackers," Alain calmly responded, now scratching his right ear with the muzzle of his Berretta. "Good luck for a boat going out fishing."

"They set off firecrackers to ward off the evil spirits—as Alain said, good luck for the fishing," Tommy explained.

"So who do we have meet with Steve?" Caroline asked, bringing the conversation back to the Society.

Tommy chuckled. "I know who."

"Who?" Chandler and Alain asked in unison, both then glared at each other.

Pointing across the deck to Jack, silently sitting at the green topped table listening to the conversation, Tommy said, "You, the English barrister, a professional interrogator, cross examining unsuspecting witnesses in order to coax information out of them in order to clear your client. You are the man."

"This entire discussion resonates more as if I have just been nominated to play the chump in a not so well thought out theatrical production," Jack mumbled, dropping his chin to his chest.

"How do we get those two together?" Chandler asked.

"Easy," Tommy continued. "We arrange for me and John Smith to meet at a common destination, accompanied. From there, I take John Smith on a walk, leaving whoever he chose to accompany him alone with whoever I chose."

"And we know that John Smith will be accompanied by his assistant, Steve," Caroline said, nodding her head.

"And I will be accompanied by Jack."

"Leaving English barrister alone with the unsuspecting witness," Chandler added, lying back down on the hammock with a smile on his face.

"Maybe not all Englishmen are stupid and incompetent," Alain said, slapping the Berretta down on the green topped table.

"Let us all hope, for the sake of the British Empire's reputation, that I do not prove you wrong," Jack groaned, looking at Alain across the table.

Raising one eyebrow, Alain asked, "I thought you were Canadian."

CHAPTER 43

Pearl Harbor, Hawaii, USA, 26 July 2006:

Stepping through the office door, John Smith locked his body at attention in front of a silver-haired man with light blue eyes and wide shoulders. "Lieutenant Smith reporting as ordered, sir."

The silver-haired man, dressed in a white shirt with black and gold stripped shoulder boards, sat behind a large mahogany desk in a room carpeted in dark blue. The walls of the office were covered in personal awards, and two flags stood on either side of the desk.

The Stars and Stripes to one side and the navy flag, with colorful battle ribbons sprouting from its top, to the other.

Looking up from a pile of paperwork on his desk, Captain Hardwick said, "Please close the door, Lieutenant."

After closing the door, John Smith moved over in front of Captain Hardwick's desk and locked his body back into the position of attention.

"At ease, Lieutenant," Captain Hardwick calmly told John Smith, looking up with his light blue eyes.

John Smith replied, "Yes, sir," before relaxing.

"Have a seat," Captain Hardwick then said gesturing to a burgundy leather chair positioned in front of his desk.

Without taking his eyes off of the captain, John Smith stepped around the chair and sat down, placing his hands in his lap.

He could feel the cool leather form around his buttocks as he settled into the chair.

"I understand you're quite clever with computers?" Captain Hardwick asked, arching one silver eyebrow.

"Yes, sir, I seem to have an aptitude for them."

"And you could easily find your way into a personal account?" Captain Hardwick asked, as he began tapping his fingers on the desk top, "A classified account?"

"Hack into a classified account?"

"Yes, I believe that's the correct terminology," Captain Hardwick replied, "You have the necessary skill to hack into anyone's account."

John Smith rubbed his hand across the top of his head and replied, "Yes, sir."

"I would like you to hack into someone's account," Captain Hardwick calmly requested, examining John Smith's reaction.

After a brief hesitation, with a quizzical look on his face, John Smith said, "I don't understand."

"I want you to hack into someone's account and acquire a certain file for me."

"Is this legal?" John Smith asked, now scratching the side of his head.

"I am your superior," Captain Hardwick said evenly. "I am tasking you with hacking into an account and acquiring a file."

"Sir, that doesn't make it a lawful order," John Smith stated. "You can't order me to do something illegal."

"Who said anything about an order," Captain Hardwick said, with a calming smile.

"Who's account?"

"Pick up that envelope, Lieutenant," Captain Hardwick requested while gesturing to a manila envelope at the edge of his desk.

Picking up the envelope, John Smith examined the address typed on its face. It read his name and was addressed to a post office box in Kansas City.

"Let's get down to business," the captain continued, still smiling. "You will hack into Admiral Whitty's classified computer account and print the contents of a file named 'OpWhalrus.' You will place that printed out file into the envelope in your hand and send it via the US Postal Service to the post office box indicated."

"Sir?" John Smith replied in a bewildered tone.

Captain Hardwick locked his light blue eyes on John Smith and coolly said, "You heard me, Lieutenant."

"I can't do this, sir."

"You will do this, Lieutenant Smith."

"I won't, sir."

Leaning back in his chair, its wooden structure faintly moaning from the change in pressure, Captain Hardwick explained, "The post office box in Kansas City was established last time you returned home on leave—"

"I did not establish a post office box," John Smith interrupted.

"A man of your general stature, similar facial features, and heritage established the box. I imagine the postal employee who handled the request several months ago will easily identify you. There is already some damning evidence in the box," the captain continued, "enough to see that you receive a dishonorable discharge and spend a few years at Leavenworth. You would find that as an ex-military con with a dishonorable discharge, your future will be limited."

"I won't do it," John Smith exclaimed, angrily standing. "I'll tell them that you tried to get me to do something illegal. You can't make me do this."

"You can tell them anything you want," the captain replied. "I brought you in to discuss your evaluation. It's marked as such on my calendar and my secretary had to remind me of our appointment. You can say what you want, and who do you think they'll believe? A lieutenant junior grade with three years of service or a captain with a long recorded history of outstanding professionalism? I will simply claim that during the evaluation you burst into a tirade about America killing your brethren overseas. We will discover the envelope in your hand and make inquiries about the post office box. We will then discover classified information in the post office box. Your career, your life, will cease to exist as you know it. You will become a just another domestic terrorist looking to undermine the safety of the United States."

John Smith's voice trembled as he said, "You can't make me do this."

"I have far more tools in my bag than classified documents in your post office box."

"It not my post office box."

"Oh, yes, it is," Captain Hardwick retorted. "And even John Smith has a past. A change of names doesn't erase your history—or baggage, Omid Sassani. You have a father who is watched by the FBI because of his ties with people who preach radical Islamism. You have the safety and welfare of your beloved mother to consider. You have a younger sister that you've become quite close to. It would be dreadful if she were to be brutally raped at the age of fifteen. Imagine the reaction of your devout Islamic father. Surely he would have to kill her to save the honor of your family."

"You can't make me do this," John Smith whimpered, quietly repeating his earlier declaration.

Laughing, the captain said, "Oh, yes, I can."

CHAPTER 44

Thongsala, Koh PhaNgan, Thailand, 11 December 2016:

The balcony provided stunning views of both Koh Samui to the south and the islands of An Thong Marine Park to the west, as John Smith stood considering the memory from Pearl Harbor all those years ago. With a soft warm breeze blowing across his face and the sun beating down on the top of his head, John Smith wondered what the outcome would have been had he not complied with Captain Hardwick's request, a request that would be followed up by many more. Where would he be at this moment in his life had he chosen country over family that day? His choice had led him down a path that bore mediocre professional evaluations but an ultimate honorable discharge from the navy.

His plans for a career in naval intelligence had been shattered by his past. He had been able to take his experience with the navy and use it to acquire a job at the National Intelligence Agency, but it was not what he had envisioned for his future, the solitary life of data collection. Minuscule fragments of information that were then collated with more fragments and passed up the chain of command.

Standing on the balcony, looking across the sound between the island at the glistening shores of Koh Samui, John Smith recalled the words of the young blue-eyed man in Kimball many years before, "Life is not fair. Life is never fair. You should never look back and worry about your past misfortune or look forward and hope for a break." The scent of wet jungle hung in the air around him as he realized that the young blue-eyed man had left one very important element out of his wise words: life was also about moral fortitude and making the right decisions, no matter the consequences.

Without righteous resolve, no one could survive the unfairness of life.

He wondered if the young man had eventually learned the same lesson as he. John Smith wondered if the young man had had the courage to make the right decisions when faced with evil in his life and, if so, where that path had led him.

Turning and limping through a large sliding glass door, his silver canes clicking across the tiled floor, John Smith maneuvered over to a long white leather couch. Seeing Steve's small stature standing behind a counter in the kitchen, digging through the refrigerator, John Smith called out to him, "Steve, get in here," as he dropped down onto the couch. Leaning his two silver canes against the couch's cushions, John Smith pulled his cell phone from his pocket and waited for Steve.

A few moments later, Steve appeared next to the couch, asking, "Yes, sir, what can I do for you?" His small beady eyes darted about as if he were nervous what John Smith's answer might be.

"Call back to Maryland and get me Tommy's current phone number. Then get me the girl."

Silently Steve turned and jogged off. After listening to a muffled conversation in the backroom, John Smith watched Steve trot back over to the couch, his pale little arms and legs bouncing in cadence with his stride.

With his small beady eyes looking as if they were pleading for approval, he handed John Smith a slip of paper and said, "Here's the last number Mr. Luck used. Apparently he's been shifting numbers quite often and Maryland is having a difficult time keeping track of his cell phone usage."

"That's to be expected," John Smith muttered, taking the

slip from Steve. As Steve trotted off, John Smith typed the number into this cell and hit the call button.

After three rings, Tommy's familiar voice answered, "Tommy here."

"Hello, Tommy," John Smith greeted his nemesis.

"John Smith, what an unpleasant surprise. Coincidently, I was preparing for the distasteful task of calling you."

"Disagreeable for both of us," John Smith mumbled. "But necessary."

"How right you are. Have you ever wondered why we keep finding ourselves on the opposite end of the playing field?" Tommy continued, "It seems every time I turn around, I find myself in a situation where I am forced to deal with you."

"Eerie, isn't it," John Smith flatly replied. "As with my back, I thoroughly blame it on you and your uncanny ability to get in my way."

"And what do I owe this conversation to? Why the call?"

"I want the hard-drive," John Smith answered. "I'm sending an emissary to pick it up."

"Before you send your emissary, I want a face-to-face meeting with you to discuss me and my friend's fate after such a transaction."

"Given the hard-drive, I will leave you and your friends alone—"

"I want a face-to-face to discuss the issue," Tommy interrupted, flatly stating his request again.

"And this was the reason you were planning on calling me?" John Smith attempted to control his building anger. "Is the face-to-face necessary? Can we not discuss it over the phone? The thought of meeting you is somewhat nauseating."

"No, we can't discuss it over the phone and, yes, a face-to-face is necessary," Tommy replied. "There is something about looking into a man's eyes when you seal a deal. I want to see your face when we come to an agreement over the hard-drive."

"You have always managed to play the honorable man façade well, but we know the truth. You are as clever and deceitful as they come, not to mention you're a drunk." And then after a brief hesitation, John Smith continued, "When and where?"

"On the south side of the pass leading into Chaloklum along the southern road, tomorrow at noon," Tommy evenly announced. "It's considered the no man's land between the Chaloklum and Thongsala mafia factions.

"You want to meet in Medeua Wan," John Smith said, acknowledging the location. "Where in Medeua Wan? It's a relatively large area."

Tommy chuckled. "That's very interesting."

"What is very interesting?" John Smith snapped back, irritated at Tommy's jovial mood.

"Your navigational knowledge makes me wonder why the comprehensive maps study of the area around Chaloklum."

"It seemed prudent, considering Chaloklum has proven to be a fortress of solitude for you and your friends."

"I wish." Tommy laughed. "Based on my friend's experience last night, it would seem you still have some influence in the area."

"Where in Medeua Wan?" John Smith repeated, ignoring Tommy's comment.

"We can meet at the Butterfly Sports Bar. There are signs around the village that will direct you there. Have your driver park at the bottom of the hill and walk up to the bar. I'll have my driver do the same."

"You obviously don't recall my condition," John Smith snarled. "I find walking difficult since our first encounter on this island."

"Very well, have your driver drop you off at the bar and then tell him to proceed back down to the base of the hill. We can mull over the fate of the hard-drive at the bar and then you can call him to come pick you up when we're finished."

"I'll be there," John Smith replied. "Tomorrow at noon." Closing his cell, John Smith slapped it down on the side table at his elbow.

Reappearing next to the couch, Steve explained, "The woman is out with a couple of the action team members. No one is sure when they'll be back."

"Oh, for god's sake, does anyone here realize how important retrieving the hard-drive is?" John Smith howled, as his two silver canes fell from their perch against the couch and clattered on the floor.

"Sorry, sir," Steve apologized, his beady eyes looking down at his feet.

Taking a moment to calm down, John Smith then instructed, "Tell the girl, when she returns, that I want her to meet with Tommy tomorrow evening. She is to drive into Chaloklum and meet with him. She is to convince him to hand over the hard-drive by telling him his life and that of his friends will be spared if he does so. Then tell the action team commanders I want a reconnaissance of a bar called the Butterfly Sports Bar in Medeua Wan today. And tomorrow at noon, I want men covering the bar itself and more watching the base of the hill. The teams must remain concealed—they cannot be seen. I want both teams prepared to nab whoever is there, on my command."

"Okay, sir, I'll let them know."

"I have one more phone call to make and then I need a nap." John Smith sighed. "Jet lag and back pains have gotten the best of me. Go find the action team commander and leave me alone."

Once again, Steve trotted off, nodding his head.

Searching through his cell phone contact list, John Smith found the number he was looking for and called. Four rings later an English accented voice answered, "Chok Dee Villas, Chandler speaking."

"Can you tell me why you've been meeting with Tommy Luck," John Smith causally asked.

"Tommy Luck is a friend," Chandler replied. "And who might you be?"

"I am the handy man for the Society Patriarchs," John Smith announced. "My name is John Smith."

After a momentary pause, Chandler asked, "And how is it you know I've been meeting with Tommy Luck?"

"It is amazing what those pesky little satellites high in the sky can pick out. We've been tracking Tommy, and we watched him arrive at your villa yesterday. We watched you greet Tommy and take him inside. So all I can think is that you, a Society agent, are meeting with a man sought by our organization without notifying your handler or seeking approval. Which immediately makes me question whose side you're on."

"I'm loyal to the Society," Chandler answered. "I met with him but I haven't given him any information that might aid him."

"That's funny, according to our agent with the Chaloklum mafia you attempted to arrange safe passage for Tommy and his friends to Koh PhaNgan. He stepped in and further arranged for them to be lost at sea, and their belongings brought to me."

"Let's not forget, your Chaloklum agent failed," Chandler retorted. "They were not lost at sea and you didn't acquire whatever it is you wanted from their possessions."

"Regardless of his failure, based on the evidence I have available you need to reprove your loyalty to the Society."

After another hesitation, Chandler asked, "What is it you wish for me to do to reprove my loyalty?"

"I want you to ensure Tommy Luck is at his building in Chaloklum two nights from now between nine p.m. and midnight. I want you to ensure he is well inebriated. Based on your friendship and his fondness for alcoholic spirits, those tasks shouldn't be too difficult to accomplish." When Chandler failed to reply, John Smith continued, "If you do not accomplish those two tasks, I will ensure your days as a Society agent are limited. I will ensure your days of breathing are limited, as well. You will be placed on the very same termination list that Tommy Luck and his friends currently reside on. I am sure you know enough about the Society to understand that's not an idle threat."

"I'll make sure he's at the building and well into a bottle of Low Kow," Chandler reluctantly agreed.

CHAPTER 45

Chaloklum, Koh PhaNgan, Thailand, 12 December 2016:

Six miles into his morning run, Tommy could still feel the nauseating effects of all the Loa Kow he had consumed the night before. Sitting on the deck the evening prior with Jack, Sandy, and Caroline, they had talked about their situation while listening to the waves breaking across the beach until early in the morning. Drinking Thai whiskey and soda water, a traditional method of getting drunk on the island, Jack had eventually fallen asleep on the hammock and Sandy on a wicker lounge. Stumbling into the main bedroom hand in hand, Tommy and Caroline had stripped off their clothes and passed out in each other's arms.

Tommy had awakened to Caroline straddling him and nibbling at his ears. Quickly becoming aroused, he and Caroline had made a quick and passionate love. All the while the dog lay on the floor at the base of the bed, ignoring them.

With distillery-smelling sweat coursing down his body and the dog at his side, Tommy ran along a jungle trail that tracked across the side of a tall mountain. Catching glimpses of the glistening Chaloklum Bay far below, he was reminded of the last time he had visited this seaside village. Just over a year ago, he had made his way back to this island for same reason he currently found himself there. Safety. He had had in his possession a small flash-drive that several vying forces desired, and John Smith had been the catalyst for that adventure, as well.

Pondering his relationship with John Smith, Tommy considered the three times he and the tall man of obvious Persian heritage had found themselves on opposing teams. The first had been when John Smith had hired him to deliver a flash-drive to Bangkok. Tommy had quickly determined that John Smith was a criminal and the delivery illegal. The two men had indirectly battled one and other for several weeks until such time that Tommy was able to extract himself from the mêlée. Each received reminders of the exploit, John Smith a damaged back and Tommy a thin scar running from the corner of his lip to the base of his jaw.

The second had been when the Society had hired John Smith to test Tommy's skills at solving complex problems. Framing Tommy with the murder of a CIA agent, John Smith had also made it appear as if he was attempting to sell a copy of the same flash-drive from the year before. During that fiasco, Tommy had fallen for a beautiful auburn haired woman named Amber that he later discovered was involved with John Smith's scheme. The last time he saw Amber, Tommy told her that if he ever saw her again, he would kill her.

Once again John Smith had entered his life. Why their paths had crossed three times in less than two years was a mystery. Was it destiny? Was John Smith and Tommy's continued conflict some required mechanism to keep the world moving forward, or were they simply a billboard as to why the world was intrinsically unfair. Had Tommy been a Buddhist, he would have believed that their discord spanned many lifetimes. Leaping over a fallen palm tree, Tommy chuckled at the thought of the two being male dogs sharing the same territory in their last life.

"What do you think?" Tommy muttered, looking down at the dog panting by his side, "Are we two dogs battling it out for the amusement of the gods?"

The dog peered up with an expression that seemed to one of amazement.

Tommy's father had told him that life was fundamentally unfair, and he had learned that lesson over and over again during his life. Once again jogging along the narrow jungle path, Tommy began to wonder if John Smith was a victim of that unfairness. Had there been one key moment that swerved John Smith down a path of crime and deceit? Or had his entire existence been so unfair that John Smith had given in and now only sought a life of hatred and misdeeds? Or was he a man without a moral compass simply due to genetics? Regardless of why their lives continued to be intertwined, despite why John Smith was the way he was, Tommy knew that this voyage would not be the last he shared with his nemesis.

Bounding out onto the main road, Tommy turned downhill toward Chaloklum. At a slow jog, he trotted past a Chinese Buddhist temple, over a small bridge, and then past a gas station. The dog stopped here and there to sniff out unusual smells. More and more small wooden bungalows spotted the interior of the surrounding jungle the closer he got to Chaloklum. As he ran by an enormous tusked elephant, the animal looked up and examined Tommy with large wet eyes. The blue-and-gray-eyed dog gave the enormous beast a wide latitude, while eyeing it with a seemingly amazed expression. The elephant quickly lost interest and shoved a large palm frond into its mouth with its trunk.

Finally, Tommy arrived at the Seven-Eleven, its red and green banner a reminder that nothing escaped globalism. The air was filled with the pungent scent of fried chilies and the sweet smell of drying squid. Jogging under a large faded banner mounted on tall bamboo pillars, proclaiming *Fisherman's Village*, Tommy turned down the main street.

Walking down the gap between the faded yellow building and the one next door, Tommy stepped out on the concrete patio. The bay was calm and flat, its waters glistening under the hot morning sun, as two tourists dressed in colorful bikinis wrapped in sarongs walked along the beach. The dog jumped off the seawall and splashed into the water.

Tommy caught sight of Jack, Sandy, Caroline, and Don in the bay. They were waist deep in water some twenty yards from the shore.

Stripping off his T-shirt and shoes, Tommy jumped down to the beach, jogged out to the bay, and dove into the shallow clear water.

The water felt cool and refreshing as he swam out to the foursome. As Tommy surfaced, Caroline wrapped her arms around him and kissed his cheek, the wide brim of her hat pushed against his forehead. Don, with his neatly combed silver hair and wide tan shoulders, laughed, and Jack, dressed in colorful swim trunks, held out an orange filled glass with his massive hand, giving Tommy a silent cheers.

Sandy, with her strawberry blonde hair wet and slicked back, splashed water in Tommy's face. "What was all that noise this morning before you headed out to run?"

"I never kiss and tell." Then pointing to everyone's orange juice filled glasses, Tommy asked, "What is that?"

"What?" Don bellowed, attempting to portray an astonished face, "Haven't you heard of a morning screw driver?"

"Other than the fact that people are trying to kill us," Sandy commented, her light blue eyes sparkling in the sunlight as she looked out over the bay. "I really enjoy this place. I'm not sure I want to go back to all the chaos of Arlington."

"The children might take issue with your absence," Jack muttered, taking a large swallow of his drink.

"Oh, god." Sandy chuckled. "I try and not think of them. He probably has them digging a bomb shelter in the backyard."

"Between hourly calisthenics," Jack added, wiping a thin sheen of sweat from his forehead with the back of his hand.

"Don't forget the daily marksmanship training," Sandy continued, as a long tail fired its noisy engine up next to the pier.

"They'll be clean shaven and clad in camouflage fatigues upon our return," Jack dryly added.

Sandy laughed. "Their future physiatrist bills will send us to the poorhouse."

Looking confused, Don asked, "Where are your children? At boot camp with the Gestapo?"

Sandy looked at Don with a perfectly straight face, saying, "Worse, they're with my father."

Jack took another sip of his drink, and asked Tommy, "When will we be departing for our meeting?"

"Around eleven thirty. Are you up for this?"

"He had better be," Caroline said. Her skin rubbing across Tommy was arousing him again.

"Venturing into enemy territory and quizzing a member of the rivaling team?" Jack calmly replied, "Actually, I'm looking forward to it. It's been nearly two days since someone has attempted to take my life. I'm beginning to find this lifestyle somewhat monotonous."

"You woke up in a hammock," Sandy announced.

"Exactly, my dear," Jack replied. "I even find sleeping in a bed tiresome."

"With a hangover," Sandy continued.

Placing his huge arm over Sandy's shoulders, Jack looked into her light blue eyes and said, "And my lovely wife was sleeping on a wicker chair next to me."

After the group stopped laughing at the playful sarcasm, Tommy asked Jack again, "Are you up for this meeting? Do you think you can wring some information out of Steve?"

Thinking for a moment, Jack asked Tommy, "What are Steve's weaknesses?"

"He's sensitive about his stature, he hates me with a passion, he has a quick temper," Tommy replied, "and he not the sharpest tool in the shed."

"He's not intelligent?"

"He's dumb." Caroline giggled. "The man is a complete imbecile."

"And he has a crush on Caroline," Tommy added.

Rubbing his chin, Jack asked, "And he angers quickly?"

"Very," Tommy replied. "What can you do with that?"

Smiling, Jack said, "Angry unintelligent hostile witnesses can be devastating to your opponent's case. The fact that he has a crush on a woman well out of his reach is an added benefit. This will be child's play."

CHAPTER 46

Madeua Wan, Koh PhaNgan, Thailand, 12 December 2016:

As Tommy stepped from the Black Toyota HiLux four door pickup, he looked up at the Butterfly Sports Bar above him. Perched on the side of a hill and surrounded by tall coconut trees and dense lush jungle, it was the perfect hideaway. One side of a concrete wraparound porch, edged with a matching rail with bright blue porcelain newel posts, contained a small bar and four tables. On the other side stood a small well used pool table. The aqua colored walls were decorated in delicately painted butterflies, each with wings designed to resemble the national flag of its visitors. A neatly trimmed garden stood before the porch, spotted with tall tropical trees. Hundreds of butterflies fluttered around the garden. A black dog lay at the top of a concrete stairway leading to the entrance.

The dog hopped from the truck's bed as Tommy began walking up a path leading to the entrance. Climbing the steps, Tommy could hear Jack turning the truck around and driving back down the road, to the intersection below. Tommy knew not to pet a black dog that sniffed at his feet as he slipped his flip flops off, because it was known to bite. The blue-and-gray-eyed dog sniffed at the black dog before also lying down at the top of the stairs.

"What?" Tommy laughed. "That dog has bitten me at least a dozen times over the years and you immediately get along?"

The blue-and-gray-eyed dog ignored Tommy's rant.

A tall man with brown and white mop like hair greeted Tommy with a North American accent as the two shook hands. Wearing wire-rimmed glasses, the man stood several inches taller than Tommy, and he had an infectious toothy smile.

Tommy greeted the man. "How's it going, Rodger?"

"Great, man," Rodger answered, "Can I get you something to drink before I get outta here?"

"Yeah, a Heineken if you don't mind. If I get more, I'll keep my own tab."

"That would be great." Handing Tommy his beer, Rodger then asked, "So this guy is really bad?"

"Very. I don't want him to even know that you exist."

"I'm headed up to my sister-in-law's," Rodger replied, gesturing up the hill.

"Don't come down here, no matter what you hear," Tommy instructed his friend. "If all hell breaks loose, hide and keep out of sight."

"Got it," Rodger said, nodding his head in acknowledgement, before disappearing around the back of the building.

Taking a seat on the porch, Tommy rested his elbow on the concrete rail and sipped at his beer, waiting for John Smith. Tommy could hear Rodger trekking through the jungle, up the side of the hill. The blue-and-gray-eyed dog suddenly let out a single bark, and Tommy shook his head.

A few minutes later, he heard an approaching vehicle and a white Chevy Colorado pickup, bounced around a bend in the road. Tommy could make out John Smith's unsmiling face sitting next to beady eyed Steve. He had to smile at the unlikely twosome, knowing that John Smith hung onto the little man only because Steve had once saved his life.

Tommy wondered how a man with that level of loyalty, a man willing to put up with the habitual incompetence of Steve, could have ever turned out so bad.

The white Chevy came to a stop, and Steve hopped from

the driver's side, racing around to the passenger door to help his boss from the pickup. John Smith, with a silver cane in each hand, shoved the little man away, telling him to get back down the hill. Steve faithfully followed John Smith's command and jumped back into the pickup, driving back down the road.

Dressed in a dark suit and tie, John Smith shuffled up to the concrete stairs, painfully taking one step at a time and stabilizing himself after each. At the top of the stairs, Tommy watched as the black dog began sniffing at John Smith's shoes. Tommy smiled as John Smith reached down to stroke the animal and was bitten.

"I assume you knew the dog bites," John Smith said, looking up at Tommy.

"I knew," Tommy replied, still smiling.

John Smith muttered, "Thanks."

"You would have done the same," Tommy commented. "The joy of witnessing that bite will stay with me for the rest of the day. On the other hand, my dog doesn't bite. Feel free to pet him."

"Why is it I don't believe you? Maybe it's because I saw your dog bite Steve at the Korea War Memorial in Washington DC not too many months ago."

Tommy chuckled. "There was that one time."

Shuffling over to the table, John Smith agonizingly sat down across from Tommy, leaning his silver canes against his thigh, before saying, "As requested, we're face to face."

"Not an occasion I enjoy," Tommy commented, taking another sip of beer. "But a necessary one, albeit."

"Necessary for you."

"Yes, necessary for me," Tommy replied, examining the man across from him. When Tommy had first met John Smith, he had been tall, strong, and healthy. Now, his dark bristly hair was touched with gray, his dark eyes hooded in tiredness, and his jaw in a perpetual clinch as he tolerated the constant pain in his back.

"You hand over the hard-drive, and I will stand down the

order for your termination," John Smith announced, gently tapping the fingers of his right hand on the table.

"Why is the hard-drive so important?"

"It is the historical database of the Society," John Smith answered. "It contains every detail of every project and operation the Society has conducted. It contains every aspect of every project and the names associated with those projects—"

"And in the wrong hands, that information could be devastating to the Society and its members," Tommy interrupted, finishing John Smith's explanation.

"That's correct," John Smith said, glaring at Tommy.

"And what assurances do I have that you will not go back on your word? What assurances do I have that my friends and I will not be hunted down by the Society after I turn the hard-drive over?"

"None," John Smith admitted. "But what alternative do you have? If you choose to attempt to maintain the hard-drive, I will eventually retrieve it, through force or coercion. You can end it all right here and now—just turn the hard-drive over."

"And what will you do with the hard-drive?"

"It will go back into a safe, to be used when the Society Patriarchs need guidance on a new project."

Looking at John Smith and shaking his head, Tommy calmly said, "Why don't I believe you, John Smith?"

"I have no idea."

"Could it be that you lied to me about the contents of a flash-drive almost two years ago? Or could it be that you attempted to implicate me in a crime I had nothing to do just six months ago?"

"I see your point," John Smith replied, nodding his head with downturned lips. "But, as I said, you really have no other alternative."

Changing the subject, Tommy asked, "Tell me how the hard-drive was stolen in the first place."

"It was taken from a secure vault in a private residence."

"Wow, the truth." Tommy chuckled. "I'm impressed. Let's toughen up the questions. How many people knew it was in that particular vault?"

"Five."

"The truth again, I'm amazed. Now tell me who of those five told someone where to find the hard-drive in the first place. Who told someone which vault the hard-drive was located?"

"I imagine it was the gentlemen assigned to transfer the hard-drive."

Laughing, Tommy said, "You're amazing. It took three questions before you finally fell on your sword and lied."

"You seem to know a lot about the Society and the theft of the hard-drive."

"It doesn't take a rocket scientist to figure out that you were involved in the theft," Tommy replied.

Suddenly the dog whimpered and looked up at Tommy.

Tommy asked, "What is it?"

Confused by Tommy's question, John Smith asked, "What?"

"I'm talking to the dog."

Shaking his head, John Smith said, "You've finally lost it Tommy. You've gone over the edge talking to dogs."

"Get yourself a dog and you'll know why I'm talking to a dog," Tommy answered, as his cell phone began ringing.

Holding up his left index finger to signify a pause in their conversation, Tommy answered the cell.

"We're surrounded by armed men. I'm coming to get you," Jack's voice erupted from the cell's small speaker, as Tommy turned and saw the black Toyota careening up the hill, bouncing across the rutted road.

Jumping from his chair, Tommy vaulted over the concrete railing into the garden and sprinted for the approaching truck. The dog hurdled over the railing and was at Tommy's side.

John Smith began fumbling in his pocket for his cell phone as Tommy grabbed the passenger door of the slowing vehicle. The dog bounded over the edge of the truck bed. Pulling the door open, Tommy leapt inside as Jack put his foot down on the accelerator and twisted the steering wheel to the left. John Smith, dropped his cell on the floor pulling it from his pocket as the truck plummeted into the dense tropical foliage surrounding the Butterfly Sports Bar, disappearing into the jungle.

Grabbing his canes and standing, John Smith yelled, "Stop them!"

But it was too late. The Toyota carrying Tommy, Jack, and the dog had vanished from sight, and was on its way back to the safety of Chaloklum.

CHAPTER 47

Standing next to the black Toyota Hi Lux, Jack examined the jungle around him. The coconut trees were tall and provided ample shade, and the dense foliage proved a visual cooling relief. Monkeys could be heard shrieking in the distance as he watched an enormous monitor lizard waddle across the rut laden road leading up to the Butterfly Bar. Glancing down at his watch, he noted that the other party should have arrived five minutes ago.

Hearing an approaching vehicle, Jack turned and watched the junction below him, where the rutted dirt road leading to the Butterfly Bar intersected a narrow paved street. A white Chevy Colorado pickup turned onto the dirt road and slowly bounced past. Inside, Jack could see a short man with beady eyes driving and a tall man, hunched at the shoulders, with short wiry black hair and bushy eyebrows. The two men scrutinize him as they drove past, and Jack could see the tall one say something to the smaller.

"John Smith, I presume," Jack whispered to himself, "And his petite sidekick, Steve."

Five minutes later, the Chevy pickup bounced back down the rutted trail it had driven past on and parked on the opposite side of the road. The small man, wearing oversized tan cargo shorts and a white muscle shirt, that emphasized his skinny arms and legs, stepped from the truck and silently looked over at Jack, once again scrutinizing him.

"You must be Steven," Jack called out as he began walking toward Steve, dust pluming each time his shoes struck the dirt road. "I was informed that you were short, but I did not expect a dwarf—a small dwarf at that."

Glaring at the approaching figure, Steve turned away, ignoring Jack's comment and kicking the dirt at his feet.

"You must either be a virgin or be required to pay for all your sexual encounters with a woman," John evenly commented, stopping next to the short beady eyed man, and looking down. "Tommy has been shagging this beautiful woman named Caroline as of late. The sounds that come from behind that closed door are deafening."

Turning and looking up at the bear of a man next to him, Steve said, "Fuck you. I've been with plenty of women."

"Did they laugh?" Jack asked with a straight face. "I mean, did they laugh when you pulled your Willie from your trousers? Based on the size of your other extremities, your Willie can't be but the size of a thimble."

"You're Tommy Luck's friend," Steve snapped, glaring up at Jack's hulking figure. "Enjoy the sunshine and good weather, your days are limited."

"I was under the impression that the requirement of my survival was being negotiated at this very minute."

With his face turning red with anger, Steve growling, "You're dead, no matter what is agreed to up there, you're a dead man, and so is your wife."

"My wife is a dead man?" Jack chuckled. "Oh, my, he was right about that as well."

"Who was right about what?" Steve's small hands and arms were beginning to shake with rage.

"In addition to lacking stature, Tommy explained that you are not a very bright man." Jack looked down at the beady eyed man with sorrowful eyes. "You should consider thinking before you open your oral cavity. Talking without contemplating what you're about to say does nothing but illustrate your idiocy. She would be a dead woman."

"What?"

"My wife would not be a dead man, she would be a dead woman," Jack corrected the small man.

"Fuck you!"

"And why?" John calmly asked with a smile, ignoring Steve's slur. "What on earth would make the information on that hard-drive worth the lives of three innocent people?"

Shaking in rage, Steve blurted out, "You're the fall guy, dumbass. That hard-drive is worth its weight in gold and your dead ass is going to be the one they blame for its disappearance. There's no way John Smith is going to let you live, it would fuck up his plans for the hard-drive."

"What are his plans for the hard-drive," Jack queried. "They can't possibly be too complex. I've been told that he is as unintelligent as you. I have it from a good source he is incapable of planning anything beyond his daily schedule. Has Tommy Luck not outsmarted him twice before?"

"Fuck you," Steve snarled again. "Whoever has that hard-drive controls the Society. Whoever has the hard-drive is in control the most influential organization in the world. He'll be more powerful than the President of the United States."

"John Smith?"

"No, of course not," Steve yelled, spittle spraying from his mouth. "And you call me and John Smith stupid? It's not John Smith you need to be worried about. We'll benefit from transaction—financially benefit in a gigantic way. But John Smith and I could disappear and you'd still be a marked man."

"Then who?"

With wide eyes, Steve abruptly took a step back and wiped his brow, first looking at Jack and then up the road towards the Butterfly Sports Bar. "Get away from me," Steve howled, looking back at Jack while pulling out a .38 revolver that had been concealed in his waistband, next to the small of his back. "Get away from me right now or I'm going to blow your fucking brains out."

As quick as lightning, Jack reached out and slapped the weapon from Steve's hand, the Smith and Wesson bouncing and skidding across the rut encrusted road. Out of the corner of his eye, Jack saw movement, a man in camouflage squatting with a short black weapon in his hand. Taking a step back from Steve, Jack turned and sprinted to the truck, jumping inside. Fumbling for his cell, he twisted the key in the ignition and the truck's engine jumped to life with a roar. He looked down at the cell in his hand and punched the speed dial for Tommy's number before stepping on the gas pedal. The truck shot forward and careened up the hill, bouncing across the ruts.

"Tommy here," squawked from the cell.

"We're surrounded by armed men," Jack yelled into the cell, sweat breaking out on his forehead. "I'm coming to get you."

Approaching the building at the top of the road, Jack watched Tommy and the dog vault over a short concrete railing, and run to the edge of the road. Jack slowed the pickup and Tommy opened the passenger door. He saw the dog bound into the truck's bed. After Tommy had jumped in, Jack slammed his foot back down on the accelerator again and turned the truck downhill, sending it crashing through the dense jungle.

With the truck bouncing past palm trees and foliage slapping the windscreen, Tommy asked, "What the fuck happened?"

The pickup bounded over a fallen coconut tree, smashing both men's heads into the overhead. Then dropping over an embankment onto a maintained paved road, both men were tossed forward, Jack's face slamming into the steering wheel and Tommy's onto the dashboard. They could hear the dog sliding across the truck's bed and smashing into the side. Straightening up, Jack turned the steering wheel hard to the right and the truck fishtailed onto the road. Once again stepping on the accelerator, Jack sent the truck racing down the road toward Chaloklum.

Settling back down their seats, and Jack replied, "I managed to obtain the information we needed—the bulk of it, anyway. I pushed that tiny man a little too far, and he pulled a weapon me. As I was taking it away, I saw a camouflaged gentleman some ten or twenty meters inside the jungle, holding a weapon and watching. It seemed an appropriate time to abandon our quest."

"Wow," Tommy mumbled.

"Wow?" Jack asked, massaging the top of his head where it had collided with the overhead.

"Wow," Tommy repeated his comment. "That took you no time at all to extract the information."

"As I explained to you this morning, stupidity and a tendency to anger quickly is not a good amalgamation of traits."

Looking over at Jack, rubbing his forehead where it had smashed into the dashboard, Tommy asked, "It was child's play?"

"It was indeed."

CHAPTER 48

Chaloklum, Koh PhaNgan, Thailand, 12 December 2016:

The moon had just risen over the mountain to the east, and lunar rays shimmered on a flat glasslike bay. Twenty or thirty fishing boats floated on the horizon, long wooden arms lined with gleaming lights, reaching out from the masts, their brightness attracting the evening's catch of squid. A soft breeze blew from the west that carried with it the scent of a wet and steamy jungle. The rhythm of an old Thai song coming from someplace in the village drowned out the soft sound of water gently rocking against the sand, as Tommy, Jack, Sandy, and Caroline strolled along the beach. The blue-and-gray-eyed dog wandered along the shore in front of them, sniffing here and there.

Shoeless and holding hands with Caroline, Tommy was deep in thought as he watched his bare feet sink into the soft sand with each step. The coolness of the sand calmed him, the warmth of Caroline's hand even more so. Jack and Sandy followed behind, holding hands as well and brushing shoulders as they peered out onto the horizon. Both had thin smiles on their faces.

Breaking the silence, Tommy looked up and said, "So we know from your cross examination of Steve that there is someone else calling the shots. He's verified our suspicions that there is someone else involved. "

"It would appear so," Jack replied, looking over at Tommy and Caroline's shadowy figures. "But I'm concerned that the little man will tell John Smith that he let that jewel of information slip out during our discussion. If he does, our plan is in ruins. John Smith will see right through your request to hand the hard-drive over to a Society Patriarch."

Giggling, Caroline said, "No way will that little twerp tell John Smith that he spilled the beans. His relentless desire to please his crippled boss will prohibit any honesty about your encounter, no matter the consequences."

"I could not have said it better myself," Tommy chimed in.

"If he doesn't, then he's not a very clever man," Sandy commented. "He must realize that not confessing what he revealed could be devastating to their plan."

"He verified his stupidity a long time ago," Tommy added. "He was validating his lack of gray matter long before I met him, no doubt."

"My favorite memory of our discussion was when I told him that the noise was deafening when you shagged Caroline." Jack chuckled. "His face turned nearly beet red."

"There was some truth to that bit of information," Sandy muttered.

Tommy laughed. "It was her. Not me."

"I was having fun," Caroline replied. "And I am usually noisy when I have fun."

"What concerns me is that Steve believes that, no matter what kind of deal we negotiate," Jack said, as he lumbered along the beach, "we will be eliminated."

"That's true, if the hard-drive ends up in the hands of the wrong man," Tommy said. "We need to determine who the shady Patriarch is and make sure it ends up with one of the other two guys. Our plan is solid. We just need to get John Smith to arrange for one of the Patriarchs to meet with me in order to hand over the hard-drive."

"And then not hand over the hard-drive," Sandy added, "because that's the bad one—that's the bad Patriarch."

"If our disappearance is a part of their scheme, it would appear that an essential element of the plan is that the Society never knows who is pulling the strings," Jack commented. "The Society doesn't know who has the hard-drive or who is using it against them. And a meeting between you and this Patriarch will not be enough to persuade the other two of his manipulative actions in order to gain control over the Society."

"So, we need to gather enough evidence for the other two Patriarchs, beyond the unknown engagement, that will convince them that their associate was scheming against the Society."

Sandy asked, "What if they're all bad? What if all the Patriarchs are in on the plan?"

"Well," Tommy said, running his hands through his hair as he continued walking down the beach, "then we *are* screwed."

"How do you intend on gathering evidence against the crooked Patriarch?" Jack said, ignoring the plausibility of Sandy's point.

"I've asked Alain to rig me out with electronics," Tommy calmly replied. "Wire me up."

"And if he checks you for wires?"

"Then, once again." Tommy chuckled. "We're screwed. But even his request to see if I'm wired and the subsequent cancelation of our meeting can be recorded and given to the other two Patriarchs. That should be worth something."

"Let's hope he doesn't check," Caroline remarked then added, "What if he doesn't say anything incriminating at your meeting? These guys aren't spring chickens. They are where they are because of their shrewdness."

"Based on what this man is attempting to do, he has got to have a big ego," Tommy explained. "Presented with the right question or comment, something that will inflate his self-esteem, he'll let something slip."

"What if he doesn't?" Jack asked.

"Then, for a third time, we are screwed."

Gently patting Sandy on the rear, Jack pronounced, "It would seem our solid plan has a few holes."

"And he claims our plan is solid," Sandy added, gesturing toward Tommy.

Stepping down to the water edge and coming to a stop, Tommy said, "Something is nagging at me about John Smith's knowledge of the terrain surrounding Chaloklum."

"What did he tell you?" Caroline asked, coming to a halt next to Tommy and wrapping her arms around his waist.

"Yesterday, while I was arranging for our meeting at the Butterfly Bar, he knew exactly where Medeua Wan was located, and when I asked him why, he said it seemed prudent to do a map study of the area."

"That seems sensible to me," Jack stated. "If several people that I was fixed on eliminating were lodging in a small and well-protected village I would examine a map of the area."

"It's not the fact that he examined a map," Tommy said, looking over at Jack's large ghostly shadow standing next to him. "It's the level of detail that he's obviously studied the map."

"A map study makes sense to me too," Sandy replied, "He studied the map in order to determine a logical route into and out of the village."

Tommy added, "With a short layover to eliminate your targets."

"And to gather up the hard-drive," Jack replied, looking over at Tommy. "What is surprising or nagging about that?"

"He doesn't have the manpower to break into this village," Tommy replied. "After Alain's handy work, he has maybe eight to ten men."

"What about the mafia in Thongsala?" Caroline inquired. "Wouldn't the crime boss there loan John Smith several of his men?"

"It would take more than several to break into this village. And no mafia boss would want throw a lot of men at this village. They would know that casualty rate would be enormous and to lose that many men would weaken them against the other mafia bosses on the island."

"So there will be no attack on the village. I still don't understand what is nagging you about his navigational knowledge," Jack said, shaking his head.

"I didn't say there would be no attack on the village. He will try something but it will need to be unconventional," Tommy explained. "I know he's planning something. He knows we're well protected in this village, but he has to get to us. Even with the entire Thongsala mafia working with him, he could not possibly succeed breaking through with a frontal assault."

"May be he intends on luring us out of Chaloklum," Jack said. "Much like today. He had his men stationed in the jungle around us."

"But he didn't attempt to kill us because he knew the hard-drive was in Chaloklum with Sandy. He might have been waiting for an opportunity to abduct us but your quick reaction got us out of there," Tommy said. "What's nagging me is that he knew about Madeua Wan before I arranged the meeting."

"So he's planning on coming through Madeua Wan," Sandy asked, "to snatch the hard-drive?"

"No way, the pass above Madeua is too well protected. He would have to use an alternate approach. But Madeua Wan is a part of his plan."

"He did a map study. He knew Madeua Wan's location," Jack said. "I don't see the significances."

Looking at Jack again, Tommy said, "He knew how to correctly pronounce the name. It's a part of his plan."

The dog suddenly raced out in front of the foursome stopped, barking once.

"Oh, shit," Tommy muttered.

Caroline asked, "The eerie doorbell?"

"The doorbell," Tommy replied.

Out of the corner of his eye, Tommy saw a slim shadow of a person approaching them along the beach and turned. Caroline saw Tommy's attention focus down the beach and rotated around to face the approaching shadow, as well.

Jack slowly turned his massive body to confront the possible threat. Sandy stepped behind Jack.

"Too small to be one of Alain's men," Tommy observed.

"Too feminine looking to be much of a threat," Jack added. "Look at the walk—that's definitely a woman."

Sandy whispered, "Maybe just a Thai woman on a nightly walk."

"They're too afraid of the Burmese men that work around the village to walk alone at night," Tommy enlightened his friends.

"Tommy?" the shadow called out, slowly walking toward them. "Is that you?"

"Oh, shit," Tommy muttered for a second time in as many minutes.

Caroline reached up and touched his shoulder. "Take it easy, Tommy."

"Based on the tenor of that voice," Jack remarked, "that shadow is definitely a woman."

"Definitely," Sandy agreed. "And one familiar with Tommy."

"A shadowy woman familiar with Tommy should not come as a revelation." Jack chuckled. "Which shadowy woman is the question."

"Thanks, Jack," Caroline remarked.

"I know who it is," Tommy muttered again. "A former associate of John Smith's."

"Did you sleep with her?" Sandy asked Tommy, punching him in the shoulder.

"Unfortunately," Tommy replied, "yes—several times."

"John Smith no longer strikes me as incompetent," Jack announced. "In fact, I would even assert that he is imaginative in his endeavors to retrieve the hard-drive."

"Tommy, Is that you?" the soft voice called out again.

"It's me," Tommy replied in a flat tone.

Out of the gloom stepped a petite woman with auburn hair and green eyes. The dog growled as she stepped up to the group. Dressed in green shorts and a beige silk blouse, the small woman stepped up in front of Tommy and smiled. Caroline and Sandy examined her with disdain.

"Tommy, I have missed you so," the petite redhead whispered, reaching out with delicate fingers and touching Tommy's face.

"Six months ago you placed my children in danger," Tommy hissed, his hands beginning to shake in rage.

"All you need to do is give me the hard-drive," the woman beseeched, "I'll deliver it to John Smith, and he'll spare your lives."

"The last time we met," Tommy continued, still shaking in anger, "I told you that if we ever ran into each other again, I would kill you."

The dog moved over to Tommy's feet and looked up, whimpering.

With his anger quickly building, Tommy looked down at the dog and said, "Make up your mind. A growl or whimper. Both don't count."

"Tommy, John Smith's offer is sincere," the small woman pleaded. "I'm sorry about what happened with your children. I didn't mean to put your family in harm's way. It was an accident."

"Maybe John Smith is not so clever and imaginative," Sandy whispered, grabbing Jack's forearm.

"Yes, darling, I smell an impending disaster," Jack mumbled.

With trembling hands, Tommy pulled a black Colt .45 M1911 from the small of his back and placed the muzzle against the woman's forehead. "You've got five seconds to get out of my face."

"Tommy, listen to me, John Smith just wants the hard-drive," the woman appealed again. "Just give me the hard-drive and I'll take it to him."

Tommy ignored the dog whimpering again and began his count, "Five...four..."

"Please listen to me," she implored, stepping back from the muzzle. "He will kill me if you don't give the drive to me."

A bright flash, followed by loud crack echoed across the beach when Tommy pulled the trigger. The petite woman was tossed back like a ragdoll when the round struck her forehead and she fell lifelessly onto the sand.

"So much for three, two, and one," Caroline commented with wide flabbergasted eyes.

"There's a global rumor that Americans have fallen behind in their arithmetic skills," Jack remarked.

"I warned her last year," Tommy said, looking down at the crumpled body. "She nearly got my kids killed for personal gain, and I told her I would kill her if I ever saw her again."

"Did she have a name?" Sandy asked, in an astonished tone.

"Amber," Caroline answered. "She was a piece of work."

"Amber," Tommy repeated, before turning and walking toward the faded yellow building with the blue-and-gray eyed dog at his side.

"Should we call someone to get her off the beach?" Sandy called out to Tommy as he walked away.

"The tide will take her," Tommy called back over his shoulder in a flat unemotional voice. "I need a drink."

"I think we are all in need of some liquid libations after witnessing that small incident," Jack remarked.

CHAPTER 49

Kansas City, Missouri, USA, 23 May 2008:

It was a hot day with no breeze blowing across the prairie to the west. The concrete buildings and glass windows of the surrounding one story buildings intensified the heat, absorbing and reflecting the elevated temperature all at once. A faded green Pontiac drove pass, leaving a dark cloud of exhaust in its wake as it cruised by John Smith, standing on the corner of the street, leaning against a lamp post.

He was wearing dark khaki pants and a red and green plaid shirt. A thin sheen of sweat had built up on his brow as he examined the grocery across the two-lane boulevard. Knowing the store had a customary lull in activity between nine and eleven a.m., he waited for the last morning customer to vacate the premises. Running his long fingers through his dark wiry hair, he watched as the owner checked a patron's goods at the register. John Smith had considered making this call at the man's house, but did not want involve his wife or daughter. He had considered making this call just before closing time, but knew the street out front would be busy with activity as the neighborhood's residents rushed home after a long day at work. This was the perfect time to confront the old man behind the counter.

The last morning customer finally arrived at the checkout and John Smith watched the old man tallying up the bill and placing the goods into a brown grocery bag. Glancing up, John Smith read the banner running across the top of the building, reading 'Sassami Middle Eastern Grocery,' and recalled the many times he walked under that sign. He remembered a childhood of working along the store's aisles, restocking the shelves and sweeping the floors. He was reminded of all the abuse he took from the old man now standing behind the counter. The memories flooded his mind, not just as he peered across the street, but each and every day since he had left and started a new life. They were the recollections of a boy of Persian descent growing up in a predominately Anglo neighborhood and amongst an intolerant Islamic minority. They were the recollections of a lost childhood at the hands of an angry and abusive father whose actions had tainted each and every day of John Smith's youth.

Watching the last customer leave the store and walk around the corner to a nearby parking lot, John Smith causally strolled across the street, pushing open the glass entrance door, with posters advertising specials on food and merchandise affixed to the inside, obscuring the interior. A faint buzzer rang out, alerting the office that a patron had entered the store. The scent of curry and coffee wafted over him and brought back even more dark memories. He calmly walked down the aisle leading to a small office at the rear of the store.

A large old man dressed in a white apron, with coffee skin and dark wiry hair, stepped from the office, abruptly stopping when he saw John Smith approaching. The smile, which had been on his face, quickly vanished and was replaced with a scowl.

"The little woman returns," the older man growled, waving his hand through the air, as if dismissing someone.

Continuing his stride toward the old man, John Smith replied, "A little woman of your making. The prodigal son has returned."

"You are no son of mine," the old man hissed, placing his hands on his hips.

Stopping directly in front of his father, John Smith

reached up and placed his hands on the old man's shoulders, examining the withered face and graying temples. "Allah entrusted two hearts to you, yours and mine, and you wasted them both. You never taught me to stand firm against wickedness. You never taught me how to overcome the unfairness of life. You never taught me that there are times when a man must reflect on what is truly right and wrong, regardless of our religious beliefs. Instead, you taught me to blame others for life's injustice. You taught me to look at life through a narrow mind. You taught me hatred."

"You dare to speak of Allah?" the man roared, pushing John Smith back. "You refused everything I taught you and sought to be one of them. You became everything I despise in this country, its weak people, and moral-less society."

"You and your religion only taught me hatred," John Smith calmly replied.

"What do you call yourself now?" the old man retorted. "John Smith, a name that heralds the failing of an immoral country."

"I chose that name because it signifies everything that you are not."

"It only signifies that you have abandoned Islam," his father spat. "You have embraced a people who kill Muslim woman and children."

"And Muslims have not killed American woman and children?" John Smith laughed. "Again, you only teach revenge and hatred. It is all you know."

"Get out of my store and never come back," the old man spat. "I will be at home by six, and I do not want to see you. I never want to see you again."

"You will never see me again," John Smith announced to his father. "And you won't be home by six," he continued, reaching around his back and pulling an eight inch knife from his belt.

Standing his ground, the old man laughed, asking, "The little woman threatens me? Has the little woman grown testicles?"

"The little woman always had testicles, father," John Smith replied as he thrust the knife through the white apron into his father's belly, continuing, "You just chose to ignore them," as he slowly drew the knife up to old man's chest cavity.

The old man's expression turned from a scowl to one of disbelief. Grabbing at his stomach, he attempted to keep his bowels from dropping to the floor. Blood gushed from the wound and the old man dropped to his knees.

John Smith extracted the knife and wiped its blade on the old man's shoulder, before repeating his earlier words, "You taught me only hatred and revenge, and now your teachings have come home to roost."

CHAPTER 50

Thongsala, Koh PhaNgan, Thailand, 13 December 2016:

Scooters and faded pickup trucks noisily whisked by in both directions along the street in front of the coffee shop where John Smith was having an early morning espresso, leaving in their wake a fine plume of dust mixed with exhaust. Tourists were maneuvering along the sidewalk, inspecting the merchandise hanging from racks in front of the stores. Two Thai men were quietly talking in front of a bookstore across the street, making arm gestures that subtly indicated that they had disagreed on something.

Sitting on a red cushioned chair next to a small round table, John Smith mulled over the day he killed his father. While he had killed his father to free himself from the hatred and intolerance that had plagued his life, that moment in time had sealed his fate, leading to an existence of crime and deceit.

That one act had demonstrated to him that he could do anything he wanted without consequences. That knowledge had been freeing and spoiling all at once. His inter-strength weakened by his upbringing, John Smith had used any and every means to get ahead in life, no matter the outcome to others.

Steve appeared in the doorway and strode over to John Smith's table, interrupting him from his memories. Pulling out the chair opposite from John Smith, Steve sat down, his beady eyes darting back and forth, his dark bushy hair glistening with sweat.

"Are they ready?" John Smith queried the small man, before taking a sip of espresso.

"They're studying the maps and getting their gear ready. They'll be ready when the time comes."

"Have you talked with Calvin and explained what we want from him?" John Smith asked, placing his espresso cup back down on the round table.

"He knows the plan," Steve replied. "I spoke with him this morning. He knows when the ruckus starts near Madeua Wan which machine gun positions to move. Are you sure this is going to work?"

"Chandler will ensure Tommy and his friends are at the building. It'll work. Tommy knows I'll try something, but he doesn't believe that I'm this daring. Even Tommy Luck will be surprised—and we both know he'll be drunk."

"But he's outwitted us before." Steve shook his head. "We've tried to eliminate him time and time again for nearly two years, and he's always been able to outwit us and escape. Look at what happened to Amber."

"Amber was a longshot and a mistake. We should have known that Tommy would not forgive her for what happened to his family. This plan is bold and daring," John Smith replied, looking over at Steve. "We'll be successful. Trust me."

"What about this Chandler guy? Are you sure you can trust him to have Tommy at the building?"

"In Chandler's world, money takes precedence over everything else," John Smith answered, looking out the window onto the busy street. "There is no such thing as honor among thieves. He will ensure that Tommy is there because he knows that the gravy train with the Society will be over if he does not."

"But he's Tommy's friend—"

"Thugs like Chandler have no friends," John Smith curtly interrupted, looking back over and glaring at the small man, his demeanor quickly changing from thoughtful to one of anger over Steve's lack of faith in his plan. "He's just like me," he continued. "Money is what motivates him, and money has no friends or relatives. Chandler is just like us."

"Alain has placed Tommy's survival above himself. He's been loyal to Tommy, even when it threatens his lifestyle," Steve insisted, his tiny hands nervously twitching on the table top and his beady eyes looking pleadingly at John Smith. "Why would Chandler not do the same? Alain and Chandler are both thugs. Why would one be loyal and the other not?"

"You are a stupid little man," John Smith hissed, slapping his hand on the table top. "Those two men are opposites. Chandler is motivated by money. Alain is motivated by ego. Chandler will ensure Tommy is at the building because if he does not, he would lose money. Alain protects Tommy because he wants to prove to the world that he cannot be pushed around by anyone—not even the Society. He would die trying to show everyone around him that an organization like the Society is nothing to him, and he *will* die trying."

CHAPTER 51

Haad Thong Lang, Koh PhaNgan, Thailand, 13 December 2016:

Sweat coursed down Tommy's face as he jogged up the narrow trail, away from the beach. The path curving upward, he pumped his arms and legs to counteract the increasing steepness. With his nose to the ground, the dog followed directly behind him. Gray coconut tree trunks picketed the trail and wide proms provided overhead shade from the sun. The trail twisted to the left and traced along the edge of a seaside cliff, waves splashing at its reddish base. Thin vines and broad dark green leafs tugged at Tommy's shins as he followed the narrow twisting path along the cliff, thinking about the previous evening's events.

Amber had attempted to implicate Tommy in several crimes last year for personal gain. In the process, Tommy's children had become the target of an immoral and deadly criminal. On two occasions there had been attempted abductions of his children. Had those attempts been successful, Tommy knew the outcome would have resulted in his children's death. In the aftermath, Tommy had issued a warning to Amber: she was to never come near him or his children again. Last night, with all the events unfolding around Tommy and his friends, he had lost his temper. Killing her was act he now regretted, but one that would find its place with all the other violent acts in his life. It would become a pebble in his pocket.

The trail wound its way through the jungle and over the mountain top. Finding himself looking down onto blue gray water churning in the small cove of Haad Thong Lang, Tommy slowed his pace and took in the sight. The path he was jogging along emptied out onto a narrow concrete road, and he jogged down the hillside, past two villas toward the bay.

Nearly at the shore, he slowed to a walk and approached Chandler's bamboo walled villa overlooking the cove.

Standing at the tall bamboo gate, with dogs barking on the far side, Tommy called out, "Hey, Chandler, you home?"

Chandler began yelling for the unseen barking dogs to be quiet, before one of the tall bamboo gates noisily and slowly clattered to one side.

"There he is," Chandler said, greeting Tommy, his green eyes mounted on an auburn-haired head peeking through the gap in the bamboo gates, before saying, "You got yourself a dog. A dog must be a fabulous running companion."

"More like the dog got me."

Scratching his head, Chandler remarked, "Although, I never thought of you as the dog type."

"Then why did you tell me it was a good idea to get a dog?"

"Does your dog have a name?"

"Yeah, Dog," Tommy replied. "Now are you going to let me in or are we going to continue this ridiculous interrogation about dogs?" Turning, Tommy pointed at the blue-and-gray-eyed dog and said, "Stay."

The dog sat down and peered up at Tommy.

"The name Dog is convenient title—a difficult name to forget, anyway," Chandler observed while pulling the gate the rest of the way open. "I see you received my message."

"Yes, this morning," Tommy answered, "Why an invitation via messenger and no phone call? Sending Don as your delivery boy seemed a bit odd."

"All in due time," Chandler replied, gesturing Tommy inside. "Come in and let's have a chat."

As Tommy stepped through the bamboo gates, the same two dogs bounded up, a yellow Labrador and a smaller black mute, tongues lapping out the side of their mouths. Both animals stopped in their tracks when they saw the blue-and-gray-eyed dog sitting just outside the gate.

Looking over his shoulder at the blue-and-gray-eyed dog, Tommy shook his head and mumbled, "What is it with you? You're like a dog Mother Teresa. Other dogs cow in your presence."

Sliding the gate closed, Chandler led Tommy into the closest villa, past the kitchen counter topped with gray granite. Tommy once again looked down at the small trash bin and saw that it was empty. They walked into the living room with its high ceiling and crisscrossing beams, passed the overstuffed chairs and large couch, and through the enormous sliding glass door trimmed in teak, onto the covered patio overlooking the Jacuzzi and swimming pool, and then the beach. Pulling a chair from the round table, Chandler sat down and looked up at Tommy.

"This must be serious," Tommy said, looking down at Chandler as he pulled a chair out from the table opposite his friend.

"It could be," Chandler replied, pulling a cigarette from his shirt pocket and tapping its filtered end on the glass table top.

Glancing over at the foliage covered beams supporting the roof over the deck and then out to the glistening water in the swimming pool below, Tommy sat down and sighed, before asking, "How have my problems been complicated?"

"I received a phone call from your friend John Smith two days ago."

"Ah, now I understand the invitation via messenger. John Smith has your phone number and is likely monitoring it," Tommy said, nodding in approval. Looking down at the ashtray, he noticed that it was clear of any self-wrapped cigarettes butts. "John Smith has a lot of technical support. He must be tracking my movements and spotted me entering your villa the other day—probably a bad idea for me to have come here."

Silently watching Tommy with his green eyes, Chandler slipped a lighter from his pants pocket and lit the cigarette, now hanging to one side of his mouth.

"And what did my pal John Smith say?"

"He asked me to ensure you and your friends were in your building between nine p.m. and midnight tonight," Chandler replied in a serious tone, the glowing cigarette hanging from his lips bobbing with each word. "And he requested that you be intoxicated."

"He requested this several days ago?"

"Yes, two days ago."

"Two days?" Tommy asked again. "Why the delay in letting me know?"

"Let's just call it a moral dilemma," Chandler answered, taking the cigarette from his mouth and crushing into the ashtray. "Between breathing and supporting a friend."

"Are you sure it wasn't a monetary issue?"

"There is the small matter of financial loss," Chandler admitted. "Which I quickly came to terms with."

"He's obviously planning on attempting to acquire the hard-drive tonight between nine p.m. and midnight."

"It would appear so," Chandler replied, nodding his head. "And I imagine there is also the goal of eliminating you and your friends."

Changing the subject, Tommy said, "Calvin is the Society agent inside Alien's organization."

"You have excellent intuition—I knew at the meeting on your deck that you suspected him. How did you figure that out?"

"Self-rolled cigarettes and Leo beer cans."

"That's why you dismissed him from the meeting the other day?"

"Yes."

"And how in the world would self-rolled cigarettes and Leo cans lead you to the conclusion that Calvin was a Society agent?"

"You delayed our meeting the other day when I called. It was an unusual request. When I did arrive, you had cans of Leo beer in the kitchen trash and the remains of self-rolled cigarettes in this ashtray," Tommy explained, gesturing to the ashtray on the table top. "The only person I know in Chaloklum that has an affinity for both is Calvin. You had obviously been meeting with him."

"I was reprimanding him on your travel arrangements from Pattaya."

"Was he the one that told John Smith about our relationship?" Tommy asked, rubbing his hand back and forth across his brown hair.

"Not according to John Smith," Chandler replied. "As you said you were spotted entering this villa via a satellite. However, Calvin has certainly been talking with him since."

"Calvin obviously knows nothing of friendship."

"Calvin is a loyal man," Chandler began explaining. "He spent a large portion of his life in the English Army where he learned that loyalty to the organization stands above all else. Friends and associates are a second tier of loyalty. As soon as John Smith discovered that I had a relationship with you, he likely called Calvin. Calvin, reacting to his training, placed the Society above all and told John Smith everything."

Nodding his head, Tommy replied, "You might be right."

Laughing, Chandler said, "That was too easy—what are you about to say?"

Looking back out to the horizon, Tommy said, "My current organization just happens to be Alain's mafia."

"You won't tell Alain about Calvin, will you?"

"I will."

"If you tell Alain who the Society agent is in his organization, Calvin is a dead man."

Still scanning the horizon, Tommy said, "One good turn deserves another. The fucker tried to get me and my friends killed on the cruise down here. Not to mention, Calvin is likely involved in tonight's events."

It was Chandler's turn to nod his head as he replied, "Good point, my friend."

Looking back over at the green eyed man across the table, Tommy smiled and asked, "You up for a rodeo?"

Smiling back, Chandler answered, "As my employment with the Society has suddenly been terminated, and my days are limited, why the hell not?"

CHAPTER 52

Chaloklum, Koh PhaNgan, Thailand, 13 December 2016:

With his light blue eyes gleaming and his silver hair neatly combed, Don slipped between the partially opened accordion doors into the building wearing green cargo pants and a red and green Hawaiian shirt, carrying a short wide muzzled weapon mounted on a wooden stock. Over his shoulder was a bandolier holding eight wide rounds tipped with flat ended green projectiles.

"Where the fuck did you get that?" Tommy laughed, as he stood next to the wooden counter with a cold brown bottle of Singha beer in his hand. The blue-and-gray-eyed dog sat loyally by his side. Wearing faded blue jeans and a tattered blue T-shirt advertising some baseball team he had once been a member of, Tommy took a long swallow of Singha.

"You can buy them over the counter in Cambodia," Don replied in a serious tone, holding the weapon up for Tommy to examine. "This was my weapon of choice during the Vietnam war."

"An M-Seventy-Nine grenade launcher?"

"Hell, yes. This baby can toss some hurt out."

"I'm not sure grenades will be much use in this building," Tommy commented, setting the beer bottle onto the counter.

"Buckshot," Don replied. "Twenty twenty-four-grain pellets—perfect for this building." Looking around the downstairs, with its two-story-high ceiling and long wooden counter, Don gestured to a large indoor balcony hovering overhead with the muzzle of his weapon. "I've always loved this old building. Where else do you see features like that?"

"Let's hope it remains intact after tonight."

A single bark from the dog and Tommy looked to the accordion doors, watching for the next attendee. Chandler slipped through the opening dressed in tan shorts and a white cotton shirt, his auburn hair freshly cut and his green eyes flashing mischievously. Resembling a tropical cowboy, Chandler had a long black barreled Colt Frontier revolver holstered on his hip.

Seeing Tommy roll his eyes at his weapon choice, Chandler said, "You're the one that said there was to be a rodeo. I selected a weapon that fit the described event."

As Don and Chandler sauntered into the kitchen and up the stairs to the second floor, Tommy leaned out the accordion door and looked down the street in both directions. Behind him, the dog barked again. From the east he could see Alain's silver Toyota HiLux pickup driving down the main road toward the faded yellow building.

Looking over his shoulder at the dog, Tommy asked, "How do you do that? His pickup is still a hundred yards away."

Parking in front of the building, Alain reached behind and extracted four twenty-one-inch Remington pump action shotguns from the rear seat before climbing from the truck.

Wearing a purple muscle shirt and blue jeans, he slipped the shotgun slings over his shoulder and stroked his goatee before asking, "Is everyone present?"

"We're all here."

"This should be amusing," Alain replied in a thick French accent.

"Where's Calvin?"

Stepping past Tommy and through the accordion doors, Alain reached down and stroked the dog's head. "This dog suits you, Tommy. He is a loyal friend that lacks the intellect to choose who to be loyal to. Just like you."

"Let's not get started on Chandler again."

Grunting a begrudging acknowledgement, Alain handed Tommy one of the shotguns, before saying, "Calvin is tending to the defensive positions around the village—making sure that John Smith's plan to get into the village will be successful, I am sure. Your plan to confront and destroy John Smith's team with an overwhelming force is very good. He will feel as if victory was very close but stolen at the last moment. He will demand au chef—ask his boss to meet with you. I like it."

"I'm glad you think so, but you might lose your chance to extract revenge on your right hand man, Calvin."

"Tommy, you think so little of my capacity. When this is over, I will find Calvin, and he will learn that it was a mistake to make a dupe of me."

Closing and locking the accordion doors, Tommy and the dog followed Alain through the bar, into the kitchen, and up the stairs to the second floor. Eyeing Alain as he stepped into the living room, Chandler was sitting on a wooden chair in the corner of the room. Jack's massive frame was slumped on matching chair next to him. Sandy was standing behind Jack with one of her long elegant hands resting on his shoulder. Don was laid out on the green couch, checking his weapon, with Caroline sitting next to him. Sitting down across the room from Chandler, Alain glared back at the Englishman, shaking his head. Jack and Sandy suspiciously eyed one another, silently wondering whether Chandler and Alain would turn their weapons on each other once the shooting started.

"Here's the plan," Tommy began, as he sat down between Don and Caroline. "We believe that there will be a diversion on one of the roads leading into the village. We believe Calvin will likely use that diversion as excuse to move one of the machine gun positions and weaken the defense on one of the other routes leading into the village. He will likely commit the reserve forces in the village. We believe that there will be a small team that uses that weakened position to enter the village. We know their target is this building—more specifically me, Jack, and Sandy. Along with eliminating us, we know they also need to extract the hard-drive."

"Which is the safe at my villa," Alain added.

"Is this your version of a pep talk?" Jack muttered, the wooden chair creaking as he shifted his enormous body.

"Why do you believe all that?" Sandy asked. "What makes you think that's the way it will go down?"

Ignoring Jack's remark and Sandy's question, Tommy continued, "We also know the men coming after us are professionals. They will want to get in and out as quickly as possible. They won't know which floor we're on so they will probably attempt to breach the building on both levels at the same time. The downstairs doors and windows are all heavy wood and locked, so they will probably use some type of explosive device to open them. They will attempt to come through either the kitchen window or back door because they're closest to the stairs. The upstairs doors and windows are all glass, but they will use the double doors just because that will allow them to get the most firepower into the building the quickest."

Don shrugged his shoulders. "Why wouldn't they just blow the building up?"

"Because of the hard-drive. They might eliminate us in an explosion but they'd never find the hard-drive."

"I want to know why you think John Smith will be using a diversion to allow Calvin to shift the defensive positions," Sandy asked again, her light blue eyes flashing. "You're basing your plan on theories."

"Because I know that John Smith is utilizing Madeua Wan in his plan, and I know that he can't send his team through Madeua Wan because that route into the village is too obvious and too heavily fortified. So it will likely be the diversion to weaken one of the other routes so John Smith can get a team in the village."

"Please allow Tommy to continue," Alain interjected. "He has thought this all out."

"We're going to make the upstairs bedrooms our main defensive position, and this room, the living room, is our kill zone. As you can see, we spent the morning cutting gun slits into the walls adjoining the living room," Tommy explained, gesturing to two long shoulder high holes cut into the living room's back wall. "Jack and Chandler get the guestroom. Don gets the master bedroom, Sandy and Caroline will be positioned on the roof top next door. It's flat, has a waist high concrete wall around it, and is full of shadows—not to mention it has great views of the upper deck of this building. Alain and I get the inside balcony. The team will likely be wearing body armor, so aim for their heads and limbs."

"Why have two people to defend the inside balcony?" Don asked, shrugging his shoulders again. "And why am I only person with no back up? I'm alone in the master bedroom, and you all got partners."

"You're alone because you've got the best close range weapon and we are an odd number. As far as me and Alain, once we find out which downstairs entrance they use, Alain and I will be dropping over the balcony onto the first floor, coming at them from behind, and trying to push them up into the kill zone. If they don't attempt a downstairs entry, consider us the reserve. We'll come to wherever they've entered the building."

"So we just shoot anything that moves in the living room?" Jack asked.

"The living room drapes will be drawn and there will be one lone dim light in the corner," Tommy explained, tossing baseball-sized hand grenades to Jack, Chandler, and Don. "The minute they breach the double doors, I want Chandler and Jack to toss these into the living room through your gun slits. Don, I want you to wait and toss yours into the stairwell five seconds later. Hopefully the timing will match each group's entry into the kill zone. Once the third grenade explodes, standup and start pumping lead into the living room. Shoot at anything moving."

Caroline asked, "And what are Sandy and I doing on the roof next door?"

"The minute the first grenade goes off, you're cleared to open fire. You need to mow anyone down who steps back out on the deck from the living room. You need to keep them in the kill zone as long as possible," Tommy explained as he took two of the Remington shotguns from Alain and handed one to Caroline and one to Sandy. "Each shotgun has five rounds, so use them wisely. Until I signal that this is over, anytime you see someone step out onto the deck, shoot first, ask questions later. We don't want anyone escaping from the back deck."

"Why all the drama?" Chandler asked, closely watching Alain for his reaction, "Why even confront them? Why don't we just move to a different building, let them come in, and find it empty, and go away? Why a confrontation at all?"

"Because we're playing head games with John Smith. We want him to feel hopelessness when this is all over. If his men were turned away at one of the defensive positions around the village or were to enter this building but had to go away empty handed, John Smith would feel like there was still hope. He would believe that he just needs to get us into the right circumstances. On the other hand, if one of his men were to return and describe the thrashing we will be meting out on his men, he will know that taking us by force is impossible, and he'll have to deal with me on my terms."

Don asked, "We're going to let one of them survive?"

"One," Tommy replied somberly. "One to describe to John Smith a massacre of his making. One to convince John Smith to play ball on my terms."

CHAPTER 53

One mile northeast of Haad Salad, Koh PhaNgan, Thailand, 13 December 2016:

At the base of a small gulch, just northeast of Haad Salad to the side of a narrow concrete road, a group of fifteen men huddled around a Ford Ranger with a map of the area spread out across its hood. The men were dressed in black uniforms, with matching black armor and web gear. Each of the thirteen men had a helmet with night vision goggles mounted on top and was carrying a Heckler and Koch MP5 submachine gun. The sun had set several hours prior and the surrounding dark jungle seemed threatening, as a soft breeze carried the scent of its wildness across the scene.

Directing the beam of a flashlight onto the map, a stout man explained how the men were to get into the village. He then moved the map aside and laid out a diagram of the building.

"The building is made up of two floors," the stout man explained in a husky voice. "The ground floor is made up of two rooms—a bar and a kitchen. The upper floor is the living quarters and is made up of a living area, two bedrooms, and two bathrooms. The floors are connected by a staircase running between the downstairs kitchen and upstairs living room on the inside, and a set of stairs on the outside leading up to a back deck."

"Where will they most like be?" one of the men asked.

"Our targets—" the stout man answered, pulling pictures

of Tommy, Jack, and Sandy out and laying them on top of the diagram. "—will most likely be in the living quarters, upstairs. We will break down into two teams. Team one will breach the downstairs back door first. Two men will proceed into the kitchen and cut the electricity, two more members of that team will proceed into the bar to ensure it is empty. Team two will drop a concussion grenade into the living room when they hear the downstairs breach and once it goes off, enter the living quarters, proceeding directly into the two bedrooms. If the downstairs is empty, team one will proceed up the stairs and back team two up. If the targets are in the bar area, team two will proceed down the stairs and back team one up."

"What of the agent who has been assigned to ensure the targets are in the building?" another black-clad man asked.

Limping forward with the moon light reflecting off his two silver canes, John Smith answered, "He's expendable. You are to terminate everyone in the building and retrieve the hard-drive."

The men all turned and looked to the east as the distant sound of gunfire began.

"That's our signal," the stout man directed his team, "We need to get moving."

CHAPTER 54

Chaloklum, Koh PhaNgan, Thailand, 13 December 2016:

The guestroom was dark and both men were silent, when Chandler heard the distant gunfire over the air conditioner quietly humming on the far wall. Sitting on the floor with his back to the concrete wall, he calmly looked over at Jack's hulking shadow next to him before laying his Colt Frontier down and picking up the grenade Tommy had given him. Placing his finger through the ring at the end of the pin, he prepared for the inevitable clash with the professional mercenaries. Looking at Jack's shadow again, Chandler watched the big man place the Saturday Night Special down on the floor and mimic his action with the grenade.

Whispering in the darkness, Chandler asked, "Are you Canadian or English?"

"How intoxicated are you?"

"Not at all."

"Then I'm English."

Cocking his head to one side in the darkness, Chandler said, "Well, whatever you are, God save the Queen."

"Just make sure you don't drop that thing before slipping it through the gun-slit," Jack whispered back, a shadowy hand gesturing to the grenade. "I would hate to have to throw a fellow countryman atop a live grenade."

"You're right about one thing." Chandler chuckled. "There's only one man in this room that's capable of tossing the other about. What shall I do if you drop your grenade?"

"Jump on it," Jack quietly answered. "Or wait for me to toss you on it."

Sitting back and waiting, Chandlery could hear Jack's heavy breathing in the darkness, and he could feel sweat building up on his brow, despite the cool air cascading down from the air conditioner. Suddenly, Chandler heard Tommy's dog on the balcony let out a single ominous bark. Five minutes later, the entire building shook from a blast someplace on the ground floor that was quickly followed by an ear splitting explosion in the living room on the other side of the wall. Pulling the pin from the grenade, Chandler reached up and dropped it through the gun slit above his head, before looking over at Jack sitting next to him and watching him do the same. Several seconds later the two grenades exploded, shaking dust from the overhead ceiling, followed by a third five seconds later.

Nodding to Jack, Chandler picked up his Colt Frontier and stood up before placing the muzzle of the weapon through the gun slits. As rounds peppered the wall on the far side, Chandler took aim at the shadowy figures and began to pull the trigger.

The guestroom echoed with the sound of the firing Colt Frontier and the Saturday Night Special, and the smell of spent gunpowder filled the room. A round from the men on the far side found its way through the gun slit and whistled passed Chandler's cheek, another two bounced off the guestroom's back wall.

Suddenly the guestroom door exploded inward, sending fragments of wood across the room and knocking Chandler to the floor. As two heavily armed men dressed in black burst into the room, Chandler brought the muzzle of his Colt Frontier up and pulled the trigger twice in a quick succession.

The first man grabbed his neck and folded against the wall, before slipping to the floor. The second grabbed his crotch and fell forward onto the floor, before Chandler put another round into the back of his head.

"Put him out of his misery?" Jack asked with a grunt in the turmoil, glancing toward him from the gun slit.

"I did the man a favor. A life with no penis is no life at all," Chandler replied, looking over his shoulder as he crawling over to the shattered door.

Continuing to shoot at the shadowy figures in the next room, he tagged one racing for cover in the bathroom next to the small refrigerator, and spinning the black clad man through the door. Aiming at another, when he pulled the trigger the hammer came down with a dry click. Rolling onto his back, away from the door, Chandler opened the cylinder and dropped the spent shell cases on the floor, before reloading his weapon. As he prepared to return to the door, the sound of the fire fight ebbed as the shadows in the living room dropped to the floor one by one.

When the return fire died down, Chandler stood up next to the wall, before looking over at Jack, who was still attempting to acquire targets in the living room through his gun-slit. Moving back to the shattered door, Chandler heard a loud blast from the living room before peering out the door. He watched Don moving from the bathroom next to the small refrigerator to the double doors leading to the upper deck. Stepping out of the guestroom, over the two bodies, Chandler moved down the steps leading to the ground floor.

At the base of the steps, Chandler turned the corner of the stairwell into the kitchen and ran headlong into Alain. Glaring at each other in the shadows for a moment, Alain suddenly raised his shotgun and pulled the trigger. The flash blinded Chandler, his eardrums screamed, and his skin burned as the buckshot sped past his neck and cheek, striking a man clad in black behind him.

Rubbing his cheek, Chandler growled, "The French are all the same. They feel so inferior to the rest of Europe that they are constantly trying to prove their manhood."

"I may be French but I am different," Alain hissed, with a thin smile on his face. "And you English are no better. You are all so proud that you cannot utter the words 'thank you for saving my pitiful life.' You are no better."

"You bloody nearly killed me, you fucking frog!" Chandler snarled, "And you want me to thank you?"

"Ah, but do not worry, Chandler, I will kill you some day," Alain spat back, "just not today," before brushing past him and climbing the stairs to the second floor.

Calling after him, Chandler said, "The day a frog gets the better of me is the day I deserve to die."

Turning and walking out of the kitchen, Chandler looked out onto the patio through shattered wooden doors in time to see a dim flash and hear a thump from the upper deck.

CHAPTER 55

The moon overhead cast a dim glow over the buildings in the village and the bay could be heard gently rocking across the beach. Silently sitting in the shadows on the roof top next door, Sandy couldn't help but flinch when distant gunfire began someplace over the ridgeline to the south. Looking over at Caroline, she saw the blonde blue-eyed woman looking back. She then glanced over to the brightly lit deck next door and wondered when the hit men would arrive and how the attack would begin.

"Won't be long now," Caroline whispered, almost as if talking to herself.

Sandy replied with a simple nod of her head.

Looking down at the Remington shotgun in her hand, Sandy wondered what her husband was thinking, knowing that he too could hear the diversion taking place. She knew that he was more than capable of taking care of himself, but after years of marriage and two children, she couldn't help but worry about a stray bullet or some event that might injure him. Silently cursing herself for worrying, she tried to concentrate on getting through the next few minutes, knowing that once the shooting began, her mind would need to be focused on the task at hand.

It was nearly twenty minutes later when Sandy heard a faint bark from within the building. It was a strange inauspicious howl that sent a shiver up her spine. Five minutes later, she saw shadows moving between the buildings, and she nudged Caroline. Twelve more shadows followed the first along the side of the buildings and split up under the deck. Crawling over to the edge of the roof, Sandy could feel bead of sweat slowly work its way down her temple and cheek.

Heavily armed men dressed in black silently moved up the steep wooden staircase onto the back deck. Hunched over, one maneuvered to the edge of double doors and pulled a small canister from his web gear. Suddenly there was a bright strobe of light and terrific explosion on the patio below, and Sandy knew that the black-clad men had just breached the first floor. The man at the edge of the double doors pushed one side slightly open and tossed the canister under the curtains and inside the upper living room. Just as the man backed off from the double doors, another tremendous flash of light and a deafening explosion, and all the windows and double doors blew outward. Shards of glass flew over the crouching men and sprayed the upper deck. Knowing it was almost time to go to work, Sandy pushed the barrel of the shotgun over the edge of the waist high wall she was leaning against. Out of the corner of her eye, she saw Caroline do the same.

The men leapt to their feet and rushed past the drawn curtains into the living room, momentarily disappearing from her sight. Two simultaneous flashes and explosions, followed by a third, from behind the curtains, and one of the armed men stumbled back out onto the deck. Sandy took aim and pulled the trigger on the Remington. The shotgun popped in her shoulder and the sound the gunpowder exploding and propelling the buckshot through the barrel, was punctuated by a bright flash from its muzzle. The man dressed in black took the full brunt of the buckshot in his chest, picking him up and knocking him over the railing. She felt a wave of calmness, as she watched his body drop into the narrow opening between the two buildings.

A second man dressed in black pushed through the shattered double doors wildly shooting back into the living room. Sandy calmly pulled the pump back on the shotgun, automatically expelling the spent cartridge and pushing a new round into the chamber, before taking aim. The man looked her direction, as she began squeezing the trigger. Realizing what was happening, he jumped back into the mayhem of the living room, avoiding the buckshot that erupted from the end of her shotgun.

Faint smoke drifted from between the curtains as the shooting slowly ebbed and Sandy lowered her weapon, breathing a sigh of relief. A few moments later there was a final flash and blast in the living room before Don stepped out on the deck. Sandy watched as he looked up and down the beach, before ejecting a spent cartridge and placing a new round in his M79. Hearing a lone shotgun blast from someplace on the ground floor, she was captivated by Don's calmness. Mesmerized, she watched him step up to the rail, lick and raise his index finger, and then cant his weapon upward and to the west. She watched in fascination as he pulled the trigger of his weapon, and with a thump, the weapon spit a projectile out that arced out over the beach.

CHAPTER 56

The dog, sitting between Alain and Tommy, let out a snarl and one menacing yowl. It was not the usual canine bark, but something that came from deep within the dog, that stood the hairs up on Alain's head. Five minutes later an explosion of the downstairs breach sent fragments of wood shards across the long wooden counter and pool table, as Alain crouched on the upper indoor balcony. Below him, he saw two armed men dressed in black step to the edge of the bar, one inspecting behind the counter, before they turned and disappeared. A muffled blast from behind told him that the armed men had just breached the living room upstairs.

Slipping over the edge of the balcony, Alain dropped behind the long wooden counter. Two more muffled explosions followed by a third indicated that Chandler, Jack, and Don had detonated their grenades. Hearing Tommy and then the dog drop down next to him, Alain slowly moved around the edge of the counter and saw the shadow of three men standing at the entrance looking into the kitchen.

Standing up in the darkness, Alain pulled the trigger of the shotgun he held at his waist. Flames erupted from the muzzle as the piercing shot echoed across the bar and tossed two of the men aside.

As he pulled back on the shotgun's pump, the third man turned and began spraying to room with rounds from an automatic weapon. The wooden counter next to him exploded into fragments as the rounds torn across the room. A second deafening shot picked the man up and threw him against the wall, telling Alain that Tommy was standing close by.

A fourth figure appeared in the wreckage of the back double door, but before Alain could bring his weapon to bear, he heard Tommy say, "Get 'em, Dog!"

The blue-and-gray-eyed dog raced across the bar and jumped on the man's chest, savagely grabbing the man's throat. Both the dog and man fell backward through the doorway onto the remnants of the shattered door. Alain could hear the man scream and the dog snarl. Within seconds it was silent.

Slipping from behind the counter, Alain cautiously approached the kitchen entrance, placing his back next to the wall on one side of the door. He saw Tommy slip past and place his back against the wall on the other side. Looking over, he nodded to Tommy's shadowy figure, and both men spun into the entrance, each firing their weapon into the space. The flash of the shots illuminated two more men standing at the base of the stairs. The two were thrown back as the buckshot penetrated their armor, dropping them to the floor.

"Sounds like its dying down upstairs," Tommy whispered. "I'm going out back to see what's going on."

"I will stay here to make sure no one escapes back down into the kitchen," Alain replied.

Watching the base of the stairwell, Alain pumped a new round into the chamber of shotgun. Hearing a rustling coming down the stairs, Alain began squeezing the trigger. When Chandler appeared around the corner of the stairwell, he reluctantly let the pressure off the trigger.

As they glared at each other, a shadow appeared from behind Chandler. Alain swiftly brought his weapon up to shoulder height and pulled the trigger. The muzzle, right next to Chandler's neck and face, let out a flash and loud crack that reverberated across the kitchen.

After watching the man dressed in black fall to the floor, Alain looked at Chandler's expression, and smiled. It was the first time Alain had ever seen the Englishman express anything but calmness. Even during their encounter at a grocery store in Thongsala, where he had killed Chandler's friend, the Englishman had never looked alarmed. But at this moment, having had a shotgun fired next to his face, Chandler's cool façade had crumbled slightly.

CHAPTER 57

With his ears ringing and the smell of spent gunpowder wafting the air, Don threw the master bedroom door open and stepped out into the living room. Inside the room, littered with heavily armed bodies dressed in black, he heard a moan from the bathroom next to the small refrigerator. Stepping over the bodies, he maneuvered up next to the bathroom door and placed his back against the wall before slipping the muzzle of the M-79 around the corner and pulling the trigger.

The bathroom flashed as earsplitting blast echoed across the living room, before he peeked around the corner to check out his handy work. His blind aim had done the job. Another heavily armed black clad man was wrapped around a shattered porcelain toilet with water spouting from a broken water line.

Turning, Don serenely walked across the room, stepping over the carnage, and out onto the back deck. Looking up and down the beach, to the west he saw two more black clad men jogging, one in front of the other, down the wide ribbon of sand away from the faded yellow building. Stepping up to the rail, Don reached into his cargo pants and extracted a single M79 round with a rounded green projectile mounted at its end. Depressing the button on the side of the weapon the muzzle swung down on small hinges attaching it to the receiver, revealing the chamber and the buckshot casing. Pulling the used buckshot round from the chamber, he dropped it onto the deck. The hollow casing hit the deck with a faint ping and then rolled off the side onto the concrete patio below. He then slipped the round-tipped projectile into the chamber before snapping the muzzle closed, as a lone shotgun blast rang out from someplace on the ground floor.

Licking his index finger, he raised it over his head and felt a slight breeze from the water. After reacquiring the two jogging men, Don aimed the M79, shifting it to account for the breeze, and pulled the trigger. The weapon jerked in his hands, a bright flash and loud thump advertising that the grenade was on its way down range. Dropping the weapon to his side, he leaned against one of the roof supports as he watched the small shadowy projectile arc over the beach in the moonlight. The grenade dropped between the two running targets, and a bright strobe like flash was followed by a faint explosion, and small plume of shrapnel and sand, knocking the two men to the beach.

"Don!" Tommy groaned, as he stepped up behind the silver haired man. "We wanted one of those guys to escape."

"Those were your instructions," Don replied, looking over his shoulder at Tommy, "but, Tommy, if I'd let them go that would have made two and you just wanted one."

"Two escaping would have been acceptable," Tommy muttered, shaking his head.

"Look, Tommy," Don admitted. "I was aiming behind the last guy and figured that with a good shot I could take him down and leave the front guy running. I could have done it back in Vietnam, but I gotta tell you, I haven't fired one of these things in over forty years. In my books, that was a damn good shot, considering the circumstances."

CHAPTER 58

Baan Tai, Koh PhaNgan, Thailand, 28 July 2015:

John Smith and Steve had just finished a late dinner, and were sitting in the hotel restaurant waiting to pay their bill. They were planning on leaving the island the next morning. A soft warm breeze blew across the outdoor restaurant and a waning moon stood high in the night sky, creating a fine network of shadows midst the palms trees surrounding them.

Both men looked tired after their previous evening at Haad Sadet. It took them nearly two hours to realize that the delivery was not going to take place on the beach, and when John Smith spotted Becky on a balcony of one of the cliff side bungalows, he knew that Tommy had once again outwitted him. At that moment, John Smith realized he would be hard pressed to ever find Tommy again. Especially if he had successfully delivered the flash-drive to Aslan.

It was then that John Smith decided to breach the organization's security protocol and approach Jainukul. John Smith had secretly kept Jainukul informed of the deliveries, hoping he would save him the trouble of eliminating Tommy, and he knew that any death at the hands of the Thai gangster would be slow and painful. He liked the idea of a slow and painful death for his deliveryman.

Jainukul still had the best chance of finding and killing Tommy so John Smith gave the Thai gangster his disobedient agent, Becky. Becky had obviously teamed up with his deliveryman and knowing that Tommy's one weakness was his loyalty, she could be used as bait. Giving Becky to Jainukul would also save John Smith the trouble of eliminating her.

John Smith was silently pondering how he would eliminate his companion, Steve. Sitting at the table next to his lone remaining agent, John Smith decided that he would enter Steve's room later that night and complete the task. He would then depart the hotel and hire a speed boat to Koh Samui before the sun came up. He could be on a plane to Bangkok before the hotel staff found the body.

Steve asked, "Did you ever reach Aslan?"

"Aslan called this morning as he was getting ready to climb aboard his employer's private jet. Considering I spent most of last night trying to contact him to find out whether he received the flash-drive, it was nice of him to have the courtesy to call back," John Smith answered with thick sarcasm in his voice.

"What about Mr. Jones?"

"He called last night wanting an update. All I could do was to tell him I thought the delivery took place but I wasn't sure. He seemed oddly relaxed at the news. After I called back this morning to confirm the delivery had taken place, he congratulated me." Then after a brief hesitation, John Smith added, "Something about this whole delivery has been off. Mr. Jones's part was far more prevalent than our previous delivery operations."

"What do you mean?"

"He provided the merchandise. He wanted daily updates. He demanded that we deliver the merchandise, even when things were well out of control. In the past, he would only call when he had pertinent information."

John Smith's cell phone began to ring, interrupting their conversation. Looking down at the cell's small screen, he saw Aslan's number on the caller ID. A smile crossed John Smith's face as he thought to himself that at least one person was truly happy with the outcome.

"Aslan, what can I do for you? I hope you had a pleasant trip back home," John Smith answered the call.

"You are a dead man," Aslan's thick Turkish accent growled.

"What's the problem?"

"You are a dead man. My organization will find out who you are. They will find out where your family lives. You and your family will be dead within the week."

"Aslan, I have no idea what the problem is," John Smith replied, sincerely confused. "Why are you threatening me?"

"You merchandise was a computer virus. It was not what you advertised. When it was downloaded, it sent all my employer's electronic files to another site and then erased everything. We are dead. I am running from them now, and like you, they will find me."

Aslan disconnected the line before John Smith could reply.

Seeing the concern on John Smith's face, Steve asked, "What was that all about?"

"According to Aslan, the flash-drive was nothing more than a virus," John Smith responded as he pushed back his chair. "I'm going to bed. Let's meet in the lobby tomorrow morning at six."

Leaving Steve at the table, John Smith walked back to his room. He was deep in thought about the recent events and all the problems he had had to overcome to ensure a successful delivery. But in the end, it appeared he had failed. John Smith was tired and confused.

The hallway was dark as John Smith placed his key into the room's lock. As he turned the handle to open the door, he felt a blade slip between the ribs in his back next to his spine. It was a quick upward thrust that buried the blade to the hilt and, before he could react, his attacker shifted the hilt of the blade. His lower torso and legs exploded in a tingling sensation, as if he had been hit with a Taser. His door swung opened and John Smith stumbled into his room, painful surges blasting down his legs with each step. His attacker entered behind him and closed the door.

John Smith turned, his back screaming in agony, but he couldn't make out his assailant's features in the darkness. He could feel energy draining from his body.

"Sorry, John Smith. Orders are orders," a calming voice spoke, strangely easing John Smith.

"Whose orders?" John Smith weakly asked, as he crumpled onto the floor next to the bed, the tingling sensation painfully accentuating his impact with the floor.

"Mr. Jones requested that I take care of you," the soft voice replied. "The inspector general's office has identified you as a member of the organization."

"Something's wrong. Someone has played me," John Smith muttered, looking up at the shadowy profile above.

"The only thing wrong is that you are dying. Goodbye, John Smith. The world won't miss you."

John Smith's last thought, before losing consciousness, was wondering if Jainukul would ever find Tommy. Little did he know that Jainukul and his remaining son had been killed just an hour earlier in Fisherman's Village on the island of Koh Samui.

CHAPTER 59

Thongsala, Koh PhaNgan, Thailand, 14 December 2016:

S tanding on a balcony overlooking the Gulf of Thailand and the distant islands of Ang Thong Marine Park, John Smith recalled the day he was stabbed in the back on this very island. He remembered waking several days later in a hospital on Koh Samui, lying on his stomach in a small room that smelt of antiseptic. He had wanted to scream as a searing pain stretched from his toes to the base of his skull. He remembered how his fingers had involuntarily grabbed the sheets of the bed and began to squeeze. The pain had been overwhelming, and he had been incapable of putting two words together. He had groaned. He had grunted. He had screamed.

He remembered how a nurse had briskly walked into the room and given him an injection. The prick from the needle had been indiscernible to the greater throbbing down his spinal cord and legs. Slowly the pain had begun to retreat.

He would learn over the next few days that it had been Steve's quick actions that had saved his life. Finding him on the floor of his room, Steve had called the front desk for an ambulance before shoving a piece of fabric he had ripped from a towel into the gaping hole in his back. Unbeknownst to Steve, that act had momentarily plugged a small hole in John Smith's aorta, stopping the bleeding long enough to get him on an operating table and save his life. Sadly, that single thrust of a knife had also nicked his spinal cord, leaving him in constant pain.

Over time, John Smith would come to blame Tommy Luck for the incident and the relentless pain he felt from the damage the attacker had inflicted. Had Tommy Luck just delivered the flash-drive as it had been scripted, John Smith would still be a whole man.

Breaking his thoughts from the not-so-distant memory, John Smith placed both his canes in one hand and took his cell phone from his pocket. Finding the contact number he wanted, he sighed before pressing the call button. A light breeze blew across the deck, carrying with it the smell of the jungle as the phone at the other end began to ring.

"What is it?" a voice gruffly answered.

"We need to go covered," John Smith muttered into the phone, glancing over his shoulder at Steve sitting on the couch.

After a brief moment, two beeps signified that the phone was in encryption mode and a now tinny voce repeated the question, "What is it?"

"Tommy called this morning. He will only give the hard-drive to one of the Patriarchs," John Smith explained.

"What of the girl and the attack on his building?"

Hesitating a moment, John Smith reluctantly said, "They're all missing. One of our people questioned several Chaloklum residents, and word is that the building was attacked, but all the attacking men were killed."

"And the woman?"

"No one knows her fate," John Smith answered. "I can only surmise she has been killed."

"And Thomas Bacon Luck survived?"

"Yes."

"And he called you this morning? Did he verify the attack took place and failed."

"He made an obtuse comment about Davey's Locker and the assault team."

After a long sigh, the tinny voice said, "You are pathetic, Mr. Smith. Even with all the assets of the Society, you can't retrieve a simple hard-drive from an unemployed drunk."

"He has very loyal friends who seem to be ready to do whatever it takes to support him."

"Excuses," the tinny voice growled. "Why does he want to give the hard-drive to one of the Patriarchs? What is he up to?"

"He didn't say."

The tinny voice was silent for a moment, then asking, "He asked to meet with one of the Patriarchs and did not request a particular one?"

"Yes."

"He left the decision up to you as to which he would meet?"

"I assume that he's leaving it up to the Patriarchs as to which one will meet with him," John Smith responded.

"Does he know anything about our business relationship and plan?"

"I can't see how he could have that kind of knowledge," John Smith muttered, shifting his weight to his left foot to relieve a growing pain in his back.

"Why does he think giving the hard-drive to one of the Patriarchs will change his situation?"

"He didn't say," John Smith repeated. "Maybe he thinks he can negotiate his survival with the Patriarchs—avoiding the middleman and going to the source."

Another moment of silence, and the tinny voice said, "You have underestimated him at every turn because you're thinking behind his decision cycle. He knows you're under orders from the Patriarchs to retrieve the hard-drive and terminate him and his friends. Why would he now want to talk to one of us? Given the facts, he must know that, even with a meeting, his situation won't change."

"I can't get to him," John Smith replied. "His friends will protect him at all cost. The only way we're getting the hard-drive is for one of the Patriarchs to meet with him."

"Something is not right," the tinny voice commented again. "Caroline knows each of the Patriarchs and could easily give him advice as to which to choose. She also knows that the Patriarchs cannot operate independently. Giving you, a man he despises, the choice of which Patriarch he is to meet reeks of naivety. And Mr. Luck is not stupid. He has a something up his sleeve."

John Smith nodded. "He's not stupid."

"And he knows you can't send a decoy because he has Caroline there to verify that he's meeting with one of the actual Patriarchs. So he knows that he will be meeting a Patriarch. He knows his current situation is due to the orders from the Patriarchs and isn't likely to change with a meeting. What's his plan? He must have something up his sleeve. He either has something he can show that will convince us to leave him alone, or he's trying to weed one of us out—and you're sure he has no idea about our business relationship or plan?"

"Absolutely. There is no way he could have that kind of information."

"I didn't rise to the level I hold by being stupid or gullible," the tinny voice growled. "I sense something dubious in Mr. Luck's request."

"I can't imagine what it could be," John Smith said, shifting his weight again while wishing he had made the phone call from the comfort of the couch. "Maybe he suspects that I plan on using the hard-drive to blackmail the Society. Maybe he thinks that by delivering it to one of the Patriarchs, he will have ruined my plans, and he can convince you to spare him and his friends."

"Ask him if he'll deliver it to all three of the Patriarchs. Let's see what his reaction is. If he agrees to those terms, then we'll consider his request legitimate."

"Won't that ruin our plan?"

"I'll show up alone and honor his first request."

"And if he says no?"

"Then we'll know he's trying to identify one of us."

CHAPTER 60

Chaloklum, Koh PhaNgan, Thailand, 14 December 2016:

The sun reflected off the crystal clear bay as colorful fishing boats bobbed next to the long concrete pier, unloading their nightly catch. The four of them were sitting on the deck of the faded yellow building, silently mulling over the events from the previous evening. Other than the shattered doors and windows, it was hard for any of them to believe that a violent encounter had occurred there the night before. Caroline was gently rocking back and forth on the red and green hammock, Tommy was sitting in a light blue cushioned wicker chair gently stroking the dog's head while drinking a bottle of cold Singha, and Jack and Sandy sat on wooden chairs next at a table holding hands.

"Your plan is coming together nicely, Tommy," Caroline commented from the hammock, sipping a glass of white wine.

"And that worries me," Tommy mumbled, now spinning the cold bottle of Singha on a small round table in front of him. "I made my request to meet with one of the Patriarchs. Soon after, John Smith countered my offer and asked if I would be willing to meet with all three."

"Have you given him an answer?" Caroline asked.

"No," Tommy responded.

Sandy turned to Tommy with a questioning expression. "Why in the world would a counter offer to meet with all the Patriarchs bother you? John smith has been defeated, and he's now been forced to call his boss and ask him to meet with you. They have decided it's best if all the Patriarchs are at the meeting. This thing is really coming together."

"Darling," Jack commented. "Tommy has gotten us this far, and I am sure he has sound reasons for being worried."

"Something doesn't feel right," Tommy replied, picking up the bottle of beer and taking a swallow. "I've got this gut feeling that something's not right."

Jack shrugged his massive shoulders and raised his thick eyebrows before saying, "I'm not sure a gut feeling qualifies as a sound reason—darling, never mind. That was an excellent observation."

Sitting up in the hammock, Caroline said, "Its standard operating procedure. The Patriarchs can't act alone. All three would have to attend. What's worrying you?"

"They know me to be pretty good at getting out of messes. They know I know the orders to terminate us and retrieve the hard-drive come from the very same people that I requested a meeting with. They also know that I know that a meeting with a Patriarch will produce nothing."

Now shrugging her shoulders, Sandy asked, "And?"

"The Patriarchs aren't stupid people. They're rich and successful. They've risen through the business ranks because of their intellect and cunning. Remember, we think that one of the Patriarchs is in cahoots with John Smith and our plan was designed to smoke that Patriarch out. Instead of agreeing to a meeting with one, which would identify the corrupt Patriarch, they now counter with an offer to meet with all three."

It was Jack's turn to ask, "And?"

"Whoever John Smith contacted after I made my request asked the same question I did and came to the same conclusion I did: a meeting is useless, so why does he want to meet with me unless he knows something or has a plan?"

"And this is your way of informing us that your plan has a hole," Jack replied, more as a statement than a question. "I recall pointing out several holes the other day."

"It's a good plan, but I think I left some needed detail out," Tommy admitted. "And I'm unsure what kind of additional detail is needed for the plan to be successful."

"I see what you're saying," Sandy replied, before taking three long swallows of beer. "It was a great simple plan, but maybe too simple. They want the hard-drive and you've offered to give it to a Patriarch. The hard-drive was to be the cheese and the bad Patriarch was to be the mouse. We figured he wouldn't care about the consequences. He just wanted the cheese. John Smith contacted him and relayed your request, and he saw through the plan. So he counters the offer with a meeting with all three. But he can't do that because it will ruin his plan. So why does he make the offer? He can't allow a meeting with all three."

"Because he wants to see your reaction," Caroline offered. "If you agree, he'll know that you simply want to give the hard-drive back. If you don't agree, he'll know you were trying to single him out. So you agree to a meeting with all three, he knows that your request was sincere, and he comes alone. He wants the cheese but needs to protect himself. At this point, we have to realize that he suspects that you suspect one of the Patriarchs is a bad apple. He won't come to the meeting with the other two Patriarchs, but he will come suspecting you're setting a trap. He'll have his own plan to protect himself from Tommy's unknown end game."

Groaning, Jack said, "So we need a new plan to protect ourselves from his plan that has been devised to protect himself from Tommy's plan. Please let me go back to the courtroom and deal with criminal deceit and lies. It's a far easier profession to understand. You'll next be telling me that he knows you will have a plan to protect yourself from his plan and therefore be required to devise another plan to protect himself, and we will need to devise yet another plan to protect ourselves from that.

"It is a bit like a room full of mirrors," Tommy replied, looking over and smiling at Jack's hulking figure.

"Do you have any ideas?" Caroline asked Tommy, as she laid back into the hammock.

"I've got one," Tommy replied, nodding his head. "It's pretty simple but it just might work—because of its simplicity."

"And you do recall," Jack pointed out, "that simplicity created the problem in the first place."

"Do you care to elaborate?" Sandy asked.

Standing up and walking over to the rail, Tommy looked out over the bay, its waters shimmering in the mid-day sun. Looking over to Caroline swinging in the hammock, Tommy asked, "Caroline, do you have the Society membership roster?"

"Emails, addresses, the whole enchilada." She laughed. "What in the world is swirling through that twisted mind of yours?"

"Simplicity at its best." Tommy chuckled back. "I won't contact John Smith with my answer—I need you to send our answer to all three Patriarchs requesting a meeting. Then we'll send a couple of emails out just as my meeting with the Patriarchs come to a conclusion."

The dog looked up and barked twice.

"The dog agrees," Tommy announced, patting the dog on the head. "And in my books that is as good as a guarantee to victorious outcome."

"This talking to your dog is becoming worrisome," Jack commented.

Looking over at Jack, Tommy said, "This dog is different."

"Like Alain," Jack muttered.

"Like Alain but his opposite. This dog has a heart."

"Please stop the bantering. It gets old very quickly," Sandy said, shaking her head. "You think all three Patriarchs will show up?"

"We want all of them to show up," Tommy said, looking back out over the bay. "We want them all there."

CHAPTER 61

Chevy Chase, Maryland, USA, 14 December 2016:

The spacious bookcase-lined room smelled of a mixture of whiskey and aftershave, as the three older men sat around the large stone fireplace. A snow-covered lawn surrounded by bare trees with icicle-laden limbs could be seen through long-paned windows edged with frost. Beyond the snowy scene, heavy traffic whisked along Connecticut Avenue, indicating that it was nearing rush hour. The dormant stone fireplace, not five feet away from where the men sat, seemed to radiate the coolness from outside. A blue and red Persian rug lined the floor and a wide silver chandelier hung overhead.

"While I trust her implicitly, I am concerned about this invitation from Caroline," Oliver Mason commented. Sitting in his customary position, a red-velvet chair to the left of the fireplace, Oliver scratched at his bald head with his left hand while holding Caroline's printed out email in his right. Looking up from the email, Oliver turned to his two colleagues to see their response to his comment.

"I believe we would be foolish to all attend such a meeting. Why doesn't just one of us attend?" Andres asked. He sat across from Oliver and on the right side of the fireplace in a high-backed and overstuffed chair covered in a floral fabric. Wearing a paisley vest over red suspenders, Andres stroked his unruly white beard with his right hand while holding a glass of bourbon in his left.

Sitting on a couch directly in front of the fireplace and

between his two colleagues, James asked, "Why on earth would he request a meeting with the same people who have issued a termination order on him? What does he have or know that would change our minds?" He began raising a crystal glass filled with sparkling water to his lips. Midway through the process, and with a faraway concerned expression, he reversed the motion and placed glass back down on the table next to the couch, as if changing his mind. "Maybe Mr. Luck has discovered the traitor in our midst."

"Please, James, I cannot possibly subscribe to the notion that one of us is involved in the theft of the hard-drive or working independently with John Smith." Oliver stated. "As I said during our last meeting, that notion is absurd."

"Let's not forget about the death of Kelley or the stolen video footage implicating Mr. Luck in the crime," James said. "An untimely interruption to an investigation that only the three of us were privy."

"The notion of one of us being a traitor is absurd," Oliver repeated in his distinct English accent. Again, looking over at his companions, he reached out to a small table besides the red-velvet chair and picked up a short glass filled with ice and brandy. "Possibly, he has some information concerning our executive assistant that he feels we need to know. Possibly, he wants to hand over the hard-drive to someone other than John Smith."

"Possibly he wants to get us all together in order to accomplish some Machiavellian scheme," Anders replied in his baritone like voice. "We would be foolish to all attend—again, I say only one of us attend."

"And when he notices that only one of us is to attend the meeting?" Oliver inquired, before raising the glass to his mouth and taking a sip of its brown liquid contents. "What if this is an honorable request that will result in an acceptable conclusion to the fiasco we find ourselves in?"

"We can ensure we're accompanied with adequate security," James commented, still appearing to be deep in thought.

"He would be foolish to attempt to harm us, considering the immense power of the Society," Oliver said, arching his white eyebrows. "He must know that the Society wouldn't take the murder of their Patriarchs lightly, and they would surely make him pay."

"And," James added. "There is the Caroline factor that we have all been ignoring. Here is a woman we all trust and respect, and we have chosen to listen to the likes of John Smith rather than observe her actions. She has chosen to fly halfway across the world to be with and support someone we placed a termination order on based on input from a man that is Mr. Luck's nemesis."

"Your attitude concerning John Smith surprises me," Oliver replied, looking at James. "Not too many days ago, you supported our temporary executive assistant, now you are questioning the same. What has changed your mind, James? I am interested in how you could have changed your mind so dramatically in such a short period of time."

"We are foolish if we all attend," Andres interjected again.

"We are foolish if we don't attend," James said. "John Smith has been outwitted at every turn by a man we attempted to hire into his position. Let's not forget why we wanted to hire Thomas Bacon Luck in the first place. We attempted to hire him because of his ability to accomplish difficult assignments, his uncanny knack for survival, his cleverness, and, most importantly, because he is honorable and loyal. The very friends who now protect him prove these facts. His word is his bond. He may be a drunk, but had we been successful in hiring him in the first place, none of this would have happened, and we would not find ourselves where we are at this moment."

"Then it's final," Oliver stated with an air finality. "We all attend the meeting with Mr. Luck—and then we offer him the job, once again."

CHAPTER 62

Madeua Wan, Koh PhaNgan, Thailand, 17 December 2016:

Sitting on the thick concrete banister, with blue porcelain Newel posts, that wrapped around the balcony of the Butterfly Bar with his feet dangling over the garden, Tommy, sat silently examining his jungle surroundings. Next to him sat Rodger's tall lean frame, toothy smile, and mop-like brown-and-white hair. The blue-and-gray-eyed dog and black dog sat at the entrance to the balcony. The two men, sitting side by side on the banister exuded a carefree aura over what should have been a tense moment.

With a high jungle-laden ridgeline behind, the Butterfly Bar provided stunning views of emerald green rolling hills and distant sparkling water of the gulf. Directly around the lone building, dense foliage, stout flowery bushes, sleek silver-barked trees, and tall coconut trees created a colorful and effervescent parameter.

Monkeys screeched and birds chirped from within, and the odor of both decaying and growing plant life mixed into a melody of scents that a light breeze carried across the balcony.

Confirming Tommy's earlier instructions, Rodger asked, "So I get to stay and see the action this time?"

Shifting on the banister, Tommy replied, "It should be safe enough, just an afternoon meeting with a several global power brokers who will undoubtedly bring a well-armed force—not to mention they have a desire to see me dead."

"That's a spirit-raising attitude. I'm sitting next to a

marked man but I'll be safe. Let's hope their marksmanship badges are up to date for my sake."

Laughing, Tommy said, "Don't worry, I've got this meeting under control. They won't hurt anyone."

The dog yapped a single bark, and Tommy said, "Ah, our visitors have nearly arrived."

Eight minutes later, both the men turned their heads toward the sound of revving engines heard coming up the dirt road below. Three black Toyota four-door HiLux pickups slowly crept rounded the corner, bouncing across the deep ruts as they moved up the road. Pulling up into a driveway below the Butterfly Bar balcony, on the far side of an enormous garden, two armed men hopped out of each of the truck beds, suspiciously examining the meeting location, and silently searching of the immediate surrounding area. Two of the men made a quick perimeter check around the building, two strode up to the Butterfly Bar and searched the balcony and bar area, and the final two walked inside the building, checking to see if anyone else was in the vicinity. After ensuring that Tommy and the tall gangly man next to him were the only two present, the six men met up back at the pickups and nodded to the passengers within.

The back doors of each swung open and six more armed men stepped from the pickups before the passenger doors slowly opened. Three old men climbed from the doors, each looking as if the time change from the United States to Thailand had been problematic.

Looking up at Tommy and Rodger, the older men mumbled something to one another and then began slowly climbing the steps to the balcony with three of the armed men following closely behind. Halfway up the steps Tommy swung his legs around the banister and stood up, all the while looking down at the men.

"That'll be far enough," Tommy called out.

A pear-shaped man, with hair resembling a balding monk, asked in a distinct English accent, "You expect us to conduct this meeting standing on a set of steep steps under a hot Southeast Asian mid-day sun?"

"It won't take long," Tommy responded.

A large portly man with unruly curly white hair and beard, loudly responded in a Scandinavian accent, "Where are your manners, young man? We've just spend sixteen hours traveling halfway around the world to a meeting you requested."

Smiling, Tommy replied, "Let's not forget you came to meet with a man you signed a termination order for and have been unsuccessfully endeavoring to retrieve a database from. If you expected good manners, then you've never learned the old adage 'you reap what you sow.'"

The final old man, slender and dressed in neatly pressed blue jeans and a white shirt, grunted in a North American accent, "Then let's get on with it," as he ran his right hand across the white stubble on the side of his bald head.

"Fair enough," Tommy replied, causally reaching up and scratching his nose.

A thump echoed across the jungle, and then sixteen simultaneous rifle shots rang out from within the jungle, piercing a racket of screeching monkeys and chirping birds. The two dogs lay oblivious to the turmoil as all twelve armed bodyguards dropped to the ground. A single grenade exploded between the awaiting trucks, flattening the tires of two. Three rocket propelled grenades flew from the jungle, between the silver-barked and tall coconut trees, striking the sides of the pickups at one time. All three trucks bucked sideways as the rounds penetrated their cabs and detonated, shattering the windows in a cloud of fire and shrapnel from within. The three older men shuddered at the violence, the pear-shaped man falling to his knees.

"What's this all about?" the slender man with a North American accent demanded after regaining his composure.

"At least one of you has been conspiring against the others and the Society," Tommy informed the trio. "And I was left with a problematic situation—one where I would have needed to find the culprit and risk my life, or one where I simply eliminate all three of you and start with a new batch of Patriarchs. Guess which one I chose?"

Pulling the Colt M1911 .45 from the small of his back, Tommy took aim on the old man on his knees and pulled the trigger. The round struck the man in the chest, and he tumbled backward down the concrete steps. Tommy then took aim on the slender old man with the white stubble and neatly pressed jeans, pulling the trigger again. The round hit the man in the left eye, and he spun to the ground before following the first and rolling down the steps.

"Please, please," the rotund Scandinavian with unruly white hair and a beard pleaded, as he dropped to his knees. "I am not the man you're looking for." Raising his hands above his head, he cried, "I know nothing about a business relationship with John Smith or any plan to coerce the Society."

"It's amazing what someone will tell you when their under duress," Rodger calmly commented, looking down at the man. "You didn't say anything about a business deal or any plan, and he just admitted to both."

Tommy sighed. "I should have just taken aim on him in the first place. He would have spilled the beans in front of his pals, and we could have all gone home," he said just before he pulled the trigger, dropping the fat man to the ground.

"Bon Jour, Tommy," Alain called out as he walked out of the jungle from the west, carrying a long scoped rifle. "What a *magnifique* day!"

Pushing a large bright green leaf aside, Don stepped from the jungle wearing green cargo pants and a blue and yellow Hawaiian shirt with his M79 grenade launcher over his shoulder. "Did you see that shot!" Don shouted in an excited New York accent, "I put that baby down right between those trucks!"

Eighteen other men wearing an assortment of shorts and T-shirts stepped out from the surrounding foliage carrying a collection of scoped rifles and RPGs, each examining the destruction at the foot of the Butterfly Bar. A tall man wearing a tattered white T-shirt walked over and nudged the obese older man with a flip-flop-clad foot. Another gently rocked the slender bald man in a similar fashion. And yet another kicked the pear-shaped man, all three ensuring that the Patriarchs were dead.

Climbing the stairs to the Butterfly Bar balcony, Alain continued, "Your plan was brilliant. You do not know which patriarch is bad so you eliminate all three. Clean the slate and start negotiations with a new set of Society Patriarchs who might see things a bit differently."

"Let's hope the new Patriarch board is a bit more lenient than the last." Tommy chuckled. "How did you manage to get all these men into position without being seen by the Thongsala mafia? They must be keeping a close watch over Madeua Wan after their failed diversion the other night."

"You think so little of my abilities, Tommy." Alain laughed as he walked up to Tommy and put his hand on his shoulder. "The failure at Madeua Wan weakened the Thongsala family and allowed me to expand my territory. Madeua Wan now belongs to me—as well as Mea Haad, Haad Salad, and Haad Yao. I have tripled the size of my territory."

Smiling at the good news, Tommy said, "Now we need to get out of here. I'm sure that John Smith probably had back up for the old men and they heard the ruckus. We don't want to find ourselves at a remake of the Alamo." Then looking over at Rodger, Tommy added, "You might want to join us for a drink in Chaloklum and allow John Smith and his crew time clean up our mess before the police arrive."

"You're not listening to me, Tommy." Alain lightheartedly laughed. "I own Madeua Wan. John Smith is nowhere nearby, and the police will come when I say it's time. I recommend we celebrate with a round of drinks and play a game or two of pool—the first round is on me."

CHAPTER 63

Chaloklum, Koh PhaNgan, Thailand, 17 December 2016:

Lying back on a lounge chair padded with red cushions on the immense deck of Alain's villa, Caroline, wrapped in a dark blue sarong, held her cell phone as she looked out over the vast Gulf of Thailand. A wide yellow umbrella above shielded her from the hot Southeast Asian sun, as she peered out beyond the deck to the bluish-green sea. She watched as a large tanker slowly crept across a horizon of calm water. She looked to west and watched a single white cloud hovering overhead, seemingly intensifying the blueness of the sky. She glanced left and then right at the dense emerald green jungle surrounding her. She was surrounded by a peaceful serenity but could not shake the anxiety that overcame her as she waited for the phone call.

"You look worried." Pann's soft voice interrupted her uneasy observations.

Glancing over her shoulder, Caroline watched Pann seemingly float out of the villa and replied, "I'm worried something might have gone wrong. The Patriarchs would not have come without protection."

"Yes," Pann softly said, sitting down on a green padded lounge next to Caroline. "But you must trust in Alain and Tommy's abilities. They live and survive in a world of constant violence—a world in which they are always outnumbered. They are among a small community in the world that violence cannot touch."

Taking a moment to look at the beautiful Thai woman sitting next to her, Caroline examined Pann's golden skin and large brown eyes. She studied her long black hair cascading over her shoulders. She scrutinized her long slender limbs and delicate fingers. She was taken in by the Pann's natural beauty and wondered why this woman had chosen such a violent man as her partner.

"Why would you choose this life?" Caroline asked, looking into Pann's large brown eyes, "Why would you chose to be surrounded by hostility when you could be anyplace with any man?"

Slowly nodding her head, Pann spoke quietly, her voice drifting over Caroline like soft music as she replied, "When you look at my husband, you see a violent and selfish man who places no value in human life. But what I see is a man who places his friends and acquaintances above his own regard. Yes, he has killed many men in his life. Yes, he seems to enjoy the excitement of the violence, but if you take a moment and think about when and why, you will see that it is never for himself. It is always for a just cause or the people he cares about." Then after a moment, she continued, "You do not see the soft and gentle man that lies down with me each night."

Lying back, Caroline closed her eyes and felt the day's heat soak into her body. It felt as if the warmth was cleansing her body of the past week's violence. As she lay on the lounge soaking up the sun, she considered Pann's words. Was it true? Was Tommy Luck one of those men who would survive anything? Maybe physically, but what about his soul? Could anyone survive what he had done and remain whole? She knew the answer.

The cell in her hand began ringing and vibrating, and she looked at the caller ID. Letting off a sigh of relief as Tommy's latest number flashed across the small screen, Caroline looked over at Pann. The beautiful Thai woman stood and smiled down at her before floating back inside the villa.

Placing the cell to her ear, she greeted Tommy with, "Tell me it's over."

"It's over, send the email."

"Did any of the patriarchs say anything?"

"I didn't give them a chance," Tommy admitted. "It didn't matter, with one being bad, I couldn't trust any one of them."

"You didn't find out which one was working with John Smith?"

"The fat one," Tommy responded, before the line went dead.

"Andres," Caroline whispered to herself, before closing the cell. Picking up her laptop from a small table to the right, she made sure the email was addressed to all the Society bishops, and then reviewed the message one last time before hitting the send button.

Dear Society Bishops,

The classified hard-drive containing a list of the Society's members and history, documenting each of its operations was stolen on 5 December 2016. This hard-drive was subsequently discovered by two individuals acting within and in accordance with the laws of the United States on 6 December 2016. Due to the sensitivity of the information contained on the hard-drive, the Society Patriarchs issued a termination order on these two individuals. The Patriarch's executive assistant has endeavored to terminate the individuals and retrieve the hard-drive.

Over the course of events, it was revealed that one of the Patriarchs was involved in theft of the hard-drive. I have personally reviewed this evidence and agree with this conclusion. Clearly the intent of the guilty Patriarch was to utilize the information contained on the hard-drive to coerce and control the Society.

Due to the inability to discover the identity of the culpable Patriarch, all three have been terminated. The hard-drive remains safe and will be returned to the Society once a new board of Patriarchs has been established. Please feel free to contact me in regards to any questions you might have.

See attached.
Best Regards,
Caroline Haney
Former Patriarchal executive secretary

Setting her laptop back on the table next to her, she stood up and dropped the sarong, revealing her sleek naked body, her porcelain skin glistening under the bright sun. Taking three steps forward, she dove into the infinity pool and swam over to the far edge. Resting her elbows on the edge of the pool, she once again looked out to the gulf. The tanker had nearly disappeared to the east, the single cloud had moved farther to the west, and three colorful fishing boats had entered the bay. She felt contentment. She never wanted to leave this place, even though it was the Wild West.

CHAPTER 64

Chevy Chase, Maryland, USA, 20 December 2016:

Two men and a woman, each chronologically somewhere in their seventies, sat in the spacious bookcase-lined study. Heavy snow could be seen falling through windows edged with frost. Beyond the falling snow, traffic moved slowly along Connecticut Avenue, providing a slow-motion light show of white headlights and red taillights flickering off of the descending flurry. Leaping flames in a large stone fireplace, not five feet away from where they sat, reflected off a polished wood ceiling. A blue and red Persian rug lined the floor and a wide silver chandelier hung overhead. The room smelled like a mixture of burned wood, fine liquors, and perfume.

Gaston Defoe, a wide-shoulder tall man with a stocky mix of silver and blond hair, sat in a red-velvet chair to the left of the fire. Dressed in gray slacks with a sharp crease and a white shirt, he looked over at the elderly woman on his right, as he reached down and picked up a crystal glass filled with a brownish liquid and ice cubes.

A small slender woman, Helen Cunningham, with shoulder-length white hair, dressed in a tan skirt and white blouse, sat across from him on the right side of the fire in a high-backed and overstuffed chair covered in a floral fabric. Holding her hands out to the fire in an attempt to warm them, she seemed transfixed, watching the flames leaping around the edges of the fireplace. Suddenly, she turned and looked over at Gaston, as if she could sense his attention was focused on her.

Sitting on a couch directly in front of the fire and between his two companions, Roland Herman, a pale skinny man with a hawk nose and long white hair tied into a ponytail, dressed in khaki trousers and a red plaid shirt, picked up a wine glass filled with a shimmering red liquid and took a sip.

"We've all seen the evidence." Helen broke their silence in a North American accent, looking back at the fire.

"Every shred is circumstantial," Gaston replied in a heavy French accent. "Our three predecessors have been murdered over evidence that would never convict a man in a court of law."

"I disagree," Helen snapped. "The theft of the hard-drive, the destruction of evidence against Mr. Luck, the relentless chase of the three Americans, and the numerous unrecorded phone calls and internet traffic between John Smith and Andres Tressel tell a story of scheming deceit."

"And what of James Tillage and Oliver Mason?" Gaston asked, before taking a large drink from his crystal glass.

"Sad, unavoidable casualties," Helen replied, shaking her head. "But for the good of the Society. Had Andres been successful, the Society and its members would have been used in ways that we cannot fathom."

"All circumstantial," Gaston said again. "And if it were true, there is no proof of his ultimate goal."

"None of that matters now." Roland joined the conversation with a hint of a German accent. "We must determine how the Society will proceed and clean this mess up."

"Nothing," Helen replied.

"Nothing?" Roland responded in an astonished voice. "We cannot allow the three Americans to survive. They've had access to the hard-drive and the information contained on it. They cannot be allowed to share that information with anyone."

"That is exactly what our predecessors believed," Helen retorted, shifting in her chair and looking over at Roland. "And look where it got them."

Gaston mumbled, "Dead."

"These three people have done us a favor. They have rummaged through our dirty laundry and discovered treachery amongst our ranks," Helen added. "And they have shown us several employees deserving of advancement."

"They cannot be allowed to live," Roland repeated. "They are like ticking time-bombs, and the minute they have a grievance with the Society or feel threatened by anyone they will share what they know."

"Actually," Gaston interrupted, "we should hire all three of them, put them on the payroll where we can keep an eye on them. They did manage to overcome incredible odds. They are obviously very resourceful and clever. It would a shame to waste such talent."

Taking another sip of wine, Roland said, "I will not allow it. They must be terminated."

"We are all members of the Board of Patriarchs and a body of three," Helen calmly responded.

"We are the Patriarchs," Gaston joked. "You are the Matriarch."

Ignoring Gaston's jest, Helen continued, "We will take a day and consider our options. Let us meet again tomorrow, discuss those options, and vote on their fate."

CHAPTER 65

Bophut Fisherman's Village, Koh Samui, Thailand, 23 December 2016:

The three sat on the small patio behind their rooms overlooking the thin ribbon of pinkish sand and sound between Koh Samui and Koh PhaNgan. Four speed boats bobbed just off shore and, in the distance, across the stretch of water between the islands, Koh PhaNgan could clearly be seen, its tall jungle laden mountains rising above emerald green valleys and long white sandy beaches. To their right, soft Isaan music played from the bar of the small hotel as Tommy rubbed his toes across the short trimmed grass growing between the stones at their feet. The blue and grey eyed dog lay next to him.

Sitting on a red cushioned rattan chair, Sandy pulled her strawberry blonde hair back and looked over at Tommy. "You've kept your opinion about our chances to yourself. What do you think?"

Looking out at the island he had called home for many years while nervously shifting in a matching rattan chair, Tommy said, "I imagine we'll find out in a couple of minutes," before picking up a glass filled with two ice cubes and two fingers of Jameson Irish whiskey from a small round table between them.

His enormous bear-like body squeezed into a chair too small for his frame, Jack commented, "You obviously believe that Chandler will know something about our fate, and he will reveal this during our upcoming meeting."

"He called and asked for a meeting with the three of us," Tommy explained. "I imagine, based on the requested attendees, he's back working for the Society in some capacity, and they've made one decision or another about our future."

Picking up a bottle of Singha beer, Sandy looked at the distant island and commented, "Do you think it was worth it?"

Tommy looked over at the tall and light blue eyed woman. "Do I think what was worth it?"

"All the violence and death," Sandy clarified. "How many people died during the course of the Society's quest to get the hard-drive back? Many of those people had families, friends, wives, or children. Our aim of staying alive ended a lot of lives."

"Darling," Jack said, reaching out and putting his large hand on Sandy's knee, "would you rather we commit suicide at the onset to avoid the subsequent death of people attempting to slay us?"

"It's just that I somehow feel dirty," Sandy softly replied. "I mean, think of the killings at the Butterfly Bar the other day. Fifteen men were killed with no thought as to who they were or who was waiting for them back home. They were just doing their job."

"They knew when they signed on with the Society that death was a possibility," Tommy offered. "It was a part of the job description. But ultimately life isn't fair. Life is never fair. We can't look back and worry about the misfortune of others or look forward and hope for a break. We just need to realize that life's not fair and forge ahead, recognizing it's ultimately out of our control. The men and women who died as a result of the Society's quest is the evidence. Their families are the evidence. In the end, happiness is based on who we associate with and how we treat the people around us. We can choose to live a life looking out for only ourselves, or a life where we choose our friends and are loyal to those friends, supporting each other when things get tough."

"That was a bit deep for me," Jack muttered, shaking his enormous head while running a large paw through his unruly brown-and-silver hair. "We deserve to live as much as anyone of the individuals killed during this debacle. It was a clear and simple choice between us or them."

"I agree, but that doesn't distract from the fact that life is not fair," Tommy responded. "We didn't elect to have the Society chase us halfway around the world, but it happened. We have chosen each other as friends and supported each other through a difficult time. Those people who worked toward the Society's goal didn't deserve to die but, once again, life is not fair and undeserving people died."

"It doesn't make me feel any less dirty," Sandy stated. "The fact I'm partially responsible for all the violence and the death keeps nagging at me."

"And it always will," Tommy explained. "Years ago, my father told me that mistakes were like putting either sand or pebbles in your pocket. Small mistakes are like sand and big mistakes are like pebbles. The sand works its way through the seams of your pockets and is eventually lost. The pebbles are always with you. But he also explained that you never want to lose the pebbles. They are what define who you are and give you basis for reflecting on a decision. I've learned that violence, whether justified by the claim of self-preservation or job description, qualifies as a mistake, making each and every act of aggression a pebble. Violence is a fact of life and sometimes required, but it's never right. And violence is indiscriminate. Whether it's a stray round or the loss of a loved one, violence effects even the innocent. As Sandy pointed out, the other day at the Butterfly Bar, we eliminated fifteen body guards and drivers at the onset. They knew that death was possible the minute they signed up for the mission. However, each one of those men likely had a family. Whether it was a wife and children or parents, they all had someone who will feel anguish over their death. Violence is indiscriminate and not right. A lot of people, some innocent and some not, pay for each act of violence."

"Get out the waders," Jack mumbled, "it's getting deeper."

"It's time," Tommy said, looking down at this watch. "Let's move over to the bar and wait for Chandler."

"Thank god, we can now put an end to this dribble," Jack muttered, pulling his body from the small chair.

"Oh, shut up, Jack," Sandy said, slapping his shoulder. "What Tommy said is true, and it made me feel a little better."

"Thankfully, it made someone feel better, sweetheart." Jack chuckled. "It made me feel as if I should take a stroll into the bathroom and slit my wrists."

The threesome walked down a narrow concrete path surrounded by tropic foliage and palm trees and into a beachfront bar. To one side stood a long half-moon-shaped counter with bottles of liquor adorning wooden shelves mounted over a large mirror on the other side. A wooden rail separated the bar from the beach and three ceiling fans turned over head. Sitting at a large round table in the center of the room, they ordered a round of drinks from a barefoot slender man with dark hair and eyes.

The waiter quickly returned, setting a Jameson on the rocks in front of Tommy, a Singha beer in front of Jack, and a shot of tequila in front of Sandy.

Looking at Sandy with a disbelieving expression, Tommy asked, "How can you drink that vile crap?"

Tossing her strawberry blonde hair aside and picking up the shot glass, Sandy glared at Tommy. "You're such a pussy. You can kill a man or woman without hesitation, but a little shot of Thai tequila is too much for you."

"Darling," Jack commented. "He does have a point. That is the worse tequila I have ever had the displeasure of consuming."

Throwing the shot into her mouth and swallowing the

shimmering yellow liquid with one large gulp, Sandy replied, "You're both pussies," before gesturing the waiter for three more shots. "Let's see how manly you really are."

The waiter, smiling as if he knew just how bad the tequila was, quickly placed three shot glasses filled with the yellow liquid on the table.

"Here's where we separate the boys from the men," Sandy joked, looking first at Jack then Tommy. Raising her shot glass over the table, she said, "And here's to our future, Chok Dee, Caw," giving them the Thai cheers.

"Chok Dee, Cup," Tommy replied, picking up his glass and touching Sandy's.

"Cheers," Jack said, doing the same.

All three drained the shot glasses into their mouths and swallowed. Jack's face immediately became pale and sweat broke out on his forehead, and Tommy stumbled from his chair and vomited over the rail onto the beach below as Sandy calmly sat in her chair watching the two men with a crooked grin.

"That was foul," Tommy sputtered, turning from the rail and wiping his mouth.

Dressed in a white Thai style cotton shirt and Khaki shorts, Chandler appeared, his green eyes flashing their usual mischievousness as he stepped into the bar. "Hello my septic friends." With a wide smile on his face, he walked over to the round table and pulled out a chair next to John.

Following him into the bar, Caroline, dressed in a floral sundress, walked directly up to Tommy, her light blue eyes shining and short blonde hair bouncing. Right behind her, Calvin, wearing a faded blue muscle shirt over his barrel chest, strutted into the bar and pulled a chair out from the table next to Chandler. His bald head glistening under the overhead light, Calvin suspiciously watched Caroline as she put her arms around Tommy's neck, stood on her toes, and began to kiss him.

"I wouldn't do that," Sandy called out from the table, watching Caroline's lips approaching Tommy's.

"I recommend a nice long embrace," Jack added.

"I just threw up a shot of tequila," Tommy explained, looking down at Caroline.

With a confused expression quickly turning to one of understanding, Caroline redirected her lips and kissed Tommy's cheek before saying, "Amazing, a man who has the ability to kill without hesitation can't keep a shot of tequila down." Then turning to the slender waiter, she said, "six more shots, please."

Turning and glaring at Calvin, Sandy asked, "What's he doing here?"

"Yes, an impending feeling of misfortune overcame me as he entered the room," Jack added, gesturing toward Calvin with his chin.

"You have nothing to worry about," Chandler explained. "Calvin now works for me."

"I am sorry about how this all went down," Calvin apologized, his soft and peaceful eyes looking at the trio pleadingly. "I was under orders." His bulldog-like face filled with sadness as he sat down next to Chandler. "I took an oath to the Society, and I believe my word is the most important asset I have."

"Chandler took an oath, as well," Sandy retorted, "but he chose to break from the Society when they asked too much."

Chuckling, Chandler said, "I only keep my word with friends and relatives."

"He was just doing his job," Tommy surprisingly defended Calvin as he walked over to the table and sat down next to Sandy. "I would have likely done the same, given the circumstances."

"I doubt that," Caroline said in a skeptical tone, sitting down next to Tommy.

"Calvin is and will always be a loyal member of the Society," Tommy stated. "We all have those that we're loyal to, and he chose what he did based on his background, just as we chose who we were loyal to because of ours."

"I am sorry," Calvin repeated. "But Tommy's right, I would make the same choice if this were to happen all over again."

"Let's talk about something a bit cheerier," Chandler said, changing the subject. "I am here on the behalf of the Society."

"There's a big surprise," Tommy mumbled.

As the waiter delivered the six more shots of tequila, Sandy said, "I hate it when Tommy's right. He knew that you were back working for the Society and this meeting was about our fate."

"Actually, I'm quite pleased when Tommy is right," Jack commented. "We're still breathing due to his accuracy over the last week and a half."

"Actually," Chandler said, "We have all benefited from Tommy's intuition. The Society has decided that what has occurred during this last week has been beneficial to the organization. Several dubious employees and at least one questionable member have been ferreted out, and a valuable database has been saved. As a result, the Society has rewarded us all."

"Please go on," Jack requested, leaning back in his chair. "This story may actually have a happy ending, after all."

Slapping Jack's shoulder, Sandy said, "Shut up and let the man talk."

"The Society has rewarded me with a promotion," Chandler continued. "I am now the Southeast Asia Regional Handler—"

"For the criminal elements, no doubt," Tommy interrupted, chuckling.

"That is correct," Chandler replied. "Calvin is now my lieutenant."

"You've got to be kidding me." Sandy laughed sarcastically. "They promoted you because you didn't robotically follow their orders, and they promoted him because he did. That makes no sense at all."

Ignoring her comment, Chandler continued, "Alain's territory, which tripled over the course of the week, has been granted a Society-free zone status. And you three have a private jet waiting at the Samui airport, ready to take you back home whenever you're ready."

Looking suspiciously at Chandler across the table, Tommy asked, "And?"

"A gentleman will be waiting for your arrival to retrieve the hard-drive, and all your sins have been forgiven. In fact, they would like to offer you the executive assistant or handy man position formerly held by your good friend John Smith—again."

Raising his eyebrows, Tommy asked, "What's to become of John Smith and Steve?"

"Everyone's a winner." Chandler chuckled. "John Smith and his sidekick were also granted forgiveness. However, they were asked to look for work elsewhere, but he was given a generous severance package—enough to keep him from causing trouble for a year or two, anyway."

"It's time," Caroline said, holding her shot glass of shimmering tequila up.

"What about you?" Tommy asked, looking at Caroline. "What did you get out of this debacle?"

"My Job back," she replied, smiling at Tommy. "Now, hold you glass up and let's toast to this being over."

Tommy reluctantly picked up his shot glass and held it out over the table. The six tiny glasses came together and everyone tossed the tequila into their mouths. Jack turned pale and sweat broke out on his forehead, Caroline choked, Calvin spewed his tequila out over the table, Chandler dropped his glass onto the table top and put his hands to his mouth, Sandy smiled, and Tommy stumbled to the rail and threw up onto the beach below.

CHAPTER 66

Suvarnabhumi International Airport, Thailand, Thailand, 24 December 2016:

S tepping through the wide turnstile glass doors of the airport, they were immediately engulfed into a sea of hawkers, calling out one deal or another: taxis, limousines, hotels, resorts, or good times. Travelers from all over the globe, dressed in an international variety of styles and colors, dragged their wheeled luggage shoulder to shoulder, all with bewildered looks on their faces.

The smell of spicy Thai food hung in the air as the trio struggled through the chaos to an escalator leading to the third floor. Carrying his leather satchel across his shoulder, Tommy was pushed aside by a tourist laboring to find his way to the exit and another tourist pulled her wheeled suitcase over Sandy's left foot. Jack easily negotiated the crowd as people around him sought to avoid the mountain of a man lumbering toward the escalator.

Stepping onto the escalator with no further injuries, Sandy loudly commented, "We could be flying over Hawaii on a private jet at this very moment, but somehow I let you talk me into an economy seat on a crowded airliner."

"Darling," Jack said behind her, "Tommy's intuition has brought us this far."

"You weren't nearly slaughtered trying to escape the bedlam down there," Sandy retorted, gesturing toward the pandemonium at the base of the escalator. "And you allow your current girlfriend the luxury of a private jet."

Looking back at his two travel companions, Tommy said, "We've made it this far because we've only trusted people I know. Placing ourselves on a private jet owned by an organization that has spent over a week trying to kill us didn't seem like a sound decision—no matter what assurances they gave us. The pilots could have easily donned their oxygen masks, decompressed the compartment, and had their way with us."

"What about Caroline?" Sandy spat, "She's riding in style."

"Someone had to escort the dog," Tommy explained. "Customs would have had my dog pinned up in some kennel for months coming from Thailand."

"What about the hard-drive?" Sandy asked, pushing a strand of strawberry blonde hair from her face with long delicate fingers.

"I'll give it back to them, but on my terms," Tommy replied stepping off the escalator at the top.

The third floor was as busy as the second, but lacked the chaos. More travelers with wheeled luggage moving about, trying to find the correct ticketing counter, but no bewildered looks or confusion. Moving down a long corridor packed with brightly clothed people, Tommy saw the sign for the United Airlines counter in the distance and strode in that direction.

Glancing to his left Tommy saw a familiar tall man with dark wiry hair, bushy eyebrows, and two silver canes leaning against his left knee sitting next to a short beady eyed man with dark bushy hair. He stopped amidst the moving crowd and turned to Sandy and Jack, standing behind him. With tourists brushing their shoulders as they moved past and wheeled luggage narrowly missing their feet, Tommy silently pointed toward the United Airlines sign and then gestured to the two men. Sandy and Jack knowingly nodded and continued on their way. Smiling, Tommy maneuvered through the bustling crowd toward the two men.

Stopping in front of them, Tommy greeted John Smith and Steve, "I hear you lost your jobs."

Looking up from his seat with a clear expression of defeat, John Smith calmly said, "We were given a very nice severance package, but, indeed, told to look for work elsewhere. Please don't tell me they offered you the job."

"Of course they did." Tommy laughed. "And of course I turned it down. You may feel comfortable working for an organization that uses less-than-sincere techniques to acquire its goals, but I don't."

Glaring at Tommy, Steve pointed a short finger from a small pale hand and added, "You had better keep looking over your shoulder. Someday we'll get even."

Shaking his head at his small companion, John Smith said, "Steve lacks the eloquence to properly tell someone that we will find our revenge. Of course, I am sure you want me to believe you were simply caught up in something out of your control and your life was threatened. I imagine you believe that we would do the same, given the same circumstances."

"Actually," Tommy replied, "I have no such excuse. Being the primary catalyst behind your failed aspirations yet again brings me joy you cannot imagine and made the entire fiasco worthwhile."

Standing up, Steve proclaimed in a whiny voice, "I will kill you one day."

"Steve," John Smith said sternly, "someday we will pay Tommy back for what he did here, and last year in Washington DC—"

"And don't forget about Thailand the year before that," Tommy interrupted. "Life's not fair, is it, John Smith?"

As if recanting some proverb from his past, John Smith said, "Life's not fair. Life is never fair. Some people get all the breaks and others get nothing. You should never look back and worry about your past misfortune or look forward and hope for a break. You just need to realize that life's not fair and forge ahead, recognizing it's ultimately out of your control."

Looking down at John Smith, puzzled, Tommy suddenly realized where John Smith had learned that adage and finished saying what he had told Omid Sassani behind the motel all those years ago: "Happiness is based on who we associate with and how we treat the people around us. You can choose to live a life feeling sorry for yourself, wallowing in self-pity, and looking out for only yourself, or a life where you choose your friends and are loyal to those friends, supporting each other when things get tough." Then he added, "but you obviously never learned that part."

Looking up at Tommy, it was John Smith's turn to slowly comprehend their past connection and, astonished, he simply responded, "Kimball, Nebraska."

Smiling down at the hunched-over man sitting below him, Tommy replied, "Kimball, Nebraska. You learned nothing from that encounter. I should have let them rape you."

Tommy turned and walked away.

About the Author

Growing up in the Rocky Mountains and graduating from the University of Colorado, Patrick Ashtre chose a career in the military as opposed to one slugging it out in the office cubicles of corporate America. After serving twenty-six years in the Marine Corps as both an infantryman and aviator he took a fancy to a horizon of water over that of mountains. Spending his final tour in Japan, Ashtre retired from the marines and moved to the small tropical island of PhaNgan, located in the Gulf of Thailand, where he owned and operated a popular beachfront pub. After ten years of living, working, and traveling throughout Southeast Asia, he has now moved back to the United States. Ashtre now lives and works in the Gunnison-Crested Butte, Colorado, area. With a misspent youth and experiences from around the globe as a canvas, Ashtre will likely fill the pages of many more books before he closes his laptop for the last time.